TRUE COLORS

BOOK 1 OF THE TRUE COLORS TRILOGY

LOREN S. OLSEN

TABLE OF CONTENTS

LORE

Moon Crossing is a sprawling metropolis in the northeastern corner of Mevania. It is the largest city in the District, a land that consists of four major cities separate from the rule of the Mevania Crown. While Bountiful Hill has pledged allegiance to Moon Crossing and provides the city with sustenance, Wolves Creek and Spring Grove have been difficult to obtain. Years ago, a rebellion rose in Spring Grove called the Deliverance and conflicted interests led to the bombing of the technologically based city. Moon Crossing took the tech for themselves and believed the rebellion to be dead.

Within the barrier that surrounds Moon Crossing, there is a strict order to the way things must be. Long ago, society's elite decided to establish Moon Crossing under an oligarchy, patriarchal system. With it, the Circle of Superiors and the Elite Council were born. While the Circle dealt with Moon Crossing's affairs with the entire District, the Council was in charge of the people's needs.

To generate the most success, the population had the option to join one of two programs enacted by the Circle: The Protectorship Program and the Edification Program.

At the age of 10, children choose which program they wish to pursue. If boys chose to become Protectors, they were then trained for two years in domestic skills. Two girls were placed as wards beneath one Protector and until the Protector was old enough, they lived with two Youth Protection Service Agents. At the age of puberty, each child was given hormonal suppressors to maintain a healthy, safe household and to decrease unwanted situations and distractions. At the age of 14, Protectors and wards then began to attend the University of Moon Crossing and in 6 years, would learn all they needed to to take up a trade of their choosing. Wards may be released early from the Protectorship if the Protector grants it. If not, they are released at the age of 23, when they have established a stable career and life for themselves.

In the Edification Program, children who choose this path are housed in dormitories on the university campus and begin their schooling. For 10 years, they are under the same rules and obligations as the children in the Protectorship Program and receive their hormonal suppressors. The Edified are offered scholarships throughout their academics based on their ability and potential. Oftentimes, these children become part of the law and justice systems of Moon Crossing and are released from the program at the age of 20, when they graduate from the University of Moon Crossing. Each graduate is required to complete a year-long internship for their desired trade and if fulfilled, is granted a job. Those who become Recons are trained at the garrison outside the city and join the District Patrol Division.

All citizens of Moon Crossing, besides those in the DPD, must abide by one rule: Never go beyond the barrier.

WELCOME TO MOON CROSSING

THE GOLD-PLATED SIGN on the wall says three simple words:

Circle of Superiors

I swipe my clearance and the twin doors breeze open. I've been working for the Circle, Moon Crossing's highest leadership committee, for two years now as their secretary and messenger. As I step into the adjacent room for their admittance, I can't help but feel like today will be…different. The muffled conversation on the other side of the opaque glass entrance trails off and a telescreen materializes in front of me with Superior Masoni's stern expression. He's older, like all the Superiors, with crow's feet and creases on his forehead from key decisions and constantly debated thoughts. His pale green eyes are fierce though, and he nods solemnly. "Miss Harte. You may enter."

The glass door opens in front of me, and I step into the Circle's conference room. I take my place on the raised dais, conveniently placed in the middle of the Superiors' bright white podiums. They have tablets to communicate ideas and facts with one another as they work, but now the tablets dissolve and they all glance down at me.

With a reserved gaze, I peer up at each one of them and explain, "All the farms in Bountiful Hill are harvesting their crops for the season. Mayor Everdon has offered a trade before the city sends their products to our stores."

Superior Cozeht asks, "And what is this trade you speak of?"

I wave my hand nonchalantly. "Mayor Everdon has asked for additional protection from the District Patrol Division for the city. They're having a problem keeping a group of people, known only as 'Worshipers' in the Blooming Woods, out of the city."

Superior Masoni inclines his head at me. "Don't be so apathetic about their request, Miss Harte. Bountiful Hill has refused our Recons in the past. Besides, we expect the Recons to have a fresh rotation of recruits this fall and there will be more to extend their boundaries to the other two cities."

I nod, a bit embarrassed at my arrogance. *Especially* in front of the Circle.

He goes on, "Thank you, Miss Harte. We will discuss this trade further. You are dismissed."

"Thank you, My Superiors."

☽ ✧ ☾

After I've returned home from work, I flop on the couch and Vanne pokes his head out of the kitchen, asking, "How was the Circle today?"

"Fine," I grumble, tugging off my boots and tossing them aside.

Vanne looks unconvinced. "You seem upset."

"I was so arrogant in front of the Circle today."

A laugh bubbles out of him. "You're upset about that? Everyone knows you're arrogant, even the Superiors."

I shoot him a glare. "Hey, you're supposed to be on *my* side and make me feel better."

"How about I pop in the apple pie that I got at the store today and top it with some ice cream?"

"You bought *sweets*, Vanne? I thought you said they'd rot our teeth out."

A smirk quirks his lips. "Did I say I was going to eat any?"

I stand. "Are you trying to fatten me up?"

He gasps playfully and shakes his oven mitt at me. "How dare you accuse me of that? I would *never!*"

I laugh and step up to him, snatching the oven mitt to draw him a little closer. "You're a terrible liar."

Vanne's gaze softens and he murmurs, "I'll be rude, too. You should shower."

"Way of the world," I say softly and let go of the oven mitt, turning on my heel.

☽ ✧ ☾

By the time I smell fresh and am ready to eat, Vanne has dinner on the table. I plop down in my chair across from him and serve myself. He watches me and I glance at him as I hand the ladle over. "What is it?"

He takes the ladle, his fingers brushing mine. "I'm still offering to be your Indefinite Protector once our term is over, you know. Then you won't have to—"

"Vanne," I cut him off, "the rules clearly state that—"

"I *know* what the rules say, Locklyn," he interrupts and sets his hands on the table, "but we don't have to stay in Moon Crossing. We can go somewhere else."

I shake my head. "This is my home, Vanne. I can't leave."

"But don't you love me anymore?"

The heartbreak in his voice is clear, and I set my spoon down, my brow creasing. "I love you, but not like I used to."

His eyes hold all the sadness in the world, the sadness I caused, as he whispers, "Why do you keep leading me on, then? A little flirting, and maybe a kiss here and there. I don't understand why you ever stopped loving me."

"Because it was getting too dangerous. Protectors aren't supposed to have romantic relationships with their wards. You knew that before I did, Vanne. We were almost discovered too many times and yes...I loved the thrill, but I knew we couldn't live like that for another decade. So it had to end."

Vanne looks away, his fingers curling. "You didn't answer why you keep leading me on."

"I…have no sensible reason for that, but I am sorry." I reach across the table to take his hand and he stands abruptly.

"I've lost my appetite. You can eat and put away the leftovers. I'm going to bed."

I wait for the slam of Vanne's bedroom door before I eat my soup again. I feel terrible, but this is the way it has to be. Vanne and I aren't permitted to be in love in this world and I moved on long ago. But he still has feelings for me and I don't know what to do about it. It's not like I owe him anything. He ruined my last relationship, so *he* owes *me* and for that, I'd like him to give me up.

☽ ✧ ☾

Since I wasn't in the mood for apple pie and ice cream last night, I trudge into the kitchen intending to eat such for breakfast. But the aroma of a proper breakfast hits me as I emerge, and I yawn as I take a seat at the breakfast bar. Vanne doesn't acknowledge me. I don't expect him to, and I watch him flip pancakes until the doorbell rings.

I get up and meander over to the door, drawing it open without even considering the state of my hair, but I'm pleasantly surprised to find my cousin Electra waiting on the other side. Even this early, she still looks put together with her strawberry blonde hair done up in a messy bun. Her electric blue eyes scrutinize me and she picks up my free hand, tsking at my nails.

"Saturday is your day off, right, sweetie?" she asks, following me over to the kitchen.

I nod as I sit at the breakfast bar. "Thank goodness. This week has been killing me."

"Then let's go shopping *and* get you a mean manicure," she suggests and searches through the refrigerator until she finds a fat-free yogurt cup and an assortment of already-washed berries.

Vanne grumbles, "What are you doing in my kitchen, Electra?"

"Serving myself, thank you very much. What? Does Lazy Bones over there ever make anything for herself?"

"It's my job to make Locklyn food and go grocery shopping," he sighs as he hands me a plate loaded with deliciousness. "Clean the apartment, deal with the bills, order takeout when needed, et cetera. I'd be a fantastic trophy husband."

"Those don't exist," Electra quips.

Vanne snorts. "I'll be the first."

He makes his own plate but sits at the table, so Electra joins me at the bar. I ask, "What are Adume and Glory up to today?"

My cousin peels open her yogurt cup and mixes in the berries, "Glory is getting ready for a photo shoot sponsored by Councilor Cristol, of course, and Adume is sick. He *really* wants you to come by and pity him."

I take a sip of my apple juice. "Hmm."

"Maybe I'll go hang with Adume today, get sick, and then make Locklyn do all the chores," Vanne suggests.

Electra glances between us and gives me a questioning look. "What's up with you two this morning? You're walking on eggshells and it is *painful* to watch."

"It's nothing," I tell her.

"Yeah, nothing," Vanne inputs.

I know she wants to go off on us, but my Mini Ardia tablet rings in my room and I get up to answer it. Quietly, I close my door behind me and pick up my Mini, not surprised to find that Adume is calling me. I tap the 'accept' icon and Adume appears on my screen. I pause when I realize that he's not at home, but in his Cube at work. He's as pale as a ghost, though, and shaking like a leaf.

My brow creases in concern. "What's wrong, Adume? Are you okay?"

He speaks frantically, "I—I overheard these guys talking...they're plotting to...you have to get out of M—Moon Crossing before they—before they..." he trails off, wildly turning toward the entrance of his Cube. Adume shrieks, turning back to me with wide, frightened eyes. "They're after me! I hear them coming!"

"Adume, calm down, okay? Do you want me to get ahold of…security…"

I type in Prime Tower's Security code and send a ping to them that someone is potentially in danger. But then…my ping is denied and I try again. Denied. Something catches my eye behind Adume, and my mouth falls agape. I watch a hooded man slap his gloved hand over Adume's mouth and yank him out of his chair.

"Adume! Let him go!" I cry, gripping my Mini in panic.

Someone else grabs Adume's Mini and smashes the screen against his desk. It glitches before I lose connection and I take in a heavy breath. I toss my Mini aside and fly out of my room, gripping my hair as I startle Electra and Vanne with my sudden presence again. Electra stands from her seat, approaching me cautiously.

"What's wrong?" she asks.

"Adume! He's in trouble! We have to get to Prime Tower!"

"How do you know he's in trouble?" Vanne counters, standing as well.

Tears erupt as I croak, "He—he called me and there was this—this hooded man and I tried to call security, but they denied me! *We have to get to Prime Tower!*"

I march over to the keys on the counter and head for the door. Vanne and Electra follow me to the parking garage. I can't drive since I'm frantic, so Vanne gets us there quickly, dodging cars and testing the speed limit. Electra and I hold on for dear life but when we get to Prime Tower, we hop out and rush inside. Vanne contacts security and the ping goes through but there's no confirmation. We're let up to the employees' Cubes with just my facial scan and race to Adume's Cube. The lights flicker and an eerie feeling washes over me. His Cube is empty, his Mini sits there still, cracked and dead. A mug of coffee steams with life and his work bag hasn't been unlatched yet.

"Adume!" Electra calls, her voice panicky.

"*Shh,*" I glance around, "the guys who took him could still be here."

"Then we ought to find him and kick some a—"

"That's a bad idea," Vanne interrupts, nervously knotting his fingers together.

"You're a wuss," my cousin bites back and marches off, taking an unhinged stapler and an envelope opener with her as weapons.

"We should stay together," Vanne tells me and I nod.

The lights flicker again before they completely go out and Vanne grips my arm. We move through the office in the morning's low light, keeping eyes at our front and our back, just in case the assailants who attacked Adume try to sneak up on us. It's a shame Electra took the two things that could be used as effective weapons from Adume's desk.

We come to a dark stairwell with its nightmarish red emergency lights and Vanne nearly faints as he pulls me to a stop. "No. *NO WAY!*"

"But what if Adume is down there?" I fire back.

"This is the stuff of horror movies, Locklyn, I've seen it! You go into a dark stairwell and seconds later, you're *dead.*"

"Then I'll go by myself!" I shake off his hand and shove open the door as he continues to object.

But Vanne doesn't join me in the stairwell, and I take a shaky step down the first one. I keep my back toward the walls as I descend, relying on the emergency lights and my fists to protect me. It's a stupid idea, but if it means I have a chance at saving Adume's life then...well maybe it would have been a better idea to wait for security instead. *Oh, stars, how stupid are we?*

When I don't see or hear a single thing, I relax a little and am glad my eyes have adjusted to the darkness. Down another flight of stairs and on a landing, I feel the hair rise on my arms and I glance back at the staircase I just came down. A looming figure stands there, head menacingly tilted toward me. I shriek and dart for the landing door, but the man moves faster than I thought he could.

He grabs me around the waist and jerks me back. My hand slips from the handle. He shoves me back against the wall, slaps his hand over my mouth, and I breathe heavily, my heart in my throat as I think of my imminent death.

But he doesn't stab me, suffocate me, or wring my neck. Instead, he waits to see if anyone heard my shriek. I'm shattered when not even Vanne comes to my rescue and the hooded man tips his head down to look at me.

I can't see anything in the darkness besides the outline of his mouth. His hood is drawn too low to see his eyes and he murmurs to me, "If you want to see your friend alive, then you will come to the abandoned Crow Factory tomorrow night. *Alone.* If you don't come alone, then consider him dead. Do you understand me, Miss Harte?"

He removes his hand and I squeak, "Y—yes."

"Good. Now get on your way and tattle to those police officers of yours."

The hooded man moves away from me and disappears down the stairs. His steps are so light I can hardly hear them once he's gone. Paralyzed with fear, I blink several times, trying to get the jitters out of me. When I still hear nothing, I rush to the door and wrench it open to an empty office space. I move through it quickly and to the elevator. I'll alert security again and hope that Vanne and Electra are safe.

In the lobby, Vanne and Electra are sitting there. My cousin is crying as Vanne comforts her. I hurry to them. "What happened?"

"We couldn't find Adume," Vanne tells me softly, "security is searching for him right now."

"Neither of you ran into the people that took him?"

They both shake their heads and Electra blubbers, "Why? Did you?"

I tense for a moment before I shake my head as well. "No. I'll go to the police station and tell them what's happened. I'll see you guys later."

"Do you want me to drive you?" Vanne asks.

"No, I'll take a cab."

He lets me go and I wander out to the street, catching the first cab that pulls up to the curb.

"To the police station, please," I request, and sit back against the seat.

"Yes, ma'am," the driver chirps and we're off.

I close my eyes, my brow furrowed in worry. Hopefully, the hooded man wasn't lying when he said that Adume was still alive. I've watched many crime shows where the kidnapper lies to lure their actual victim to their demise. But that was fiction, this is real life, and Adume isn't just some actor who gets to play dead for a few hours and then go on with his life afterward. He may not be able to and that thought terrifies me.

Why me though? What do I have to offer?

☽ ✧ ☾

I meet with Detective Cyrus Caine at the station and tell him everything I know. He asks that I bring in my Mini another time—to view the recording it automatically takes of each video call—and I feel daft for not even thinking of that. So I promise to bring him the Mini tomorrow once I get my wits about me and he sends me home with two officers to watch over our apartment. They dispatched another two to Electra and Glory's apartment for the night.

When I get home, Vanne is eating leftover soup on the couch, staring at the blank TV. He startles when I shut the door and glances at me. A shadow passes across his expression. "That took a long time."

I shrug. "They wanted to rehash everything and make sure all the details were correct. I have to go back tomorrow with my Mini."

Vanne stands and approaches me. "I feel you know more than you're letting on, Locklyn."

"Why would you say that?" I counter as I try to move past him, but he grabs my arm.

"Because you're trying to avoid me and you looked…frightened when you came into the lobby earlier."

"Of course I was frightened, I was worried about Adume."

"But what else are you hiding, Locklyn?"

I huff. "Vanne, let me go. I'm not hiding anything."

He releases me. "So you say, but I know something's up. You can have leftover soup if you're hungry."

I make myself a bowl of soup and hide in my room, contemplating my meeting with the hooded man tomorrow night.

AN ACCUMULATION OF ASHES

IT'S EVENING AGAIN.

I let the officers download the recording of Adume's call but I have heard nothing back yet. So I borrow the car, say I'm going to see Electra, and drive to the abandoned Crow Factory on the outskirts of the city. It's not hard to miss, considering the structure is charred as it nearly burned to the ground years ago. My mom was working when it caught fire, but thankfully, she wasn't in the restricted area. She was bitter about losing her job and ended up being a stay-at-home mom to me and my brother. I don't think she's ever really gotten over it.

In my sweatshirt pocket, I carry pepper spray and a taser, in case I need to use them. I park outside the dilapidated factory and wait a moment longer before I get out. This is stupid, I know, but I seem to do a lot of stupid things lately and I don't know if I'll stop. So I walk through the factory's doors that hang off their hinges and crinkle my nose at the eternal scent of ash and death. People died here in that fire and I could be walking on their remains at this very moment.

Oh, stars. My stomach turns and I pause to collect myself.

"So you really came," a voice echoes from somewhere above me.

I glance up, startled, and whimper softly, "Wh—who's there?"

I turn as three hooded men emerge from the still-standing concrete stairs. One of them drags a body bag after him. I hear it rustle when they come to a halt in front of me. I stare at the bag to make sure I'm not hallucinating, and it moves again. Like a fool, I rush for it, but another one stops me, hooking his arm around my waist and hauling me back.

"Adume?" I ask, my voice trembling.

I hear a muffled version of my name and then a muffled, frustrated cry for help. Tears blur my vision. "Let him out of there! Let me see his face!"

The middle one clicks his tongue and they tear the bag open. Adume is dumped to the ground. His glasses are broken and askew, a slab of duct tape covers his mouth, and his wrists and ankles are tied together. He has a minor scratch on his forehead but otherwise, looks unharmed. His gaze turns to me, wide-eyed and terrified, and I share the same look with him.

"Now, let's get down to business, Miss Harte," the middle one claims.

"What do you want from me? I have nothing valuable to give you," I spit, struggling against the man that still holds me back.

"Oh, we want nothing from you." He paces around me and I stiffen at how close he passes. "Something...drastic is going to occur within the next few weeks and the entire city will blame you for it. That is, if you agree to take the blame and keep your mouth shut about what we're discussing."

"Why would I take the blame for something I didn't do?"

He comes full circle and tips my chin up. "You will, or everyone you love will die. I can guarantee that. I know who you are, Miss Harte. I know who your father was and what he did to this city. Caused it so much grief and pain. Your father's sins have fallen on you and you are *just* like him. You will be just like him."

I look away. "What do you know about my father? He was a good man."

"He was a *murderer!*"

My pulse quickens and my gaze flickers. "What—what are you talking about?"

A low chuckle rumbles out of the man, cruel in its intent. "Oh, so they have kept you in the dark on the details, huh? Well, let me enlighten you. Your father engaged in illegal trading outside the barrier and one night, a deal didn't go as planned. He murdered two innocent people in cold blood and still didn't get his money. It terrified everyone that a Superior, their leader, could murder innocents so the people rallied for his execution...and their wish was granted."

I say nothing because even though I don't know why my father died; I know he engaged in illegal trading. That was our little secret we kept from my mom. I don't want to believe that my loving and kind father would outright murder two people...but I know what his relationship with greed was and it was complicated.

That relationship destroyed my father's soul.

"Speechless, huh?" The man moves over to Adume. "Tell me, do you want your friend to die or will you take the blame?"

"Why must you be so cruel? Who are you?"

"People with a cause. Now, am I going to slit your friend's throat?" he grabs Adume's hair and yanks his head back, pressing a savage-looking knife against his neck.

I push against the other man. "No! Stop!" My voice breaks and tears well in my eyes as I relent. "I'll do it, I'll take the blame."

The man tsks. "I'm not feeling it. Try again."

"*I'll do it!*" I sob, "I'll do it..."

"Good." He pulls the knife away from Adume's neck and drops him on the ground. "You'll get your friend back when the event occurs and you're arrested. I'll be looking forward to seeing your face again behind bars, Miss Harte." He motions to the one holding me. "Get her out of here and make sure she doesn't come back."

I am drawn away and even when I struggle; he picks me up and carries me out of the factory. I shove him away when he sets me down and turn my back on him, running my fingers through my hair. *This is absolute madness! What am I going to be blamed for and will it lead to an execution? One life for another?*

"You should really get out of here," the hooded man tells me.

"Give me a moment, my life is ending before my very eyes," I snap and lean my hands against the car, taking in uneven breaths. "*Heavens above.*"

"Miss Harte," he warns, setting his hand on my shoulder.

I turn on him and hiss, "Your comrade says you are people with a cause but do you even have a conscience?"

His hand hovers near me before he drops it and his shoulders fall, defeated. "Just get going before he comes and makes you."

I get in the car without another push and drive far, far away from the Crow Factory.

☽ ✧ ☾

I don't sleep for a few days as insomnia plagues me.

But as I lie in bed, waiting for the sun to rise on the third day, my Mini rings on my nightstand. I roll over and pick it up. One of my best friends from college, Malini, is calling and I can't help but wonder why so early. That girl used to sleep through class and party all night long. Her image appears on the screen and she glances me over.

"Hey, Mal," I say groggily as I yawn and rub insomnia from my eyes.

She squints at me. "Why are you up?"

"Because you called me and I haven't been able to sleep a wink for the past three days."

"That's not healthy."

I shrug. "I know. What's up?"

"Well, I was going to ask if you wanted to come to the club with me tonight and be my wing woman, but maybe you should stay home and get some rest."

"No, I can go out. I probably won't sleep, anyway."

Malini sighs. "Will you be an *alert* wing woman, though?"

A small smile lifts my lips. "I'll chug something before going to the club. Don't worry, I'll scope out the hotties for you."

"Okay...but if you scope out the weirdos, then I'm taking you home."

"Sounds good."

"Now get some sleep. I'll see you tonight. Love you!" She blows me a kiss and hangs up.

"Oh, I've tried," I grumble and get out of bed, deciding that I should probably take a shower.

☽ ✧ ☾

The mood is somber in the apartment as the search for Adume continues. I've been itching to tell the police exactly where he is, but I fear that if I do, his kidnappers will kill him, anyway. Hopefully, they're feeding him or at least giving him some water. If Adume dies, it will be my fault and I can't live with that guilt. He's my friend, a human being, and at least I have a conscience to recognize that.

Vanne has only a bowl of cereal sitting in front of him, but he glances up when I emerge from my room. "Morning," he mumbles.

"Morning," I mumble back. "I think I'll just get something at the café today."

He nods and drops his head again. Adume is his best friend. We've all been close—Vanne, Adume, Electra, Glory, and I—since we enrolled in the Protectorship Program. Clover, my companion, was our close friend, too, but then...she was unexpectedly murdered four years ago and the police never caught her killer. None of us can bear to lose another friend.

It looks like it's going to be a little chilly today, so I grab my plum peacoat, button it up, and head out. I've been stuck doing desk work for the Circle this entire week but hopefully, I'll have their response to Bountiful Hill's proposal and be able to send it on its way. Then I can get on to planning the biggest event of the year, the Autumn Charity Ball. I probably won't even be able to attend because I'll either be in prison or dead...

I make a run for it to the café across the street from my apartment complex and shiver in my coat. The line is already long so I stand there, quietly shuffling forward with everyone else who looks about as tired as I feel. I yawn behind my hand and blink slowly, trying to gauge the time from the clock across the way, when someone taps me on the shoulder.

Like a startled gazelle, I glance over my shoulder and am surprised to see an incredibly handsome man from my past standing there. I turn to him with a smile. "Stryder Monroe, is that you?"

He looks a little taken back and he blushes. "I didn't think you'd remember me, Locklyn."

"Of course I remember you." I bite my lip. "That kiss on the gondola was all I could think about for weeks after."

Stryder chuckles lightly. "Yeah, me too."

We move forward in the line and I ask, "So how have you been? I know you had to transfer to Bountiful Hill after the fight."

"I've been good. I got a degree in Bountiful Hill before I had the chance to be kicked out. I've been there since but thought I'd set foot in Moon Crossing again."

"And you came to the right place. Must be fate if we're meeting again after all these years."

His blush deepens and he rubs the back of his neck. "Must be."

I move to stand next to him so I'm not shuffling backward and I tip my head at him. "I remember you being nervous about our date, but surely you've talked to other girls by now. Why are you so nervous?"

"I don't know. I'm not a smooth guy, I guess? And...it's great to see you again, Locklyn."

"You as well, Stryder."

We chat until we come to the counter and order. I'm about to pay for mine when Stryder insists that he's got it and hands his card over. As we move aside, I can't help the flutter in my chest at his gesture. "Thanks."

"Any time." He winks at me.

As I get my cider and scone and Stryder gets his hot cocoa, we wander over to the door and I turn to him. "Hey, I know this is last minute, but would you like to go out tonight? My friend and I are heading to a club downtown and I'd like to spend some time with you."

His eyebrows quirk in surprise. "Oh, um, sure."

I draw my Mini from my pocket. "What's your code?"

"35032."

I type it into my Mini and his profile pops up. I friend him so I can contact him later.

"I have to get to work but I'll message you later."

I turn to leave, but Stryder asks, "Were you planning to walk? I could give you a ride if you want…"

A smile comes to my lips. "A ride sounds much better than walking, especially in this weather."

He smiles as well, his mouth a little lopsided to make it crooked. "I agree."

He opens the door for me and we walk to his car, a dingy little number that looks about ready to fall apart. I pause and glance at him. "Are you sure your car won't break down the minute we sit in it?"

Stryder laughs. "It won't, I promise. I drove it from Bountiful Hill so even though it might look on the edge of death, it'll still get us places. I'm saving up to buy a new car, anyway." He pops open the passenger door and sweeps his hand inside.

"Thanks." I slide in. He closes the door and runs around to the driver's side. Once he's in and we've successfully pulled out into the road, I ask, "So what do you do for work?"

"Odd jobs here and there. I'm not very…good at holding down a job."

"Oh."

He cringes. "I mean, I've found nothing that interests me yet."

I cock my head at him. "Well, what did you study in college?"

"General studies. Although I probably should have done political science, economics, or law."

"The Circle of Superiors is thinking of having a trade school built in the next few years so maybe you could go there and find your passion."

"Ah, I'll be too old by then." He glances at me. "Where do you work, by the way?"

"Oh, Prime Tower. I'm the Circle's secretary."

"Fancy."

"Not necessarily."

"Good pay, though?"

I laugh lightly. "You seem stranger than I remember."

Stryder shrugs, "Life happens."

I regard him for a long moment and he seems stressed. His shoulders are tense and he grips the steering wheel tighter. I guess not being able to find a steady job is a pretty terrible situation to be in. He also doesn't seem *that* motivated or interested in anything. But maybe, if he'd be down for office work, I can talk to the Elite Council about him as a temporary secretary. Theirs is taking maternity leave in a few weeks and I've been juggling both theirs and the Circle's work.

Before I can tell Stryder about the offer, we come to Prime Tower and he pulls up right behind Councilor Cristol. Stryder stares at him as he gets out of his car for a moment with Glory. They embrace—as if everybody can't already tell that they're madly in love with each other—and then she heads for the modeling department. I gather my purse and open the door, climbing out.

"Thanks for the ride, Stryder," I smile as I lean back down. "I'll see you tonight."

He waves, "See you," but is still distracted by the Councilor.

I shut the car door and turn around, surprised to see Councilor Cristol standing there, his hands in his pockets as his wary gaze follows Stryder's car as he leaves.

"Good morning, sir," I say softly, dipping my head in respect.

Councilor Cristol's baby blue eyes shift to me and he tips his head in greeting. "Good morning, Miss Harte. May I ask why you were with that lowlife, Mr. Monroe?"

I crinkle my nose at him as we walk into the lobby. "I wouldn't consider him a lowlife. I've yet to see him in The Moonlight Times and at least give him a little credit for offering me a ride to work."

He presses the elevator button and taps his foot. "I *suppose* that was kind of him. Nonetheless, seeing him again hasn't made my day."

I nearly roll my eyes. Back in college, Councilor Cristol and Stryder couldn't stand each other and they got into fights all the time. The worst fight they got in left Stryder partially deaf in one ear and Councilor Cristol with a nasty scar across his collarbone. They were expelled from Moon Crossing University. Councilor Cristol finished his schooling in Bountiful Hill before interning in Moon Crossing and becoming a member of the Elite Council. No one knew why they hated each other so much and everyone was terrified to ask. Even me.

As the elevator doors slide open and we each swipe our different clearance cards to go to different levels of Prime Tower, I ask, "How are you and Glory faring? I hear there might be an engagement in the works?"

Councilor Cristol's expression lights up at Glory Troisi, his lifelong friend, and supposed lover. "I will not tell you a single thing because I'm sure you'd just blabber everything to Electra and *she'll* tell Glory."

"So you are planning to propose? Her term ends this year."

"I know. You'll just have to wait and see what shows up in The Moonlight Times, Miss Harte." He tips his head to the side. "What about you? Thinking of running back to Blake after your term is over?"

My cheeks heat and I look up at the panel, watching the numbers rise. "Blake Carmichael and I can't possibly be together again after what happened. It was so embarrassing."

"Well, Blake talks about you all the time when we go out for drinks. He's still a lovesick puppy, you know."

"It's been almost a year. He has to get over me eventually."

Councilor Cristol leans back against the elevator wall and I glance at him. "Do *you* still love him? I mean, you agreed to marry him."

I grumble, "But then my Protector helped me see the light in how foolish and young we were to be thinking about getting married."

"We all know Vanne is still in love with you, too."

My shoulders tense and I sigh. "I'm not in love with Vanne *or* Blake anymore. Maybe I'll take up with your most favorite person in the world—Mr. Monroe."

His brow furrows and he snorts. "I'm sure your mother would be so proud of you."

"For once, I'd like her to be." I snap and then clear my throat. "Sorry. But I don't much care what you think of Stryder. I like him and maybe I'll see if there's a chance between us. You never know, sir, love comes in mysterious ways."

"That it does," he regards softly. "But, so you know, he isn't faring as well as I am so if you're okay with living in a trailer, or even that dumpy car, then that's your choice."

The elevator dings as we come to the Elite Council's floor and the doors open. Councilor Cristol steps out without another word to me and I shake my head. Whatever grudge he has against Stryder, I don't want to know. Tonight, I just want to spend some time with a great guy and not worry about a single thing.

THE TIDE OF MENACE

MALINI PICKS ME up at 10:30, thirty minutes later than she said, and I climb in. She glances me over in my short, black lace dress and strappy heels with a matching lace choker. "Um, who are you trying to impress because you look *hot!*"

I laugh. "You wouldn't believe who I ran into today."

She leans her elbows on the center console. "Who?"

"Stryder Monroe."

Malini gasps, "That guy you went on a date with when you were with Vanne?"

"Yes, so I invited him to the club. I told him we'd be there by 10:30-ish so we better hurry before he leaves."

"I am on it!" She barely checks both ways before pulling out into the road and almost runs a red light.

I hold on to my clutch and tighten my seat belt. "You don't have to drive like a maniac, goodness. At least get us there alive."

"*Psh*, you know I was in a gang back in the day and street racing was my specialty. I'll get us there *and* successfully avoid the police in record time." She pokes my leg. "So tell me about Stryder. Are you two going to find somewhere nice and quiet?"

I blush and snort softly. "Malini! Who do you think I am?"

"A woman who likes troublesome men, of course. Come on, tell me you'll at least kiss him tonight."

"If the moment arises."

"*If the moment arises,*" she mocks in a stately voice. "By how you are dressed tonight, I *know* you want him to kiss you."

"Maybe…but our key point is to find a guy for you. Tell me what you're looking for this time."

Malini flutters her fingers. "Tall, gorgeous, and has impeccable lips. I'm also feeling the successful type? So maybe like a physician or a lawyer. Well-settled into life, too."

"So an attractive, rich guy who is also a good kisser?" I clarify.

"Exactly," she sings with a big smile and glances at me, shimmying her shoulders. "I'm looking for a sugar daddy."

I roll my eyes. "Of course you are." Then I change the subject, "Oh, I ran into Councilor Cristol earlier."

She huffs. "What did His Gorgeousness have to say today?"

"That he might propose to Glory soon, but don't tell Electra because we both know she'll blab."

"Huh, somehow it's still hard to believe that they're *actually* together. I always thought Glory was obsessed with him like every other woman in Moon Crossing."

"They've been dating since college, Malini. Electra told me and then I told you. Besides, Glory isn't the kind to 'obsess' over anyone, guys obsess over her."

"I know you told me. I still don't see Cristol as the 'settling down' type, though."

"He hasn't been caught in public with anyone else so I think he's completely committed to Glory." I sigh. "They are so painfully cute together but sometimes, I wonder how she tolerates him. He can be a pain."

"Did he question you about Blake again?" Malini asks as we pull into the club parking lot.

"As always. He says that Blake still talks about me and is still hopelessly in love."

"Well, forget about him because I see your new man right there."

I wildly turn around in my seat to see Stryder leaning against the wall outside the entrance, tapping at his Mini. Mine buzzes a second later and he's asking when we're getting there. I type back, *Look up*, as I get out of the car. He does and his eyes widen when he sees me, his mouth falling open.

I smile, knowing I look good, and saunter up to him. "Hey."

His ears are already tinted pink and his gaze wanders to mine. "Hi. Um, wow, you look great."

"Thank you."

"Ahem," Malini takes my arm and we both look at her, "what about me, Monroe?"

Stryder nods. "You too, Russo."

"Good."

She heads for the club entrance and we follow behind. Stryder shyly glances at me again and offers his arm. I take it, glad he's gentlemanly, and we're let into the club. The music is booming and the lights pulse all along the dance floor. We move up to the lounge on the balcony with booths and tables with low lighting. Where we're able to hear each other. I slip into the middle of the booth, with Malini on my left and Stryder on my right.

First off, I have to find Malini a man to occupy herself with for the rest of the night so I can spend some time alone with Stryder. So I scan the area. Stryder nudges me and asks if I want a drink. I tell him I'd like Bliss, and he wanders over to the bar.

"Ooo, would you look at that hunk that just entered." Malini gestures to a tall, handsome, and physically fit man. Two scantily clad women become leeches on his arms in an instant and whisk him away. "Well, what a bummer."

The next one up the stairs is a man of average height with buzzed umber hair and costly-looking apparel. I nudge Malini, "Hey, how about him? He looks rich."

She studies him for a long moment, her eyebrow piqued in interest. Then she nods, scooting out of the booth. "I'm taking it. Adorable, probably has a pleasant personality, doesn't look like a rip-off, *and* he has great taste." She blows me a kiss and winks. "Wish me luck!"

"*Psh*, you don't need it."

"You know that's right."

I watch Malini make her approach and take a seat next to him, crossing her legs to emphasize the mini length of her dress and his eyebrows rise in surprise. She touches his embroidered collar, probably complimenting it, and a smile immediately comes to his lips. Malini is a master in the art of flirting.

Stryder comes back a few minutes later with our drinks and slides in next to me again. "Sorry it took so long. I didn't think many people drank Bliss."

"It's okay." I take a sip of my drink and it sizzles with sweetness on my tongue. "*Stars*, that hits the spot."

He glances around. "Where's Malini?"

"Occupied with that one over there." I gesture to the other side of the lounge.

"Wow, that was quick." He scoots a little closer and I have to bite my lip to keep from smiling. "This just turned into a quiet evening."

"She can be loud, can't she?"

"Yeah. But enough about Malini. Besides being the Circle of Superior's secretary, I don't know what else you've been up to."

"Well, I attended Moon Crossing University, received my degree in Legal Office Management, Public Relations, and Marketing, and interned at Prime Tower before they hired me. I don't know, my life revolves around work."

"You do nothing outside of work?" he asks.

I think for a moment and then a smile comes to my lips. "Okay, I have been taking roller skating lessons and I really want to join the local roller derby team but, honestly, I'm terrified. I've been to a few of their races and it's so aggressive! I don't know if I can be *that* aggressive."

"It doesn't hurt to try, though, right? Maybe you can go to their practices and learn some techniques."

I nod. "Maybe I'll do that this weekend. I know the league practices Saturday nights."

My gaze wanders to Malini as she comes toward us, towing the man she met. "Hey guys, we're heading to the dance floor and you should join us. This is Domenico, by the way."

Domenico smiles, his gaze vibrant and Stryder stands to shake his hand, although I catch them sharing a knowing glance. I wonder if they've met before, or maybe Stryder's being cautious for Malini's sake.

"We'll join you in a minute," I tell her and tip my glass against my lips as Stryder sits down again.

Malini and Domenico head for the dance floor and I ask Stryder, "Do you know him?"

He looks at me. "Yeah, we had a few classes together in Bountiful Hill."

Stryder downs his drink and I take another swig before moving out of the booth. He takes my hand as we go down to the dance floor and butterflies erupt in my belly. I didn't quite think this through, how club dancing differs greatly from the dancing at the formal events I attend. But Stryder doesn't pull me against him. He draws me close and I settle my arms around his neck. At least we're not in the middle like Malini and Domenico are, being squished by other sweaty, pulsing bodies. We dance for a good half hour, unable to talk because the music is so loud and once we return to the lounge, I excuse myself to freshen up in the ladies' room.

A few minutes later, Malini bursts through the door and startles me and another girl at the sinks. She swoons as she says, "Okay, don't be mad but Domenico and I are leaving."

"Where are you going?"

"We're getting dinner. I'll send you my location and if I'm in trouble, I'll call."

"I'll hold you to that."

She looks at me and then tosses her arm around my shoulders. "Why are you hiding in here when you've got a cute guy waiting for you?"

"I'm not hiding," I claim, even as my cheeks flush. "I'm freshening up."

"So it's going good then?"

"Yeah, I mean it's been…such a long time since we last saw each other so I guess it's a little awkward."

"Just loosen up, Locks. I know he's a gentleman, so he won't make you uncomfortable. I'd say go in for the kiss."

"*Malini.*"

"What? You've kissed him before. Let those sparks ignite again." She kisses my cheek. "Call me if you need rescuing, okay? Love you!"

"Love you, too," I mutter as she leaves, letting the door swing closed behind her.

I glance over myself in the mirror as the other girl leaves and I'm all alone. I look good and confident, but I don't feel that way. Is it too soon to look for a new relationship? I'm technically not allowed to date exclusively yet, but I've slipped around the rules with Vanne and Blake. I know Stryder is a great man. A bit of a temper, maybe, but he wouldn't force me into anything I don't want.

The lights flicker a second before they completely shut off and I sigh as the emergency light comes on. This club is known for its power outages because of all the LED lights they use on the dance floor so it's not like this is the first time. But I guess that means I have to face Stryder again and I head for the door. Until guilt rears its nasty head in memory and I wonder why I am even out of my apartment when I know about Adume…and I can't tell anyone.

I drop my head against the door and close my eyes. I stay there for a moment, my body trembling. How can I push Adume's situation aside? He's probably cold and hurting from being bound up in the Crow Factory. How can Adume's kidnapper expect me to act like everything's okay?

I have to keep Adume on my mind because if I don't, then he's dead.

The lights flicker back on and I recheck my makeup in the mirror before leaving the ladies' room. Stryder is still waiting at the booth and stands to let me slide back in. Before he can sit down again, I ask, "Could you get me another drink?"

"Sure."

I drink the rest of my first Bliss and try not to look gloomy when Stryder comes back. When he sits, I drape his arm around my shoulders and snuggle up to his side, drink in hand. I gaze up at him, a soft smile on my lips as I say, "You don't mind if I snuggle up to you, do you? I'm a little cold."

He smirks. "I don't mind."

We talk softly as I finish my second drink and I'm feeling warm and bubbly again. I laugh at his jokes and flirt to my heart's content and pretty soon, my mind's hazy. Stryder is enjoying himself and blushes as I playfully press a kiss to his jaw. Against his skin, I whisper, "Let's get out of here."

Instead of enthusiastically agreeing, he asks, "Are you sure? You seem a little...tipsy."

I gaze at him, rubbing my thumb along his jaw. "Would I ask you if I didn't trust you?"

He says nothing so I get up and drag him to his feet. "Come on, cutie."

Stryder follows me out of the club, supporting me since I can't walk straight, and we get in his car. He starts it up, puts on the heat for me, and then asks, "Should I take you home?"

I shake my head. "No, let's go to Cascade Plaza. It's near the west gate."

"Okay," he agrees, "but remember that this was your idea, not mine."

"Stryder, it's okay. We're adults."

"But I don't want to be blamed for something I didn't do."

My pulse spikes at that and I lean my head back against my seat. "You won't, I promise."

He nods and we drive in silence to Cascade Plaza. The barrier's west gate is closed. But past it, I can see the outline of the Blooming Woods in the distance as we pass by. We're the only car in the parking lot and Stryder parks away from the streetlights, turning off the headlights.

He clears his throat as we sit in silence before his gaze finds me. "I can sense that there's something wrong."

I look away. "It's nothing."

Stryder takes my chin and turns my head to him. "You said you trust me. Just tell me."

"I can't!" I blubber and the waterworks begin. I cover my face, embarrassed that I'm sobbing in front of him.

"Did someone hurt you at the club? Make you feel uncomfortable?"

I shake my head, unable to speak proper words. Stryder pulls me from my seat and embraces me. I cry against his chest and he lets me, rubbing my back. At least we're not at my apartment, so Vanne can shoo Stryder away and try to comfort me himself. He'd probably try to grill me, but Stryder doesn't do that. He lets me sob.

When I've run out of tears, I clutch his shirt in my fingers and confess in a whisper, "I'm worried about my friend. He was kidnapped earlier this week and...the police haven't been able to find him yet. I hope he's okay."

He says softly, "I'm sorry about your friend. I hope he's found safe and well."

I wipe away my tears with my hands and sit up, nodding. Stryder cups my cheek. "Let me take you home."

I climb back over to my seat and curl into myself. Stryder offers me his hand as we drive to my apartment and I trace his fingers, feeling the strength in them. He's such a good man and would never take advantage of me when I'm vulnerable. I love that about him. He is not like other men I've come to know.

Stryder walks me up to my apartment and we pause outside the door. I rise on my toes and lean into him to give him a goodnight kiss. He cups the nape of my neck, so gentle and kind, and nuzzles my nose.

"Goodnight, Locklyn," he murmurs against my lips.

"Goodnight, Stryder," I draw back, "and thank you. For listening."

He nods. "I'm here for you whenever you need me."

A small smile lifts my lips and I turn toward the door, fishing my key out of my purse. But it flies open and Vanne stands there in his pajamas, looking peeved that I'm coming home at nearly two in the morning—with a man, nonetheless.

"Who are you?" he snaps at Stryder, stepping across the threshold.

I stop him with a hand on his shoulder and he glances at me. "Vanne, don't."

He watches Stryder hurry away and then moves back inside, pulling me along. Vanne practically slams the door behind us, startling me, and crosses his arms.

"*What the hell, Locklyn?* I was so worried about you! Why didn't you message or call?"

"Because I'm not a child, Vanne," I tell him with a sigh as I kick off my heels.

"*But* you are my ward and I'm your Protector. I'm supposed to know where you are at all times. So where were you tonight with that—that random guy?"

I rub my forehead as a headache comes on. "I went to Club Aura with Malini and Stryder, the 'random guy'. *I've* actually met him before in college so he's not random, just a past acquaintance. I was with Stryder for the rest of the night."

Vanne's cheeks turn a deep red and he spits, "Do you want me to turn you in for breaking the rules of the Protectorship?"

I scoff. "As if *you* ever cared about the rules! I didn't break any rules, Vanne. Stryder and I kissed, just like you and I, and me and Blake used to. You're always jealous and I'm *tired* of it. I don't love you! I've moved on! So get over it!"

I turn away and stomp to my room, slamming my door behind me and plopping on my bed. Vanne opens it anyway and stands there, his fists clenched. "We're not done talking, Locklyn. This has nothing to do with my jealousy. Have you forgotten what happened to Adume? Our *friend*? He was kidnapped and no one saw anything! You could have been next!"

"Well, I'm home now so you can go to bed," I grumble, tossing my purse aside.

"Locklyn," he says softly and approaches me, kneeling at my bedside. I look at him, my brow furrowed, as he goes on, "Adume is my best friend. You are the only woman I've ever loved and I don't want to lose you, too."

"Nothing will happen to me, Vanne."

He sighs, "I can only hope."

Then he stands and rubs his hand through his copper hair. "I hate being at a crossroads with you, but your safety means everything to me. Promise you'll at least message me next time you're out late."

"I promise," I tell him softly and he nods.

"Goodnight then, Locklyn."

"Goodnight."

He leaves, gently closing my door behind him, and I fall back on my bed. What a night it's been.

A LESSON IN ESPIONAGE

THE NEXT DAY, I am called to the police station to talk about Adume's recording. I'm not thrilled to watch my friend freak out again before being kidnapped, but Detective Caine said that there's something in the recording I should see. So I leave without breakfast and take the car to the station. Vanne told me to be back by one o'clock so he could go grocery shopping, but if the detective needs me any longer, there's always public transportation. He despises riding the metro, though.

As I sit in the waiting area for Detective Caine to greet me, my Mini buzzes in my coat pocket. Stryder has sent me a message and I smile as I open it.

Good morning, gorgeous, can I stop by later this afternoon?

Of course! I get off work at five and good morning to you, too, handsome. I write back.

Great, I'll see you later!

See you then!

"Miss Harte?"

I glance up and slip my Mini back into my pocket as I stand. "Good morning, sir."

"I wouldn't be saying that yet," Detective Caine mumbles and gestures for me to follow him.

We wander past all the desks and come to his office in the back, hidden but spacious. He closes the door behind me as I sit in the armchair and he sits at his desk. He powers on the TV on his wall and pulls up the recording that was taken from my Mini.

Detective Caine then sets the remote down and steeples his fingers. "As you know, I've called you here to show you something I found on the recording. You were the last person Mr. Hines was in contact with before he was kidnapped. You also are the Circle's personal secretary, which I believe will come in handy once I show you what I've found."

With that, we turn to the TV and he plays the recording in a slower setting so we can observe the details. My stomach turns at Adume's frightened face and when the hooded man appears behind him. Then Detective Caine stops the recording right before it ends with Adume's Mini being smashed to bits.

"Tell me what you see," he says, quizzing me like I'm a detective in training.

I scrutinize the paused image, my nose scrunched up as I analyze. The hooded man has Adume by now and is lifting him out of his seat. His hands are gloved and the camera cuts off his head so we have no close-up visual. It's dim in Adume's Cube, which is different. My gaze travels down to the bottom, where the other kidnapper's hand rests on Adume's desk as he prepares to smash the Mini. This one doesn't wear gloves and even though it's a little blurry, I make out the distinct statement ring on his pinky finger.

A statement ring that I know only Elite Council members wear.

"Oh," I gasp, touching my hand to my chest. I turn back to Detective Caine. "Do you think that someone in the Elite Council kidnapped Adume?"

"That *or* someone impersonating a Councilor could have kidnapped him. We all know the Councilors wear statement rings on their right pinkies but anyone could simply do that. I've sent the recording to our forensics department and their video expert is going to clear it up a little so we should have better results in a few days.

"That being said, you have better access to the Elite Council than we do, and I'll need you to gather information. Find out where they were Thursday morning. Just bring it up in casual conversation or whatever. I'm leaning more toward an impersonator than one of our Councilors, but you never know who can be corrupted in the government these days."

I bite my lip, nerves roiling in my belly. "Don't you have other detectives to dispatch and question the Elite Council?"

He rolls his eyes. "The Elite Council and Circle of Superiors are basically untouchable. I would have to go through the court first to get a search warrant and ask questions. They're not above the law, of course, but pretty close to it and I don't think we have time to wait for a warrant to be signed. So I'd like to enlist your help, Miss Harte. You'll be a detective for the day. Do you think you can do that?"

I think for a moment and knot my fingers together. I mean, I could simply ask each Councilor what they were up to Thursday morning. I'll have to make sure I'm not too invasive; otherwise, they might figure out I'm trying to gather information for the police. So I nod, "Yes, I can do it," and hope that no one becomes too suspicious.

The first Councilor I talk to is Councilor Carmichael in the elevator.

"Good morning, Blake," I chirp.

He glances at me, a smile on his lips. "Good morning, Locklyn. You seem chipper."

"Well, I went on a lovely date last night."

Blake's smile drops and he scratches his ear, glancing away. "Oh. With who?"

"You wouldn't know him. So, what have you been up to? Did you do anything interesting this week?"

He shrugs. "I've been bowling every evening this week. The league has a tournament coming up and I'm trying to brush up on my skills."

Ah, yes, Blake is in a bowling league with others who are retired and over fifty. But honestly, Blake himself, even at the young age of twenty-three, is an old man at heart.

"Sounds exciting. How about Thursday morning?"

"I was trying to motivate myself to go to work and then still struggled to get out of bed." Blake's gaze wanders to me again. "Why do you ask?"

"I'm curious about what you do on Thursday mornings."

"Okay..."

"So what time did you come into the office?"

"Shouldn't you know? You have access to the Council's time sheets," he casually mentions.

I turn to him. "Wait, I can see the Elite Council's time sheets? I thought only Zoie could."

"You're the secretary of secretaries, Locklyn. Did you really not know that?"

"*No*, I only thought I could see the Circle's time sheets."

He cocks his head at me. "Why are you asking, anyway?"

I scoot closer and lower my voice. "Don't tell any of the other Councilors I said this but...the Circle is having me investigate the Councilors to make sure they aren't slacking off. I know you aren't, of course, but the others might be. I even overheard them talking about possibly changing up the Council."

Blake straightens his coat jacket. "Then I will do my best to be on time from now on."

I pat his shoulder. "Good."

Before the elevator comes to his floor, Blake wrings his fingers together and says, "So, I know you might be too busy and everything, but our first tournament game is next Friday, and I...think it'd be great if you came. You always enjoyed coming, right?"

I did.

"I'll think about it." I brush a loose curl behind my ear.

He looks a little disappointed but nods. "Okay."

The elevator comes to his floor and the doors open. He waves to me as he exits and then hurries to the Council Room. I ride alone to the top floor, eager to look at the Council's time sheets.

At home, after a grueling day of secret detective work and planning the Autumn Charity Ball, I take off my heels and collapse on the couch with a small tub of rocky road ice cream for one. Vanne isn't home, so I have the apartment to myself. I stretch out and wave my hand at the TV sensor. It flickers to life and I find my favorite show, *A Collection of Hearts.*

A little over halfway through the episode I'm watching, there's a knock at the front door. I pause my show and get up with my ice cream and slippers, shuffling over to the door. Through the peephole, I see it's Stryder and I facepalm. *Totally* forgot he was coming over. I shrug. At least I'm still wearing the dress I chose for work today.

I swing the door open with a smile and gesture for him to come in, "Hey there."

"Hi." He steps inside and glances around. "Hmm."

"What?" I ask, closing the door behind him and trotting back over to the couch before I sit down again.

"Your apartment is immaculate."

"Vanne likes to keep it spotless. He cleans when he's bored."

Stryder joins me on the couch. "Is…is Vanne here right now? Is he going to kick me out?"

"Oh, no, he's gone." I snuggle up to his side and purr, "It's just the two of us."

His ears tint pink and he gestures to my ice cream. "Bad day at work?"

I sigh, "A little stressful, if I'm being honest, but you know, ice cream can fix almost anything."

"True."

I set my ice cream on the coffee table and turn toward him, my fingers crawling along his knee. "So, what did you stop by for?"

He gulps. "Locklyn, I need to tell you something."

I lean into the couch, tucking my legs beneath me. "Proceed."

Stryder gazes at me, his pretty almond eyes so sincere. He reaches for my hand and takes it, his thumb rubbing against my palm. He reaches for my hand and takes it, his thumb rubbing against my palm as he says, "I want to explore our attraction a little more. I'd like to take you out again and get to know you."

I glance away, my fingers curling around his. "So...you want to date me?"

"Yes." He leans down, so he catches my gaze again. "What do you say?"

I stand and move toward the wide window that looks out on all the silver skyscrapers that make up Moon Crossing. In the far, far distance, I can even see what's left of the Crow Factory and I bite my lip, thinking of Adume. If I'm going to take the blame for something supposedly huge, then I shouldn't involve Stryder. I won't be able to tell him the truth without Adume's life still in danger and I certainly can't risk it. I don't want to break his heart before anything can really begin between us. I shouldn't lead him on.

"Locklyn?" he asks, sounding less confident by the second.

I turn to him and rub my arms as goosebumps emerge on my skin. "I...I can't pursue you, Stryder. I can't...date you right now."

His cheeks flush in embarrassment. "Why not?"

"There's something..." I trail off as he stands and walks up to me, standing so close that I lose my train of thought.

Stryder's gaze strikes me like lightning. In a soft voice, he admits, "I like you, Locklyn, I really do. I've liked you since the moment we met and I haven't stopped thinking about you since. I came back to Moon Crossing for you, hoping that the spark between us was still there. I know you're going through a tough time right now, but I want to help you. Please, let me be there for you."

"My heart wants to, but my mind can't," I whisper. "I'm sorry."

He says nothing, only nods slowly and turns away. I watch him walk over to the front door and run his hand through his hair. Before he leaves, he glances back at me. "That's all I wanted to tell you. Have a nice evening, Locklyn."

When he swings the front door open and walks out, I feel my heart drop into my stomach. Whoever is holding Adume hostage is doing a good job at ruining my life before they even plan to. I want to date Stryder, but I can't. For his own good. Even justified, it doesn't sit right with me.

THE REUNION

TWO WEEKS HAVE passed since my investigative work for Detective Caine began and they still have no leads. One night, I forced myself to drive out to the Crow Factory to confront Adume's kidnapper, but no one was in sight. It was like they had never been there at all, so now I don't know where they've taken Adume or if he's still alive. The anticipation of this so-called "drastic event" is driving me insane and I'm hardly able to focus on work. I've become paranoid and cannot sleep most nights.

Stryder hasn't talked to me. Electra and Glory are still worried sick about Adume, and Vanne doesn't talk much these days either. I went to two of Blake's bowling games, just to get out of my routine of going to work and coming straight home to binge *A Collection of Hearts.* I'm waiting around for the police to arrest me and I hate that I want it to happen sooner rather than later…so Adume can be free.

This weekend, my mom, Maisie, and my brother, Jesse, are in town. His son, Baden, will stay with our stepfather in Bountiful Hill. I don't quite know what she wants or why she insists on coming this weekend at all when I have to finalize plans for the Autumn Charity Ball next weekend. But Vanne thinks it's a good idea to have my family around. He's visiting his brothers in Bountiful Hill.

A sharp knock at the door gets me off the couch and over to the door. I swing it open and Mom saunters in with my brother lugging their bags. She hugs me, kisses my cheek, and then glances around at the messy apartment. Vanne hasn't even been gone for 24 hours and I've already made it messy.

She quirks an eyebrow at me, joking, "Where's your semi-permanent manservant?"

I roll my eyes. "*Vanne* is visiting his brothers this weekend and he's not my manservant, Mom, he's my Protector."

Jesse sighs as he sets their bags down in the living room and pops his back. "Ma, why did you bring so much stuff? We're only staying for three days."

"I need everything. Don't judge me."

"Too late," he grumbles as he ambles up and wraps me in a bear hug.

I squeak as he squeezes me. "Do you like being Mom's semi-permanent manservant?"

He snorts. "Shush."

I smile as he lets go and we sit on the couches. I turn off the TV and fold my blanket in my lap. "So, what did you have in mind for our 'fun family weekend'? I have some work that needs to be done before Monday morning."

Mom folds her hands in her lap. "Well, first off, you and I are booked for a spa treatment tomorrow morning, the whole deal. Jesse gets a massage and a sauna experience."

My brother nods slowly. "Is that all you brought me up here for?"

She cocks her head at him. "You've been so tense and wound up lately, sweetie, I think you need a relaxing get-away."

"Hmph."

"But we'll go to dinner tonight. We have plenty of catching up to do."

Both Jesse and I grumble, not looking forward to this 'supposedly relaxing' weekend and Mom frowns, tsking at us. "Stop moping about it. You are adults now, *not* children anymore. Besides, Locklyn, I know you're probably working yourself too much and Jesse, you rarely get out of the house to do anything with Baden."

"I know, I know," my brother sighs, rubbing his forehead. "It's been difficult...without Dalia."

Mom's brow creases and she sighs as well. "I know how hard it is. I've been there, but you still have your son to think of. Dalia wouldn't want you to be stagnant."

I glance down at my hands as silence falls over us. Jesse's wife, Dalia, passed away nearly a year and a half ago from a rare form of brain cancer. Their son was only five years old so Jesse has been raising Baden by himself since. He and Baden have been living with my mom and stepfather for the past few months until he can get on his feet again since he got laid off. I don't know the pain of losing a spouse, but I know the pain of losing someone you love. My father.

"I have planned nothing for our last day. I wanted to leave that up to you two."

"Okay." I look at my brother. "I'm sure we can figure something out."

He nods. "Yeah, sure."

As promised, Mom takes us to dinner that night at the Cinnamon Lounge—a high-end restaurant with a pretty price tag. But she strolls in like she's VIP and tells the Maitre D' that we have a reservation under Stretton. I've only met my stepfather once—when he and my mom got married—but I still find it strange to hear her go by Maisie Stretton rather than Maisie Harte or Maisie Hillen; her maiden name. At least Jesse gets to keep our last name forever.

Dinner is incredibly tasty and it's probably the best food I have ever consumed in my life. My mom has come a long way from being a deadbeat college student to a single mom and now the Chief Marketing Officer at an entertainment company in Bountiful Hill. So I guess she and Oisin are doing pretty well for themselves. I should visit sometime and see what life is like in Bountiful Hill. If I could escape this situation with no consequences, then I would gladly go to Bountiful Hill.

To my surprise, Superior Masoni and Superior Cozeht are out dining with their wives and Mom encourages them to join us. I'm surprised that they don't look down on her—considering what my father did—but they seem genuinely happy to see her. Jesse and I sit back, chatting while the older adults talk.

"I should have worn my wedding tuxedo to this place," he tells me softly, glancing around at all the other expensively dressed men.

"You look nice enough. Maybe someone will think you're the valet. That's not an inferior position."

He gives me a side-long glance, unamused at my joke. "You're mean."

I laugh lightly. "Only to you, Jesse."

My brother straightens as the server drops by and asks if we need anything. He smiles and asks for another glass of Winter Gin. I sip on my drink until the server walks away and then nudge my brother, my eyebrows raised.

He plays dumb. "What?"

"You think the server is cute."

"So what if I do? I like to admire beautiful women sometimes."

I tip my head at him. "So have you been going on dates?"

"Didn't you hear Mom say that I hardly get out of the house? Of course I don't go on dates."

"Why not?"

Jesse's hand curls into a fist on the table. "I'm not thinking about dating at this point. I want to focus on Baden."

"Understandable."

"What about you? Any dating after the incident with Blake?"

I glance at the two Superiors and lower my voice so they can't hear. "Keep quiet, okay? The Superiors weren't happy with me and Blake about the whole situation." I sigh. "But no, I mean, not really. I went on a date with someone but...it won't work out."

"So you say."

"So I *know*."

He shakes his head. "Locklyn, Locklyn, Locklyn."

The server comes by again with Jesse's drink and then says to me, "Ma'am, could you follow me for a moment?"

I share a look with Jesse before standing and moving away from our table. I follow the server over to the bar—tucked away in a far corner of the restaurant—and she picks up two glasses of a fizzy drink I can't quite name as she turns to me.

"These are special orders for Superior Cozeht and Superior Masoni. I would deliver them myself, but I know that you're their secretary and I think they'd appreciate the drinks more if they came from you."

I don't make a move to take the drinks and instead ask, "Who ordered them?"

The server shakes her head. "He gave me no name, but he said he knows the Superiors personally and wanted to send them the drinks."

"But…you don't want to deliver them?"

"Well, I can't. The man who sent them wants you to."

"That's…strange. I'm a guest here, not a server."

She shrugs. "I know, but I have to follow the customer's orders."

After a moment of thought, I hesitantly take the two glasses. "Okay then."

Feeling a little awkward, I wander back to the table and clear my throat. Everyone looks at me and I set down each drink in front of Superior Cozeht and Superior Masoni. "Complimentary drinks for gracing us with your presence tonight, My Superiors."

"Thank you, Miss Harte," Superior Cozeht says with a smile and takes a sip of his.

Superior Masoni nods and sets his aside for a moment. They chat again and I take a seat next to Jesse once more. He leans over to me. "What was that?"

"I don't know. Someone wanted me to deliver their drinks," I shrug and pick up my glass again. "Maybe the server was too nervous to address the Superiors herself."

"But it's weird that she'd have you deliver the drinks and not another server."

"I know...really weird."

We eat in peace for the rest of the night and both Superiors finish their complimentary drinks. We say goodbye, get in the car, and drive back to my apartment. In the elevator, Mom comments on my kindness in bringing the Superiors' drinks, but I say little on the subject. Who knows where those drinks came from? But both Superior Cozeht and Masoni seemed absolutely cheery once we left them.

As we walk down the hallway to the apartment, I'm shocked to see Stryder waiting outside, tapping his foot impatiently. He straightens when he sees us and his gaze glimpses over Mom and Jesse before settling on me. I hurry to him and take his arm, stepping aside so Mom and Jesse can get to the door.

"What are you doing here?" I ask quietly.

"Who's this?" Mom asks, stepping up beside me.

I turn to her. "Mom, this is my friend Stryder."

She sizes him up. "Nice to meet you, Stryder."

He nods. "Nice to meet you as well, ma'am."

She steps back and introduces my brother. "And this is Jesse, my son."

I watch my brother and Stryder shake hands, nodding in a silent greeting, and then I hand Mom the keys. "I'll be in soon."

"Mhm." She glances between me and Stryder and then slips into the apartment, my brother following her.

Once the door is closed and we're alone, I guide Stryder to the stairwell. There, I release him and cross my arms. "So?"

A frown creases his mouth. "You don't look thrilled to see me."

"I thought you'd never see *me* again after what I told you."

"Yeah, well...something's changed." His fingers make a mess of his hair. "I'm going to Bountiful Hill tomorrow and I was hoping you'd come with me."

I blink at him. "Come with you to Bountiful Hill? Why?"

"I want to spend more time with you. Out of Moon Crossing. I would still like to be friends."

"Stryder, my mom and brother are here to spend the weekend with me. It'd be incredibly rude to up and leave."

He groans and rubs his face. "*Blazes*, can't you come with me for one day?"

My brow furrows. "What's wrong with you? Usually, *I'm* the one who's a mess."

Stryder paces. "This city isn't safe. I've always felt like that with Moon Crossing and it makes me antsy to be here. I'm sure you could use a break from the city, anyway."

"I have a lot to do this weekend, between spending time with my family and finalizing plans for the Autumn Charity Ball next weekend, Stryder. So I don't have time to gallivant around Bountiful Hill with you."

"Fine." He throws his hands up in defeat and then rubs his face again.

I watch him pace to the other side of the landing and back. "Okay, there's something wrong with you."

Stryder shoots me an annoyed look that actually startles me and he snaps, "Stop asking what's wrong with me."

"Hey, there's no need to get testy with me." I walk to the door and turn the handle. "If you're done talking then I am, too."

"Wait, wait," he counters and bolts over to me, pushing the door closed with his fist. I glance up at him, puzzled by his nature tonight. He goes on, his voice low and sincere. "I'm sorry for snapping at you. I'm stressed out right now. What you told me about your friend has me worried about you so I was...hoping you'd like to get out of Moon Crossing until all this passes."

I sigh, tipping my head to the side. "But that's the thing, Stryder, I can't leave Moon Crossing. It...won't be safe for my friend if I do, or for anyone else I care about. So you go to Bountiful Hill, get out of this insane city," I shuffle closer and press a sweet kiss against his cheek, "and forget about me."

He steps away from me. I swing the door open and head to my apartment without looking back.

A CITY OF HAUNTED HEARTS

A T THE SPA the next day, we happen upon Superior Dunn and his wife. I try to unwind, I really do, but it's incredibly hard with everything that's going through my mind. So I listen to Mom drone on and on to Mrs. Dunn until she mentions someone I've never heard of.

"Wait, wait," I interrupt, "who's Nadia?"

She turns to me and bites her lip. "Nadia is my daughter."

My eyebrows shoot to my hairline. "*What*? You never told me you and Oisin had a baby."

"I thought you wouldn't care, seeing how you behaved towards Oisin at our wedding. I had Nadia a little over a year and a half after we were married. Jesse came down to see me after the birth, but I didn't want to tell you because...well, you were still angry with me."

"I would have loved to know about my half-sister!"

"Shh," she glances around before eyeing me, "keep your voice down, sweetie. I would have told you sooner, but you never wanted to talk anymore. I didn't want that negativity around Nadia as well."

I sit back in my chair and glance down at the attendant giving me a pedicure. "Well, I hope you'll grant me the chance of meeting her someday."

Her brow furrows and she reaches over, taking my hand. "Of course you'll get to meet Nadia, dear."

I abruptly pull my hand away.

Mrs. Dunn clears her throat and leans around Mom. "So, Locklyn, how have you been since I last saw you?"

"Well enough," I quip.

Mom gasps lightly and I push myself up, even at the protest of my attendant. Mrs. Dunn and Mom glance up at me. "Excuse me, I need to take a moment."

"Miss Harte, your pedicure—"

"Will be fine, thank you."

"Locklyn—"

I turn on my heel and waddle across the room, unbothered by the stares. The attendants, particularly, are looking at my pedicure, but I'm doing my best not to mess it up. How could Mom keep such a secret from me? Granted, our relationship wasn't the strongest after my father was executed, but we've been working on it. I feel...left out. She wasn't even going to tell me anytime soon.

I push open the doors, walk through the lobby in my robe until I come outside to the courtyard. I startle Superior Dunn, who is taking a smoke break, and he waves me over to sit next to him.

"Hello, Miss Harte. You look tense," he comments with a chuckle.

"You seem tense yourself, My Superior." I quirk an eyebrow as I sit. "We're at a spa, and yet, it seems to be the least relaxing place right now."

He takes a drag and exhales a puff of smoke. "You remind me of your father. Never taking the time to unwind, even while on vacation. I guess we're all alike. What's stressing you out, Miss Harte?"

I shift on the bench and fold my hands on my lap. For one, I'm surprised that Superior Dunn mentioned my father. None of the Superiors talk about him in my presence and two, I obviously won't tell Superior Dunn what I'm really upset about.

So I say, "My mother, first and foremost, and then the Autumn Charity Ball."

He nods and reaches over, patting me on the shoulder. "Family matters can be tough. But, I'm sure you'll do a splendid job on the ball, Locklyn, like you always have."

"Thank you, Superior Dunn. May I ask why you're smoking at a spa?"

Superior Dunn takes another drag and his brow furrows. "You know about our Recon scouts in Wolves Creek, yes?"

"Yes, sir."

"Well, we've lost contact with them and we don't know where they could be or even if they're alive. The O'kshah deny that they've been in contact with the Recons, but that's hard to believe. We've been looking for a reason to boot their *darga* and assimilate the tribe. I suppose we have one now."

I frown. "If the O'kshah have done nothing, then why would you unleash the Recons on them?"

"We won't be 'unleashing' the Recons, Locklyn. Assimilation should be a peaceful movement."

I take in a breath and clutch my robe in my fingers. "Sir, I don't agree and it's not my place to say anything but maybe...maybe those Recons disappeared for a reason."

He gives me a sidelong glance. "You're right, it's not your place to say anything. We have Bountiful Hill under our thumb and we *need* Wolves Creek as well. To unite the entire District, of course, and protect all of us from outside forces."

"Protect us how?" I ask, treading carefully.

"Well, Moon Crossing is well-equipped, as you know, and having the District united, with soldiers of distinct skill sets and such, gives us a unique advantage." Superior Dunn shrugs. "In a few weeks, we'll be heading to Wolves Creek to do away with their *darga*."

I sit there for a moment, grasping my robe as I try not to let my annoyance show. I never really approved of them sending Recons to scout out Wolves Creek and spy on their *darga*. They've earned their right to their own land and I don't think we need to interfere with that. But who am I to say anything about it? I'm only the Circle's secretary and they decide what's best for the city, for our people.

"Locklyn," Mom says behind us.

I stand and bow my head to Superior Dunn. "My Superior."

He nods back. "Miss Harte."

I move past Mom into the spa's lobby but she grabs my arm in passing. "Darling, now that you've had time to cool off, can you be pleasant around others?"

"I can try," I huff and we head over to our seats to get our pedicures finished.

At home, I crash on the couch and tuck a pillow under my head. My Mini buzzes on the table and I reach over to grab it. I have a message from Superior Wells saying that he'll drop by to check up on the charity planning. I've made reservations for the venue, catering, and music. All that's left is a revision of the final guest list and to send the rest of the invitations out. Since nothing has happened, maybe I really will attend the ball. At least have one night feeling luxurious and rich as I dine with the elite of Moon Crossing.

Mom and Jesse are in the kitchen cooking dinner, so I'm the one who has to get up when Superior Wells knocks. I smooth out my blouse and cardigan before opening the door and let a smile come to my lips. "Good afternoon, Superior Wells."

He nods to me. "Good afternoon, Miss Harte. Do you have the reservation receipts?"

"Yes, please, come in."

Superior Wells walks into the apartment and makes himself comfortable at the breakfast bar. I head to my room to retrieve my folder of documents and as I pass by my dresser; I catch sight of the azure pendant that my father gave me many, many moons ago. I pause for a moment and rub my thumb over its crystalline surface. I should visit his memory stone before night falls. I usually go every week, but I've been so disoriented as of late that I haven't been. No matter what Adume's kidnapper said about him, I will always love him for who he was and pay my respects. Dad deserved as much.

I pick up the necklace and tuck it away in the pocket of my cardigan before heading back to the kitchen. Superior Wells chats with Mom and Jesse but turns to me when I reappear. I hand him the reservation receipts and tell him what else still needs to be done. He nods, asks a few questions I answer flawlessly, and then promptly leaves before we eat.

"Sounds like everything is coming together for the Autumn Charity Ball," Mom says as she sets a plate of roast beef, a baked potato, and vegetables in front of me.

"Slowly but surely," I tell her. "Thanks for dinner, Mom."

"Hey, I helped, too," Jesse scoffs as he sits next to me, digging into his plate already.

I clear my throat. "I'm going to visit Dad's memory stone after dinner."

Mom sits across from us. "I should go, too, while I'm here. Do you want us to come with you, honey?"

"No, I want to go alone tonight."

"Of course, darling," she says softly.

We fall silent, lamenting the future event of visiting Dad's memory stone. I need to tell someone what's happening and even though his body won't be there, I feel his spirit might listen to me.

It's cold and hazy as I drive to the cemetery. Lucky for me, there's only one other car in sight as I park and get out. I draw the hood of my coat over my head and clutch a candle and lighter in my pockets, along with the azure pendant. I pass through the iridescent gates and wind down the cobblestone path. The cemetery isn't as creepy as it could be, with fresh mounds and positively green patches of grass, since all citizens of Moon Crossing are cremated, their ashes given to their families. Mom took Dad's urn to Bountiful Hill so the memory stone is what I have left.

Since Dad was executed, his memory stone is nowhere near the others. Though he was a leader of Moon Crossing, his stone isn't in the crypt with past leaders.

He was too good for them, anyway.

On my way, I catch sight of a figure kneeling at a memory stone near a weeping willow tree. Hunched over, murmuring something as their candle flickers in the slight breeze. I move on. We all have our dead to remember, and it's best not to disturb anyone while they utter a prayer.

Dad's memory stone is almost on the other side of the cemetery, but once I reach it, I'm glad to find that no one has moved other stones close to his. For now, only his stone weighs into the ground, his memory eternal. I kneel at the stone and brush away the leaves that have fallen on its granite surface. It reads:

HERE RESIDES THE MEMORY OF CICONE HARTE—THE LOVING FATHER OF JESSE AND LOCKLYN, HUSBAND OF MAISIE, AND A SUPERIOR OF MOON CROSSING. MAY HE REST FROM THE TERRORS HE FACED AND START ANEW ON THE OTHER SIDE.

I trace Dad's name, tears pooling in my eyes. I remove the candle and lighter, set the wick aflame, and let it illuminate the engraved letters. As I close my eyes, I clasp my hands together and whisper a prayer of hope that my father's soul is well, that he's been accepted and his wrongdoings are forgiven for.

After my prayer, my eyes flutter open and the tears slip silently down my cheeks. I lean down, press my forehead against his memory stone, and keep my voice low. "Papa, I wish you were here. You would know exactly what to do and I really need your help right now. My friend's life is in danger and I can't do anything but let his captors ruin my life. I might—" I pause as a strangled sob escapes me. "I might see you soon if they truly succeed. I don't know what they want and I don't know how to rescue Adume without paying the consequences of my own life, or others.

"You were always there for me, even when I stubbed my toe and bawled about it for nearly an entire day. You never told me to toughen up and fight through the pain. You always told me to embrace it, that it's okay to feel and know how those feelings affect you. But I can't embrace this pain, Papa, and I don't want to lose my life. I want to live to see Moon Crossing change for the better, to see *your* vision for the District put into action...

"But I suppose...if it's meant to be, it will be, right? If I'm to die, for something I didn't do, to save Adume's life, to save Mom, Jesse, Electra, and everyone else I love, then I think I can accept that. I'll try to and I hope someday that everyone will remember me in a way as I remember you. I love you more than anything, Papa, and I hope you're behaving up there...I—I—"

I'm cut off by a shriek and I sit up, whipping my head around. Chills chase down my spine and I stand, moving away from Dad's memory stone. All I see through my misty gaze are shadows from the trees as the moonlight casts a bright glow on the grounds. I wipe my tears on my sleeve as I quickly wind up the path again, and my gaze catches the other mourner still here. However, they are no longer hunched over the memory stone and muttering words. Now, they lie on their back, gasping for air.

I race over and kneel next to them, glancing up at their face only to find that it's Superior Roman. My heart pounds in my chest and I rasp, "M—My Superior? *Oh, blazes!* Sir!"

His eyes shift back and forth rapidly. "I see—I see stars."

"Stay with me, sir, it's going to be okay. I'm calling an ambulance."

With one hand, I fumble to get my Mini out of my pocket and dial an ambulance, practically screaming at the operator to send one to the cemetery. My other hand falls on the knife hilt sticking out of Superior Roman's stomach. He wheezes as I carefully try to remove it.

"*Argh!*" he groans and shoves my hand away. "Don't! It's no use!"

I shift to cradle Superior Roman's head in my lap. "I'm sorry, I'm so sorry..."

He shakes his head, eyes glazing over. "Oh, *s—stars and s—skies above…t*—take me…take me to my f—final resting place."

"No, sir, you have to—"

His gaze finds mine. "Salana? I—is that y—you?"

My eyelids flutter. I glance at the memory stone to see it says Salana Roman. *He thinks I'm his late wife.* I brush my hand along his cheek. "Stay with me, okay? You'll make it."

A wobbly smile curls his lips and I hear the sirens as they approach the cemetery. Superior Roman stares at me, but I realize the light fades quickly from his eyes. So I ask one last question, "Who did this to you?"

He gulps in air and his eyes roll. "I—it was…it was—"

Superior Roman falls slack in my arms, his eyes blank, and I slide his lids closed. According to his weak pulse, he's still alive but barely and I suspect he's passed out from shock. Hopefully, he will wake up and tell us who is committing treason in this city.

The paramedics transport Superior Roman to the ambulance quickly and blaze off towards the hospital. I follow in my car, not caring that there's blood staining my clothes and hands or that I'm smearing it all over my steering wheel. My tears have dried, at least, but now I have an aching headache. I should call Mom and tell her I'm okay, but I forgot my Mini at the cemetery and I don't want to go back right now, in case whoever stabbed Superior Roman was looking for me as well.

I screech into the parking lot and fly into the emergency room. I'm immediately stopped by a hunky nurse, who says, "Excuse me, miss, but this is a restricted area…" his gaze falls over me and he asks, "Is that your blood? Are you injured, miss?"

I shake my head. "No, Superior Roman is and I—I found him. Where is he? He should be here by now."

The nurse's expression falls and he takes me under his arm, leading me over to an empty seating area against the wall. "Superior Roman…didn't make it. He was dead on arrival and had DNR orders. There was nothing we could do for him." He sighs. "He was our last one."

I glance at the nurse. "What do you mean our last one?"

He looks around and then snatches a shock blanket off a nearby table and wraps it around my shoulders. For a moment, he studies my face before he nods. "You're Locklyn Harte."

"Yes, I am. Now, what do you mean that Superior Roman was our last one? Last one of what?"

The nurse rubs a stubborn crease on his forehead. "Superior Roman was our last Superior. I'm probably not supposed to spread the news yet, but the other four—Masoni, Cozeht, Dunn, and Wells—were all assassinated this weekend. They're all dead, Miss Harte."

I am stunned into silence and I have to turn away. I gnaw on my lip and bury my face against my hands. *How? Why? Is this...is this what I'm going to be framed for? The murder of the Circle of Superiors?*

The nurse rubs my back and explains, "Masoni and Cozeht were rushed in this morning for what seemed like food poisoning but turned out to be arsenic poisoning. They died within minutes of each other. Dunn was shot behind a spa uptown and Wells was found dead by asphyxiation not even an hour ago...now Roman is gone, too. The police didn't even have time to send out anyone to protect the remaining Superiors, but I hear the Councilors are all under lockdown and being protected. It's been a terrible night."

I say nothing and curl into myself, hiding under the shock blanket. The nurse leaves me be and my grief drowns all the noise of the ER out. I saw every single Superior this weekend, alive and well. But now, they are all dead and I can't help the pit of dread in my stomach that this will all fall back on me. It's ingenious, really, blaming the personal secretary who surely would have access to many restricted files and discussions the Circle has and could certainly disagree with. But I'm not a murderer and I know exactly who did this.

I get up and drop the shock blanket. As I do, someone grabs my arm and I look to see Detective Caine standing there. His dark eyes bore into me as he simply says, "Miss Harte, I need you to come with me."

ON BORROWED TIME

*T*ICK, TOCK, TICK, *tock, tick*—

"Miss Harte, you were at the cemetery when Abrahm Roman was attacked. What were you doing there?"

My gaze flickers to Detective Caine and my shoulders hunch forward as I clasp my hands together in my lap. "I was visiting my father's memory stone and I noticed there was someone else visiting, but I didn't know it was Superior Roman at the time. I passed by him. I was in the middle of my visit when I heard a scream. I got up and ran to discover Superior Roman lying on the ground, a knife sticking out of his stomach. I..." I trail off and take a deep breath, "I tried to help him but it was...it was useless and I called an ambulance."

"Did you see anyone else around the cemetery? Hear anything?"

"No, I didn't see anyone else or hear anything. As you can imagine, I was...pretty caught up in visiting my father's memory stone."

Detective Caine asks a few more questions before he steeples his fingers. "The forensics team dusted the knife hilt and found your fingerprints on it. Care to explain that, Miss Harte?"

I brush a loose lock of hair behind my ear. "I tried to take the knife out but, of course, that was a foolish idea. I wasn't thinking properly."

"Yes, you shouldn't touch evidence, especially in the case of murder. So our only lead on Superior Roman's attack is *you*."

My pulse quickens and I glance at Detective Caine. "You know me, sir, and I would never kill *anyone*, especially a person I've admired for years."

He spreads his hands and shrugs. "I do know you, Miss Harte, and I know your arrest history. I'm not trying to speculate anything quite yet, but it's my job as a detective to consider every factor. And, well, we all know what your father did."

I stand and slam my hands against the metal table. "My father was a good man! No matter *what* he did, he was the best father to me!"

Detective Caine stands as well, albeit cautiously, and stares me down across the table. "Did you have any quarrels with Abrahm Roman?"

I blink. "No. Sure, I didn't always *agree* with the Circle but that doesn't mean that I would kill any of them! I'm *not* a murderer!"

"Again, Miss Harte, I'm not making any speculations or accusations. Simply asking a couple of questions."

"I'd like a lawyer."

"That might be a good idea."

I work my jaw and turn away, crossing my arms. "Am I allowed to go now?"

"Yes, you are. Thank you for your time. I've asked Officer Rase to take you home."

"But I have my own car—" I counter.

"I know and I don't care. You will let Officer Rase take you home and you can come back for your car tomorrow."

"*Fine*, fine."

I push out of the interrogation room and am met by Officer Rase. She takes my arm, without even a glimpse at me, and walks me out of the police station. She opens the passenger door of her patrol car and practically pushes me in. I sit there quietly as we drive to my apartment in silence. It's late now and I'm sure that Mom and Jesse are worried about me.

The crescent moon shines bright and I lean my head on my hand. I wonder when the police will let the rest of Moon Crossing know about the Circle's deaths. They probably won't until they have more evidence...more evidence against me, apparently. I close my eyes, worry creasing my brow. This can't be a coincidence—their deaths—and I feel foolish for not being suspicious that I saw each of the Superiors within two days. Outside of work, I hardly see them…but I do wonder if having me see them all was done on purpose…by whoever is holding Adume hostage.

The city is quiet and calm as I get out of the patrol car and head toward the lobby. Officer Rase watches me until I disappear through the front doors and punch the elevator button. It comes slowly, as if I'm waking it up, and I tuck my hands in my coat pockets, taking in a quiet breath. I don't even know if a lawyer would be worth paying if I have no intention of winning the case anyway—for Adume's sake and for the sake of everyone else I love.

The elevator dings and opens. I step inside and it's a quick ride to the fifth floor. My heart is heavy as I make my way to my apartment and slip the key in the lock. But the door flies open before I can even turn the key and Mom stands there, eyes wide as tears slip down her cheeks.

"Locklyn!" she gasps and drags me inside, wrapping me in a tight hug. I feel her shudder as she inhales sharply and it brings me back to when my father died. Mom hugged me like this, in hopes that she wouldn't lose me either. "*Heavens*, sweetie, I was so worried about you!"

I hug her back, gripping her sweater in my fingers. "I'm okay. I was at the police station."

She draws back and wipes away her tears, her voice raspy. "An officer at the cemetery told us that it was closed off because someone had been stabbed and they wouldn't tell us who it was. I thought it was you! So I sent Jesse out to look for you to…to make sure you weren't attacked."

I nod. "Well, it wasn't me. It was…it was Superior Roman. I was at Dad's memory stone when he was stabbed, but I didn't see anyone else around so I don't know who did it. At the hospital, I learned that—" I choke up and Mom guides me to the couch to sit down. I fan my face. "All the Superiors are dead, Mom, assassinated. They all died today."

She glances away and runs her trembling hands through her hair. We sit there for a moment, lamenting the deaths of our leaders and friends. Her shoulders hunch as she begins to cry again and presses her palms against her eyes.

"I told Detective Caine everything I knew and then he practically accused me of stabbing Superior Roman. But I didn't. You know I would never kill anyone, especially Superior Roman."

Mom reaches over and takes my hand. "I know you wouldn't, sweetie, and I'll get a lawyer for you. One from Bountiful Hill so they're not biased."

"Thanks, Mom."

She sniffles and reaches for her Mini on the table. "I guess I should tell Jesse you're home safe and sound." Her fingers prance across the screen as she sends my brother a message. Then she stands, leans over to kiss my head, and whispers, "I think I need some time alone, but I'm so glad you're okay, darling. Sleep tight if you can."

"Goodnight, Mom," I murmur and she heads to the office, closing the door behind her.

I sit back on the couch and pull my knees against my chest. The lamplight is dim and I stare out the wide, picturesque window across from me. Moon Crossing glimmers in the night, with life and laughter. It has yet to know that its leaders are gone, all assassinated within two days. How could every single Superior be picked off so quickly? They had the most well-trained security detail, ten agents assigned to watch over each Superior, outside of their home or always a few steps behind wherever they went. But, now that I think about it, I didn't see any security. How could they fail Moon Crossing and the Circle of Superiors? Maybe they were paid off. That's the only reasonable explanation.

I hardly slept, of course, especially after scrubbing Superior Roman's blood from my clothes and skin. When I wake, I trudge out into the living room and flip on the TV. Jesse rises from his bedroll set up in the corner and rubs his eyes. I keep the volume low but the top story running is Superior Roman's stabbing. The news anchor plays it as if he is recovering in the hospital and I don't see anything about any of the other Superiors.

"Huh," my brother says and pulls a t-shirt over his head, "I wonder why they're keeping the other assassinations hush-hush."

"They probably won't reveal it until they're ready to. Maybe they don't want everyone to fly into terror mode." I lean into the fridge and pull out a yogurt cup.

I don't have much of an appetite, but Mom will be short with me if I don't eat something today. So I plop down at the breakfast bar, crack open my yogurt, shake some granola into it and dig in. Jesse joins me and the news continues in the background.

He peels a banana and takes a bite. "But I think we all ought to know that our leaders are dead, that Moon Crossing is completely hopeless and vulnerable now."

"We have the Elite Council still so we're not completely hopeless and vulnerable," I point out.

"*Pft*, the Elite Council are like the privileged children of the Circle. They don't have as much authority for a reason."

I wave my spoon around. "Say what you want, but I think that at least Councilor Cristol or Councilor Carmichael would be perfectly capable of running this city as the Circle did."

Jesse gives me an unconvinced look. "Moon Crossing is moving in a direction that neither of them can keep up with. If anything, I'd place my money on Ridge and Cunningham becoming Superiors. They're old enough and have plenty more experience."

"Blake is a good man and he can pull Moon Crossing out of the dark pit it's falling in. He'll want to help Bountiful Hill and Wolves Creek rather than enslave them. Did you know that that was what the Superiors were planning to do with Wolves Creek? Basically, get rid of their *darga* and force the people to labor for the District? If Dad was still alive, he would have never let this happen."

"Yeah, he wouldn't have," my brother agrees, tossing his banana peel in the trash can.

I eat another spoonful of yogurt. "And, above all else, I have to work tomorrow and act as if nothing happened."

"You could call in sick, you know. That's a thing."

"I'm aware of that, but I wonder if the police will find it suspicious—since I'm apparently the only lead they have on Superior Roman's attack."

Jesse rubs his chin before he snaps his fingers. "What if you get Blake to vouch for you, huh? Certainly, they'll trust his word."

My brow furrows. "But I wasn't with Blake at all this weekend."

Jesse rolls his eyes. "Not for an alibi, to vouch for you on your character. He's someone who knows you personally, deeply, and if I'm right, he's still in love with you."

"I can't use Blake's feelings like that," I tell him, even as my cheeks flush pink, "it wouldn't be right."

"Locklyn, you don't have to make googly eyes at him to help you. As you said, Blake is a good guy and he'd help you if you were ever in need. You're in need now, to defend yourself from the police. Detective Caine questioned you, right?" I nod and he goes on, "I know he's had it out for you forever because you were such a troublemaker back in the day. So he'll probably try to build this case against you, solely relying on the fact that you happened to be at the cemetery when Superior Roman was attacked."

I eat the rest of my yogurt before I respond with, "Fine, I'll ask for Blake's help, but only *if* I'm taken to trial."

"Good, and once you are proven innocent, I will start planning the wedding that didn't happen between you two." He smirks.

"Oh, hush." I roll my eyes.

Jesse reaches across the island and pokes my cheek. "I'm only kidding. Although, I was looking forward to it."

"Me too."

☽ ✧ ☾

I stand outside of Blake's apartment, my fingers curled against the door as I prepare to knock. I haven't been to his apartment in over a year—when I came to break up with him. I push down that painful memory and knock. It takes a few moments for Blake to open the door and his eyes widen behind his glasses. Quickly, he tucks his dress shirt back into his trousers and runs his hands through his hair, ultimately making it more unruly.

"Hi, Locklyn, um…what are you doing here?" he asks, his midnight blue eyes filled with hope—as always.

"I need to talk to you. Can I come in?"

"Oh, of course." He steps aside and I stride in. "Can I take your coat?"

"Sure, thank you." I shrug out of my coat and hand it to him.

From the kitchen ambles out his big, fluffy border collie, Harper, and I grin, kneeling as she nearly tackles me to the floor. Her tail wags so vigorously and I scratch behind her ears as she licks my cheek.

"How's my girl, huh?" I coo and she prances around me, unbelievably excited.

Behind me, Blake says, "I see that Harper missed your ear scratches."

"And belly rubs," I laugh as she flips over on her back and I scrub my hands along her belly. "Who's a good girl, huh? You are, Harp, *yes you are.*"

I kiss her head as she gets up again and follows us over to the couch, where she snuggles her head against my legs. Blake smiles at me as I glance at him and then he scratches his ear, clearing his throat. "She hasn't been this excited ever since you…since you…"

"Broke up with you," I nod and curl my fingers over my knee, "but I don't want to talk about that, Blake. I came here to ask for your help. I'm sure you've heard what happened to the Superiors?"

His expression grows grim and he nods. "Yeah, I received the news last night."

"Did they tell you that I was the one who found Superior Roman?"

"No."

"Well, I did and I called the ambulance for him. At the hospital, I learned about the other Superiors and then Detective Caine took me down to the station for questioning. Seemingly, I was the only other person at the crime scene and Detective Caine has a hunch that I stabbed Superior Roman." My fists clench in my lap. "Of course, I didn't. I was visiting my father's memory stone when I heard him scream, but if Detective Caine tries to pin the evidence on me, would you be willing to testify to my character if they take me to trial? I know it's a lot to ask—"

"Yes, I'll do it," he states quite matter-of-factly.

Relief floods me, warm and bright. "I hope Detective Caine doesn't try to take me to trial. I've done nothing wrong...well, I did try to yank the knife out of Superior Roman, which was very stupid of me, but I was panicking..."

Blake reaches over and clasps my trembling hand in his. My gaze wanders to his, so soft and loving as usual. "I believe that you're innocent, Locklyn, and I will help you if it comes to trial. Ultimately, it'll be the Elite Council judging you, but I'll do it, even if the other Councilors say I can't."

"Thank you, Blake," I say softly.

Without thinking, I lean into Blake and let him cup my face. He tilts his head down to mine and our mouths brush ever so slightly. My hand falls on his knee and he closes the short distance between us. We haven't kissed in over a year and it feels euphoric. My shoulders relax and Blake slips his fingers into my hair, drawing me closer.

But then, I begin to think of Stryder Monroe and the kiss quickly turns sour. I abruptly pull back and he blinks at me, puzzled. Then he stands and tousles his hair once more. "I'm sorry. I—I don't know what came over me."

"Your feelings," I tell him and add, ever so quietly, "and mine."

Blake stares at me but I look away to rub Harper's head again. He doesn't say anything until I get up and face him. "You still have feelings for me?"

"Apparently." I rub my temple as a throbbing headache begins to emerge. "I think I'll always love you, Blake. Our breakup was premature and if we did marry, we would be happy. But maybe the universe was telling us this wasn't right. In some bizarre way, we simply weren't meant for each other?"

"I don't agree, I think that we are—that we were."

His glasses have slipped down his nose and I push them up. "I don't know, Blake, maybe." Then I sidestep him and head for the coat rack.

Blake follows me and helps me slip back into my coat. He asks, "I have a feeling that you're hesitant because of someone else, yes?"

"Possibly."

"Well, if it does work out between you two then I wish you the best, Locklyn."

I turn to him with a small smile. "Thanks, and I wish you the best as well."

He nods and opens the door for me. I kiss his cheek before stepping out and I head to the elevator, wondering if I made a mistake telling Stryder to forget about me.

THE AUTUMN CHARITY BALL

TONIGHT IS THE Autumn Charity Ball and I'm glad this week is over. No police officers have approached me or arrested me out of the blue. I've been keeping my head low at work, though most of the other employees have taken off considering the Superiors' deaths. Moon Crossing now knows of the assassinations and the city has held vigils every night this week for each Superior in Cascade Plaza. I've attended each, out of sight and out of mind.

I'm surprised that we're still holding the Autumn Charity Ball tonight, but Councilor Cristol insisted that this would be what the Superiors wanted...and ultimately, what Moon Crossing needs at this point. The charity selected has shifted—from a chosen organization—to the Superiors' families.

I wear a soft sapphire gown with black lace trim at the hem and a modest neckline. On my arm, I wear a black band, like everyone else, with the symbol of Moon Crossing on it—a red-handed scythe capturing the moon. I thumb the band as I get anxious, waiting for the rest of the designated guests to arrive. All the Councilors are here already and Councilor Cristol brought Glory as his plus one, of course. When she spots me, she leaves him and wanders over with a furrowed brow.

"Locklyn," she says softly and embraces me.

I hug her back. "Hey, Glory."

She draws away and holds me at arm's length. "You look lovely."

"Thank you, so do you," I remark, gesturing to her dusty pink gown with a sparkling bodice of diamonds.

Glory tips her head. "Are you going to be okay, honey? I can't imagine how difficult it must be for you—"

"I'll be fine," I interrupt, "and I'll feel better once we get the auction going."

"Ah, yes, was it your idea to have the proceeds go to the Superiors' families instead?"

"No, it was your beloved Councilor Cristol's idea."

She glances back at him, her cheeks tinting to match the color of her gown. "Of course it was." Glory turns her tawny gaze back to me. "He's always been so selfless."

I nod and a smirk quirks my lips. "Speaking of Councilor Cristol, when is he going to pop the question?"

Glory brushes her hand along her bodice and snatches a glass of red wine from a nearby server. "I would like to know the answer to that question, too. We've talked about it, you know, but I think he might be a little shy."

"Him? Shy? That's unbelievable."

"It is, but you know how O—"

"Excuse me."

Glory and I both turn to find none other than Stryder Monroe standing there. He shares a nod with Glory and she wanders back into Councilor Cristol's arms. I get my glass of wine and tip it against my lips as Stryder watches me. His expression strains and he lets out an awkward chuckle. "Hi, I, uh, I hope I'm not intruding."

I turn and let him follow me to the side of the stage. "Well, I know for a fact that you didn't receive an invitation, and the only other person who could have granted you one doesn't even like you."

"Believe it or not, Councilor Cristol *was* the one who invited me. I think he wanted me to see how 'selfless and rich' he's living," Stryder counters.

I take another sip of my drink. "That certainly sounds like him. But why are you talking to me instead of your 'oh so gracious' host?"

His head tilts. "I'm sure that I don't need to tell you why. We keep leaving on terrible terms and I want to make it right once and for all."

"So, what are you going to do? Donate all twenty-four credits you made this year to the Superiors' families?" I gibe.

Stryder laughs, which is not the response I expected, and boops my nose. "You're a funny one. Actually, I made *twenty-five credits* this year, which I consider a feat since I do absolutely nothing. Don't tell me that's not a valuable life skill."

I smile despite my feelings toward him right now. "I don't quite understand what 'skill' you have in obtaining only twenty-five credits. Did you find money on the street and pick it up or did you steal it?"

"You may never know how I acquired the money, but I would like to donate," he tells me and slips a check into my free hand.

My eyes widen as I gasp, "Stryder!"

"Just a token of my appreciation for you and all you do."

"This is...*way more* than twenty-five credits. I don't...I don't know if I should accept this or not."

"Please accept it. I won't take it back."

I touch his arm. "Thank you, Stryder."

"My pleasure." He dips into a bow, and then Councilor Cristol pushes him aside.

"Miss Harte, it's time," he tells me.

I blink away my awe and bob my head. "Yes, of course."

I hand my glass to Stryder and turn away. As I ascend the stairs to the stage, I tuck the check against my back and grab the microphone with my free hand. I test it quickly and then clear my throat to catch everyone's attention.

"Welcome to Prime Tower's Autumn Charity Ball. Tonight, our auction proceeds will go to each of the Superiors' families, the Masonis, Cozehts, Romans, Dunns, and the Wells. May we remember our beloved leaders tonight and bring comfort and love to their families. So, without further ado, let's begin. Miss Zoie Goodwin will head the auction."

Applause is given as Zoie steps onto the stage with the first item to be auctioned off. Stryder hands me my glass back and we move to the nearest table, where my clutch sits. I slip Stryder's check into my clutch and watch Zoie's charismatic smile as she auctions off the items.

After we have sold a few, I glance at Stryder and ask, "So, how did Bountiful Hill treat you this last week?"

"Fine. I took up a week-long job helping with the harvest so the next time you have corn on the cob, I'm probably the one who picked it."

"I'll remember to pay homage to you when I eat corn on the cob."

The corner of his mouth lifts. "How was your weekend with your family?"

"It was okay. I mean, it wasn't relaxing at any point, but I'm glad I got to see my mom and brother."

"Well, maybe you'll get to relax one of these days."

My heart catches in my throat and I glance down at the auction paddle in front of me, running my finger along the number's grooves. "Yeah, maybe."

Stryder is quiet for a moment before he scoots his chair closer to mine and leans on his arm, gazing at me. "Locklyn."

"Don't give me that look," I counter and brush a loose lock of hair behind my ear.

His eyebrow quirks. "You're not very good at hiding your emotions, you know. So I won't ask what's wrong. But I will ask what you're doing after this shindig?"

"Still trying to ask me on a date, huh?"

He shrugs. "Worth a shot, right? And who said it was a date?"

I reach out and set my hand on his. "In that case, I'm not doing anything. I should go home and sleep, but I won't be able to sleep anyway...I'm babbling on. What did you have in mind?"

Stryder flips my hand over and draws a circle on my palm. "Have you ever heard of Sapphire Point?"

A blush warms my face. "Yes, I have. It was my parents' favorite spot. That's where my father proposed to my mother and where they got married."

"Ah, so it has a reputation for romance, eh?"

"Yes. Should I bring my swimsuit?"

"Sure." His fingers crawl up my arm and my pulse quickens. "Would you mind if we took your car instead? Mine will probably break down and then we'll be stuck out there."

"Would that be such a bad thing, though?" I bite my lip, trying not to smirk.

Stryder draws my hand up to his mouth and brushes his lips along my knuckles, eyes twinkling. "I would think not."

My smirk breaks through. "Where should I pick you up then?"

"I'm staying at the Ruby Vista Hotel."

"Great, I can't wait for our non-date."

"Eh, how about sort-of-date?"

I grin. "Okay, Stryder, it's a sort-of-date."

☽ ✧ ☾

Despite trying to leave as quickly as I can, I'm stuck in traffic for about an hour, so I pick up Stryder quite late. When I pull up to the curb, I reach for my work Mini, while mine is in repair from the incident last weekend, and I message Stryder that I'm here. As I sit there, I think of how well the auction went. Nearly every item was sold at a remarkable price. I don't know how much we've raised, but I get to collect and dispense it evenly among the Superiors' families when I go back to work...if I don't get arrested and executed first.

The passenger door opens, startling me, and Stryder slips in. I reach over and bat him on the leg. "Announce yourself before you get in, *heavens.*"

He chuckles. "Sorry to startle you. Should I get out and announce myself?"

"No, let's go." I check over my shoulder before pulling out and the lights of the city glitter in the night.

We chat on our drive to Sapphire Point and I keep thinking about my parents. They were so in love and I remember wanting to find a love like theirs one day. They had their fights but in the end, they always made up. They knew how important it was to set an example for Jesse and me about a healthy relationship. One thing that helped destroy it was my father's secrets. I was the only one who knew about his trading outside the barrier and his greediness, but he never let it affect his relationship with Mom or with us.

Which is why it puzzles me to think he'd do something so horrific as he did. He grew up poor, but he made his way in this world of his own volition. He was kind, smart, and goofy. He was also good at bargaining. My father's guilty pleasure truly turned out to be his downfall.

"Locklyn?" Stryder asks, startling me yet again from my thoughts.

I glance at him. "Hmm?"

"You missed the turn."

"Oh, sorry." I press gently on the brakes and turn around.

I can still feel Stryder's gaze on me, but he's kind enough not to ask. So instead, he says, "I hope it doesn't rain while we're here."

"Was it cloudy earlier?"

"During the auction, I noticed it. And, well, my weather app says there's a storm approaching."

"Always trust the weather app, right?"

"Hey, sometimes it's more reliable than the news, so yes, I trust the weather app," he chuckles.

We come to Sapphire Point and I park under one of the fully-fledged palm trees. Hopefully, no coconuts decide to kiss the ground and hit my windshield instead. Stryder and I get out and grab two blankets from the backseat, wrapping one around me. He takes a satchel I hadn't noticed and brings it along. I let him lay down the other blanket on the sand and then we sit side by side, watching the waves lap gently on the shore.

The Glass Sea reflects the starry night sky perfectly. The moon, as bright and round as ever, looms high above, now revealing the possible rain clouds moving in. This is one of the most beautiful places I've ever been and it brings back fond memories of beach days with my family. I glance down the wide, white sand beach, wondering where my dad proposed to my mom. The beginning of their happiness.

"I often forget that we live on an island," I say to fill the silence.

"It is vast," he remarks, tipping his head back to look at the sky.

"We've never left the District and there's so much more to explore out there." I rub my hands together with a sigh. "I wish I could leave but...well, you know how it is with our citizen trackers."

"I...don't have a citizen tracker."

My eyes widen as I glance at him. "You never got one? You should have when you were born. Weren't you born in...actually, I don't know where you were born."

He leans closer and drops his voice. "I probably shouldn't tell you this, but I wasn't born in the District. I was born...elsewhere."

I reach for his arm and push his sleeve up, turning his bicep to find the little tracker scar but he has none. "How did you get into the District? How did you enroll at Moon Crossing University and Bountiful Hill University?"

"I had to lie," he admits, his gaze shuttered in shame. "Believe it or not, it was safer for me in the District at the time so I became a citizen—claiming my birth records were lost—but that I was born in Bountiful Hill."

"When did you come to the District?"

"When I was twelve. I lived in a foster home."

"What about your parents?" I ask softly.

He looks away, his jaw clenched in unsettled pain. "They died when I was young. So, as an orphan with no other family around, I had to come here."

I draw him into an embrace. He takes a moment before he wraps his arms around me, pulling me into him. I tuck my cheek against his shoulder and whisper, "I'm sorry about your parents, Stryder."

"It wasn't your fault," he whispers back, his voice raw with emotion. "Besides, you lost your father, too."

I pause and clutch his shirt in my hands. "How did you know that?"

"I heard it on the news when it happened but never mentioned it because, well, our tragic pasts aren't a delightful conversation."

"You're right. What do you say about testing out the waters?"

"Sure."

I shed my blanket and stand, removing my outer clothes. I'm glad I wore a tankini because the chill in the wind proves to be so and I shiver. Stryder strips off his shirt and kicks off his shoes before tucking me under his arm. He holds a small glass sphere in his hand and tosses it in the water before we reach it. I watch in curiosity as the sphere glows a soft blue and the water bubbles.

"What the—is the water *bubbling?*"

"Yup. The sphere is a reusable water heater I got a while back."

I step forward into the water and it warms my chilly toes. Moving further, I ask, "Where did you get it?"

"Spring Grove, before it was destroyed."

He joins me in the water and the sphere follows, warming the surrounding waters. I swim out until I'm up to my shoulders and then I dip my head under, sea salt in my hair. I hover there, staring at Stryder across the surface of the water.

He laughs. "Are you a crocodile?"

I creep toward him. He flaps his arms comically. "*Oh, no!* Help me! I'm about to be eaten!"

When I reach him, I wrap my arms around his waist and pop out of the water, giggling. I tug him closer and press a kiss along the bottom of his jaw. "Mhm, you taste good."

He cups my head and I tip it back into his hands, gazing at him. I stand on my tiptoes in the water and he leans his face down to mine. Our eyes shutter and our lips brush gently. My pulse goes a mile a minute and I can't help feeling what I do when I'm around Stryder. He's so unique in his own way and mysterious in another. I'm drawn to him, like a moth to the flame.

Before he truly kisses me, he whispers, "Our lips have to stop meeting like this, Locklyn."

I laugh lightly and slip my hands to his back, feeling his taut muscles and smooth skin. "I know. We can't seem to stay away from each other."

With that, he kisses me. I sigh softly, letting him gently bite my lip. He is perfect and I want, more than anything, to be with him. I feel safe in his arms, out of Moon Crossing and out in the world. In reality. He feels like life, a breath of fresh air into deflated lungs. *Would it be so terrible if I left with him?*

☽ ✧ ☾

After a bit of swimming, we lie on the blanket and toss the other one over us to keep us warm. I tuck myself against Stryder's side and we gaze at the stars, pointing out constellations we find. The sphere sits in a small towel of its own, dark for now.

I lean my cheek on his shoulder, craving his warmth. In a quiet voice, he remarks, "You confuse me, Locklyn."

"Why?"

"Because you flip back and forth between liking me and telling me to go away. I know you said we couldn't date and I gave you your space." He pauses and I feel his fingers glide through my damp hair. "But then things like this happen and...I don't know, it's hard *not* to fall for you. I'm trying, Locklyn, I really am, but it can't be like this forever. Do you have feelings for me?"

My fingers curl around his side and I gaze into his sweet and innocent almond eyes. Softly, I admit, "I do have feelings for you, Stryder."

His eyes fall closed and his smile is happy. "What a relief."

I remain quiet for a long moment and glance out at the ocean again. It's so serene out here, under the full light of the moon and the mist of the Glass Sea. I wish the serenity could transform how I feel on the inside right now. My heart catches in my throat and before I can stop myself, I spill, "I'm being framed for the Circle's assassinations. So that's why we can't date, Stryder, because once the police link everything to me, I'll be executed." Tears well in my eyes, "And I don't want you to live with that grief."

"*Little fox,*" he whispers, his voice filled with pain and worry. "Why didn't you tell me before?"

"Because I couldn't. At least not while we were in Moon Crossing." I rub away a few stray tears and sniffle. "But we're safe out here. I'm safe with you."

His expression shifts and he draws me into him. "I'll keep you safe. I always will."

"How are you going to do that?"

"You'll see."

TO CAGE A BIRD

T HE NEXT WEEK, I go to the police station to view a set of four security videos. Each of them details the Superiors' last hours of healthy lives. Conveniently, I'm in each one and Detective Caine is now as suspicious as ever. We sit in an interrogation room and he winds back to the first one, which is set at the restaurant Mom took me and Jesse to.

"Care to state your case for your appearance in each video?" Detective Caine asks.

"My lawyer isn't here yet."

"Are you sure your lawyer is coming?"

My eyes narrow on him. "Yes, just running a little late."

"Hmm."

He clicks his recorder off. We sit there in silence for a bit, staring at each other, and I pray my lawyer shows up soon.

Finally, the door to the interrogation room opens and my cousin rushes in. "Sorry! I was having lunch with a co-worker and lost track of time."

"That's quite all right," Detective Caine tells her and Electra sits down, fixing her suit coat and brushing a few loose strands from her bun behind her ears. "Now, Miss Harte, would you care to explain why you're in these videos?"

I stare at Electra, a bit terrified. Mom was supposed to get me an unbiased lawyer from Bountiful Hill, not my cousin. Electra is definitely biased.

"Let me see the videos first," Electra interjects and Detective Caine turns the Mini toward her.

My cousin watches the videos with a furrowed brow and once the last one ends, she asks, "Who sent these in?"

"They were sent in anonymously from each location."

"So how do you know that these aren't just videos of someone stalking my client? I question their credibility."

"Well, the question is *why* Miss Harte is seen with each Superior *before* they die. The source of this evidence is irrelevant at the moment."

Electra presses on, "But what if these videos are fabricated? Spliced and a complete hoax?"

Detective Caine huffs. "You're not conducting this interview, Miss Harte, and I'd like to take my lunch break as soon as possible. So," his sharp gaze falls on me, "are you going to answer my question or not?"

I glance at Electra and she nods. I tell Detective Caine, "My mom and brother came to town that Friday, and she treated us to dinner. We bumped into Superior Cozeht and Superior Masoni while we were there. It wasn't planned by any means and I didn't expect to see them there."

"Why did you bring them drinks? And who was that server you were talking with?"

"I don't know who she was. She told me that someone else had requested the drinks."

"Who requested it?"

I shake my head. "She didn't say, only that the man gave her no name and that he knew the Superiors personally."

Detective Caine rubs his chin. "How interesting. There are not many people who knew the Superiors *personally*, but of course, that could have been a lie as well."

"Have you questioned any of the Councilors for Adume's kidnapping? Maybe one of them was involved in this too."

"I questioned them and they all have solid alibis. One of the Councilors did notice that his ring went missing the weekend before and we searched his office. Someone clearly broke in and stole it. But without it, we can't trace the theft to anyone and Mr. Hines has…" he trails off, glancing at Electra, "he has yet to show."

"Show up dead, you mean," my cousin bites.

Detective Caine nods. "It's possible."

Electra clears her throat. "Well, that's not the case we're discussing right now. But I think that my client makes a good point, that whoever kidnapped Adume might be involved in framing Locklyn for the Superiors' assassinations."

"In Adume's recording, he said that he overheard something so…I wonder if he overheard the plan to kill the Superiors," I add.

"That could be it." Detective Caine laces his fingers together on the table. "But we won't know for sure without Mr. Hines' statement on whatever he heard. So you've explained yourself at the restaurant. How about the spa and the cemetery?"

"My mom took my brother and me to the spa. We were having a family weekend and we saw the Dunns there. I went outside to…cool off and found Superior Dunn smoking. We sat and chatted, then I went back inside. I didn't see him for the rest of our time there. As for the cemetery, I was visiting my father's memory stone and I didn't know Superior Roman was there until I heard his scream. I saw him as I walked by, but I didn't see who it was at first."

"Then Superior Wells visited your apartment to collect receipts for the Autumn Charity Ball expenses, correct?"

"Yes and then he left. I didn't harm any of them, Detective, and I have alibis for each time, witnesses to where I was."

He sighs. "This is such a mess. But I will contemplate what you've said today, Miss Harte. However, I can't let you go quite yet so I'm going to detain you for the night."

My eyes widen and I sputter, "On what charges?"

"No charges, just reasonable suspicion. I know you've worked for the Circle for years and could have developed ill feelings toward them in that time, considering all that they do. You don't seem like an evil person but you do seem like an advocate for justice and with what the Superiors did in all their years, you might have wanted to seek it—for those in Wolves Creek, in Bountiful Hill," he pauses, "and especially those in Spring Grove."

My fists clench in my lap. "What they did to Spring Grove was horrible."

"I know and I didn't approve of it either, but I'd rather not be on the losing side against Moon Crossing. The District is restrictive, to say the least, but at least we're kept safe from the outside world. We are privileged to live in Moon Crossing, even more than Wolves Creek and Bountiful Hill. We are safe within the barrier, within this system." Detective Caine stands. "Now, please, if you would follow me, Miss Harte."

I glance at Electra but she shrugs. "You're not being arrested, just detained for the night. He has the right to do that."

Reluctantly, I stand and follow Detective Caine out of the interrogation room. Electra hugs me before I go and I take the walk of shame through the station. All the officers stare at me, suspicious, and one steps in Detective Caine's way. I glance up and my stomach turns when I see Commander Keeva Westing standing there. She tips her head at me, her stare intense, but talks to Detective Caine.

"Are you finally incarcerating this troublemaker?"

"Only for the night. On reasonable suspicion," he tells her.

Commander Westing glances at her partner, Commander Ore. "What do you think of that, Ore?"

"Should be fine," he agrees, looking at me with ice-blue eyes and a slight frown.

Commander Westing nods and steps aside. "Off with her then."

I drop my gaze as we pass and catch Ore's hand lingering on Westing's back. The rumors about the two of them have been going on for years, but no one knows for sure whether they're together or not. Either way, they would make an incredibly powerful couple, since they already make a powerful partnership. The best in both their classes and the best overall. I hope they don't take this case from Detective Caine.

Right as I think it, Commander Westing says, "Wait, Caine."

My shoulders tense and I stand still as Detective Caine turns to the commanders. "Yes, ma'am?"

"Ore and I will be taking over the case regarding the Superiors' assassinations," she states and I can hear the smirk in her voice. "But you can stay on, Caine. Now, take her away."

When Detective Caine grabs my arm again, it feels like a zip tie being cinched around my skin and I know he's just annoyed but it hurts. Once we're out of earshot and heading toward the cells, I tell him, "You're hurting me, Detective."

He loosens his grip. "Sorry, I'm irked."

"I can tell."

"It's just that *I'm* the Head Detective of this precinct and *I* was put on this case by Chief Teller. Then the commanders stroll in here and decide to take it over!" he complains. "*Gah,* sometimes I wish I was more than a detective so I could tell them no."

"I'm sure that's not a word they hear often."

"*Exactly,* and they know the depth of their authority so they can use it to their advantage." Detective Caine stops at a cell and punches in a code. The door glides open and he directs me inside. "But anyway, I can't do anything about it. Goodnight, Miss Harte."

"Eh." I shrug and sit down on the padded bench as the cell door closes.

At least I have my own space and it's concealed by padded walls. I lie down on the bench and fold my hands on my belly, closing my eyes. The bench is actually quite comfortable but I can't deal with the fact of my detainment in the first place. Whoever is framing me thought out every minuscule detail. Exacting revenge typically isn't a spur-of-the-moment kind of thing.

I turn over on my side and Stryder slips into my mind. I hope he doesn't find out about my detainment here. It's embarrassing and I'd rather he not think of me as a low-life criminal right now. Our relationship is still new and fresh, not official but fragile. I'd like to keep my criminal history out of everything.

Somehow, I manage to fall asleep and my dreams are filled with a life outside of Moon Crossing.

CAPTURE AND RELEASE

A S MY EYES flutter open the next morning, I see a figure standing at the entrance to my cell. I push myself up and run my fingers through my hair, squinting as I try to make out who's on the other side. But the light from behind them casts them in shadow. Then the door opens with a hiss and the figure steps into the dimness of the cell. I look up at Stryder, my cheeks flushing in embarrassment.

Quickly, I turn away toward the wall and fold my arms around my waist. He comes to sit by me, the cushion on the bench dipping, and I see his hand fall near my knee. I focus on his slim and tan fingers, not brave enough to look him in the eye.

"Good morning," he begins.

"To some, it is," I say softly and grip my sides.

Stryder hmphs. "I guess so. But I'm here to escort you home."

My gaze finally wanders up to him. "Escort me home? Why?"

A crooked smile lifts his lips. "I guess you ought to know that I'm a private investigator."

"What? Who sent you?"

"Someone who wishes to remain anonymous."

I turn to him and grasp his hand. "Did my mom hire you to watch me? Make sure I was okay?"

Stryder shakes his head. "That's not what a private investigator does, Locklyn. I gather intel and I investigate. I came originally to investigate the Circle and the Council but then you fell into that mix, too."

My gaze shadows over and I draw my hand back, a frown creasing my mouth. "So...all the moments we shared? That was you investigating? Were you using me to gain intel on the Circle and the Council?"

"No! Of course not!" he claims, his eyes wide.

I give him a cynical look and cross my arms. "I don't believe you."

His neck grows warm with heat and he looks me dead in the eye. "Locklyn, I never used you to gain intel. You turned out to be a...a distraction."

"A distraction?"

"In a good way! I've been working like a dog for years now and I needed to live a normal life for a bit, go on a date, kiss someone, things like that."

"So you used me for your own pleasure is what you're telling me."

He rubs his forehead, letting out a groan. "No, no, that's not what I meant. When I saw you at the café, I was simply getting breakfast before I was going to tail Superior Masoni. I remembered you instantly and thought of our date, how it was the best first date I'd ever had. So I got distracted in that daydream and honestly, you were more interesting than what Superior Masoni was probably doing. I didn't mean to develop feelings for you but...it just happened."

"Oh."

His eyes brighten with delight. "Believe me, darling, you were well worth it."

I blush and my eyelashes flutter. "Now what?"

"I get to question you myself."

"How fantastic," I grumble and rise to my feet.

Stryder stands and guides me out of the cell, out of the police station, and to his junky car. We sit in silence as we drive to my apartment complex. I'm surprised that Commander Ore and Commander Keeva didn't stop us on our way out. I imagined they would, but they didn't even look up from the reports they were reviewing. So much for being fiercely observant.

When he parks and we get out, he takes my arm, leading me up to my apartment. I glance at him, wondering how I didn't realize who he was. He turned up a few weeks ago and couldn't seem to leave me alone. He said those times were his feelings getting the best of him, but he must have been gathering intel as well. Gauging my reactions and interactions. He's been watching me, studying me, and for who?

At my apartment, Vanne is sitting on the couch, twiddling his thumbs. He shoots up when we enter and darts over, pulling me into a tight embrace. Stryder lets go of my arm as Vanne squeezes me to him.

"I've been waiting all night for you," he murmurs against my ear.

"Didn't Detective Caine tell you he was detaining me for the night?" I squeak.

"Yeah, but I worried anyway." Vanne draws back and his gaze finds Stryder. His brow creases in annoyance. "What are *you* doing here?"

I'm about to explain when Stryder steps forward himself and holds his hand out. "I don't think I've formally introduced myself. I'm Stryder Monroe, a private investigator from Bountiful Hill, and right now, I need to question Miss Harte."

Vanne's eyebrows rise in surprise and he asks, "Who sent you to investigate Locklyn?"

"My client wishes to remain anonymous," Stryder tells him. "Now please, I need to question her in private."

Hesitantly, Vanne steps back to grab his keys off the counter. "I'll be at the store. Do you need anything, Locklyn?"

I shake my head and we wait for Vanne to leave. Once he does, I flop down on the couch and lean back, watching Stryder as he pulls up a chair in front of me. He sits and leans his elbows on his knees, steepling his fingers. I cross my arms and rub my hands along my cold skin. I still don't know what to think of him being a private investigator.

After a moment, Stryder begins, "I know you said you were being framed for the Superiors' deaths, but can you elaborate a little more on that?"

"Well, it began with Adume's abduction. He called me and was trying to tell me something, which I assume now was about the Superiors' deaths. He was trying to warn me. Videos of me with each of the Superiors before they showed up dead were sent anonymously to Detective Caine. I imagine that more evidence will be planted and it won't seem like a coincidence to the police anymore. As I said before, I took the blame because if I don't, they'll kill Adume and everyone else I care about…which would include you as well," I pause and his expression grows cold but he nods.

Stryder rubs his chin, thinking. "Did he give a time when Adume would be released if you took the blame?"

"When I'm behind bars."

"Do you have any idea who could be behind this?"

I lift my shoulders in a shrug. "All we got from Adume's recording was someone wearing an Elite Council ring but their alibis checked out. So an impostor. And, there are at least three of them involved in this. All men."

"I'll look into it then and see what I can find," Stryder stands, preparing to head out. "You keep your story straight and don't give anyone a reason to find you suspicious. The police won't make an arrest until they have enough evidence and as far as we both know, they only have those videos. If you end up going to trial, I'll be there, okay?"

I stand as well, gazing up at him. "I hope you can help me get out of this mess, Stryder, that would really be something."

His almond eyes linger on mine and then he takes my hand, rubbing his thumb against my palm. "I hope I can get you out of this mess as well. I'll probably be investigating so don't worry if you don't hear from me."

"Okay…thank you."

"Of course."

I lie in bed for a couple of days, only getting up to go to the bathroom or retrieve food, and then trudge back to my room to hide under my covers again. I've heard nothing from Stryder and nothing from the police. It all feels so strange, how quiet it is.

When my door creaks open, I stiffen with a hand clasped around a tub of ice cream and a spoon stuck in my mouth. I'm still under the covers but they're abruptly drawn back and I hiss against the daylight, shading my eyes. I glance up at Electra as she sets her hands on her hips.

"Vanne told me you were in a sad state but I didn't think it would be *this* terrible," she sniffs and her nose crinkles. "When was the last time you showered?"

I sigh, taking another scoop of sweet Rugged Route ice cream. "I don't know. Wednesday night?"

Electra frowns. "It's Saturday morning, Locklyn. And what about work?"

"I called in sick for the week."

"You're hiding."

I shrug, not giving her the verbal pleasure of being right.

"How was your detainment?" she asks briskly.

"Cold. Lonely." Tears pool in my eyes. "I don't want to go to prison, Electra."

"You won't be going to prison, Locky, not while I'm representing you." Electra sits on the edge of the bed and takes my hand off the ice cream tub, concealing it in hers. I sniffle and wipe away my tears with my sleeve as her expression softens. "I won't let them take you when you've done nothing wrong, okay? We're family and we stick up for each other."

"Thank you," I whisper.

Electra pats my hand before standing and smoothing her fingers over her gingham pants. "Now get up and take a shower. Detective Caine wants to see us at the station."

My shoulders fall. "Are Westing and Ore going to be there?"

"I doubt it. They hardly work on Saturdays."

I nod and take another bite of ice cream before Electra wrangles it out of my hands and shoos me into the bathroom. I turn on the shower and strip off the long-sleeve oversize tee I've been wearing for the last few days. My hair is greasy so I wash it and when I smell squeaky clean, I dress in a pair of striped pants and a blouse before joining Electra in the living room. She sits on the couch with Vanne and they stop talking when I emerge.

Electra pops up as Vanne averts his gaze and suspicion rises in me. I narrow my eyes at them. "What were you two—"

My cousin grabs my hand and drags me over to the door. "Let's go. We're late as is and have no more time for chit-chat."

Just when she's about to slam the door, Vanne grabs it while lifting his coat off the coat rack. "I'm coming, too."

"Why?" I ask, still suspicious.

"I want to see what evidence they're trying to plant on you."

I sigh and we head down to Electra's car. I call the passenger seat so Vanne has to sit in the back and Electra taps her manicured nails against the steering wheel, not helping one bit with the stifling silence. I'm about to ask them what they were talking about when Electra speaks first.

"So, Locky, Malini was telling me you've been seeing Stryder Monroe," she glances over and winks, a wicked grin on her lips. "How's that working out?"

"I—I've hardly been *seeing* him as much as…well, seeing him with my own two eyes."

"That's not an answer, honey."

I flush pink and sink low in my seat. "Why are we talking about this?"

"Because I enjoy gossiping about your love life so give me some details."

"There are no details."

Electra sighs. "You're a pain, you know that? I'm just trying to have some girl talk."

I turn slightly to Electra and see Vanne shift uncomfortably out of the corner of my eye. He continues to tap away at his Mini, acting like he's not listening, but I know he holds on to every word that leaves my mouth. I gaze out at the road ahead and give in to Electra's meddling.

"I like Stryder…a lot, actually."

"Have you kissed?"

"A couple of times."

She ventures on, whispering, "Have you guys—"

"No!" I retort and my blush deepens. "*Heavens above*, it's forbidden."

Electra shrugs. "That doesn't stop some people. But I get it, it's too risky. Are you going to make it official then?"

I lean my head back against the headrest. "No."

"Why not?"

"It's just...this mess is too much for me to handle right now and pursuing a relationship with him—when there's a possibility that I'll be thrown in prison soon—would be a disaster."

"He's a private investigator so I don't think you should trust him in the first place." Vanne contributes from the backseat.

Electra's brow furrows. "Hold on. *Stryder Monroe is a private investigator?* Why didn't you lead with that?"

"Because I didn't think it mattered." I glare back at Vanne and he shrugs, glancing at his Mini again. I turn forward with a sigh. "But yeah, he's a PI, and honestly, I don't know if all we have is a lie or not. His job is to sneak around and gather intel on people, who's to say he wasn't doing that with me?"

"Well, you have feelings for him, don't you?"

"I do, but how do I know if those feelings are true?"

"You just do, Locky, everyone knows that. I doubt he'd manipulate you or use you if you're not the person he's investigating."

I bite my lip and glance out the window. "Yeah."

"But anyway, I think it's mature of you to not lead him on when something silly *could* come of this mess. You're smart, honey, and if he sees that, he'll understand."

"I told him why we couldn't be together and he gets it. It's for the best."

"*Ugh*, can we talk about something else? This conversation is getting me down," Vanne complains.

Electra gives him a sharp glare through the rearview mirror. "Oh, I'm so sorry that our important conversation is *boring* you, Vanne. Should we talk about you now?"

I can hear the smirk in his voice as he says, "What a marvelous idea."

My cousin bites out, "How was your date with Amira?"

I whip around, my eyes wide as I stare at Vanne. "You went on a date and you didn't tell me?"

His ears grow pink and he rubs the back of his neck. "It was a few weeks ago—before this all started—when we...fought that one night. I told Electra to set me up on a blind date."

"So I did," Electra chimes. Her gaze pierces Vanne again. "How was it?"

"It was pretty great, but I haven't called her back since. I should, though."

"Yes, you should, because she's been flapping her lips at the gym ever since and I can't *stand* it. She had a great time, though, and hopes you'll call her soon."

Vanne nods, looking like a little schoolboy as he drops his gaze to his Mini once again. I cross my arms. Electra glances at me, her eyebrow quirked, but I lean my head back and close my eyes.

Electra strolls into the police station like she owns the place before an officer steps in her way. "How can I help you?"

She tosses her strawberry blonde hair over her shoulder and sets a hand on her hip. "Detective Caine called us down here."

The officer glances past her to me and nods. "Ah, yes, Miss Locklyn Harte."

He steps aside and sweeps his hand toward Detective Caine's office in the back. We walk through and I hate the stares, the unblinking eyes, and the silent judgment of each officer in the station. Surely, they all know about the evidence that is being gathered against me and most of them must think me a monster.

So be it.

Electra barges into Detective Caine's office without knocking and he glances up from the paperwork he's filling out, sighing as he gives Electra a look.

"What?" she asks.

"Don't you know how to knock?" he retorts.

She leans over to see what he's working on and then shrugs. "It seems that you're not doing anything important and you asked us here in the first place, Detective, so please, don't waste any more of our time with this idle conversation."

He chuckles. "You sound like your mother."

Electra stiffens at the remark but takes a seat and gestures for me to sit as well. Vanne stands by the door with his arms crossed, waiting patiently. I fold my hands in my lap and Electra sets her hands flat on Detective Caine's desk.

"So?"

He looks at me. "Miss Harte, I've had a warrant approved by the Elite Council to search your apartment. I wanted to bring you down here in case you'd like to confess to anything before we find something. So, do you have anything to hide that we should know of?"

I shake my head. "No, sir."

Detective Caine looks unconvinced. He continues, "Do you have any experience with shooting a firearm, Miss Harte? Or wielding a knife?"

"Don't answer that," Electra guides me.

His mouth presses into a firm line and his dark eyes bore into me. "My apologies. Did your father ever take you shooting? He certainly must have, considering how well he could wield a firearm that night fourteen years ago."

My jaw clenches and my cousin sets a hand over my fists. "He's trying to bait you, Locklyn."

"I'm not baiting her, only asking a simple question."

"You want me to confess, don't you," I say through gritted teeth.

"That would solve this problem."

I stare at him, thinking of all the lives in Moon Crossing, each breath being taken, each heart beating, each laugh. This is my city and these are my fellow people. I'll be seen as a monster, but at least I can lift this heavy weight off my shoulders and relax behind bars.

My mouth opens as Vanne steps up beside me and leans his hands on Detective Caine's desk. "She did nothing. She's innocent."

Detective Caine's eyebrow quirks. "But is she really?"

He spins around in his chair to a filing cabinet and searches for the file on me, which includes all my past crimes that he's had to deal with. I've been arrested many times before, and Detective Caine will always remain suspicious of me. Though now I'm older and have a respectable job, I've toned down my wild side.

With the file in his hands, he slaps it down on the desk and opens it. "Let's review Miss Harte's criminal past, shall we? At age seven, she removed her father's memory stone from the cemetery and tossed it in the canal. At age twelve, she was caught shoplifting frequently with Miss Russo and Miss Electra here as well." He looks up at Vanne with a smirk. "From ages fourteen to sixteen, she engaged in a forbidden romantic relationship with you and had to do one hundred hours of community service for breaking the rules of the Protectorship.

"In between that, at age fifteen, she was caught out on a romantic endeavor with a boy named Stryder Monroe, and I increased and specifically monitored her hormonal suppression supplement dosage. At eighteen, Miss Harte was caught drinking underage at a party with her so-called friends once again. Finally, last year, she was engaged to be married to Councilor Carmichael, which was illegal since she wasn't released from the Protectorship Program and you refused to sign an early release form for her. So tell me, Mr. Heppin, do you really think that Miss Harte *can't* cause any more trouble for us?"

Vanne's skin is flushed, both in anger and embarrassment, and he turns away, hurrying out of the office. I knot my fingers together and bite my lip.

He didn't know I went on a date with Stryder when we were dating, or that my supplement dosage had been increased. That's why I fell out of love with him as my feelings became numb and then nothing.

"Are we free to go?" Electra asks.

"I suppose so," Detective Caine sighs and shoots me a sharp look. "A couple of officers will follow you back to search your apartment."

My cousin stands, drawing me up next to her. "Why so quickly?"

Crinkles form around his eyes as they narrow on me. "So Miss Harte doesn't have any time to hide anything she doesn't want us to find."

"Well, she has nothing to hide."

"I don't need your assurance, I need hers."

I see Adume in my mind and I say nothing, no matter how much I want to. Electra ushers us out of the office, but she doesn't wait for us to leave the station before a curse slips past her painted lips.

"You being so quiet is making him more suspicious, Locklyn!"

"You told me not to answer any of his questions!" I snap and pull my hand out of hers, marching toward the entrance.

Electra trails after me and asks with caution, "You really don't have anything to hide...right?"

"Are you on his side now?"

"No, of course not!" She claims with a snort. "But seriously, Locky, no nighttime magazines or something?"

I snort now and Electra snickers. *"Skies above."*

We get in the car, where Vanne waits, deathly quiet. I can tell he's brooding in the backseat as we drive back with a patrol car behind us. It's been rough between us for years now, but his silence feels like a stab in the stomach. Vanne is my friend and I don't want him to hate me forever, even if I continue to hurt him. *Unintentionally.*

Electra parks outside and we head up with the officers to the apartment. Vanne opens the door and lets the officers in to do their search. He then gives

Electra a look that makes her skedaddle away faster than a cheetah and we wait outside, awkward and quiet.

"Vanne—"

"Why am I even surprised that you went out with Stryder Monroe when we were dating?" he shakes his head and leans on the door jamb, his hazel eyes hot with betrayal.

"Glory set me up on a date with him and I thought it was harmless. He just needed help getting out of his shell, that's all."

"Well, you must have done *something* with him to get your supplement dosage increased."

I lean my head on the wall. "Vanne, don't do this to yourself."

His nostrils flare. "You think *I'm* the one making myself miserable?"

"Why are you still hurt by every romantic decision I make in my life?" I retort, "We broke up *six years ago!* You should be over it by now. I know I am."

Vanne's voice falls low, his tone cold. "You were my first love, Locklyn, and no one forgets their first love or how it made them feel. I've tried to move on, but nothing else ever seems to work out and I always come back to you. Do you think I want to obsess over the times we had for the rest of my life? *No!* I really don't want to and I can't *wait* for you to be released. I've wanted it for six years."

I shift on my feet, a bit taken aback by this truth coming to light. "If you felt this way, then why didn't you release me when I was engaged to Blake?"

His nose crinkles, his mouth twitching. "Because I didn't want you to be happy while I still struggled to connect with anyone."

"That was cruel of you," I whisper.

"I know, but I don't regret it. You've moved on from Blake now and you have Stryder Monroe again," he shrugs, "maybe that will go somewhere."

I turn away from him, leaning back into the wall. We've both been terribly cruel to each other and it's time for it to end. I close my eyes and breathe out. "I'm sorry for everything I've done that hurt you, Vanne. I'm sorry for being naive and thinking it was harmless to go on a date with Stryder. I'm sorry for the mixed signals I've sent over the past six years, for not telling you about my dosage increase, and for being dishonest about why I wanted to break up."

He's quiet for a long moment and I turn my head, glancing at him. Vanne clears his throat. "I'm…I'm sorry for pressuring you to come back to me and ruining your relationship with Blake. I'm sorry for being a pain, for whining about everything, and for impeding your other relationships. I want the best for you. Clearly, that's not me and I get it. I want to sign a release form for you."

My eyes widen. "Really?"

"Yes." Vanne bobs his head. "I don't think we should be living together anymore. We need to live our lives separate from each other."

I stride over to him and pull him into an embrace. "We'll always be friends, Vanne, I promise that."

He hugs me and then steps back. "I promise, too."

From inside the apartment, we hear, "Well, well, well, what do we have here?"

Vanne and I step inside and I blink. I completely forgot that the officers were here, searching for evidence, and my heart seizes as I see what one officer holds up.

A slick black handgun with a silencer on it.

I swallow. In my desperate state of mind, I forgot about the gun. When they run the serial numbers, they'll find that the handgun is actually registered to me, a gift from my Uncle Tiran because he knew my father would have wanted me to have a way to protect myself. However, the silencer isn't mine, but I don't think they'll care about that detail. They've found a weapon, one of such that was used to kill Superior Dunn.

The officer grins at me with malice. "Locklyn Harte, you are under arrest for possession of a prohibited firearm while in the Protectorship Program."

I take a step back as two burly officers advance, ready to put me in handcuffs, and I protest, "But it's registered and I have a license to carry!"

He tsks. "That won't make a difference if forensics matches the ballistics to their report on Superior Dunn's murder."

I glance to Vanne for help and his brow furrows. We both know he can't do anything. So they grab me and spin me around, pressing me hard against the door like what once happened to my father. They jerk my arms behind my back and clasp the heavy cuffs around my wrists. Tears pool in my eyes as they lead me down to the patrol car. Vanne remains at the entrance to the complex and watches with watery eyes as I'm taken away.

I guess I don't need that release form now.

THE TIGHTENING OF A NOOSE

M Y NEW CELL is far away from everyone else and smells damp. I sit on the bench with my head hung as the police officers guarding me jeer in spite. I tune them out and wonder how Stryder plans on rescuing me from this situation now. If he's even still in Moon Crossing. Maybe he bailed when he realized it was impossible. And I don't know what Electra is going to do either. Everything is closing in fairly quickly and there's only so much she can do, so much she can say.

I hear through the grapevine that my handgun's bullets match the one used to kill Superior Dunn. It's a special bullet that only works with my handgun, a rare model of its kind. Uncle Tiran and my dad loved collecting rare things.

The knife to stab Superior Roman was dusted and my prints were discovered, of course, since I did stupidly touch it as I tried to yank it out of him. With two deaths accounted for, it was easy to explain the other three. I apparently snuck out to acquire some arsenic from some shady fellow at Cascade Plaza, when I was really with Stryder that night. And then after Superior Wells left my apartment, I followed him and strangled him before going to the cemetery to kill Superior Roman.

It's all pieced together, my ultimate demise, and I can't say I'm thrilled about the matter. Who would be, anyway? But I know the answer to that one. Whoever is holding Adume captive must be positively happy about all the work they've done to destroy me. They've basically won by now and they must know it.

At least two or three days have passed before a guard clears her throat outside my cell and announces, "You have a visitor."

I turn over and stand as she unlocks my cell, stepping inside to place handcuffs on me. We walk up to the visiting room and I wander in with tired eyes and an aching body. That bench definitely isn't comfortable to sleep on and I hope Detective Caine and the commanders take me to trial soon so at least I can sit in a comfortable chair for hours on end.

My gaze glides across everyone in the room and I have to do a double-take on a man sitting at one table, waiting patiently. My eyes widen when I recognize him. Despite the scraggly beard and longish hair, I'd know those bug eyes and new, thick glasses anywhere. I cry as I rush over to him and flop down at the table.

"Adume! *Oh my stars*, you're alive!" I cry, my mouth trembling.

He flinches at the sight of me and his brow creases in worry and fear. "Why did you do this, Locklyn?"

I blink. "What?"

Adume reaches across the table and clutches my fingers. "Why did you take the blame?"

"For you, of course."

"But *why*?"

My shoulders fall. "You're my friend, Adume."

He sighs. "You're letting your life be ruined for a simple friend?"

My jaw clenches. "Aren't you happy they released you? That you're *alive*? And..." my gaze drops to our hands, "it's not just you I'm saving. It's everyone else I care about, too."

My stomach twists and then my eyes go wide again. "Wait, Adume, do you know who he is? Did he ever show his face?"

He shakes his head. "No, but he said that I would recognize him if he showed me his face. So I know who it is but...I don't."

"Was he wearing an Elite Council ring?"

"Only once, when I was first taken." Adume rubs his scruffy chin. "I wouldn't put it past anyone in the Elite Council to want the Superiors dead. It would promote at least five of them and give them ultimate power over Moon Crossing and the District. Maybe someone who wanted to expand past the boundaries of the District as well."

"Maybe." I lift my cuffed hands to scratch my ear. "If we can find out who is doing all this, then we can stop him before anything happens."

"We?" he snorts softly, "It'll be up to me."

My skin heats. "Yes, but there's a guy I know who has been looking into it for weeks. His name is Stryder Monroe. You should get in contact with him. He's a PI from Bountiful Hill."

"Why were you hanging around with a PI?"

"It's a long story."

"Hmph."

We sit there for a bit, staring at each other, and I notice the healing cut on his forehead. I huff in anger. "They hurt you."

Adume touches a hand to his forehead as if he forgot all about it and shrugs. "I got a little beat up when they first took me, but I'm fine now. No broken bones or anything. Just plenty of bruises from sleeping on concrete."

"So...you're really free?"

He nods. "They dumped me at my apartment the night you were arrested and Electra and Glory had me report to the police the next day. But I couldn't give them much on my captors so now I have an officer following me everywhere." He gestures to a broad-shouldered woman I hadn't noticed standing against the far wall, looking as bored as ever. "But after this, I'm heading over to the courthouse with Electra and Glory to sign early release forms for them. I don't want to be a Protector anymore and I don't want to live in Moon Crossing. I'm moving to Bountiful Hill as soon as possible."

My eyebrows rise in surprise. "Oh."

"I'll still contact Stryder Monroe and get to the bottom of things. I'll tell the police everything I heard and maybe it can stay your trial. I won't be back once I leave."

I bob my head. "That's only wise, especially after everything."

"Yeah, so this is goodbye."

I glance up at him, at his unruly hair and the dark circles under his eyes. The scruffy beard really does nothing for him and neither does the hunch of his shoulders. As kids, we would always bond over books we were reading and geeky TV shows we binged together since no one else in our group of friends cared for them. I became instant friends with Adume when I first met him, even though he was four years older than me, and we both enjoyed having someone to geek out with.

"I'm sorry...about everything," I whisper, clasping his fingers again.

"You don't need to be sorry for anything, Locklyn," he responds in kind and offers a smile, though it's filled with sadness. "This life isn't for me anymore. But I'm really glad we became friends. It was nice to talk to someone else about things we both liked and...you never made me feel alone. I hope we can remain in touch, though."

"Of course," I promise.

But we both know it's an empty promise, considering the situation I'm in now. Adume fishes through his pocket and takes out a small token from a bet I lost years ago. He places it in my palm and closes my fingers over it, reminiscing, "*The Cosmos Chronicles* wasn't better than the *Dream Cycle* series. I lied because I wanted the token."

A small laugh bubbles out of me. "That debate took *months* to resolve, but I enjoyed both."

Adume chuckles. "You've always liked overdramatic stories." We stand and he stuffs his hands in his pockets, saying, "I don't think I'm allowed to hug you."

"Probably not."

He pushes his glasses up. "I'll see you around, Locky."

"See you around, Adume," I say softly.

He turns from me and his officer perks up. I watch them depart and Adume gives me one more glance with a little wave. I wave back and feel queasy once he's gone. Now I've lost two of my closest friends and I'm sure I'll lose more if whoever is behind this charade has anything to say about it.

☽ ✧ ☾

Stryder flipped through the channels as he sat in his hotel room, bored beyond compare. He had spent the day trailing an underground criminal who had made threats against the Circle of Superiors on multiple occasions. All it led to was Moon Crossing's underground Moonless Market, which didn't surprise him, considering that he saw shady people waiting by the barrier to make trades with outsiders earlier that night. He would continue to look, though, for Locklyn's sake.

She had been arrested nearly three weeks ago and it was such a pain to keep away, but he had to continue investigating. If only he could get a better lead before they took her to court. Her friend, Adume Hines, had talked to the police about his captors and what they intended to do to Moon Crossing. He'd also contacted Stryder, but it wasn't much help, so Stryder insisted on working alone. The city had been on lockdown since and set a curfew. Anyone out past midnight would immediately be arrested, simply for being suspicious. They lined the streets and had even brought in Recons.

Moon Crossing's eyes were open and alert, but no other threats had been placed. And the Elite Council had decided that there would no longer be a Circle of Superiors. So the ten of them, mere children, everyone thought, were now in charge of the city and the District. Moon Crossing was at a crossroads, in a state of disarray like it never had been before. Its leaders were gone. It was vulnerable. Stryder felt like he shouldn't be here. But he stayed for Locklyn.

Always for Locklyn.

He fell back on the bed and stuck with a news channel, where the news-caster droned on and on, reminding everyone of curfew and the consequences of being caught outside after midnight. Stryder closed his eyes and dug his fingers into his hair. He had remained in Moon Crossing for too long now and it was killing him. This city was ripe with pompous folk who thought themselves better than everyone else, and who disregarded other cities, other nations, and their independence. It was the self-righteous city it made itself out to be and he was sick and tired of it all.

"In recent news, Commander Westing and Commander Ore have taken the case of the Superiors' assassinations to court." Stryder shot upright, his eyes opening as he stared at the TV. The newscaster went on, "Locklyn Harte, the former secretary of the Circle, was arrested three weeks ago for owning a prohibited firearm. Since then, detectives have linked evidence in two of the individual cases to Miss Harte. She will appear in court before the Elite Council this Friday for a hearing of the charges that are set against her. It will be a closed hearing but once her trial begins, anyone will be welcome to sit through it. There will be a select few from the population who will be jurors in this case so look out for a letter of invitation this week, folks. In other news—"

Stryder waved his hand over the monitor and the TV powered off, whirling before it fell silent. He groaned and flopped back on the bed again, shoving his palms against his eyes. Locklyn was going to trial and he still had no lead...but maybe he didn't need a lead. The Elite Council was impressionable and they would make the final judgment on Locklyn's case. He was a PI; he had a license, and he would be at her trial. He could talk to one of the Councilors, maybe Carmichael or Cristol, who were friends with Locklyn, and convince one of them to make sure the Council didn't seek her execution.

He smiled at the ceiling as a plan formed in his mind. Locklyn would be free, he'd make sure of it, and she would live to tell the tale.

☽ ✧ ☾

I am petrified that I am going to trial so soon and when a night and day pass, I ask to make a call. The guards roll their eyes but comply and take me to a Mini Ardia tablet station for prisoners. There are walls between each booth and I take an empty one, quickly typing in Stryder's code. I plug in a set of headphones and draw them over my ears, waiting anxiously for him to answer.

It takes five rings before Stryder picks up and it looks like he's in a dark alleyway, a black sweatshirt on with his hood drawn low. His eyes widen when he sees me and he whispers, "Locklyn? Why are you calling me?"

My shoulders fall and I lean closer to the screen. "I'm basically your part-time lover. So, have you found anything? Any trail leading to who could have done this?"

He shakes his head. "No, I'm sorry."

"Oh."

"*But* I have a plan in mind and I—" he glances to his right, "I'll have to tell you about it later, okay?"

"Wait!" I cry softly and he pauses, looking at me again. His almond eyes soften and I bite my lip. "Can you visit me and tell me then?"

A small crooked smile lifts his lips. "Yes. I'll be there tomorrow."

"Thank you."

He nods and ends the call. I remain leaned over the Mini so the guards don't see that the call has ended and I type in my mom's code. She answers almost immediately, and her expression is pinched in worry. Her eyes are red and watery. I blink, surprised that she's actually been crying.

"Why have you been crying?" I ask.

"I saw the news, sweetie. You're going to court on Friday?"

"Yeah…the commanders were growing impatient. They've collected enough evidence to take me to court. At least I get to bathe before showing up." I laugh lightly but it holds no humor.

A tear slips down Mom's cheek and she wipes it away. "Oh, Locklyn, I can't stand it anymore. It's all happening again."

"What do you mean?"

"This is just like what happened with your father," she says, her voice hoarse as more tears slip down her cheeks. "He committed the crime and the next week, he was arrested. His own friends—his co-workers—betrayed him. You have a personal history with Blake and I fear he will betray you, too."

"I already asked Blake to testify to my character during the trial and he said he would, but I don't know if it will mean much. And I grew up alongside Councilor Cristol…but he's strictly business, so I doubt that he'd let his personal feelings get in the way. If he has any, he's about as closed off as Moon Crossing's barrier right now."

Mom nods. "I'll be there to support you on Friday, darling, and I'll help you get through this mess."

I fold my arms around myself, feeling insecure. "Mom, you don't have to come. It's going to be long and stifling hot and…I don't want you to see me like this."

She lifts her chin, defiant. "Locklyn, I've seen you at your worst and I've seen you at your best. Let me be there for you since I…wasn't there for you all those years ago. I know it won't make up for the neglect I inflicted on you, but I'm your mom and you are my child. I love you."

My shoulders shake and tears well in my eyes. "I love you, too, Mom."

It's rare when she tells me she loves me since she struggled with postpartum depression after I was born and was jealous of my father's affection for me. We struggled to even be in each other's presence after my dad died and we were both in our own heads for too long, but she didn't leave me in the Protectorship Program without promising to make amends. And we have been, for the past eleven years. I wish I could be in her arms right now and curl into her warmth. Alas, I'm stuck in jail instead.

"I'll see you Friday, sweetie," she breathes.

"See you Friday," I reply and end the call.

I sit there for a few more minutes before my guard nudges me and tells me my time is up. I pull the headphones off and stand, letting them cuff me again and lead me back to my cell. I have two days until I'm taken to court and I hope that Stryder's plan, whatever it may be, will solve all of my problems.

☽ ✧ ☾

Stryder breezed into the police station and asked the receptionist if he could see Locklyn. She blushed and sent him to the visiting room, which was equipped with tables and chairs, a fan spiraling above, and a few police officers dotted about the perimeter. They were far enough away from the tables that they couldn't overhear people's personal conversations—which Stryder was glad about since this particular conversation was not meant to be overheard.

She was brought in from the far corner and Stryder stood, sticking his hands in his pockets so he wouldn't be tempted to touch her. If he did, he knew a guard would body slam him and tell him not to touch the prisoner. Or they would take Locklyn away and he couldn't have that either. Her smoky gray eyes brightened when she saw him and she hurried over. She was a beautiful mess in an ugly gray and white striped jumpsuit, her ebony hair tousled and dark circles beneath her eyes. His pulse quickened as she smiled and the genuineness of it actually reached her eyes. No one would even guess that tomorrow, she'd be going to court to be accused of murder.

"Stryder," she breathed and they sat down. Locklyn immediately reached out and clasped her fingers around his. It pleasantly surprised Stryder when no guard body-slammed him. She went on, "I'm so happy to see you. It's been so long."

"I know," he tilted his head at her, "how are you?"

Locklyn's long lashes fluttered and she looked down at their hands. "Not terribly well, but I've accepted what's being handed to me."

"Don't accept it yet, little fox. I have a plan, remember?"

She leaned forward; her gaze finding his again. "Of course I remember. I've been waiting all morning for you to come by."

Stryder glanced around once more before he lowered his voice. "I've had no luck in finding the people who set you up, but I spoke with one of the Councilors yesterday. I know that if you're found guilty, the city will want an execution, but the Council makes the final verdict. The Councilor I talked to thinks that an execution would be too easy a punishment."

Her mouth drooped into a frown and her gaze narrowed ever so slightly. "If I don't get executed…then what's the other punishment?"

"Exilement."

Locklyn gnawed on her lip and Stryder got distracted for a moment, thinking about those lips on his, her fingers in his hair, and her breath growing rapid. He blinked as Locklyn sat back and thought for a long, long bit. A little line formed between her eyebrows as she thought and Stryder leaned his head on his hand, admiring her.

Finally, she leaned forward again and tentatively asked, "Where would I be exiled to?"

"Outside of Moon Crossing," he told her and then remembered what the Councilor had said, "or to Silverwater Penitentiary, which resides underground, outside of Spring Grove. I think that's the likelier choice rather than only being exiled from the city."

"Silverwater Penitentiary?" she shivered. "I've heard horror stories about that place, Stryder. I don't want to go there either."

He couldn't bear seeing her so distraught, so he nodded. "If you're exiled there then…I'll take you myself. Get you out of Moon Crossing and then we can just…run away."

Locklyn's shoulders dropped. "No, I won't drag you into this with me. We'll both be wanted fugitives if we simply run away." She straightened, her gaze hardening in an instant. "I'll go to Silverwater and I'll endure it."

Stryder reached for her hands again and took them in his, so small and cold, with dirt under her fingernails. He knew she would never tolerate this kind of state any other time, but she had been broken and his heart ached for her. Firmly, he said, "I want to be dragged into this with you. I don't care if it means we're on the run for the rest of our lives, I want to be with you, Locklyn Harte, and no one, not even you, can change my mind."

She gazed at him, her pretty eyes were soft and watery. He felt like he loved her already, but he knew the process was only beginning, that his feelings would deepen, grow into the earth, and plant roots far from his reach. Locklyn Harte was a beautiful thought in his mind that seemed to see him for who he was and cared about what he thought, too. He cared for her immensely, and it terrified him a little. How close to his heart she was getting. But Locklyn drifted there nonetheless and it seemed like she belonged there. He didn't mind that.

"You're something else, Stryder Monroe. You're my hero."

His heart seized and he lifted her hands to his mouth, pressing delicate kisses across her knuckles. "No, you're *my* hero."

TRIAL AND ERROR

I T'S FRIDAY MORNING.

The sun has just risen outside of my cell window and casts a sliver of light directly across my eyes. I groan and push myself up as I hear police officers clomping down the corridor, ready to retrieve me for my 10 AM court hearing. They'll take me back to my apartment, where I can shower and get dressed, before bringing me to the courthouse. I've been waiting all month to sit in a comfortable chair and that luxury will finally be given to me today.

"Excellent. You're up already."

My head whips toward the cell door and I groan again, muttering, "Good morning, commanders."

Westing smiles wickedly, her forest-green eyes intense. "I've been looking forward to this day for a while now, seeing you permanently placed behind bars. Today's going to be fun, don't you think, Ore?"

She turns to her partner, who shrugs. "Let's get it over with."

Westing's smile drops and she turns back to the cell door, opening it. She steps in and yanks me to my feet. "Let's go, Miss Harte."

I follow her and Commander Ore without handcuffs since Westing's grip is incredibly strong and I wouldn't dare run away from her. She's the best of the best and she aims to kill. I'd rather not die a fool today when I can die a fool later on.

She tosses me in their patrol car and we head off to my apartment. It's incredibly silent. Which becomes awkward in an instant. To fill it, I blurt, "Are you two together?"

Ore nearly swerves into the other lane and Westing turns so sharply to glare at me that I swear she might get whiplash. "What kind of question is that?"

I shrink away. "An...honest one?"

For a minute, she stares at me. Her nostrils flare before she laughs harshly. I cringe, it's as if this woman is mad. Which she very well could be and we're all praising her for it. She glances at her partner and asks, "Ore, what do you think of her question?"

"I think it's too personal."

"I agree." She looks back at me, "It's too personal, you little snipe."

I glance between them as she turns forward again. Commander Westing runs a hand through her hair and I nearly miss the tan line around her ring finger. Even though they terrify me, I can't seem to keep my mouth shut and I say, "Well, I'd be surprised if you two *weren't* together because the chemistry seems pretty raw and real between you."

She stiffens. "Shut that mouth of yours."

I'm getting to her. I smirk. "I also couldn't help but notice the tan line around your finger, Commander. Seems that you wear a ring when you're not on the job."

Commander Ore sighs and glances at his partner. "She's too observant for us to keep denying it."

"Ore!" she scolds and smacks his arm. *Definitely a wife move.*

He is unfazed by her smack and looks at me through the rearview mirror. "We're married. We've been married for two years."

"Congratulations then."

Ore looks a little confused. "Thank you?"

His wife sighs in frustration and she glares at me. "If you tell anyone, and I mean *anyone*, about what my lovely but doltish husband just told you, then I will slit your throat. Do you understand me?"

I nod vigorously. "Yes, ma'am."

"Good."

We fall silent again and as we walk up to my apartment; I keep my head low, both because I don't want to incur Commander Westing's wrath and because I don't want anyone to see my face. I knock on the door when we get there and Vanne opens it a few seconds later. I hear the lilting laugh of a woman behind him and his smile drops when he sees us.

"Oh, um, hello."

Westing shoves past me into the apartment, setting her hands on her hips. "We're here to let Miss Harte get ready for her hearing today."

"Right." Vanne nods, rubbing the back of his neck.

I'm ushered by with my head held low, my skin flushed in embarrassment. I glimpse the woman on the couch and she stares with wide eyes as I walk past. She's voluptuous, with full lips and a mass of pretty curls atop her head. Definitely nothing like me, scrawny and boyish. And I can't help but see that she's wearing an oversized t-shirt and shorts as if...as if she spent the night here. My gaze wanders to the kitchen and I see two empty plates on the table.

So Vanne has moved on. That's refreshing.

I wonder if she's the one Vanne went on a date with. I shake my head and open the door to my room. It feels so odd being back and there's a film of dust on my dresser. I pull out a lacy blouse and a pair of houndstooth patterned pants, bringing them to the bathroom with me. The shower is magnificent and I know I'm taking too long when Commander Westing pounds on the door, shouting at me to hurry up and get out. So I do. I get dressed and I quickly blow-dry my hair, pulling it back into a sleek bun. A stubborn curl won't stay back, so I go with it, making another curl on the other side of my head to match.

When I walk out, Commander Westing is asking the woman, "Miss Solomon, are you officially released from your Protector?"

"Yes," she tells her as she glances at her nails, not even terrified of the Commander. "I'm 25 so I've been released for two years."

"Hmph," Westing glances at Vanne, "and you've signed the release form for Miss Harte, yes?"

He bobs his head, keeping his gaze lowered. "Yes, ma'am."

Commander Westing sighs. "*Blazes,* I was hoping to arrest someone today." She turns to me and grabs my arm. "But I guess I'll just take this little snipe to the courthouse."

She drags me out of the apartment and I feel like a child being dragged from the candy section by her mother. Ore follows and we descend to the patrol car. After enduring another awkward car ride, we make it to the courthouse and head inside. The marble all around us feels so cold as we walk through to where the Elite Council, the jury, and my private audience are gathered, which should include Mom and Stryder.

Westing pushes open the doors to the courtroom and strides in, tucking her hands behind her back. Ore guides me past the pews to a table on the left side of the Elite Council's dais. On the right, the commanders sit alongside Detective Caine. Electra joins me and takes my hand under the table, giving me a reassuring squeeze. But it doesn't make me feel any better. I couldn't even look up at Stryder or Mom as I passed by. When this trial goes public, it's going to be so embarrassing.

The bailiff moves to the center of the room and says, "Please rise." We all do and she goes on, "The Court of Moon Crossing is now in session, the Honorable Elite Council presiding."

With that, the Elite Council walks into the courtroom and takes their seats on the dais. I lower my gaze when Blake looks at me and he takes a seat that is across from me. *Blazes.*

Councilor Cristol remains standing and folds his hands behind his back. "Everyone may be seated but the jury. Miss Asch, would you do the honors of swearing in the jury, please?"

He sits as Bailiff Asch turns to the group of ten jurors, all of them blank-faced and cold. "Raise your right hand," they do, "do you solemnly swear that you will listen to this case in truth and provide a true verdict to this defendant?" They all agree and she nods. "You may be seated."

Councilor Cristol turns to the jury. "Your duty today will be to listen to the charges being made against the defendant. In the coming week, your duty during the trial will be to determine whether or not the defendant is guilty or not guilty by the facts and evidence that will be presented in this case. The prosecution must prove that the defendant is the person who committed the crime." He glances at the bailiff. "Miss Asch, please state the case."

"Yes, Your Honor. The case is The City of Moon Crossing versus Locklyn Harte."

"Is the prosecution ready?"

Detective Caine stands. "Yes, Your Honor."

"Is the defense ready?"

Electra stands, her electric blue eyes aflame. "Yes, Your Honor."

Councilor Cristol lifts his chin. "Let's begin."

Detective Caine makes his way to the podium and addresses the court. "Your Honors and members of the jury, my name is Cyrus Caine. I'm the head detective assigned to this case and have been working under Commander Keeva Westing and Commander Anton Ore. We are representing the people of Moon Crossing and wish to prove that Miss Locklyn Harte is guilty of the crimes she has committed against our city. That being, of course, the assassinations of at least two members of the Circle of Superiors. I hope we can bring justice to this disaster together. Thank you."

Once he sits down, Electra makes her way to the podium. "Your Honors and members of the jury, my name is Electra Harte. I am representing Miss Locklyn Harte in this case. I intend to prove that Miss Harte is not guilty of the crimes being charged against her and to attest to her character. Please know that I have known Miss Harte all my life and she would never do something as drastic as this. Look at her. Does that look like the face of a murderer? I hope you come to know Miss Harte as I do during this trial. Thank you."

As per Electra's request, the members of the jury stare at me and I flinch. They're all so serious and distant. I don't know any of them, which means they're unbiased toward me, but certainly, they'll be biased toward Moon Crossing. They live here anyway and the Circle of Superiors were their leaders. At least none of the Circle's family members are on the jury. Otherwise, I would be as good as dead.

Commander Westing and Commander Ore rise to present the evidence against me and then Councilor Cristol closes the session. We'll continue the trial on Monday, with a courtroom full of angry people, and it gives time for the jury to develop particular hate for me. I don't doubt that the Elite Council held my trial like this, with two days for the jury to mull over the evidence against me, for a reason. I can't even defend myself until Monday and it feels downright awful.

I stand and Electra hugs me, rubbing my back as she whispers, "We've got this, Locky, don't worry."

"The jury is getting two days to think about the accusations against me. It's pointless to have any hope," I mumble and draw away, letting Commander Westing grasp my arm once more.

Electra frowns and watches us leave. I pass by Mom and Stryder and I share a glance with them. "Locklyn—" Mom starts but I am quickly ushered past and out the doors.

"Oh, I can already feel my blood pumping," Westing says with a sigh and a smile. "This trial is going to be one of a kind, Locklyn, and I get to be a part of it."

"You're strange for wanting to ruin a person's life so terribly bad."

Her gaze snaps to me and narrows. "Ruin *your* life? How many lives did you ruin when you killed the Superiors, huh? Have you ever thought about that, *you heartless little snipe?*"

I bite out, "I didn't *kill* anyone! Why would I kill the Superiors? They gave me a job, a way to sustain myself! I had a *life* because of them."

"Have you so easily forgotten what happened to your father, Locklyn? They were his friends. They didn't even give him a second chance. You're lucky that the Elite Council is being more lenient with you, though I don't know why if the evidence is so clear, but they're only babies. They'll learn."

"Aren't some Councilors older than you?"

She shrugs and opens the door of the patrol car for me. "Perhaps, but they haven't been out in the field like I have. I've been doing this since I was eighteen. All they do is sit in their cushy chairs and chat all day. If you were being held on trial in Wolves Creek, you'd be dead by now."

My brow furrows before I get in. "They don't hold trials for murder in Wolves Creek."

"*Exactly.* A crime is committed and punishment is delivered immediately. I much prefer the O'kshah tribal system than our oligarchy system."

I slip into the patrol car and she does, too. We wait for her husband and I ask, "You really think I'm capable of killing five grown men?"

She turns to me and studies me for a long minute. Then she says, "When I was a mere intern at the police station, I got my hands on your father's case because I was curious about how he could have exploded into such a rage. I always knew him as quiet and kind when I was growing up and he was the Superior I admired most. He seemed to not have a single violent bone in him. But then I discovered he had engaged in illegal trading outside the barrier for years and he was having a terrible affair with Lady Greed," she inclines her head at me when I wince, "which you must have known. So when he didn't get what he wanted, the *money* he wanted, he exploded. Guns fascinated him, so it wasn't a surprise he knew how to wield one and I'm sure he taught you and your brother how to shoot as well.

"For you, I suspect it was a crime of passion rather than greed, like your father. You must have been so angry when they simply slaughtered him, not even a month after he was arrested. That's when you started getting in trouble, too, as your file shows. So yes, I think you're quite capable of this explosive rage, Locklyn Harte. I think it's highly possible."

My nose crinkles in anger and I snap, annoyed that tears well in my eyes. "What do you know about losing a parent, huh?"

Commander Westing's eyebrows lift and then her eyes grow furious. "What do I *know*? Let me tell you what I *know,* Locklyn. A deranged man killed my father and baby sister when I was only nine years old. He stabbed me and left me for dead before he went after..." her voice breaks, "after Wila. He killed her and slit my father's throat before my mom shot him, but he escaped, anyway. I'm not a fan of innocent people being killed for no reason."

We stare at each other, tears welling in our eyes but not daring to be the first one to let them spill. Finally, I break the silence. "Did you take revenge for your father and sister?"

She lifts her chin. "You don't need to know that."

Commander Ore enters and she turns forward again, her fists clenched in her lap. He looks between us and I lean my head on the window, staring out at the city I once loved but has now turned against me.

A Dangerous Approach

I'M PLACED UNDER house arrest—which I'm happy about—and I'm definitely not going to miss that jail cell at the police station. I have two shadows now, though, who don't let me out of their sight, unless I'm in the bathroom. Even when I'm sleeping, they keep watch outside my door and they have sealed my window shut so I can't escape that way. It's nice to be home—besides the fact that another girl is living here.

Saturday morning, I wake, crawl out of bed, and wander out into the kitchen. Vanne's supposed girlfriend, Amira Solomon, stands at the stove, making herself an omelet. I met her briefly yesterday when I returned from the courthouse and she and Vanne were heading out. She's in her pajamas again and I open the pantry, snatching my favorite cereal.

"Good morning."

She startles and glances back at me, her hazelnut eyes wide. Then, she relaxes with a smile. "Good morning, Locklyn."

I grab milk and a bowl before making my way to the breakfast bar to take a seat. "I don't mean to be rude, but can I ask why you're here?"

A laugh trickles out of her and she finishes cooking her omelet, sprinkling some parsley on top. She joins me at the breakfast bar before answering. "I guess you ought to know that I'm living here. I needed a place to crash after I got evicted and Vanne has been so kind to let me stay."

"Are you two sleeping in the same room?" I ask, stirring my bowl of cereal.

Amira blushes. "No, I'm staying in, oh, what was her name…"

My shoulders tense. "You're staying in Clover's room?"

"Ah, *Clover!* Yes, I'm staying in there."

I take a bite and chew, trying to keep my mouth shut. Vanne shouldn't let her stay in Clover's room, even if she's dead. We've left everything the way it was before. I'm sure now Amira has moved things and made it her own space. I hope they haven't thrown anything out.

Amira tips her head at me. "I can tell you're not too thrilled that I'm staying in her room. Why's that?"

"Did Vanne tell you that Clover died? That she was *murdered?*"

"In that room?"

I clench the spoon in my hand. "No, but she's dead and I don't like that you've disturbed her space."

"Sorry, but Vanne refused to let me sleep on the couch, so I took the room. Otherwise, I would have taken yours."

"Hmph."

She delicately cuts her omelet as she asks, "How was your hearing yesterday?"

"It's none of your business."

Another laugh bubbles out of her. "You're one tough cookie to crack, Locklyn."

"So?" I snap. "The trial is going public on Monday and you can see then how it was."

"I'll take your invitation to come."

"That *wasn't* an invitation. I was just informing you on the matter."

She glances sidelong at me. "You don't like me, do you."

I answer honestly, "Not particularly."

"Is it because I'm with Vanne?"

I nearly spit out my cereal and shoot her a glare. "*Blazes*, no. I'm glad Vanne has moved on. He deserves it. I don't like you because you're a stranger."

A frown creases her mouth. "But everyone you've ever met and those close to you now were all strangers once before, were they not?"

"Besides my family, yes. But," I sigh, slipping my fingers in my hair, "I'm not in the mood to make friends."

"Then what are you in the mood for?"

"Sleep. Ice cream. Spending time with the guy I like."

Amira leans closer in interest. "Ooo, you like someone? Tell me who, maybe I know him."

I scoot away from her, hunching over my cereal. "Go away. I don't need to tell you anything."

"Fine, I'll stare until you do."

She stares at me, her eyes almost unblinking and round. I turn my gaze away, but I still feel it and I hate it. It feels like spiders are crawling up my spine and burrowing beneath my flesh. I squirm and Amira taps her long nails against the granite counter.

I relent. "Stryder Monroe."

Her fingers stop tapping and she gasps, "*Really?*"

Tentatively, I glance up at her. "You know him?"

"Know him? He's my cousin!"

I blink. "What?"

Amira laughs, her smile bright as she repeats, "Stryder's my cousin."

"I—heard you, I'm just...surprised."

"Why are you so surprised? Don't we look alike?"

I glance her over. She and Stryder have the same skin tone, a warm caramel with a few freckles here and there. Her hair is nearly the same shade of chestnut, but darker and curlier rather than wavy like Stryder's. Her eyes are more round and open, her nose smaller but still broad. There's enough of a resemblance that I can see it. My mouth presses into a firm line. It doesn't mean I have to like her, even if she is Stryder's cousin.

"So? What do you conclude?" she asks, blinking at me.

"That you're right," I grumble, "although, don't expect me to like you now."

Amira shakes her head. "I can see why Stryder likes you. You're certainly a challenge."

"What's that supposed to mean?"

But before she answers, there's a heavy-handed knock at the door and I get up to answer it. One of my shadows answers it instead and I'm glad to see that Stryder has stopped by. His fist almost falls on the officer's face, but he catches himself in time and then his brow furrows in confusion.

"Umm…"

"Over here," I say as I stride up to him.

The officer bars me from stepping any further and asks Stryder, "What business do you have with Miss Harte?"

"I'm dropping by for a visit," he tells the officer. "She's still allowed to have visitors, right?"

"*Ugh*, what a despicable system," the officer grumbles and drops her arm.

I bounce over to Stryder and swing my arms around his neck. I pop up on my tiptoes and press a kiss to his cheek. I'm thrilled to see him. My heart is alight, and someone clears their throat behind us.

Stryder draws back and glances over my head, his ears tinting pink. Then his eyes widen and he sidesteps me. "Amira? What are you doing here?"

I turn and simmer with my arms crossed as Stryder hugs his cousin before holding her at arm's length. She smiles, as charming as ever. "I got evicted and I'm dating Vanne so he's letting me stay here for the time being."

Seeing them together now, they look like they could be siblings rather than cousins. I wonder…

Stryder reaches for my hand and drags us both over to sit down on the couch. My two shadows make themselves cozy in the kitchen, talking to each other as they cook breakfast. At least they're giving us some space, which I appreciate. I wish Amira would go away so I'd have some time to talk to Stryder, but she remains.

"How are two of my favorite people getting along?" Stryder asks, looking so hopeful.

I snort softly when Amira says, "I think we're going to be *best* friends."

"Oh, *by far.*"

He looks between us and I lean my head on his shoulder as he states, "Clearly, you don't get along well but that's fine. I like you both as is."

Amira tucks her legs underneath her, smiling mischievously. "Both of you failed to tell me you're dating. Strydy, you used to tell me everything."

"Oh, well," I feel his shoulder tense up and I lift my head, a blush blooming along my cheeks as we share a glance, "we're not dating."

"Yeah," I agree, though a frown tugs at my mouth.

"Why not?"

My jaw clenches and I look at her. "I don't think it would be wise, considering everything that's happening."

"*Oh, that.* I guess that's a good reason."

I walk my fingers up Stryder's hand and ask, "Where's Vanne?"

She shrugs. "Still sleeping, I assume. We stayed up pretty late last night."

"Aren't you tired then?"

Amira shares a smirk with Stryder, some unknown memory being passed between them. "Not one bit. I was a party animal during my college years and I swear, I had the power to stay up all night and not get tired."

"You could have insomnia," I comment.

She laughs. "I sleep regularly, Locklyn, and when I do, it's easy to fall asleep."

My nose crinkles and I lift my shoulders. "Just saying."

Her hazelnut eyes sparkle and it bothers me how carefree she is about everything. "Should I go wake him?"

"I don't care whether he's awake or asleep, I was just wondering where he was."

"*Sure.*"

Amira stands and makes her way to Vanne's room. I watch her peek inside before she slips in and closes the door behind her. I quickly turn to Stryder, now that we're alone, and ask, "Any updates?"

He tucks an arm around my waist and draws me back with him as he leans on the couch. His voice is low, his face tilted toward mine. "I talked to the Councilor again and with how this trial is being set up, he's pretty sure that the jury is going to find you guilty. The Council has been talking about punishments and he brought up exilement to Silverwater. Some Councilors think execution would be fair but others like the Silverwater idea."

"Would you be able to take me there?"

"I haven't talked to him about that bit yet, but I know you would need an escort. Usually, they'd assign a Recon or a Commander to bring you to Silverwater, but if I can make a case that *I* should be the one to bring you, they might let me."

I worry my lip. "How do you know that they'll trust you to bring me? If they found out that we're...entangled, won't they think you're trying to get me out so we can disappear?"

"I'm pretty sure none of the Councilors are really looking into your romantic life right now." He tips his head from side to side. "Besides Blake maybe, but the others? They don't care. And if we remain professional at all times, during all our interactions, then they won't suspect a thing."

"So how will you earn their trust? You're not a Recon or a Commander."

"But I *am* a private investigator and there's this little thing called *blackmail*—"

My eyes widen and I whisper harshly, "*Stryder!* You can't do that! The Elite Council leads Moon Crossing now, they lead the District. They're too powerful!"

A crooked smile curves his lips. "Blackmail is a powerful tool and I'm under no obligation to them. Remember, I'm not from here."

"You still have citizenship in the District."

He shrugs. "My citizenship doesn't matter. I don't plan on staying here forever, so if I lose it, that's fine. The only thing that I don't want to lose is *you*, Locklyn."

My heart flutters in my chest and I smile before I come to reason and shake my head. "No, you can't blackmail the Council."

His gaze shadows over and he glances away. "Then what else am I supposed to do?"

I take his chin and turn his head to me. "I don't know but I'm sure there's another way."

Stryder cups my face. "You're too kind and reasonable to be framed for this, *little fox*. Why can't anyone else see that?"

"They don't want to see the truth," I resolve quietly. "They want to see someone put away in the name of justice, even if they are as innocent as the air we breathe. They see my father's outburst and they pin that reaction on me as well. They'll take lies for the sake of blaming someone else, and I'm the chosen scapegoat. I have the motive, means, and opportunity so of course, they blame it on me."

His expression pinches in emotional distress. "We'll make it through this and we'll get you out of here."

"You keep giving me hope, Stryder, but I don't know—"

Stryder leans close and I feel his warm breath on my mouth as he whispers, "*Never* give up hope, Locklyn, not for the infinitesimal hardships and not for the colossal nightmares."

I bury my face against his neck. He's been so supportive and so kind. So hopeful and bright. But my world is ending and I don't know that he'll ever really accept that. I'm not destined for anything remotely great and I get that. I accept it. But Stryder won't ever accept it. I grip his t-shirt in my fingers to try and quell the tremors that take over me.

So we shouldn't be together. We have become too attached, too dependent on each other for emotional support, and have selfishly craved the thrill of falling in love. I know that my heart will be sore when the sentence is given and Stryder's will be sore, too. We set ourselves up for heartbreak, simply because we couldn't stay away, and I...I regret it. If we hadn't met again and reconnected, I don't think that we would have later on. Maybe it would have been better if we'd never met at all.

I reach up and cup the nape of his neck, turning my head to whisper in his ear, "I think you should go."

Stryder draws back and glances down at me, questioning, "What? Why?"

"Because we failed at protecting ourselves, protecting our hearts, and I think it best if we—if we part."

"Locklyn—"

"Stryder," I interrupt, "please, don't fight me on this."

He shakes his head. "No, *no*, I *will* fight you on this and I *will* fight to be with you! Stop thinking that you're doomed because you're *not*, okay? You don't need to push everyone away and wallow in your own self-pity. I'm not leaving you alone right now, not when you're thinking like this."

I detangle myself from his arms and stand from the couch, running my hands through my hair. "Don't talk to me like that. We both know what's going to happen, Stryder."

Stryder stands as well, towering over me, and he grips my shoulders. "I've seen you as bright and bubbly before, but this is the raw truth of things and this is the raw truth of me. I find you extraordinary, a rarity, and you have a heart that feels for everyone. You make me want to be better, Locklyn. *So* much better and I don't think there's anyone else out there like you. So please, I know this is hard, but I'm here for you and I'm here to help you and only you. Talk to me about anything and everything, I'll always be here to listen."

My tears fall like rain and I hastily wipe them away. I'm slipping and losing a grip on myself. I feel hollowed out, empty and cold and alone. *So utterly alone.* And yet Stryder is here, willing to fill that emptiness, to give me a second chance at life, and I feel like I don't deserve it.

He watches me cry with his mouth pressed into a firm line. Out of the corner of my eye, I can see Amira and Vanne emerge from his room and make their way over to us. I turn away, hiding my face against my hands as I try to control myself. But it's difficult when I can feel all the eyes in the room on me.

"Locklyn? Are you...okay?" Amira asks.

I hear Stryder grunt and he sets an arm around my shoulders, leading me back to my room. I hear the heavy footfalls of the officers following us, as alert as ever, and the door creaks open. We step inside and he lets me fall back on my bed. I curl myself around a long body pillow, my tears soaking the fluffy material. Stryder rubs my shoulder, letting me have my release. So I do.

It's raining Monday morning, which is fitting for this dreary day.

I shower, dress, and am escorted to the courthouse, all in a state of complete numbness. We stand for the Councilors; we sit down, and the session begins. I know the pews are filled to the brim behind me. Electra holds my hand on the table, but it gives me no warmth, no reassurance, and I keep my gaze straight ahead, unwavering.

Councilor Ridge stands at the podium. "As we move through this trial, each assassination will have its own day, or more, to be examined. Today, we begin with Superior Masoni's assassination. The prosecution may call your first witness."

Detective Caine stands and straightens his suit jacket. "Thank you, Your Honor. I call to the stand Miss Bibiana Kendricks."

"Will the witness please come forward and be sworn in by the bailiff?"

Out of the corner of my eye, a woman emerges from the pews and walks forward. I don't really recognize her and I try to rack my brain as she's sworn in and sits on the stand. Detective Caine walks up to the front of the courtroom and paces as he addresses Miss Kendricks.

"Miss Kendricks, you are employed at the Cinnamon Lounge, correct?" he asks.

She nods. "Yes, sir."

"And do you recall seeing Miss Harte at the Cinnamon Lounge on August 2nd, the day that Superior Masoni was poisoned?"

"Yes. Superior Masoni and Superior Cozeht joined her when they arrived at the Cinnamon Lounge."

"Was Miss Harte at the restaurant by herself?"

Miss Kendricks, who I now recognize as the server, shakes her head, "I believe that Miss Harte was there with two other family members."

Detective Caine nods. "Did you notice anything suspicious about Miss Harte while she interacted with the Superiors?"

Electra stands. "Objection, Your Honors. Counsel is leading the witness."

Councilor Ridge nods. "Sustained."

The detective's jaw tightens and he asks, "What were your interactions with Miss Harte like?"

Miss Kendricks shifts in her seat and glances at me. "Well, we talked little at first, but then a patron ordered special drinks for the Superiors. The patron's only request was for Miss Harte to deliver the drinks to them. So I told her what had been requested. I have to follow the customer's orders, of course, and, eventually, Miss Harte took the drinks to them."

"What do you mean by eventually?"

"She was confused at first and hesitant."

My heart pounds in my chest. What she's saying basically tells the Council that I am being framed.

Detective Caine clears his throat. "Do you recall who sent these drinks in the first place? Who ordered you to give them to Miss Harte?"

The server glances around the courtroom and beads of sweat appear on her brow. She shakes her head. "He gave me no name and I didn't recognize him. He said he was close friends with the Superiors so I thought...that it would be okay."

"Clearly not."

Commander Westing stands. "May I make a suggestion, Your Honors?"

The Council nods in unison and Councilor Ridge gestures for her to come forward. She does, folding her hands behind her back. "Miss Kendricks *saw* who requested those drinks so this man must have known that there was arsenic in them. What we don't know is *who* made the drinks at the Cinnamon Lounge. Certainly, an employee must be an accomplice with that man and possibly, with Miss Harte as well."

"So what is your suggestion?" Councilor Cristol asks, tipping his head at her.

"I suggest that Miss Kendricks meet with a sketch artist to describe this man. If we find him, we can question him about his accomplices and see whether or not Miss Harte was indeed an accomplice."

The Elite Council share glances and my stomach fills with knots as they nod in unison once more. Commander Westing sits down, a catlike smile on her lips as she looks at me. It's obvious that she still thinks I did it, but now I have accomplices in the matter. I'm surprised she didn't bother to question the server, who is indeed an employee at the Cinnamon Lounge and could have been lying to me about the man who sent those drinks.

I nudge Electra and she leans closer as I whisper, "She could be lying about not knowing the man."

My cousin's eyes narrow and Detective Caine sits down, claiming he has no more questions. Blake speaks up and says, "The Defense may cross-examine the witness now."

Electra pops up and smooths her fingers over her midi dress before strutting up to the stand. I can see the server tense as Electra nears and I work my jaw, wondering what she has to hide. Electra reaches out to shake her hand and Miss Kendricks takes it.

"Good morning, Miss Kendricks, I'm Electra Harte." She pulls away and stands aside, facing the witness and the jury. "My first question is about this man. Were you attracted to him?"

Detective Caine stands, "Objection, Your Honors. This question seems irrelevant."

"I promise there's a good reason for this," Electra states.

Blake smiles. "Go on."

Electra turns back to Miss Kendricks, her perfect eyebrow quirked. "So?"

Miss Kendricks blushes. "Y—yes. He was quite attractive."

"Was he dressed well?"

"Very well."

"So would you say that he came from money?" Electra asks.

She bobs her head. "Yes, I would say so."

"Was he wearing any noticeable jewelry?"

"A...ring."

I catch on to what Electra's getting at and I lean forward in my seat as she continues, "A statement ring perhaps?"

Miss Kendricks's eyes widen and her expression strains. She presses her mouth into a firm line and before she says anything, Detective Caine shoots to his feet again. "Objection, Your Honors! Counsel is leading the witness *and* implying a theory that has already been proved erroneous!"

Electra whips toward Caine and counters, "In Adume Hines' kidnapping, *your* theory was but not in the assassinations of the Superiors."

He glances to the Council, his brow lined. "Your Honors?"

We all look to the Elite Council, who know what theory they're talking about, and I hold my breath as Councilor Cristol waves his hand at Electra. "Continue."

She turns back to Miss Kendricks and leans close. "Was the man at the restaurant wearing a statement ring?"

I see her swallow and then she lifts her chin, her gaze unwavering. "No, it was a regular old wedding band."

Even from here, I can tell that she's lying and my gaze turns to the Elite Council. They all look regal, sitting up straight and poised in their seats. I wouldn't think any of them would be capable of murder, but does anyone really know our leaders? The Circle of Superiors, not the people, elected them. They're the most qualified of the law students and are now in equal standing as the Circle was. Promotion to more power can certainly be a driving factor.

My gaze wanders down the line as Detective Caine calls another witness to the stand and questions him. Blake is too cuddly and kind and I've never seen him hurt a fly, let alone another human being, so he's out. Councilor Fraze is older than the others and was close friends with some Superiors. Even now, I see the heavy weight on his shoulders and melancholy creasing his brow.

Councilors Ridge, Cunningham, and Zimmer are strict and follow the law no matter what. Councilor Graves is too clumsy. Even now the pen he's twirling in his fingers hits his wrist and flies out of his hand. Councilors Vaughn and Castillo hardly talk or do anything in the Council. Which leaves Councilors Cristol and Marsh. They sit side by side, both undeniably hand-some and charismatic.

Cristol was the best in his class and the first to be elected to the Elite Council. I sort of grew up with him—from a distance. But he was always over at Glory and Electra's apartment because, lo-and-behold, he and Glory were into each other. I used to be jealous of her because he's so gorgeous, but they suit each other well. He's incredibly intelligent and can be a know-it-all, but he's dedicated to the Elite Council. If he had to kill to be promoted...I wouldn't put it past him.

Marsh is cynical and he has had a few run-ins with the law in his youth. I often saw him at the station when I was brought in. But being a top student, they sent him to a correctional facility and got some sense knocked into him. He was the third candidate for the Elite Council and he's always with Cristol. He would even come over and try to woo Electra, but she didn't like him that much. Of all the Councilors, Marsh would be an excellent hitman, though he claims he's 'changed', *I* think that a change isn't always made. On the outside, maybe, but not always on the inside.

The trial drags on well into the afternoon and we begin talking about Superior Cozeht, since he and Masoni were poisoned in the same place at the same time. I remain numb and get a little bored, hiding a yawn behind my hand. Witnesses come forward that I don't even recognize and I wonder if Detective Caine and the commanders found random people off the street to accuse me in court. It could be possible and quite frankly, I don't care at this point. Because Electra breaks them down.

Eventually, the session ends and we can all go home. I get up and stretch, my back popping. Electra leads me out of the courthouse and to her car, where my two shadows soon join us. We drive home and I trudge inside, taking a nice, warm shower before collapsing in bed. I fall asleep the minute my head hits my pillow.

WATERSHED

"**I** STILL THINK the server was hiding something," Electra says as we make our way to the courthouse for day two of my trial.

"She was, I could tell."

"*Ugh*, I wish we didn't have to fight Detective Caine and the commanders on this and prove that you're completely innocent."

"It would take years of my past to unravel for Commander Westing to believe I'm innocent," I sigh and press a hand to my cheek.

"She's tough and terrifying, but certainly, she wants the truth in justice, right?"

"Yes, but she's already against me and her mindset will not change on that. About me or my father."

Electra glances at me. "What does she have against Uncle Cicone?"

I clench my skirt in my fist. "She thinks he simply snapped and that I'm capable of the same outburst of violence. I don't know what happened that night and I'm sure that the story on the news was embellished."

"Of course it was embellished," she shakes her head, "he was a Superior, but the proof was there and the Circle was unforgiving."

"I know, I know." I look at her. "Yesterday, when you were questioning the server about the statement ring, did you really think one of the Councilors could be behind all this?"

Her fingers curl around the steering wheel and she glances at the two officers in the backseat through the mirror, telling them, "We're only stating our opinions, not making any accusations so don't prance off and tell the

Councilors we find them suspicious or anything because we *don't*." To me, she says, "I bet you that Councilor Marsh is behind all this."

"You two have bad blood," I laugh, "but I agree. It seems plausible, considering his past."

"*Exactly,* and I mean, our records aren't squeaky clean either, but Marsh was sent to a *correctional facility.* Neither of us had to go to one."

"Maybe Detective Caine should request alibis for each Councilor on the nights of the murders. They may all have alibis for Adume's kidnapping, but I wonder who was where that night."

Electra sighs. "If only we could take this case into our own hands and figure out who's pulling the strings."

"That would be nice, wouldn't it?"

We fall quiet as we come to the courthouse and my gaze narrows when I catch sight of Amira entering on the arm of Vanne. I still don't like her, and I especially don't want her here to accuse me at home. Electra gets out and as we walk, she says, "Oh, look at that. The gushy couple is here."

"I don't mean to be rude, but I don't like your friend," I tell her.

"Amira?"

I nod.

"Well, she can be a bit much sometimes, overbearing and pushy, but she's a great laugh to have around. And honestly, she knows so much gossip it's kind of insane. I hear *everything* from her."

"Where did you meet her?"

"She lived in the same complex I do, and we met at the gym. I'm terribly sad she got evicted so now I don't have a gym buddy."

"How long has she been in Moon Crossing?"

Electra taps her chin. "About a year and a half now, said she's originally from Spring Grove then moved to Bountiful Hill before coming here."

I tense. *Amira couldn't have been in the Protectorship Program then. So why is she showing up now?* I push open the doors to the courtroom and strut with Electra to our designated table. We sit and there's a buttered bagel with steaming apple cider waiting for me. I turn and catch sight of Stryder in the pews.

He winks and I blush, facing forward again. Electra tries to snatch my bagel, but I break it in two and hand half to her. We eat as the rest of the courtroom fills and then stand for the Council to enter. My eyes follow Councilor Cristol and Councilor Marsh, my two prime suspects. They're neatly shaven and dressed in well-spun suits. Both of them have their statement rings on their pinkies, like the other Councilors, but it irks me that the server isn't telling the truth. Unless, of course, she's being blackmailed by the Councilor behind this. *That would make plenty of sense.*

Blake opens the session, and then he holds his hand up when Detective Caine stands. The courtroom is silent as Blake looks out at those gathered today and his midnight blue gaze finds me as he states, "I would like to begin with my testimony of Miss Harte's character. I have known Miss Harte for years. First, as an acquaintance, then as a friend, and then on a more personal level. She is brave and not afraid to speak up. She is kind, intelligent, and caring. Locklyn cares deeply for others, far more than any of us could imagine, and she loves fiercely.

"I do not see a murderer before us today and I never will." His smile is soft. "I know I may be biased, given our history, but I attest that Miss Harte would harm no one. Not in a million years. She doesn't need revenge or money or any other unreasonable satisfaction to live her life. Locklyn, I know you know better than that."

My entire body heats as he nods to Detective Caine and sits. They call an attendant from the spa forward and the trial begins. But my eyes don't leave Blake's and I can feel my pulse pounding and pumping. I'm glad he's testified to my character and I know it probably won't help my case much, but it certainly helps me to see the bright things in life. Blake Carmichael was a steady foundation for me to hold on to when we were together, and now I feel like he always will be.

☽ ✧ ☾

Bibiana was glad to be out of the courthouse on the second day of Lock-lyn Harte's trial. She had attended today for Superior Dunn's assassination examination, but that would be it. The courthouse was stuffy and old, with fans circulating above that didn't push down enough air, and it was a pain to sit through hours and hours of questions and objections and evidence.

She was making her way to her car when a shadow passed just beyond her vision and she pivoted, glancing about in the dark. A hand slid around her waist and she squeaked as she was pulled back into the shadows. A giggle lilted out of her as Viktor's lips skimmed her neck, his fingers brushing gently along her stomach.

"Were you going to leave without me, baby?" he whispered against her skin.

Bibiana turned in his arms and glanced up at him, a smile on her lips. "Of course not."

When he leaned down to kiss her, her eyes fluttered closed. They had kept their romance on the down low for the last year. They had officially met when she was eighteen and he was twenty-five. Viktor had sauntered into the Cinnamon Lounge with his high-end friends, and Bibiana had immediately caught his eye. Though young and not yet out of college, he still asked her out. Their love blossomed. He had proposed only a few weeks ago. She had accepted with glee. Bibiana drew back as her hands settled on his chest.

"I have something to tell you," she whispered.

He nuzzled her nose. "First, I want to tell you that you did well in there."

"Thank you. Electra was a bit...forward, but I kept my wits about me."

"Yes you did, my sweet." Viktor slipped his fingers into hers and they made their way to her car. He asked as they settled in their seats. "What were you going to tell me?"

Bibiana glowed and she grabbed her purse, reaching in to pull out her most treasured picture. She handed it to Viktor, and he glanced at it in the moonlight. For a long moment, he was quiet, and Bibiana worried her lip, afraid that he would be mad and leave her. Viktor had told her repeatedly that he didn't want children, but it was purely an accident. A happy accident, at least to her.

"Are you…are you happy? Excited?" she asked, treading with caution.

Viktor glanced up at her, his expression a mixture of emotions. "I'm…not sure. How did this happen?"

Bibiana tucked a loose wave behind her ear and shrugged. "I thought you would be excited."

"I am," he claimed, though his hoarse voice said otherwise.

Her heart twisted. "I know you said you didn't want children, but you said you love me. Aren't you happy that we're having our own baby?"

Viktor handed back the ultrasound and leaned his head back on the rest, running his fingers through his long, dark hair.

"Viktor?"

"I'm sorry, Bibi, but I really don't want kids."

Her heart stumbled in her chest. "What are you saying?"

His dark gaze found hers. "We should break up."

Bibiana clutched the ultrasound in her fingers as tears spilled down her cheeks. "Because I'm pregnant? You had a part in this too, Viktor! Believe it or not, it takes two people to get pregnant, and I certainly didn't force you! I want you in our baby's life." She sniffled and looked at him again. "I covered for you in the courtroom, and I did what you asked me to do that night at the restaurant. Will I never be enough for you? Or have I always been a plaything?"

Viktor said nothing, and she threw open her door, getting out. "You bast—"

Someone stuffed a gag in her mouth and shoved her into the backseat of the car. They tied her hands in an instant and she screamed against the gag, trying to blink away the tears in her eyes to see who was now taking her hostage. The car sped off down the street and she fell against the backseat. Her chest heaved and she could make out Viktor, still sitting in the passenger seat. He was staring at her, a line of worry between his thick eyebrows.

Then, he tsked. "You're a terrible liar, Bibi, and Electra saw right through you. If they bring you to that sketch artist, I know you'll accidentally describe me and then I'll be behind bars. So you have to go."

Her eyes widened as she realized what he meant, and fresh tears stained her cheeks. She sobbed against the gag, and Viktor watched her. She thought he loved her, why would he propose if he didn't? And so what if he was high-class and she was low-class? Viktor had made her feel special, feel seen, and with him, she could tell him her opinion without getting backlash. But now, the Viktor who was staring at her wasn't the man she knew or loved. He was a blank, expressionless monster who didn't even care about their unborn child.

Bibiana feared for their—*her* child's life more than her own. Her baby's life had only just begun, and now it would end with her. It was so unfair, so cruel, and Bibiana knew she had to fight. She started working at the restraints on her wrists, trying to slip out of them. Viktor turned forward and muttered something to whoever was driving. Bibi couldn't see his face, as he was wearing a hood, but she knew who it was, anyway. Another high-class snob who trusted Viktor, a snake, and a liar.

They sped through Moon Crossing and then came to the outskirts, where a raging river passed by right outside the barrier. It led to Bone Falls, a place of horrors near Wolves Creek. They yanked Bibiana out of the car and they passed through a hidden door with Viktor's clearance. The hand on her arm was like a vice and she jerked a few times, but he held on. This merciless man who she had always been afraid of and yet, still worked alongside him to poison Superior Masoni and Superior Cozeht.

She could hear the river as they came closer, and her heart pounded. Bibiana fought, finally able to pull her arm out of the man's grip, and she stumbled away. The rope loosed from her hands and she ran as quickly as she could, nearly tripping on a root erupting from the ground.

Bibi gasped as an arm snaked around her waist and yanked her back. Viktor was holding her too tight to be kind, and madness gleamed in his eyes. "If you don't struggle, it'll be less painful."

"I wish I never met you," she bit out.

Anger flashed in his eyes, and he picked her up, tossing her over his shoulder as he carried her back to the river's edge. She kicked him in the stomach and he grunted, holding her legs against his chest. She clawed at his back and tried to reach for the gun at his hip, but then Viktor tossed her to the ground. She gasped again as the air expelled from her lungs and stars burst across her vision.

Viktor removed his gun and handed it to his dearest friend. The last thing Bibiana heard as his friend leveled the barrel at her was Viktor sneering, "Careful now. She's *pregnant.*"

☽ ✧ ☾

After the third trial day, I slouch on the couch with a tub of pistachio ice cream. Vanne and Amira sit next to me, holding hands as she flips through the channels. My two shadows have gone to bed, though it's not even that late. I guess they're exhausted from watching me sit in a courthouse all day. My own eyes flutter with sleepiness, though, and I hide a yawn behind my hand.

"Hey, isn't that the witness from the first trial day?" Amira asks.

My gaze wanders to the TV and a picture of the server, Bibiana Kendricks, lingers in the corner above the newscaster's head. Amira waves her hand at the sensor and the sound turns up. "This afternoon, Miss Bibiana Kendricks was reported missing by her former companion, Miss Riva Thorne. Miss Kendricks testified against Locklyn Harte in the opening trial on Monday morning and was last seen yesterday evening leaving the courthouse. She is nineteen years old, 5'3" with long brunette hair, hazel eyes, and was last seen wearing a light pink blouse with a black skirt. If you see her, please call the police station. A volunteer search team will be dispatched at dawn."

I can feel Amira looking at me. I glare at her. "What?"

"Did you have her kidnapped or something?"

My blood boils and I toss my arms up. *"NO!* For Heaven's sake, I didn't have her kidnapped or anything!"

"Locklyn, calm down—" Vanne starts.

I shoot to my feet, knocking the ice cream tub out of my lap, and my hands curl into fists at my sides. *"Don't tell me to calm down, Vanne,"* I hiss, absolutely lethal. My glare turns to Amira. "And don't come into *my* home and accuse me of having some girl kidnapped!"

Amira stands and I hate that she's two heads taller. She crosses her arms and juts her hip out. "You're on trial for *murder.* Having someone kidnapped must be such a breeze for you, even *boring,* huh?"

Vanne stands and moves between us. "Amira, stop it."

My jaw clenches in anger, but I turn away and march over to the living room balcony that looks over the city. It glitters in the night, with light and life below. But then the barrier in the distance tells the truth. We're trapped here. We can't escape and no one is let in without special clearance. Moon Crossing is a prison, a wretchedly beautiful prison made out to be a utopia. If I'm to be exiled from this two-faced city—and I want to with all my heart right now—then I should start playing the part.

Not a victim anymore, but a villain.

"I didn't have that server kidnapped," I begin softly and then turn, my eyes blazing, "but whoever did has done me a favor. She was lying in court that day and we should remove liars from the equation."

Vanne's hazel eyes are cautious and a worry line creases between his eyebrows. "...Locklyn?"

A catlike smile comes to my lips. "I think I should get some sleep. Tomorrow's the final trial day."

Numbly, I head to my room and softly close the door. Only the lights from the city illuminate the space and then my Mini buzzes on my bed, casting a halo on the ceiling. I walk over and pick up the Mini. A simple message from Stryder reads, *My place. Midnight. Room 384.*

I blink at the message and then set my Mini aside, trudging into my bathroom. I take a bath, complete with ominous candles, a glass of Bliss, and bubbles. With my shadows exhausted, it will be easier to sneak out, but I can't say the same for Vanne—if he and Amira are still up. If my window wasn't sealed, then I could sneak out of here, but then...I'm pretty sure none of the other windows are sealed in the apartment.

After I wash off in the shower and dress in a pair of black joggers and a long-sleeved t-shirt, I shrug on a jacket and boots. It's a half-hour before midnight, but it takes just as long to get to the Ruby Vista Hotel, where Stryder is staying. I crack open my door and peek out into the living room. The TV is on with a comedy show playing and Vanne and Amira are quiet, but I can hear the soft smacking of their lips as they kiss. *Bleh.* I roll my eyes and glance over to the office where my two shadows are sleeping. Neither of them moves on their cots, and I wait for a few heartbeats, listening to their steady breathing.

Once I'm sure that neither is going to wake up, I stuff pillows in my bed and then zip across the hallway to Clover's old room. I slip inside and gently close the door behind me. My nose crinkles at the overpowering smell of Amira's fruity perfume, and I step over the explosion of clothes across the floor and bed. She's incredibly messy and I nearly trip on her suitcases by the window. I catch myself on the windowpane and then ease it open.

Clover's room is right by the fire escape and when we were young, we would sneak onto the fire escape—whenever there were blackouts—and climb to the roof to watch the stars. Vanne never liked us teetering on the edge of the fire escape, only because we're up so many floors, but when we dragged him along one time to see the stars, he joined us every time after that. It was magical, knowing that Moon Crossing, that the District, wasn't the only place that existed.

I climb out the window and scurry down the fire escape to the ground. My keys jingle in my pocket as I make my way to the parking garage and head for my car. I haven't driven by myself in over a month and it feels exhilarating to do so. I zoom down the streets of Moon Crossing, past flashing lights and smiling faces. People laugh as they leave the clubs, heading home to make curfew. I'll definitely be out past curfew, but the police can't do much to me if they find out. I'm already on trial for murder, anyway. I'll get what I deserve.

The Ruby Vista Hotel comes quickly into my view as I make my way downtown and I park in a shaded alleyway, walking in the shadows to the hotel entrance. I slip into the lobby with my head down and move toward the elevator. The reception desk is empty, thank the stars, and once the elevator opens, I step inside. This hotel is very nice for being downtown and it's classy, with gold stenciled walls and rolling marble floors. I come to Room 384 and rap my knuckles against the polished dark wood.

It opens fairly quickly, and Stryder takes my hand, pulling me inside. I instinctively grab his tank top and draw him toward me, my arms slipping around his waist. His almond gaze is soft and light as he tips his face down to mine and then our eyes flutter closed. I kiss him first, slow and passionate, my teeth nibbling on his lower lip. He scoops me up and brings me over to the bed, where he sets me down gently. Stryder leans over me, his mouth brushing against the skin of my neck, and I curl my fingers around his shirt hem, burying myself against him.

"I saw the news about the server," I tell him, my voice soft and intoxicated.

He draws back but keeps his arms on either side of my head. A few lovely waves of chestnut hair hang in his eyes and I reach up to brush them back as he says, "I saw it, too. Someone didn't want her to see that sketch artist."

"Someone in the courtroom."

Stryder nods. "Yes, someone in the courtroom."

"Why do you and Councilor Cristol hate each other?" I ask, completely off-topic.

His eyebrows quirk in surprise, and then his cheeks flush with anger. "Cristol has always thought himself superior, especially over me, and I couldn't stand him walking all over me in college. He thinks I'm a worthless lowlife, lazy and unmotivated, a follower not a leader." Stryder's brow furrows, and he grips the comforter beneath me, gaze ready to burst into flames. "He's always thought of me as a scared little child and so, I thought I ought to think of him as a hard-hearted, unfeeling hunk of flesh."

I tip my head at him and he slips his fingers in my hair, easing down next to me. "Why does he think of you as a scared little child?"

Stryder pauses for a moment as his jaw clenches. "I don't know. Maybe you should ask him why."

"I don't want to talk to him, I want to talk to you."

"Then can we talk about something else?" he asks, a hint of frustration in his voice.

I skip my fingers along his side and slide my arm around him, drawing him against me again. "Tomorrow's the last trial day. I'll receive my sentence before nightfall." Stryder gazes at me but says nothing. I cup his stubbled jaw and press a kiss to his chin. "Have you had any luck becoming my escort to Silverwater?"

A low chuckle rumbles out, vibrating from his chest into mine, and I gaze at him, my expression quizzical. His crooked smile lifts his lips. "Please don't be mad, but I had some exceptional blackmail on several of the Councilors, including Cristol himself. So, if they decide to exile you to Silverwater over execution, then I will officially be your escort."

"Hmm."

"Are you mad?"

I shake my head. "No."

"No?" he asks, surprised.

"I'm not mad because I want to be exiled and get out of here. I don't care if blackmail is shady and illegal, if I get to leave here with you then that's all that matters to me."

Gently, he knocks his knuckles against my forehead and I laugh. "Are you sure everything's okay up there?"

I take his hand and brush my lips along his knuckles. "Definitely not after the month I've had, but you know what, I'm getting used to being a criminal. Even falsely so."

Stryder tsks, "Not falsely so. I got curious and hacked into the files from the police station one night. *Yours* is loaded with stories. I quite enjoyed reading about all your arrests."

I snort. "I'm sure you've been arrested before?"

"Actually, I've never been arrested," he murmurs, "not even when Cristol and I were expelled."

"So you're smarter about skirting around the law than I am."

His arms come around me. "Wait, how did you get out of your apartment?"

"I snuck out of my old companion's room. Hers is right next to the fire escape and my two shadows were zonked out on their cots. It's kind of silly how they wouldn't think to seal *all* the windows in the apartment. Sometimes, I wonder how some people are even hired. They have quite a few dull ones."

He chuckles again, and it warms my heart to hear. "I'm glad you came. It's nice to see your cute little nose and tempting lips rather than the back of your head for hours upon hours each day."

"Get a good look then because tomorrow will be even longer than before."

Stryder's eyes glow mischievously. "I'd like a good taste, actually."

A giggle bubbles out of me as he kisses me again. His kiss leaves me breathless, but wanting more. I should go, though, before my shadows wake up.

But Stryder is intoxicating.

I don't leave until two hours later, with my hair a tangled mess and my lips a little sore. It always feels like a hazy, beautiful dream with him, and I wonder what our life is going to be like outside of Moon Crossing. Because once we cross outside of the barrier, we're home free.

A MOON OF TWO FACES

J UDGMENT DAY.

I wear a flattering black jumpsuit with heels and a white blazer. My hair hangs in loose curls around my face and I brush it over my shoulder as I sit, folding my hands neatly on the table. Electra looks as ready as I am to get this over with, but we both have different objectives today. She wants to win while I want to lose. I swallow. This won't be easy.

We stand for the Council; they enter and sit; the session begins. We're examining Superior Roman's death today, and I keep my expression blank as they lay the evidence before me. The knife with my prints on it is definitely winning over the jury, but then, Electra's heartfelt recall about my visit to my father's memory stone brings the jury to a standstill. Some look at me with compassion while others hold on to the evidence. I don't want anyone's compassion. I want to be exiled from this city.

With the evidence presented, it's time for closing statements, and Detective Caine stands to address the jury. He rubs a hand along his jaw before beginning. "I've been a detective for nearly twenty-two years and I've never felt so sure about a case in my career. I have a soft spot in my heart for each of the Superiors because we all grew up together and attended the Edification Program. Though I delved into the justice side of things and they went into law, we all had a common purpose—to keep peace and to keep our people safe. Moon Crossing is the most advanced city in the District with the most intelligent people.

"I do not doubt that the Superiors were in charge for a reason and they did all they could to improve and build our society. Like the scythe guides the moon in the sky, the Circle of Superiors guided us. Now, they are all gone and there will never be a Circle of Superiors again. So I will carry on our common purpose of keeping the peace and bring justice to our beloved leaders. Thank you."

He sits, and Commander Westing gets up to make her closing statement. My stomach turns, but this is perfect. She'll condemn me for good. She paces in front of the jury, her uniform pristine and white, and her hair, perfectly straight, cascades down her back. A line creases her brow and her eyes are alight with power as she begins. "I didn't know all the Superiors on a personal level, but I had worked with them frequently and I will never forget the wisdom they incited. People need vigorous leaders. Leaders who have strength, might, and intelligence. Leaders who think strategically and can rescue us from the riskiest of situations. The Circle of Superiors were those leaders and we hope that the Elite Council can take up the helm as they did."

Her gaze wanders to the Council and they nod. She goes on, "I can sympathize with the Superiors' families." Commander Westing's voice takes on a rare tone of emotion and she hesitates. "I...I have lost loved ones, too, right before my eyes. It is unfair to lose the ones we love, especially when they are innocent and still taken away from us. This case strikes close to my heart and as Detective Caine stated, our purpose is to bring justice, and that's what I have worked so long for. Justice for the innocent. I hope that you, the members of the jury, can also bring justice for the innocent. Thank you."

The members of the jury glance at one another as Commander Westing sits down. She takes in a deep breath and I can see Commander Ore hesitate a moment before he reaches out and settles a hand on her shoulder. Baring her heart like that just to condemn me is something I never thought she would ever do. But Keeva Westing did and as quickly as her walls came down, they built up again, her expression going stone cold.

Electra stands and smooths her skirt before making her way over to the jury. "I know that the evidence seems pretty condemnable, but I have fought this case with everything that I am because I know my cousin and I know who she truly is. I wish, like everyone else, that the Superiors may rest in peace, but I know they won't be able to rest in peace if the wrong person is accused. So please, look deeply into your hearts and your minds about your final verdict. I know our leaders are gone, but that doesn't mean we have to depend on others. We can all be our own leaders and take charge of what we believe in.

"That's what I strive to do every day and what I strive to do in court. This city has already experienced so much loss and heartache. It has taken a toll on everyone. Our city is meant to thrive in unity and strength and we can't have that if we're divided. We are all reasonable people, with families of our own whom we love and support. So let's stand side by side and be our own leaders. Thank you."

My heart pounds as Electra makes her way over and Councilor Ridge stands. He glances at me. "Miss Harte, you may now defend yourself if you so wish."

I get up and my legs feel like jelly as I walk over to the jury. They stare at me, eyes unblinking and judgmental. I stop before them and wring my hands together. "I know there's probably not much I can say that may change anyone's mind about me. I have lived in this city my entire life, enclosed in its walls and integrated into the Protectorship Program. I have made friends here and have left my family to be a genuine member of this community. I used to love this city but now, I see it is two-faced. I worked for the Superiors for only a year. In that time, I saw the cruel intentions behind Moon Crossing's smiling eyes. They destroyed Spring Grove because their people knew the truth of Moon Crossing before any of us ever did—or ever will.

"Innocent people died standing up for themselves, for refusing to help further Moon Crossing's tyrannical reign. Fear that Moon Crossing will retaliate against them if they step out of line has oppressed Wolves Creek and

Bountiful Hill for years. I've taken no one's life and I never want to. Yet, here I stand before you and you will most likely claim that I am capable of such an atrocity. But the Superiors, though they thought they were doing good, were not in the slightest. *They* slaughtered the innocent, not me. This city has changed for the worse. I don't condone the shedding of innocent blood and I no longer want to live in a city that does. So, make your verdict. Destroy my life. That's what the people of Moon Crossing do, anyway."

I turn on my heel and trail back to my seat as stifling silence follows my closing remarks. Electra looks stunned as I sit next to her, but I keep my head down. Finally, a Councilor stands and closes out the session, telling the jury to head to the jury room to make their final verdict. I'm not allowed to leave the courthouse so as everyone else files out, I remain in my seat, gaze lowered to the wooden table before me.

"Locklyn, you just—what you said was near *blasphemous*," Electra says softly, her hand on my shoulder.

"I don't care if it was or not. I want this nightmare to end and if that means I die or...then whatever."

"But *I* care—"

"Locklyn, what was *that*?"

I tense, and we both glance up at Blake. He's already run a hand through his perfectly coiffed hair. It didn't take him too long to become unkempt. I clench my fists in my lap.

"It was the truth," I retort.

His midnight blue eyes shine with fear while his brow furrows. "You don't outright say how much you *hate* the city that's putting you on trial for murder! The jury's going to think you did it—"

"So what if I did or didn't?" I stand and step back, away from my two confidants. "I'm done. That's it."

"*Locklyn—*"

They both begin, but I pivot and hurry out of the courtroom. Outside, someone catches my arm and I glance up, ready to confess to a crime I never committed. But it's only Stryder, and I follow him through the courthouse to the quiet library. Luckily, we aren't followed by any police officers. We sit on a cushioned window seat, complete with pillows and a shaft of light illuminating the dusty books and maroon carpet. I sit across from Stryder and tug off my blazer, setting it aside so my arms can breathe. He gives me a curious tilt of his head and regards me in silence for a long, long moment. I regard him as well before I look out the window, to the lush courthouse garden and a fountain spewing crystal clear water.

"This is it," he mumbles.

I nod and fold my arms around myself. He snatches a book off the top shelf and cracks it open. The spine is worn and yellow. I lean into a pillow and close my eyes. The jury will be gone for quite some time, so I might as well nap.

☽ ✧ ☾

Stryder wakes me up with a kiss on my nose, and my eyes flutter open. His voice is gruff as he tells me, "The jury is ready."

I stand, muss my hair, and pull my blazer on. We walk back to the courtroom, keeping our hands to ourselves, and make our way inside. The nap I had in the library was the best sleep I've gotten all month and I wonder if my mind has finally accepted the fact there's no way I'm going to get out of this. After my closing statement today, I would say that my mind knows exactly what's happening.

Electra doesn't even look at me as I sit and neither does Blake. I can feel the tension in the air, but my gaze drifts to the jury. Rather than staring like they usually do, not a single one makes eye contact, and my brow creases.

Councilor Cristol stands, his voice strong. "Jury, have you reached a verdict?"

A tall woman stands with a paper clutched in her fingers. "We have not, Your Honor. We could not agree unanimously."

"Then what was the majority vote?"

Her skin pales and her expression falls as she tells the court. "That Miss Harte is guilty on two accounts."

Councilor Cristol glances around the courtroom, "Then it's settled. In the case of The City of Moon Crossing versus Locklyn Harte, the defendant has been found guilty of assassinating two members of the Circle of Superiors. Thank you for your service this week, members of the jury. The court is adjourned. Miss Harte will receive her sentence in a half-hour as the Council makes their final decision."

The verdict reading is so quick that I hardly blink and the Council hurries out of the room to discuss my sentence. Everyone remains seated and chats amongst themselves, although it's all whispers and quite tense. Electra gets up to chat with a guy I've never seen around. He's wearing a sleek gray suit and has dark wavy hair neatly swept to the side. I watch him embrace Electra as she shakes with a sob and they move out of the courtroom for a moment. My mom and Jesse are embracing and crying as well in the far back. I'd forgotten that they were even here. I should comfort them, comfort Electra, but I can't bring myself to it.

What's the point, anyway?

I watch Stryder signal to me in the back and I get up, telling the officers that come to attention that I need to use the ladies' room. My shadows follow me out and then stand guard around the corner from the bathroom. Stryder walks by, acting as if he's going to the men's bathroom, but we instead meet in the little alcove between, behind a pillar, and out of sight.

"It's torture to wait another thirty minutes," I whisper, my cheeks heating in annoyance.

"Technically, you spent half of it sitting in the courtroom already," he chuckles softly, but when I give him a look, he clears his throat. "Sorry, but *little fox*, you have nothing to worry about."

"Tell that to my family. They think I'm going to be executed. Are you *sure* that the Council is considering Silverwater?"

"*Yes.* Knowing how in love Blake Carmichael still is with you, he'd reject any sentence of execution, even though you've been found guilty."

"Falsely so," I poke his chest, "but if the Council pulls a majority vote like Cristol just did with the jury's decision, then I'm as good as dead."

His skin pales and he rubs a thumb along his bottom lip. "Huh, I hadn't thought of that."

Tears well in my eyes and I crumble his button-up in my fists. "I thought I was ready for anything, ready to take the blame and go, but I'm really not ready to die, Stryder."

"You won't," he whispers and cups my face. "Our plan is foolproof, and the blackmail I have on the Council is sound. I demanded that you be brought to Silverwater and if they reject my demands then...well, I have a Plan B in mind."

"And what's that?"

"Steal a Councilor's clearance ID and escape outside of the barrier. We'll really be fugitives then, but I don't care. This mess needs to be over and done with."

I sigh and pinch the bridge of my nose as he steps back. "I wish it never even *began.* But I suppose it benefited me. I realized how terrible this city is and if I'm not executed or we're not gunned down when we escape, then I want to join the Deliverance underneath Spring Grove's ruins."

Stryder's eyes widen and he sets a finger against my lips, quickly glancing around as he mutters, "*You shouldn't speak of the Deliverance when you're still in Moon Crossing! They'll kill you on the spot!*"

I simmer. "So what? Let them."

His expression changes as he hears the raw truth of my heart. I'm frustrated and tired and this is just *torture.* I want nothing more to do with this life, and if I could die and be reincarnated, then I would gladly accept my fate. My father could have escaped if he wanted, but his burden was heavier than mine, and he paid the ultimate price for it. I've caused plenty of pain and heartbreak. I've thought of myself as higher and mightier than the other citizens of the District. I *worked* for the Circle, made plans and executed them, and sent out their orders. I never read the confidential orders to the Recons, to the police, to the people alike.

I'm as terrible as the Circle.

"Locklyn," Stryder says softly, his voice full of pain and regret, "I—I have to tell you something—"

"No, don't." I shake my head and lean into him. "Let me have a moment with you."

"But it's—"

I cut him off with a kiss, fervent and true, as I wind my arms around his waist. He sighs, his hands braced on my hips to ease me off, but I don't let him go. I turn us and press him back into the pillar. I don't want to hear what he has to tell me, whether it be that he's actually not a PI or that the Deliverance doesn't exist or this will end up being a hopeless cause. After all this, I can't lose him now. He's the only one I can talk to in truth.

"*What* is the meaning of this?"

Stryder jerks back, smacking his head on the pillar, and I cast a glare at whoever disrupted us. Councilor Cristol has just emerged from the men's bathroom, and his icy gaze lingers on Stryder.

"I *said, what* is the meaning of this?" Councilor Cristol states again, his voice borderline furious.

"I—we were—"

"We're done and if you've taken the time to dilly-dally in the men's bathroom then I'm guessing the Council has decided?" I ask. My voice is borderline venomous.

Councilor Cristol blinks at me and then scowls. "We have and that is no way to speak to a member of the Elite Council, Miss Harte."

"Who cares? It's not like you'll have any authority over me for much longer."

He huffs as he walks beside us. "I suggest you keep your head level until you hear your sentence, and then you'll *beg* the Council to have authority over you again."

I gaze at him sidelong, my lips pressed thin. "I highly doubt that."

Councilor Cristol's baby blue eyes narrow as he barks, "Monroe, I need to speak with you."

We reach the courtroom, and Stryder follows Councilor Cristol a distance away. I move inside, not caring to hear their hateful banter, and take my seat at the front for the last time. Electra joins me, a handkerchief in hand that isn't hers, wiping away the tears still streaking her cheeks. She looks at me and her electric blue eyes blaze.

"Why aren't you upset?" she asks. "They have convicted you of murder!"

"But they haven't sentenced me yet and anyway, what I said about Moon Crossing still stands. I want to leave."

"Even by death?"

I flinch and drop my gaze to my balled-up hands in my lap. "I hope the Council has a solution other than death."

"Oh, Locklyn," she cries and wraps me in a hug.

I lean into her and sniffle. "The jury decided that I have no heart anymore. The Council will decide that I have no life."

Electra buries her face against my hair and then she pulls away, turning me to look at her. "No matter what happens, know that I love you. You're my best friend and my favorite cousin. We've been through thick and thin and I'll never forget all the good times we had."

I cup her cheek, wiping away a stray tear. "I love you, too."

We hug again, clinging to each other until the Council enters. Councilor Marsh, who hasn't really spoken during the trial, remains standing. His dark eyebrows slant as he glances out among the court and at me. His eyes pierce me to the bone with so much loathing I'm quite taken aback. Councilor Marsh has little reason to hate me this much. I've heard him talk trash about the Superiors behind their backs so he must be glad they're gone.

"This case has been a delicate one for our city and we have moved through this trial in under a week to bring the justice that the Superiors deserved. Under regular circumstances, a murderer would be met with their own medicine, imminent execution." Councilor Marsh pauses and works his jaw. The courtroom is so silent you could hear a pin drop until he continues, "But with Miss Harte, the Elite Council has decided that execution would not be enough. Therefore, Locklyn Harte is to be exiled to Silverwater Penitentiary outside of Spring Grove where she will serve two life sentences for each life she took. There will be no chance of parole and Miss Harte will live with this weight on her shoulders in solitary confinement. Case closed."

My chest deflates with relief and Electra squeezes my hand, but Commander Westing rises, protesting, "All she gets is *exilement?* She *murdered* our leaders, and she gets to *live* the rest of her days in solitary confinement? Does the blood of the innocent mean *nothing* to anyone? *She committed treason of the highest degree!*"

Blake's expression shadows over, and he steps off the dais to address Commander Westing privately. The rest of the court clears out, and I try to hold back my grin as I exit as well. Mom and Jesse attack me, holding on as they sob and I keep my expression somber, even shedding a tear or two. But then I am wrenched away and ushered into a patrol car, where I'm promptly taken back to my apartment. My two shadows tell me I can pack a small bag of things and then I'll be taken to the barrier Saturday morning, where I'll meet my escort.

It makes my skin crawl that they don't tell me who my escort is, and I also wonder why Councilor Marsh didn't mention it either. Hopefully, Stryder has made his point, and he shows up because if he's not my escort, then I really am going to Silverwater Penitentiary.

AN UNEXPECTED COMPLICATION

WITH SATURDAY ONLY hours away, I can see Mom and Jesse today, along with Electra, Malini, Blake, and Glory. Vanne and Amira stayed in a hotel for two nights so they were not shacked up with a "convicted criminal" but I get to say my goodbyes to Vanne as well. It's hard to keep the tears flowing, but I manage until I get to Blake.

His expression is so crestfallen that I feel terrible for being so happy about my sentence. We sit on the balcony, away from everyone else, and he takes my hand in his. For a good bit, he rubs circles into my palm, and I watch the tears glisten on his handsome face. Other than Stryder, I had a genuine connection with Blake. A relationship that was positive and real. I genuinely love him and it feels wrong to keep my true intentions from him. But I bite my lip. He can't know, he's part of the Council.

"I tried, Locklyn, I really did, and yet, I still failed you," he remarks softly.

"You didn't fail me, Blake," I tell him. "I appreciate all that you've done for me."

Blake shakes his head. "I never wanted you to end up rotting in Silverwater, but I couldn't think of anything else before Councilor Cristol proposed it...and then everyone was agreeing and I thought it'd be better than execution but now...I realize that it's worse. Solitary confinement is worse, Locklyn, and I agreed to it."

"The entire Council agreed to it, not just you, Blake." I offer a smile, hoping that it's warm. "I'll be fine, okay? At least I'm still alive."

His fingers cinch around mine, eyes fearful. "You don't know what Silverwater is like. I could only stomach one visit and even that was too much for me. The guards are ruthless, they'll beat anyone to a pulp for talking back, and the other prisoners...well, they are there for their own reasons. It was rare that the Circle of Superiors sent prisoners to Silverwater. I...I don't want you there."

"Blake," I sigh, "I'm capable of handling myself—"

"Locklyn," his gaze is pleading and his voice drops as he leans closer, "escape when you get outside of these walls. I'll help any way I can."

He presses something into the palm of my hand before kissing my cheek and standing. I watch him weave through everyone else and leave before opening up my palm. Blake has given me a tiny chip the size of my fingernail and as I inspect it, a small symbol catches my eye. One I've seen from old footage the Circle reviewed of Spring Grove. I gasp quietly and quickly slip the chip into my pocket, my heart pounding in my chest. My wary gaze wanders around the room, making sure that no one has caught on to my surprise, and my skin heats. The chip bears the marking of the Deliverance.

Blake is part of the Deliverance.

☽ ✧ ☾

With my pack and my goodbyes in order, I'm taken to the east gate, where I can hear the raging river on the other side. If we follow the river, it will lead us to Wolves Creek. But I hope Stryder, or whoever my escort may be, doesn't lead us to Bone Falls. I've heard a few stories about the Ar'iks that live among Bone Falls and consume human flesh. The thought makes me shudder, and I glance around again, hoping that Stryder shows up.

"Who are you looking for?" one of my shadows asks, her nose crinkled.

I look at her. "Where's my escort?"

She lifts her shoulders in a shrug. "Should come with the commanders or with the Council, I don't know."

Just then, a slew of cars pull up and Commander Westing gets out, with her husband and Stryder on her heels. He has his own pack of provisions and looks ready to go on an adventure. I refrain from running into his arms as the Council emerges from all the other cars. We're outnumbered now, but Stryder comes to stand by my side.

Councilor Cristol steps forward and shades his eyes against the morning sun. "Miss Harte, the Council has entrusted Stryder Monroe to escort you to Silverwater. He is under obligation to the Council and not to you." He nearly rolls his eyes but turns to Commander Westing. "If you would, Commander."

She steps toward us and removes a gun. My eyes widen and I step back, but one of my shadows grabs my arms and holds me in place. They do the same to Stryder, and I glance wildly at Blake, who isn't looking at me. Then I look at Stryder and he seems just as confused as I am. *They're going to kill us.*

Commander Westing snatches my jaw and tips my head to the side. I struggle as she places the gun against the side of my neck and grunts. "Stop struggling, you little snipe."

"I thought—*ow!*"

A sharp but small pain enters my neck as she pulls the trigger. It feels like a little needle has been inserted and she moves on to Stryder, injecting him as well. The officers hold on to us and my head feels a little funny. I blink several times.

"Commander Westing has inserted tracker devices into your necks," Councilor Cristol explains, "if you so much as leave the District or never make it to Silverwater Penitentiary then we will activate the devices. Once activated, they will release a lethal toxin into your bloodstream and you will be dead within minutes. So, don't get any ideas about escaping. Or removing them, either. They self-destruct if they're tampered with and well, I think you'd like to keep your heads, wouldn't you?"

I clench my jaw as Councilor Cristol smirks and my two shadows lead us over to the gate with the commanders and Council. Cristol swipes his clearance and the gate glides open with ease. Commander Westing is practically giddy as she takes my arm and shoves me out beyond the barrier. I stumble and trip, falling hard on my right knee. Stryder walks out and helps me up, keeping his expression blank.

To the Council and the commanders, he states, "You have my word that I will bring the prisoner to Silverwater Penitentiary."

"Good," Commander Westing grins, and then she waves at me as the gate closes again, "bye-bye, little snipe."

Once it's closed, all I can hear is the raging river behind us and it fills my head. I turn to Stryder as a mad giggle bubbles out of me. He takes my arm, tugs me away, and we begin our journey, walking along the river. I tentatively press a finger against the injection spot and hiss. It hurts to touch still, but I can feel the tiny dot underneath my skin.

"We need to figure out how to remove these trackers as soon as possible."

He gives me a wild look. "Did you not hear what Cristol said? These trackers will blow up if we mess with them!"

"Then…you're actually taking me to Silverwater?"

Stryder groans and curses under his breath. "No, I'm not." He taps his chin. "We would need an extraction gun like the one Commander Westing has, but…I don't know where we can find one."

I think for a moment before I snap my fingers. "Moon Crossing stole all the tech from Spring Grove before they destroyed it. So, if the Deliverance went underground with some tech, they might have an extraction gun!"

Stryder lights up. "You're right! So clever, my *little fox*."

"Not clever, just knowledgeable. I was the Circle's secretary, anyway. I know plenty about their dirty deeds and stealing."

"Which makes you a great asset for the Deliverance."

I smile. "We ought to make it to Spring Grove soon, then."

"Soon. It will take us a week to get to Wolves Creek, and then I was thinking we could rest there for a bit. Try to get in contact with the Deliverance about the trackers and then join them as well."

"That sounds like a dream."

The night approaches quickly and we've entered a lush forest that is fed by the river. Stryder and I find a clearing big enough to set up the two-man tent he was given. I'm tasked with the search for kindling and wood to start a fire while he sets up the tent and traps a wild chicken. He's slaughtered the chicken, plucked its feathers, and cleaned it in the river by the time I make it back and he teaches me how to build a fire.

I sit on a mossy log and prop my arms on my knees as I ask, "Is where you come from…primitive?"

He laughs as he strikes the flint and a few sparks catch the kindling on fire. "Do you think everywhere else outside of the District is primitive?"

I shrug. "You tell me. I've never left Moon Crossing before."

"Well, I've traveled around the District and my homeland as well. I learned these skills from the Blood Hunters in Wolves Creek when I hunted with them for a few months."

"Blood Hunters?" The name sends a shiver down my spine.

Stryder nods and builds a little spit for the chicken over the fire. I kneel to help as he wraps the twine around a few sturdy logs. "The Blood Hunters not only protect Wolves Creek from the flesh-eating Ar'iks and the scavengers in Morlam Canyon but also hunt for the tribe and such. Anyone can join, even if you aren't a native. Their *darga* isn't even a native. He's from a tribe in a different country."

"Huh."

Once the chicken is on the spit, we wash our hands in the river with a rough bar of soap Stryder was given. Then we sit side by side on the mossy log and turn the chicken as it cooks. I lean my head on Stryder's shoulder and watch the flames lick the meat, cooking it to perfection.

"What's your home like?"

He tucks his arm around my waist. "It's like Wolves Creek, without their yurts and traditions. But a forest surrounds my home, like this. There are mountains and rivers and villages. The land is basically untouched and plenty fertile. We farm and raise our own livestock. We value both industry and agriculture. We have Hovercrafts and TVs as well."

"That sounds peaceful."

"It is."

I tilt my head up. "Will you take me there someday?"

Stryder's gaze warms and he smiles. "Only if you want to, I'd gladly take you there."

My hand settles on his leg and my heart thumps in my chest. "I'd love to."

His smile becomes crooked as it broadens, and he leans closer, nuzzling my nose. "Under the witness of the stars, I promise I will take you to Iluro one day."

"Iluro," I repeat with quiet reverence, "sounds heavenly."

Stryder's lips brush mine. "About as heavenly as you are in this lighting."

I snort and he kisses me, gathering me onto his lap. I wonder if he'll ever be able to keep his promise since we have plans to join the Deliverance. Certainly, I wouldn't mind leaving the District behind and living in Iluro with him...my pulse quickens at the thought. *Living in Iluro with Stryder. Having a blissful future with him. Well, that sounds downright lovely.*

"Hey," I whisper, my eyes fluttering open, "let's make it official."

His jaw drops. *"Really?"*

"Yes. We're free of Moon Crossing, free of the trial and whoever framed me. And once we get these trackers removed, we'll have a chance."

"I would want nothing more," he states softly, his gaze never leaving mine.

A smile lifts my lips. "Then, under the witness of the stars, we are officially dating."

He pops another kiss on me before the flames spark and we smell burnt chicken. I practically tumble off of Stryder's lap as he abruptly stands. Then he catches me. "Sorry, *little fox.*"

"It's okay." I straighten and he snatches the chicken off the spit with makeshift tongs, setting it on a clean cloth from his pack.

We sit on the ground around the chicken and dig in. I get a juicy leg and am glad to find that it doesn't taste like char, though the skin is pretty dark. I laugh at our little blunder, and Stryder smiles across the way before he bites into the other chicken leg.

"I think we're made for each other," I tell him, "both inattentive and clumsy when we're gazing into one another's eyes."

"Hey, what can I say? Your eyes draw me in all the time. It's like a void I get sucked into—"

"My eyes are a void? That doesn't sound romantic."

He amends, "A pretty void? Of cool smoky gray?"

I shake my head with another laugh. "I don't think 'void' would be the right word. How about a nebula?"

"Poetic. Also true. Sure, a nebula. Of cool smoky gray." He snaps his fingers. "Your eyes are a monochromatic nebula!"

"Better..."

His crooked smile makes my neck heat with a blush and I take another bite of my chicken leg, trying to hide it. Stryder leans back against the mossy log and asks, "So, what should our sleeping arrangements be on this week-long journey?"

I blink and my blush creeps up to my cheeks. "Oh, um, well we have the tent." I gesture across the way to the two-man tent, which *definitely* isn't designed to fit two people.

"Yes, there is that...or we can sleep under the stars, which might be more comfortable. I like to flop out like a starfish when I sleep so I wouldn't want you to be squished to one side of the tent."

"I guess sleeping under the stars it is then because I, too, flop out like a starfish."

"Perfect."

As we continue eating, silence falls over us and when we're stuffed, Stryder wraps up the rest of the chicken, tucks it into a small, waterproof pack with other food we've been given, and ties it to a tree far away from the tent. I toss sand from the riverbank onto the fire until it's out and then rinse my hands, running water through my sweaty hair. I wouldn't mind washing off, but the river is frigid and if we're sleeping under the stars, I can't imagine that I'll get warm during the night.

"Tomorrow, we'll reach an oasis where we can bathe," Stryder suddenly says behind me and it startles me.

I nearly face plant into the water but I catch myself, my hand sliding against a sharp rock. "Argh, *ow!*"

He is at my side in an instant, a curse tumbling from his lips. "*Blazing suns,* are you okay? I didn't mean to startle you."

"It's okay. I'm fine," I claim, even as I sit back on my legs and look at my hand. It's a minor cut and blood pools from the wound at the rate of a sloth moving.

Stryder curses again.

He helps me to my feet and hurries me over to his pack set up outside the tent. I sit down as he kneels and searches for a first aid kit. When he finds it, he pulls it out and cracks it open, digging around for a small bottle of antiseptic to sanitize the wound. We don't know what bacteria lives in the river and I cringe as he pours a little antiseptic on the wound and cleans it as it foams. Once the blood is gone, he applies a salve to the cut and wraps it in a sterile bandage. I'm glad he's kept a level head about it and his shoulders fall as he sits back with a sigh.

"I'm sorry."

"Stryder, it's fine. Just a minor cut," I reassure him, placing my uninjured hand on his arm.

He glances at me. "Are you sure?"

I nod and he deflates even more. A droplet of water hits my forehead and cascades down my nose. I glance up to find that rain clouds are creeping in and shading the full moon. A cool breeze lifts my hair off my shoulders and I stand. "It's raining."

Stryder looks up too and scrubs his face. "Two-man tent it is then."

I pull off my boots and crawl into the tent, being mindful of my hand. I help Stryder roll out the cushy sleeping pad and the two sleeping bags, which fit snugly in the tent. He tosses an extra blanket inside. I pull off my outer sweatshirt and tuck myself into one of the sleeping bags. He tosses a tarp over his pack after he's washed his face and hands, then crawls in and zips up the flap. I watch him over the top of my sleeping bag and am glad it's too dark for him to see me blush as he strips off his sweatshirt and then his shirt.

My gaze travels along the taut muscles of his back and I catch sight of a tattoo I hadn't seen fully before. It snakes around his left side and hugs his rib cage, but it's too dark for me to figure out what it is. Stryder unzips his sleeping bag and crawls in, arranging the blanket over us. Then he lies down and drapes his arm over his eyes, letting out a frustrated sigh once more.

"Stop whining," I mumble.

He lifts his arm to peek at me. "What?"

I prop up on my elbow. "I said, stop whining. The rock didn't slice off my hand and I don't have hypothermia so stop whining about it. I'm not dead."

"I know. I'm just a little...annoyed with myself."

"You don't need to be."

Stryder turns on his side and runs his fingers through his hair. My gaze wanders...then he tilts my chin up, his smirk teasing me. "My eyes are up here, *little fox.*"

My skin heats to the temperature of the sun's surface, but I sit up and unzip my sleeping bag, then his before I zip them together. Then I move closer, pressing against him. "Sorry, but you're a distraction."

He chuckles and cups my warm cheek. "Oh, I know, but listen to me for a moment."

I nod, gazing into his almond eyes.

"I guess...that I take the pain of others a little hard sometimes, especially if I cause it." His expression pinches and he leans his forehead against mine, our eyes falling closed. "I grew up privileged, I'll tell you that, and I used to care little about others' feelings. But then, I hurt someone close to me and it changed my perspective entirely. He has never forgiven me for what I did and I don't blame him...I haven't forgiven myself either. On and on, I keep hurting people and I hate the feeling that comes with it—the regret and the despair. I despise that part of me. With you, Locklyn, I never want to hurt you. I want to be done with hurting people."

"I understand where you're coming from and I feel it, too," my fingers graze his ear, "but you can't be too hard on yourself, Stryder. You're the only one that can forgive yourself. Other people not forgiving you is their own problem."

"I see."

Cautiously, I ask, "Was it that fight with Councilor Cristol back in college?"

His head bobs once. "I almost cut his throat. I was so angry with him."

"He hit you in the head with a crowbar."

"That doesn't mean I had to pull a knife on him."

I lean back. "How's your hearing these days?"

Stryder sighs. "Locklyn."

"I'm just saying he probably deserved that cut on his collarbone. He hurt you first."

"But that's not the point I'm trying to make." He flops over on his back and presses his palms against his eyes. "I want to make amends with him, but he's so *stubborn*. We have a lot of bad blood between us and I'm really, truly surprised he even let me escort you."

"Not without lethal trackers, of course. If we don't get them removed soon, I'm sure that Cristol will have no problem killing us from afar."

"*Ugh*, don't remind me."

"Look, I know you want to make amends and that is wise of you to do so. Everyone could learn a thing or two about making amends with those that have hurt us and those we've hurt."

"But our world isn't perfect, and I'm sure Cristol will hate me for the rest of his life. Which is fine, I suppose. I forgave him for causing my partial deafness and all the other things he's done. At least one of us can be at peace."

"You don't look like you're at peace, though," I remark.

His head rolls in my direction and he laces his fingers together on his stomach. "You're right. I'll never be at peace." His nose crinkles. "Do you have a grudge against anyone?"

"At the current moment, I'm holding a grudge against Detective Caine and Commander Westing...and the Council, I guess. But they won't have any sway over me once this tracker is removed." My gaze glows as a teasing smile lifts my lips. "I can't wait to be a fugitive on the run."

Stryder's mouth lifts ever so slightly at the corner. "It'll be something, won't it."

"Yes, it will." I scoot closer again and draw back the blanket and sleeping bag covering him. "I couldn't help but notice the tattoo along your side. Can I see it?"

"You can't get enough of my bare skin, can you?"

"Oh, *certainly not.*"

He sits up and turns his back to me. I prop up on my elbows as I examine his tattoo of a black-inked tiger crouching low in tall grass, its piercing, golden eyes staring right into my very soul. The tail sweeps around his side and words in a language I don't understand swirl like the wind above the tiger's head.

Quietly, he explains, "My parents used to call me *Tigris Sol,* which means Sun Tiger. It's my Spirit Guide, and my father always told me that this tiger was an Ancestor existing among the cosmos who watches over and protects me. I received my tattoo when I was eight, the age when we were taught about our Ancestors and able to understand what it meant. And able to make this promise to them." Stryder's fingers brush over the words as he recites, "*Vivere con forza e coraggio, in indipendenza e uno spirito libero, come la potente tigre.* My promise to 'live with strength and courage, in independence and a free spirit, like the mighty tiger'."

My fingers graze the tattoo again and I can feel him shiver beneath my touch. "What an honorable animal to watch over you."

He says nothing, only draws me near, and settles his arms around me. I lean my head on his shoulder as he buries himself against me. After a long moment, he whispers, *"Mi sto innamorando di te, piccola volpe."*

I hold him close, glad that he feels comfortable enough to share something very important to him, very sacred to his culture and how he grew up. The rain patters gently against the tent as we lie side by side, still wrapped in each other's arms. My fingers slide into his silky chestnut hair as I rest my head on his chest. He rubs circles into my back and I fall asleep to the steady beat of his heart beneath my ear.

A DAY IN THE WILD

WAKING UP NEXT to Stryder should feel like the best thing in the world, but we were both right about sleeping like starfish. Somehow, I'm halfway strewn across his chest on my stomach, like I've been thrown over him, and he's in the middle of the tent, taking up most of the space. One of his hands rests heavily on the back of my leg and the other is tucked under his head, tilted to the side while his mouth is parted ever so slightly. I'm surprised he doesn't feel my knee digging into his ribs, and I gently straighten out the best I can.

Droplets of rain have collected on the tent's dipped roof and I shiver, feeling the morning nip in the air. I grab the blanket and draw it around me as I sit up. Stryder stirs, only to turn on his side and I get to see his tattoo in the light. It's still beautiful and even more so. Steady and skilled hands inked his tattoo and I wonder again what Iluro is like. I also have yet to ask him what he said last night in what I assume is his native language. It sounded beautiful.

I ruffle my hair as I take in Stryder's still sleeping form and poke him in the stomach with my toes. He doesn't move. Apparently, he sleeps like a rock. I sigh and crawl over to the front of the tent, ready to unzip it. Stryder's leg suddenly swings up and hooks me around the stomach, dragging me away from the zipper. I fall on my back and blink at the roof of the tent. He sits up with a laugh and smiles at me.

"*Ha!* You thought I was still sleeping."

I cut him a sharp glare. "Are you always annoying in the morning?"

"Possibly."

I roll my eyes and unzip the tent, pulling on my boots as I get out. My spine pops as I straighten and I wince. Sleeping in that tent is definitely not going to work out for us. As I make my way over to the tree where our food is stashed, I see animal tracks in the mud, and I pause, my eyes widening as I glance around. Of course, no animals are scurrying about that I can *see*, but it still sets my stomach into a tumult. I hurry back over to the tent and dive in as Stryder's trying to get out, knocking him onto his back this time.

"*Ow*, what the—what are you doing?" he asks.

"There were animal tracks in the mud," I whisper as if any animals who hear us can understand what we're saying.

"So?"

"*So?* There could be wild animals still lurking near the campsite! I don't think it's safe to go out yet."

Stryder chuckles. "Wild animals are the least of our worries. If you had seen human footprints, then that would be cause for concern."

I knock my knuckles against his forehead. "Are you *mad*? I wasn't planning on getting mauled by a bear or attacked by a cougar today!"

He snatches my hand. "Calm down, okay? Animals only attack when they feel threatened or are provoked. I snuck a couple of knives into my pack in case we run into any trouble."

I sit up, straddling his waist, and cross my arms. "What are a few measly knives going to do?"

"More than sitting here crying about it."

My mouth presses into a firm line. "I'm not crying."

"Not yet," he teases and eases me off.

I hide in the tent as he gets out, puts his boots on, and inspects the animal tracks. He crouches down to get a closer look, counts how many paces away the tracks are from our camp, and then simply hops over them to retrieve our bag of food. I glare at him as he comes back and pulls out a granola bar, handing it to me.

"Here's breakfast."

I take the granola bar and break it open. "Thanks."

He reaches for my hand and pulls me out of the tent. "I'll take down the tent, redress your wound, and then we can head out. There's some fruit to eat, too. We should reach the oasis early this afternoon and then we can camp there for the night. I'll teach you some wicked hunting tricks."

"Mhm."

I take an apple from the bag and a canteen of water before I perch on the mossy log. Stryder brings me my pack, and I open it to grab a fresh sweatshirt. But my hand falls on the stone pendant my father gave me. I pull the pendant out and gaze at it in my hand. The teardrop stone still glistens in the light after all these years, deep indigo with veins of glimmering gold throughout. I haven't worn it in a while and I packed it last minute when I saw it in my dresser.

Now, I unclasp the pendant and put it on. It falls heavy on my chest and I rub the beautiful stone, lost in a memory of when Dad gave it to me.

"I've done something horrible, my sweet Locklyn. I'm so sorry. I pray you will forgive me someday for the wrong I've done. I love you. I love you with all my heart," he whispers, his voice breaking as he gently strokes my hair. *"Remember the good times, not the bad."* He pauses and I listen to him breathe for a heartbeat. *"Remember me."*

Then he places something on my nightstand, and I hear it thud. He plants a kiss on my forehead and is gone.

Little did I know that the horrible thing he did was take two people's lives. Allegedly. I still feel like something shady went down and he was never the monster everyone made him out to be.

Stryder sits by me with a banana, a granola bar, and his own canteen of water. He does a double-take of the stone in my hand and then his gaze widens as he breathes, "A *lapis lazuli*? Where did you get that?"

"My father gave it to me," I tell him and glance up. "He gave it to me the night before he was arrested."

His gaze shadows over and then he peels his banana. "I've never seen a *lapis lazuli* in person. Do you know where he got it?"

I shake my head. "No."

"Oh." He takes a bite of his banana and chews thoughtfully. "This is tasty."

I nudge his side. "What did you say last night in your native language?"

A smirk curves his mouth. "Nothing."

I reach for his pack and take out his Mini. There's a translation app already installed, so I open it and turn to him again. "Just say it one more time." I press the microphone icon.

"*Non ti dirò cosa ho detto, piccola volpe,*" he rattles off.

I glance at the translation and almost shove him off the log. *I won't tell you what I said, little fox.* I scoff. "Why not?"

"It's personal."

"It *can't* be that personal if you were willing to say it to me!"

He takes a swig from his canteen. "In Italian, yes, but not in English. Not yet."

My eyebrows quirk. "Italian?"

"Yes, *Italiano.*"

"Oh."

Stryder's eyes sparkle with amusement. "What language did you think I was speaking?"

I take a swig of water. "I don't know, refined gibberish? I'm not a linguist so I just knew it was foreign but...Italian. It sounds romantic."

A blush tints his ears pink. "I'm glad you think so because now, I'll just start speaking Italian and I know you'll fawn all over me."

"*Pfft,* as if."

He leans over and whispers, "*Baciami ora. So cosa vuoi.*"

I narrow my eyes at him. "Stop it."

"*Baciami, piccola volpe.*"

"I know that—pardon my Italian—*piccola volpe* means little fox."

"Correct." His eyes grow dreamy and he sets a hand on my leg, making butterflies erupt in my stomach. He moves closer and nibbles on my ear before saying once more, "*Baciami.*"

"And that means?" I ask, nearly out of breath from simply sitting here with him.

"Kiss me."

His lips skim my neck and I want to get lost in him, but then I hear a twig snap and I jerk away. Stryder's hand tightens on my leg to keep himself from tumbling over as I whip around. A few deer are wandering through the woods and have found a spot to graze. My racing heart calms and I set a hand on my chest, taking in even breaths.

Stryder sighs. "The deer ruined my chance at a morning kiss."

I look at him again and smirk. "You're right. They did. Now can we go? I'm eager to get to that oasis."

He takes my hand from my chest and unwraps the bandage. "Let me redress this first and then we can go."

I feed him the rest of his banana as he redresses my wound and then we stand, ready to head out. We talk and remain alert on our way to the oasis. I hold his hand; he makes silly jokes, and I feel like I'm having the time of my life with him. We had a breakthrough last night, but I don't know if I've ever told him how I've felt about my past. He knows about my father; he knows I was a privileged snot in Moon Crossing. He opened up about his culture, about his home, and I feel like I should give him something in return. A truth for a truth.

I squeeze his hand gently as a lull of silence overtakes us and he glances at me. A blush blooms along my cheeks as I tell him, "I'm really glad you feel comfortable enough to tell me about your culture and your home. I think it's really beautiful."

"Thanks. I think so, too."

"And I'm glad that you believe your ancestors are watching over you."

His brow furrows. "Is everything okay, Locklyn?"

Unexpected tears pool in my eyes, and I glance away. "Yeah. I mean, you have ancestors who give you hope and strength and love. When my dad died, my mom withdrew from me. She was always in her room and only came out to make me food, and to check on me once a day. I prayed many times that she would feel happy again and not be so sad over my dad's death. Our conversations were awkward. It was so quiet in the house, and when I told her I knew about his trading...she kind of blamed me for not telling her.

"If she had known, she could have convinced him to stop, convinced him it was too risky. But I promised my dad that I'd always keep his secret. I even knew he had a trade that night, and it didn't sit right with me all day long. I should have told him how I felt. Maybe I could have prevented it, too, and I regret not doing anything. Then he did the unexpected, and everyone withdrew from each other. I believe that there is a higher Being above, but it's hard to feel anything from that belief. So...I guess I'm searching for that reassurance and comfort."

"I believe in a higher Being, too," Stryder states softly, "but I think I'm not worthy of love or acceptance from that higher Being. I've done terrible things."

I look at him again and we come to a stop, turning to each other. "So what do we do? We've both done things we regret."

A small smile lifts his lips. "I think that hope and faith go a long way and we can try to be better. To each other, to others, and ourselves."

My heart skips a beat and I draw him closer, embracing him. "You're right, Stryder."

He cups my head. "We ought to learn how to forgive ourselves for the things we've done; otherwise, they'll be in our minds forever and make us miserable. I think a higher Being would want us to make it right with ourselves and with others. I imagine that a higher Being would want us to be happy."

"You're wise for your age."

"I have opened my eyes to the truth of things."

I draw back and smile, my heart warm in my chest. Stryder Monroe is like nobody else, and I'm falling in love with him.

☽ ✧ ☾

By the time we reach the oasis, I'm exhausted and my legs ache. So I simply fall onto the lush grass, curl my fingers around it, and take in the beautiful little spot from the ground. A high stone wall, covered in moss, surrounds the oasis and is hidden by wide and tall trees. The tree canopy protects us from the harsh sun but still lets light in here and there. The grass I'm lying in is impeccable and the ground isn't even too hard to lie on. A gleam of light filtering through the canopy catches on the crystal clear waterfall cascading from the canyon wall above. The pool of freshwater is tempting but my eyes flicker, sleep—a much more tempting fate for me right now.

"This used to be a lookout post for the Recons," Stryder says to my left, where he's now setting up the two-man tent again.

"So like a temporary military base?" I ask.

"Yeah, something like that. Do you see those slits in the walls? Those were for their sniper rifles so they could pick off anyone who was coming too close. Since the walls are covered in moss and there are trees all around, it's practically invisible."

I flip over on my back and stare up at the canopy, trying to catch snippets of the clear blue sky above. "How do you know all that?"

Stryder clears his throat before he says, "Well, um, I was part of the Blood Hunters when they raided this place."

My head tips toward him and I prop up on my elbow. "Wait...how recently was it raided?"

"A week or two before I went to Moon Crossing..."

I gasp and sit up, my eyes wide. "So Wolves Creek *did* take the Recon scouts prisoner?"

He shrugs. "Yes, but they weren't being tortured or anything. We were trying to figure out why they were spying on Wolves Creek."

"Lucky for you, I know the answer to that. The Circle sent the Recon scouts to spy on Wolves Creek's *darga.* They wanted a reason to boot him and assimilate the village."

Stryder's brow crinkles in annoyance. "Kaer is a saint so they would find nothing…unless…" he trails off and then turns away, "never mind."

I crawl over and plop down at his side, lying on the grass again as I gaze up at him. "Unless what?"

"Nothing."

I nudge his foot and he moves to the other side of the tent, setting up the poles. "I'm not the Circle's secretary anymore and I'm certainly not in league with the Elite Council so tell me."

"It's nothing, Locklyn."

I stand, set my hands on my hips, and level him with a glare. "Why don't you trust me?"

His expression strains. "I do trust you…but I think it'd be better for you to see for yourself."

"See what?"

"Kaer's wife…she's from Moon Crossing."

"Oh, so I might know her? What's her name?" I ask, stepping closer.

Stryder shrugs again and continues to work. "Something that starts with a letter in the alphabet. I barely spent time around her. Kaer didn't want any handsome, young fellows talking to his wife."

"So he sheltered her away so he can be the only one she looks at?"

"No, I'm saying that Kaer was always with her, or she spent time with the other women in the tribe. Personally, I never acquainted myself with her."

"Mhm." I trail back to my spot and lie down again. "Why would the Recons care about a woman from Moon Crossing? If she left, she left. There's nothing Moon Crossing can do about it and they have no sway over any citizens who choose to give up their citizenship and leave."

"True, but Kaer didn't want to take any chances in case the Recons were going to alert the Circle and force his wife back to Moon Crossing. We only took them prisoner because Kaer wanted to protect her. She's pregnant."

"That's sweet and that's a good man right there, not letting Moon Crossing push him around or take away his happiness. I wouldn't go back even if someone *paid* me to."

Stryder chuckles. "Are you sure about that?"

I glance at him. "Yes. That city is the embodiment of hell. The people, too, no doubt. I'll be content out here."

"With me?" he asks, a crooked smile curving his lips.

My cheeks flush as I grin and crawl back over to him. "I'll be the most content woman in the world with you by my side, Stryder Monroe."

He cups my cheek and I kiss him first, helpless to the energy between us, and we tumble over in the grass, a tangle of limbs. Stryder musses my hair with one hand, while the other draws me closer to him. I feel like a giddy teenager, falling in love for the first time with someone way out of my league. But I suppose that was true, way back when we were, in fact, teenagers.

I never forgot Stryder Monroe, and whenever the memory of our date came up, I cherished it fondly. A beautiful gondola ride through the city beneath a clear, midnight sky. It was beautiful and simple. Even getting busted by the police was a fond memory because that was the first time we got in trouble together. Now, we're deeper than ever before, but I feel like things will work out this time if we play our cards right.

"Hey, do you hear gushing water, or is that just me?" Stryder whispers against my ear.

My lips stray from his neck to his ear as I whisper back, "Do I smell terrible? Is this your way of telling me I should go bathe?"

A low chuckle rumbles in his chest. "Possibly...but I imagine I smell terrible, too."

"Like dirt and sweat."

"How sweet of you to say."

I laugh as I sit up and he does too, running a hand through his unruly hair.

Once we're both standing, our faces flush again and he states, "Neither of us brought a swimsuit, did we?"

"Uh, no."

"Hmm."

I rock on my heels. "Should we bathe one at a time? *No peeking, right?*"

He nods vigorously. "Right, of course. You can go first. I'll, um, be out hunting...or wandering around aimlessly."

Abruptly, we part ways and I gather fresh clothes out of my pack, along with the bar of soap and towel I brought. I hide behind a shrub as Stryder disappears to catch us dinner and then I strip. I also grabbed his little orb that makes the water warm, and I toss it in before I slip into the pool. It warms up and I sigh, glad to scrub myself with soap and get all this dirt and grime off of me. We've only been gone for two days but it's felt like forever since I took a bath.

I take my sweet time before I get out, dry off, and get dressed. Stryder comes back a half-hour later with three unidentifiable creatures. I help with the fire and create a makeshift spit. He skins the creatures, skewers them with sturdy sticks, and leaves me to cook them while he bathes. I keep my back turned, even though I'm deadly curious, but he was a gentleman about my bathing so I have to be a lady about his. He startles me when he plops down on the ground next to me and I nearly fling one of the skewered creatures away.

Stryder leans close to my face and quirks an eyebrow at me. "Did you peek?"

Though a blush tries to betray me, I firmly shake my head. "No. I was a lady about the matter and kept my back turned the entire time."

He sits back, smirking. "Did you want to?"

I laugh. "Oh, *heavens above*, who do you think I am?"

"Someone who would like to take a sneak peek at this rare attraction, eh?"

"In all honesty, I wasn't curious at all," I tease, keeping my tone level and my expression blank.

Stryder purses his lips. "Oh, really?"

"Yes, really."

His hand finds my knee, and I gnaw on my lip. "If I recall correctly, you were all over me three times today."

I flick his hand from my knee and shift away. "Doesn't mean I was purely attracted to the physical aspects of you."

He gathers his arms around my waist and draws me back into him. "That's a shame. I think I'm quite handsome."

"Oh, you are. But you didn't hear it from me," I joke.

Stryder gasps. "So rude."

I laugh and between bites of our meal, we talk about anything and everything.

THE CALL OF A SHIKOBA

I WAKE EARLIER than usual and crawl out of the tent. We slept in it because it rained again and was too cold outside. I stretch and yawn as the crisp air nips me and I pull on a sweatshirt before slipping into my boots. Slowly, I make my way over to the pool and kneel at the edge, splashing water on my face and rubbing the sleep out of my eyes. I hope there are proper beds and showers in Wolves Creek because I would rather not live like a camper for the rest of my days. I don't want to complain, but I miss my privileged lifestyle.

A soft call from the trees makes me glance up and I see a little bird with black and white plumage perched on a branch above. It stares down its sharp beak at me, eyes black and beady. It makes a sound again, its chest puffing out as it shifts on the branch. I shake my head and stand, lest it try to release some natural goop on my head, and I wander over to the pack of food. As I sit on a log with my breakfast spoils, the little bird keeps making its call and after a bit, I pick up a small stone and chuck it at the branch. The bird squawks and takes flight, only to perch on a branch a little higher in the tree.

It continues its call.

"*Ugh,*" I groan, giving the bird my best glare, "go away!"

It stares at me and, as if mocking me, makes an even louder call than before.

"To hell—"

"What was that?" Stryder suddenly asks behind me.

I glance at him and point to the bird. "That thing won't shut up."

He looks to the trees, squinting until he finds the bird, and then his eyes widen. "We have to leave."

"What?"

Stryder takes my arm and draws me to my feet. "We have to leave. It won't be safe here for much longer."

I blink, stumbling as he drags me back over to the tent. "What are you talking about? Is that bird calling all his friends to devastate the oasis with their natural goop?"

"Ah, not quite." He hastily rolls up our sleeping bags, the pad, and ties them to his pack. "It's a Shikoba Sparrow, and its friends are the flesh-eating Ar'iks I was telling you about."

My heart skips a beat and I help him. "Oh, *blazes.*"

Stryder nods. "The Ar'iks have been training Shikoba Sparrows for years to be their eyes beyond Bone Falls. They're trained to find other people and then emit a call to come and slaughter us. So we really have to get going."

"Agreed."

Once our packs are ready, we tear down the tent, and I cringe every time the Shikoba Sparrow makes its call. I follow Stryder as we make our way to the entrance of the oasis, and he pokes his head out, glancing left and right. I don't know how far away Bone Falls is from the oasis, but it took us a good minute to pack up so the Ar'iks surely could be on their way...unless they're already here.

I curl my fingers around Stryder's shoulders and whisper in his ear, "Do you see anything?"

"No, but we have to watch our backs. The Ar'iks are masters of stealth and they won't stop their hunt for anything." He reaches up, takes my hand in his, and gives it a reassuring squeeze. "We'll be okay, Locklyn. If they find us, I know where we can go."

"Wolves Creek?"

He draws me out and we both remain alert, glancing about as we hastily walk away from the oasis. Stryder shakes his head. "We're too far away from Wolves Creek. So, if they find us, we'll go to Mirror Lake, which is conveniently on our way to Wolves Creek. *And* the Ar'iks won't even set foot on its banks."

"Why?" I ask, pulling closer to him as chills run down my spine.

"Mirror Lake is where they dump the bones of the people they've consumed. They believe that if they set foot on the banks, the spirits of those they've killed and eaten will rise and drag them down to a watery death."

My chills multiply, and I glance up at Stryder. "That's *incredibly* unnerving! How do they dump the bones if they don't even set foot on the shore?"

He shrugs. "Attach them to arrows? Toss them in? I don't really know. I've yet to witness such a ritual."

"And I hope we never have to...or worse, be a part of it."

He snorts softly. "True. I'd hate to have front row seats to that."

"Why did they turn to cannibalism?"

"If I remember correctly, I believe their leader brought home a fresh kill one day and they all had a taste of human flesh for the first time. The Ar'iks are actually those that have been banished or forced to leave their homes. Most are from Spring Grove, after it was destroyed, but there's plenty from the other cities as well. They continue to hunt and kill anyone they find out of revenge. You could have joined them if you told them you were exiled."

"Oh. That's...I didn't know that."

"Not many do."

We fall silent as we continue the constant scan of our surroundings and no matter how much distance we put between us and the oasis, I still hear the Shikoba Sparrow's call echo in my ears.

The day goes on without interruption, and we rest under a rock outcropping with our eyes trained on the wide and open meadow. We eat leftover meat, drink water, and relax against the cool rocks. The sun's heat is sweltering today, just some absolutely *fantastic* autumn heat rolling in before winter comes about. I lean my head back on a smooth plane of rock and watch a swirl of butterflies as they land on flowers and then off. Bees buzz, a small herd of deer is grazing in the far distance, and the space between trees is empty.

Watching the butterflies flit around in the meadow, carefree, reminds me of a happier time, of course. Times that are now long gone.

"Where are we going to camp tonight?" I ask once we've finished our meals.

"I suppose it depends on how the rest of the day goes. Would it creep you out too much if we stayed on the banks of Mirror Lake? The Ar'iks know there are people out here and I wouldn't want to risk waking tied up and about to be sacrificed."

I stand and knot my fingers together. "Yeah, we should head to Mirror Lake now. Call it a night even if they don't trail us there."

He nods and offers his hand to me, which I gladly take. "To Mirror Lake we go."

We don't get far before the call of a Shikoba Sparrow stops us in our tracks. Stryder and I tense and look behind us. There, on the branch of the nearest tree, is a Shikoba Sparrow, eyes focused on us. For a moment, we stare at the bird and it continues to stare. Then Stryder squeezes my hand and yanks me away. I stumble before I catch my footing and we fall into a steady running pace. My heart, however, is unsteady in its rapid beat and sweat trickles down my temples.

The Shikoba Sparrow being here can only mean that the Ar'iks are still on our trail, and they could be close, for all we know. We could be running into a trap. *Blazing suns! Why did I think being banished and hunted by cannibals would be better than death?* My gaze turns to Stryder as he huffs next to me. His face is red and sweaty and he looks very unwell. But I imagine I do, too. We *have* to get to Mirror Lake, no matter what, even if the Ar'iks aren't on our tail.

As we duck under a scraggly set of branches, something whizzes past my ear and I feel a small but stinging graze on my earlobe. I jerk to the left, into

Stryder, and blink as I catch sight of an arrow lodged in the tree's trunk to my right. We breeze past it, but I gulp and look at Stryder again.

"Serpentine," he breathes, "they're onto us."

I follow Stryder, gripping his hand for dear life, as we serpentine through the trees. A few more arrows are let loose—and they miss. Mirror Lake comes upon us quickly, and terrifying shouts fill the air as I focus on the lake's reflective surface. Of a sky too calm for a situation like this, with lazy and puffy white clouds, birds flying with ease, and the sun smiling its warmth all across the land. Personally, I think it should rain right now, with thunder and lightning casting crackling energy in the air.

Each step closer means the shouts get louder—and closer. Though my legs burn, I press on…until I trip and my arms dart out to catch myself. Stryder is faster, and he catches me around the waist, hefting me into his arms. I glance over his shoulder and my eyes widen when I see at least a dozen Ar'iks chasing after us. Their faces are painted like skulls, their clothes aged and torn, and their eyes hungry and wild. A girl with red stripes in her blonde hair shoots an arrow directly at us. I squeak and curl in Stryder's arms, but he grunts, stumbling.

A curse slips from his lips. *"Blazing suns above."*

"We're almost there," I reassure him.

He grunts again and presses on. Finally, we make it to the shore and Stryder sets me on the white sands. Hastily, he removes his pack, rips mine away, and tucks them underneath a small rock outcropping. I now see the arrow sticking out of the back of his calf and I wonder how he could run with it in.

"Stryder, there's a—"

"I know." He kneels, reaches back, and takes the shaft in his hands before he snaps it as close as he can to the wound. He grunts and tosses the broken arrow shaft away. "We need to get in the water."

I nod, absolutely bewildered by his strength, and we trample into the water. Stryder's wound is bleeding, and yet he reaches back to take my hand

and make sure I stay afloat. My stomach turns as we swim out to the middle of the lake and the crystal clear water turns a murky red with his wound. Stryder's breathing becomes heavier and I glance out across the shore. The Ar'iks surround us and sure enough; they stand at the treeline, staring in silence. As I look at them, I notice they vary in look and age and clothing style. One even wears a now ratty and once-white lab coat. Their eyes seethe with anger and spite and for a moment, I wonder who they all were before they became cannibals.

I shiver, and he leans his head against mine as we wade into the middle of Mirror Lake.

"If we are going to die today, I have one request."

A soft chuckle escapes him, but he holds on tighter. "What's your request?"

"Tell me what you said that night."

He cups my cheek as he tilts my face to his. His almond eyes are soft and kind as he admits, "I said that I'm falling in love with you."

"Oh," I whisper, a bit taken aback.

Before he can say more, a volley of arrows breaks the water surface around us. I flinch and cling to Stryder.

"Hold your breath," he instructs.

I do, and we dive into the lake. Stryder guides us deeper and deeper into the lake, and my chest burns as darkness closes around us. A school of fish swims by, eyes bulging and wide as they try to decipher what species of fish we must be. I grip Stryder's hand and kick my feet faster. A few moments later, he reaches out and grips a stone dome covered in moss that I hadn't noticed. He pushes me toward the dome's entrance. I swim beneath the arch and pop out into a wide cave, surfacing quickly.

Gasping for air, I grip a nearby stone jutting out of the water as I blink, wiping the water from my eyes with my free hand. I hear Stryder pop up behind me and his hand settles on my back, patting gently.

"Are you okay?"

"I—I think so…" I cough and my fingers curl. "*Ugh*, I'm not made for this kind of 'excitement'."

Stryder chuckles. "So it seems. Come over here, we can sit on a ledge."

I leave the safety of my stone and swim over to the ledge with Stryder. He rips his flannel sleeve off, rolls up his pant leg, and makes a tourniquet for his calf. He bites his lip as he ties it and then sits back with a sigh.

I reach for his leg. "Shouldn't we take the arrowhead out?"

He shakes his head. "No, the Ar'iks use borbilite arrowheads, which shatter if not removed correctly. I'm sure I've already done some damage by breaking off most of the shaft but it had to be done."

"Don't you feel any pain?"

"Of course," he grunts softly, "but I'd rather be in pain than both of us dead and roasted."

My brow creases and I look at his wound. Blood seeps onto the rock and dribbles into the water. "You're still bleeding heavily. If you lose too much blood, you'll pass out and I won't be able to carry you back to the surface."

Tentatively, I crawl over him so I'm on his wounded side and instruct him to lie down on his stomach. He does, grumbling that it's fine, and I assess the wound. The arrowhead hasn't pierced his calf too deeply, but I see that the smooth white stone is fractured. I don't want to risk it shattering in his leg, especially since I don't know how to remove arrowheads.

"The arrowhead isn't lodged too deep," I tell him.

"Is it still bleeding?"

"Now that you're on your stomach, it's slowing down."

"Then leave it be." Stryder glances at his watch and sets a timer. "I can only have the tourniquet on for two hours. Hopefully, by then, the Ar'iks will be long gone."

I sit back on my legs and knot my fingers together. "Do you think they'll leave? What if they camp out by the treeline?"

He folds his arms under his head and closes his eyes. "If we haven't surfaced by now, they'll think we've drowned. And since they won't even set foot on the shore, they have no way of knowing there's a cave down here. It should be safe to go up in two hours."

"How far away are we from Wolves Creek now?"

"About another two days of walking. But I have a kit in my pack so I can bandage the wound when we get back to shore."

I nod and gently rock back and forth. I don't know how he's staying so calm in this situation, especially since he's the one that's injured. My hands tremble and I ball them in my shirt, glancing away from Stryder. I'm not cut out for this kind of ragtag life, running away from Ar'iks, sleeping in the wilderness, *actually* trying to survive. I've been sheltered and it makes me feel insecure about my upbringing in Moon Crossing. I've always been safe in the city with its enclosed barrier and cushy living. Though really a glorified prison, I thrived in that society. I was an elite. Out here, I'm nothing, I have no smarts in what it takes to *really* survive in the world and that is terrifying.

"Stryder?" I whisper.

He shifts slightly and peeks at me. "Hmm?"

"How did you know about the cave?"

A blush colors his cheeks. "Er, would you believe me if I said I was psychic?"

I snort. "No. So what's the truth?"

"Someone showed it to me."

"Oh? Why would someone want to show you this cave in Mirror Lake, the Ar'iks' dumping grounds?"

He dips his hand in the water and swirls it around. "Her name was Inaya, a girl from Wolves Creek I fancied once upon a time...anyway, she showed me this place."

I wrap my arms around myself. "What happened here with Inaya?"

"Locklyn, *nothing* happened. I found out a week later she was a Worshiper, so that ended pretty quickly."

"Ah, well that changes things."

"It did." He chuckles. "I'm glad I've found someone better."

"You think I'm better?"

"Yeah. Much better because as far as I know, you're not a Worshiper," Stryder smirks as he looks out across the water, "and, you're far more beautiful."

I blush. "Keep talking like that, and I might have to kiss you."

"*Baciami.*"

"You know what I'd like to tell you?"

He twists his head toward me. "Yes?"

"I'm falling in love with you, too."

He grins and I ease myself down next to him. I'll admit, I'm a little jealous that another girl was here with him before. We may be in danger and hiding in an underwater cave until the Ar'iks go away, but at least we're together. Wet and exhausted. Stryder's injured. I'm terrified. But all that seems to drift away as I lie with him, safe for now.

"If the Ar'iks aren't gone in two hours," he murmurs after a bit, "how do you feel about living in this cave?"

A light laugh bubbles out of me. "It needs some decor, but I think we can make it into a home."

The corner of his mouth lifts. "Anywhere is home with you, my love, even here."

A SHADOW OF THE PAST

WHEN WE BREACH the surface after two hours of being underwater, I'm terribly glad to find that there are no Ar'iks in sight. There aren't any Shikoba Sparrows either. Those pesky little birds have nearly brought death on us *twice.* If I ever see one again, I'll knock it out of the tree with a makeshift slingshot. Of course, I'd have to ask Stryder how to make one first.

The moon has emerged since we've been underwater and the nightlife of the forest is awake, mosquitoes zipping along the surface, frogs croaking on the shore. Stryder kneels next to our hidden packs and tugs his out, searching for the first aid kit. I stand at his side and when he finds the kit, he lies down. I kneel and look at his calf in the moonlight, taking off the tourniquet. His skin is pale and crusted with dried blood. Meticulously, I take a pair of small tongs and extract the arrowhead at his will. I exhale in relief once the arrowhead has been removed, unshattered, and his wound bleeds a little.

I clean it, wrap it with gauze and a bandage, and give Stryder some pain relievers. He stands once it's wrapped and directs me over to a rock outcropping on the shore that would enclose us from anyone else's sight. I'm iffy about the idea of sleeping on the shore in the dead of night, but the cave ledge was not comfortable at all to lie on. I swing my arm around Stryder's waist, and we hobble over to the rock outcropping with our packs. I let him slip in first, and then I build a barrier to the outside elements with our packs, making sure that I grab a few snacks as well.

Stryder and I sit back against the rock, which is thankfully smooth and not covered in moss or bugs. I make sure he eats first and enough to cover for losing blood today. He drops his head on my shoulder once he finishes, and I shift, enveloping him in my arms. Stryder drifts off in a matter of minutes, his chest rising and falling as he spirals into a deep slumber. I lay my hand against his forehead and gnaw on my lip, he's warm. Hopefully, his wound won't get infected from being directly exposed to the lake water…but I mean, we don't know what could be in the water.

Once we get to Wolves Creek, he is seeing their physician, whether or not he wants to.

☽ ✧ ☾

The next two days are arduous, with Stryder's wound slowing him down. He has developed a limp but explains that his limp is from an old injury and it's acting up because we had to run away from the Ar'iks. I'm not sure that I believe him about the old injury, but at least he doesn't have a fever and his wound doesn't look infected.

When we're nearing Wolves Creek, I ask, "So what was your old injury?"

Stryder chuckles for a long moment and I give him a look as he stops to double over, tearing up as he laughs.

"Uh, are you okay?"

He waves at me, bobbing his head. "Yes, I'm fine. I'm just—*ha*, it's such a stupid story."

"We have plenty of time for a stupid story." I nudge him as he straightens. "So hit me with it."

He cringes before beginning and we continue walking. "I was in Bountiful Hill when it happened, so I was around fifteen or sixteen years old? Anyway, my buddy and I were hanging out at the train station one night—totally not trespassing." His mouth quirks at that and I snort. "We went down to the tracks and heard a train coming. We would always hop on the train to go uptown and sneak into the kitchen of this fancy restaurant that served the best ice cream in the world.

"It goes along the outskirts, so it passes through tunnels and snakes through the Blooming Woods. My friend dared me to climb on top of one of the train cars and stand up. Being a dumb teenager, I did. But we were in the Blooming Woods and I...kind of got spooked by an owl in the trees and tumbled off the train. I broke my leg—which was a nasty wound to witness—and my friend had to call an emergency Hover to airlift me out of the Woods."

I have to look away so he doesn't see the smile come to my face, and I cough into my elbow, my attempt at obscuring my laugh. Stryder sighs. "Go ahead and laugh. I told you it was stupid."

"Why do you think I'm going to laugh?" I ask, trying in vain to keep the humor from my voice.

Stryder leans around to look me in the face. "Because I can see it on your face and hear it in your voice."

That breaks me and I let out a laugh, which turns into a snort or two. Stryder shakes his head and tosses his arm around my shoulders. "Laughing at my pain. So sad and yet, *you're so adorable.*"

"I'm not laughing at your pain. I'm laughing *with* you, of course." I smirk.

"Ha, of course."

I reach back for my canteen and take a swig. "Do you think the people of Wolves Creek will be fine accepting a criminal like me?"

Stryder strokes his stubbled chin. "If you're not a hardcore patriot of Moon Crossing, then they'll love you."

"Well, I guess I'm all good then."

Before long, we come to a clearing that leads to the entrance of Wolves Creek. As we approach, I tense when I catch sight of two muscular O'kshah men standing sentry at the entrance gate. They stare at us as we approach, expressionless, with dots of white paint splattering their exposed arms and shoulders. A stark contrast to their beautiful skin and dark eyes. My gaze wanders to the gate, made of what looks to be bamboo and twine. A wall of...what looks to be mud, sturdy and thick, surrounds the village. The wall is at least twelve to thirteen feet tall, with sharpened bamboo sticks along the top to act as spikes. It doesn't look too inviting, but I imagine they weren't going for an "inviting" look, anyway.

We stop before the sentries, and they stamp their spears against the ground. Stryder says, "Mohe, Yansa, are you still going to pretend that I don't exist?"

The sentries glance at each other and then smiles break across their stoic expressions. "Oi, what brings you back to Wolves Creek, *milk chocolate*?"

"*Milk chocolate*?" I laugh and all eyes turn to me.

Mohe and Yansa grow curious, their eyebrows lifted. Stryder draws me out from behind him and tells them, "Believe it or not, this is my girlfriend, Locklyn, and I thought I'd take her on a wilderness adventure. Wolves Creek seemed like the perfect place to start."

The sentries look at one another again and the taller one, Yansa, steps up to the gate. "Wolves Creek is about as adventurous as you can get in the District. Welcome, Miss Locklyn. If you're with Stryder, we welcome you into our village."

"Oh, thank you." I blush as I'm led forward and glance back when Mohe claps Stryder on the shoulder. He murmurs something to him before Stryder joins me inside and I give him a quizzical look. "What did he say to you?"

Stryder's eyes sparkle and he slips his arm around my waist. "Let's just say he was right in what he said."

My nose crinkles and I'm about to counter him when someone demands, "Halt."

Both Stryder and I startle to a stop and glance at a broad-shouldered man. His skin is dark umber, his hair a clean-cut array of tight coils on his head, and he has a stark red handprint on his exposed chest. Eyes as dark as a moonless night pierce us, especially me, and my stomach turns.

The man looks at Stryder, but his expression doesn't soften one bit. "Monroe, who is this, and why have you brought her here?"

Next to me, Stryder shifts on his feet, nervous as other O'kshahs gather around to stare at us. "Can we talk in private, Kaer?"

My gaze snaps back to the man before us. *Kaer. So this is the* darga *of Wolves Creek that the Circle wanted to take down.*

With a sigh, Kaer waves us over to a canvas yurt with small puffs of smoke emerging from its center hole. I can feel the other O'kshahs' eyes on us as we walk over to the yurt. I'm glad when Kaer holds the flap open for us and we step inside. A woman is kneeling on a set of thick quilts as she stokes the fire and stirs a boiling pot of soup above it. Her gaze finds me and her eyes widen the same time mine do.

Our jaws drop as Kaer says, "This is my wife—"

"*Clover?*" I breathe, crumbling to my knees as I take her in.

She stands and waddles to me since she's nearly at full term in her pregnancy. I watch as she takes my trembling hands in hers. We stare at each other and tears well in my eyes. I knew I missed her, but I didn't think I'd feel this much emotion over Clover Parrish. We were companions, good friends who had our quarrels, but we still stuck by each other's sides and that was all that mattered.

"Locklyn," she smiles softly, "I—it's so lovely to see you."

"How—how are you even *alive?*"

Clover's forest-green eyes fill with guilt and she drops my hands to cradle her belly. "It's a long story."

I rub my eyes and blink. "*Blazing suns,* is this real?"

Kaer interjects with a frown as he asks, "How do you know Clover?"

I turn to him and Stryder helps me up and over to a pillow to sit on, while Clover moves over to Kaer's side and leans on him as he wraps an arm around her. I can't stop staring at Clover, but her gaze focuses on the flames before us. Her cheeks are flushed a soft pink.

"We were in the Protectorship Program together in Moon Crossing," I explain. "We were companions, like roommates, and so we lived in the same apartment with our Protector."

"Ah, so you hail from Moon Crossing, Miss—?"

I glance at Kaer. "Oh, I'm Locklyn. Locklyn Harte." My brow knits in confusion as I address Clover. "Can I at least hear a summary of what happened to you? All I know is that one minute, you were with us having a good time, and the next, you went missing and then were pronounced dead, *murdered*—I wept so terribly when I found out..."

For a moment, Clover remains quiet, and then she sits up, her eyes lifting to mine. In a guilty voice, she tells me, "I'm not originally from Moon Crossing, Locklyn. I was born in Spring Grove, but my parents are from Wolves Creek. I enlisted as a child to be part of the..." she hesitates and glances at Stryder, "does she know about, uh, *that* group?"

"Yes," he answers.

Clover nods and continues, "I became a part of the Deliverance when I was ten and was sent with other children to infiltrate Moon Crossing by posing as orphans. That was the day they raided and blew up Spring Grove. They took us in after the fact. They integrated us into the Programs. Vanne and I were assigned to you because of your name's sake."

"Wait, what do you mean 'Vanne and I'? And my name's sake?"

"Oh, he's my cousin. They assigned us to you because your father was an early benefactor of the Deliverance."

My jaw drops again. "*What?*"

"I guess he kept that secret from you?"

"Yes, he did." My head is spinning. There's more to my father than I ever knew about.

Clover shrugs. "Vanne and I were both in the Deliverance as children. Fast forward a couple of years and I was dying to get out of Moon Crossing. Kaer had emigrated to Wolves Creek and was looking for a job. My mom hired him to help me escape. He did. We made it seem like I had been murdered, and so they wiped my name off all records in Moon Crossing. And...we fell in love, which was unexpected." She glows as she smiles at Kaer and he draws her closer, pressing a kiss against her forehead with his own smile.

"And now you're expecting a little one. Congratulations." My smile is less enthusiastic but as warm as it can be.

Kaer's steely gaze turns to Stryder. "So why are you here?"

Stryder clears his throat. "We're on our way to the Deliverance so we're passing through, really."

"We were attacked by Ar'iks," I add with a mutter, "speaking of which, Stryder sustained an arrow to the calf that needs to be tended to as soon as possible."

"Of course, you can go to Rhyn once we're done here." Kaer nods and continues. "Any reason you're going to the Deliverance?"

Next to me, Stryder tenses, and we share a glance. I sigh and look at Kaer. "If you haven't heard the news yet, then here it is. All the Superiors from the Circle were murdered a couple of weeks ago and I've been framed. I was banished from Moon Crossing and Stryder is my escort to Silverwater Penitentiary. We have no plans to go there, of course, but Commander Westing injected us with trackers that are supposed to release a lethal toxin if we don't go to Silverwater or if we leave the District. We need to find an extraction gun to remove the trackers and we're hoping that the Deliverance might still have some of Spring Grove's tech. Somehow, we need to relay a message to them to see if they do."

"Why not remove them here? I'm sure my mom can do it just fine," Clover says, but I shake my head.

"The trackers are sensitive and they will self-destruct if not removed properly. So we need an extraction gun. That's the only way."

Her brow furrows. "Whose idea was it to inject you with these trackers?"

"Councilor Cristol," Stryder huffs.

"Oh, *of course.*" Clover rolls her eyes. "That man could bring down this entire nation if he wanted to."

Kaer rubs his chin. "With the monsoon season kicking in, it will flood the canyon for several weeks. We can send a messenger to the Deliverance before the rains start. I'll grant shelter and food for as long as you need it."

"Thank you, Kaer, that means a lot."

"But I expect you to join up with the Blood Hunters again, Monroe." His gaze turns to me. "Clover can find something for you."

"You can work with me, Locklyn, no worries."

"I can't express how grateful and bewildered I am at your kindness."

Clover shrugs. "Must be the baby that's making me so kind."

We all share a laugh and then stand, departing from the yurt. Stryder heads for a long log building that I guess is the clinic, while Clover shows me to a spare yurt where I'll be staying.

I ask, "Where is Stryder staying?"

Her dark eyebrows lift in surprise. "Oh, uh, I thought he'd shack up with the other Blood Hunters in the garrison."

"Oh."

A mischievous gleam comes to her eyes and she smirks. "Why? Were you hoping he'd stay with you?"

I shuffle on my feet. "Maybe."

Clover pulls me inside the yurt and we sit down on the padded floor. She cradles her belly as she asks, "Are you two dating, perchance?"

"Yes, and…I enjoy having him nearby when I sleep."

"So all you do is *sleep* when you're with him?"

I blush as I realize what she's getting at and I snort softly. "Clover, you know me. I'm a tortoise in relationships."

"Uh-huh," she leans her elbow on her knee, "*sure.*"

I knot my fingers together, give her a look, and then change the subject. "Clover, why didn't you tell me you were coming here? Why did you let me believe you were murdered?"

Her smirk drops and she sighs, rubbing her hand through her inky black hair. "It was easier to let you believe I was dead, to let the entire city believe it. Otherwise, they would search for me. I didn't even tell Vanne until I wrote to him last year. He visited me only a couple of weeks ago and insisted on coming to my baby shower, even though he was the only guy." She laughs lightly.

"But, really, Locklyn, it was for the best and you were working for the Circle, so I couldn't tell you. When the Recons were spying on us, I thought Vanne had blabbed and Kaer and I were terrified that they'd take me away. We still don't know why the Recons were spying on us. They haven't said a peep about their mission since we captured them."

"So you're still holding the Recons captive?"

She bobs her head. "Until we find out why they were out here. If we let them go, we risk them telling the Elite Council things they might have overheard about our operations in Wolves Creek. Some want to go home but...it's a bit of a tricky situation. Kaer and I didn't quite think it through."

I lean back on my hands. "The Recons were spying on Wolves Creek because the Circle wanted to boot Kaer and take the village. Certainly, if they found out about your...courtship then they would have sufficient evidence he committed treason by deceit and illegally removed you from the Protector-ship Program without a proper release by Vanne."

Clover's face pales even more than its usual pallor. "Moon Crossing would have killed him and brought me back." Her fingers tremble as she runs them over her belly. "I suspect they would have forced me to have an abortion and then send me to a correctional facility."

I shudder as I think of that. "It could have been that cruel, yes, but the Circle is gone and the Elite Council probably doesn't care as much about assimilating Wolves Creek."

"Thank the stars that those terrible men are gone. Although, I don't think that the Elite Council will be better."

"I feel like Blake will be a valuable asset in their decisions. He's levelhead-ed and has too kind of a soul to do anything cruel."

Clover gives me a wary look. "And yet, he let you get banished to Silver-water Penitentiary with a lethal tracker in you."

I tip my head at her. "Did you know Blake is in the Deliverance?"

Her eyebrows rise in surprise. "Blake Carmichael, the all-too-perfect citizen of Moon Crossing and a member of the Elite Council, is in the *Deliverance?* How is that possible?"

"I don't know, but he is. He gave me a little chip before I left and I don't know what it's for. It has the Deliverance's symbol on it, though."

"Can I see the chip?"

I turn to my bag and dig around for the chip, which I stored in the pouch with my pendant from my father. Once I find it, I hand the tiny thing over to Clover and she inspects it, careful not to drop it or crush it between her fingers. Finally, she hands it back with a shake of her head.

"I'm not sure either, but that is the Deliverance's symbol. Huh, didn't know Wonderboy had the nerve of rebellion in him."

"Yeah, me neither."

"It's kind of hot, isn't it?"

I wave her off. "I'm over Blake, at least, as a romantic interest...wait, how did you know we were together?"

"I didn't, but you just told me. We have so much to catch up on."

I grin. "We sure do."

After talking with Clover for a bit, I make my way over to the clinic to check on Stryder. When I walk in, I'm greeted by a buzz of nurses and physicians tending to what I assume are a few of the Blood Hunters. My brow furrows as I move past them to the back, where Stryder sits on the edge of a bed. Across from him is a woman I recognize and I hurry my step. They're having a hushed conversation and then her gaze lifts to find mine and she shrinks into herself, turning away.

Once I reach them, I snap, "You're the server that went missing! What are you doing in Wolves Creek?"

Stryder grabs my hand and pulls me down next to him, his expression stern. "Locklyn, how did you get back here? This is an authorized area—"

I ignore him as I ask the server, "You were working for someone on the Council, weren't you? I *knew* you were lying in court that day."

She glances up at me, her hazel eyes frightened. "I—I don't know what you're talking about."

Stryder sighs. "Bibiana, tell her about Viktor."

My head whips toward Stryder. "Wait, you know her?"

"She's...she's Inaya's little sister."

As my nostrils flare, I cross my arms and scoot away from him. There are so many things he hasn't been telling me. It's starting to add up and I don't like it. So I wait eagerly for Bibiana to talk. She's quiet for a long, long moment and then says softly, "Viktor Marsh put the poison in the glasses and asked me to have you deliver them."

"Did you know there was poison in them?"

"Initially, no, but I found out after."

I stand, my hands clenched into fists. "You and Councilor Marsh framed me then."

Bibiana wraps her arms around herself as tears well in her eyes. "It was Viktor's idea."

"How do you even know him?"

She takes in a steady breath before telling me, "He is—was—my fiancé. We met a year ago and now...now I'm pregnant with his child."

I glance her over. Her long brunette hair hangs around her youthful face. She looks like a scared little doe and I see the bandage wrapped around her chest as it peeks out of the tunic she wears. Beneath, her belly is rounding out with new life. I sigh and run a hand through my hair, my brow knit in confusion still.

"What happened to you?"

Bibiana looks at Stryder, or rather, past him, as she recounts what happened with a haunting look in her eyes. "I thought I had done well giving my testimony about what happened, but Viktor didn't seem to think so. He took me outside the barrier, to the river that leads to Bone Falls." She pauses and her voice breaks. "I was shot in the chest and tossed in the river, left for dead. I drifted down the river, but the Blood Hunters found me before I made it to Bone Falls. On our journey here, we were ambushed by Ar'iks and some of the Blood Hunters were taken. We got back four days ago and I've been in here since."

My gaze wanders back to all the Blood Hunters behind us and it twists my gut to see so many bandaged up. The Ar'iks must be hungry if they'd attack such a large group of people. Stryder and I were probably going to be simple little snacks. I turn back to Bibiana. "I'm sorry that Viktor betrayed you like that. He's always been shady but I...I never imagined that he would try to kill the woman carrying his child."

Her expression hardens as she stares at me. "He doesn't care and he never did. But if he finds out I'm alive, he'll make sure that I end up dead somehow. Me and my baby."

"Then we should make sure he never finds out. Are you going to stay in Wolves Creek after you're healed?"

"Oh, no, I can't stay here." Bibiana's fingers glide over her belly. "Wolves Creek is a place of tradition and they look down on an unwed, pregnant woman. I've already received so much scrutiny from the Blood Hunters and even some nurses. My child and I wouldn't be accepted into their society so I plan on heading to Bountiful Hill...whenever I can figure out how to get there."

Stryder says, "Well, there's no way you can go through Moon Crossing. We've been told that the monsoon season is coming so Morlam Canyon will be flooded for a few weeks. After that, we're heading to Spring Grove. You can come with us and then I can take you to Bountiful Hill."

Her eyes widen in surprise. "Really? You'd let me tag along?"

"Of course."

"Why are we chatting over here and not resting like we should be, hmm?"

We all turn to the physician, a short, curvy woman with raven black hair and piercing green eyes. She stands there with her gloved hands on her hips and a smear of blood on her otherwise pristine, white apron. I stare at her for a long minute before I say, "You look like Clover."

The woman nods. "That's because she's my daughter. You must be new here." Her gaze glides over me. "And your hand is wrapped so you must be injured."

She kneels at my side and snatches up my hand, unwrapping it to reveal the cut on my palm. Her eyes lift to Stryder. "Your handiwork, I presume?"

He chuckles and shrugs. "I tried."

"Mhm, I don't know about *tried*, dear Stryder. What's your name, honey?"

"Me?" I ask.

"Yes, *you*."

"Oh, I'm Locklyn."

The woman smiles as she lifts me to my feet and brings me over to a small standing table with supplies strewn all over it. "Lovely to meet you, Locklyn. My name is Rhyn, the leading physician in this clinic. Now tell me, how long ago did you sustain this injury?"

"Um," I crinkle my nose, "about four or five days ago, I believe?"

"And what happened?"

"I was washing my hands in the river and someone startled me." I shoot a glare at Stryder. "So my hand got sliced open on a rock."

Rhyn nods. "I see. I'm going to disinfect your wound, wrap it again, and then send you on your way. Come back tomorrow so I can check it and make sure it isn't prone to infection."

"Thank you, Rhyn."

"It's just my job." She grabs the disinfectant and gets to work, bending over my hand. "So how do you know my Clover?"

I wince as it stings the wound. "We were companions back in Moon Crossing. Vanne was our Protector."

Rhyn glances up at me. "*Oh,* you're Locklyn *Harte*."

"Yes...why is everyone so interested in my last name?"

She shrugs as she focuses on my hand again. "Everyone's interested in the news and information that has been *associated* with that last name. Your father was Cicone, right?"

"Yeah."

"I met him once when he came here on business. A very kind man—incredibly attractive, too. It's a shame what happened to him, though."

My brow furrows. "I don't understand why he did what he did but...it doesn't matter anymore." I change the subject. "Does your husband work in the clinic as well?"

"I'm not married," Rhyn states.

"But...you have Clover. Isn't Wolves Creek very traditional?"

"Yes, but I clearly failed at keeping traditions. I had Clover when I was nineteen. I was in love with the blacksmith's son, Ezra Cline, and I didn't want to be the village's prosecutor once my mom retired. Oh, and I didn't marry the man my father wanted me to, the *darga* before Kaer. So, I still had Clover, but Ezra and I aren't married."

"Well, I think people can do whatever they want. Do people look down on you?"

"They do, and at the beginning, it bothered me more so than not. But now, I'm the person who has the most sway over whether people live or die." She laughs lightly, though it isn't filled with amusement. "But all I wanted was to raise my baby with the man I love and become a physician. I got all that and everything's rosy."

"I'm glad for you."

Rhyn looks at me, surprised. "You don't even know me, honey."

I shrug. "Doesn't mean I don't wish you well in your life. My father taught me to be kind to everyone, no matter their life circumstances."

"Wise man."

"He was."

Once Rhyn has bandaged my hand, she wanders away to tend to another patient. I sneak over to Stryder's bed again before anyone can kick me out.

He's lounging back on his pillows now and Bibiana is reading. I sit on the edge of the bed next to Stryder and reach out to poke his chest.

"I need to have a word with you," I say, keeping my voice low.

He looks wary. "What is it?"

"You fail to mention very important things. Things that would be very nice to know, like how you happen to know Bibiana."

Stryder gaze trails away as he gulps, his Adam's apple bobbing. "I just...I don't have an excuse."

"You leave things out on purpose." I work my jaw. "I feel wary about trusting you, Stryder. If you actually cared about my well-being, you should have told me."

"I do care, but—but, *ugh*, I don't know, Locklyn. I'm just...there's a lot of thoughts swirling in my head and I need to collect myself."

I shake my head. "From now on, just tell me. Stop keeping secrets."

"I can try," he hangs his head, "but keeping secrets is all I know how to do."

"Then trust me enough to let me keep them too."

I stand and leave the clinic. My yurt is warm, and Clover has provided me with blankets and pillows. I set up my bed and lie down, staring at the hole in the yurt's top. The night sky is beautiful but I'm still troubled. My father, a benefactor to the Deliverance. Stryder, a stalwart secret keeper. If I don't trust him, he won't tell me anything but I fear that if I do, he'll end up breaking my heart someday with one of his secrets. Eventually, after tossing and turning fitfully, I fall asleep.

UNFURLED DISCOVERY

WE'VE BEEN IN Wolves Creek for about two weeks and Stryder has shacked up with the other Blood Hunters. We're working on trusting each other but I'm still a bit hesitant. I miss his warmth, though. Although now, I'm not alone in my yurt.

My new yurt mate is Bibiana, and she's a pretty decent yurt mate. Some nights, however, she has nightmares and whimpers or wakes up screaming. She tells me it's always the same nightmare, of Viktor standing over her saying, *"Careful now. She's pregnant"* before someone she has yet to disclose shoots her.

I typically crawl over to the bucket of rainwater we have sitting outside the front of the yurt, dip a washcloth in it, and dab away the sweat on her face as she cries. I can't imagine being betrayed and almost killed by the man I thought I loved and the father of my child as well. Bibiana has had terrible luck in love. Even though I'm not too keen on the idea of her helping Viktor poison Superior Masoni and Superior Cozeht, I hope she finds someone who can truly love her and her baby. It terrifies me that Viktor could do something so cruel to a person he at least had affection for. Had Electra really given in to him, I wonder if she'd be the one lying here, pregnant, and haunted by nightmares of him.

No, Electra wouldn't be so naive. Bibiana is young, barely an adult, and now learning how cruel the world can be. Even when someone says they love you, they could be lying. She was blinded and dragged into this terrible situation. Under normal circumstances, I would never take her to be an accomplice in two assassinations. Cruel, cruel Viktor Marsh. He needs to be stopped before he hurts other innocent women like Bibiana.

One morning after Bibiana's fits, I emerge from the yurt groggy and wish I could have fallen asleep after waking up. But I lamented about a plan to take Councilor Marsh down. I thought about writing to Electra, but I fear the letter will be intercepted once it reaches Moon Crossing. Then when the police determine the letter is from me, I'm sure someone will make sure it never gets to Electra. I could call her on my Mini, but I know that any transmissions from my device will be recorded or my access could have already been cut. I haven't been on my Mini much, seeing that there's an entire world out here I've yet to explore.

On my way to the mess hall, I notice a bit of a commotion near the gate of Wolves Creek. A group has flocked to the gate and I decide to make my way over there, too. Luckily, I find Stryder in the crowd and slip my fingers through his. He startles and then presses a kiss to the side of my head once he realizes it's me.

"What's going on?" I ask, standing on my tiptoes as I try to see over everyone's heads.

"Riders are approaching far off," he tells me.

"Riders?"

"Yeah, people on horses. Kaer isn't fond of riders who pass through the land, typically looking to trade."

"Isn't trade a good thing though?" My brow crinkles in confusion as I catch sight of the riders approaching. "There's only three. Doesn't seem like such a threat."

Stryder shrugs, and we all disperse when Kaer demands us to. "Anyone coming from the direction of Moon Crossing is *always* treated as a potential threat."

Everyone still lingers in the square, but we've scattered apart now. Once the riders have reached the gate, Kaer steps out along with several muscled Blood Hunters and the two sentries, Mohe and Yansa. It takes only a few minutes before the gates open and they welcome the riders in. They're wearing cloaks, which means they must have ridden through the night and needed to stay warm. The riders slip off their horses. Stable hands run out to guide the horses away, and Kaer directs the riders to his yurt, along with Clover. He glances around until his dark gaze lands on Stryder and me and beckons us to the yurt as well.

The O'kshah watch with curious eyes as we all head into the yurt and sit down. The riders finally remove their cloaks and I almost faint seeing their faces. Clover gasps and jumps up, ambling over to Vanne as he stands with a grin to embrace her. Stryder stands to shake hands with Domenico, the man Malini went on a date with long ago, and then he hugs Amira. My nose crinkles at her presence and she gives me a sour look as well.

"What are you doing here, Vanne?" Clover asks once she's settled down again, next to Kaer.

Vanne glances between Amira and Domenico before he states, "Their business is with, uh," his hazel eyes flicker to Stryder, "Mr. Monroe. I came along so I could see you again, cousin."

Clover glows. "I'm happy you're here."

Domenico asks Stryder, "Is there somewhere we can talk in private?"

"Sure, follow me."

I watch as Amira, Stryder, and Domenico stand and depart. Clover, Kaer, and Vanne fall into simple conversation, but I have a knot in my stomach that needs to be untied. Without protest, I sneak out and glimpse Stryder across the square. He's entering the garrison with Amira and Domenico. I hurry over, trying to be as stealthy as I can so he doesn't spot me through the windows, and I trail around back. I drop to the ground when I hear their voices inside and seat myself under an open window.

"There's no one else in here," Stryder says, and I hear a chair creak as he sits. "What did you come to tell me?"

Domenico goes first. "It's about Orb. He resigned from the Elite Council and moved back to Iluro. He took a woman named Glory Troisi with him and we believe he plans to marry her."

A long moment of silence passes before Stryder asks, "Amira, has Aunt Khione told you if she's relinquishing the throne to him?"

Wait...is Amira a—a princess?

"She called me when he arrived and...it *is* his rightful inheritance. I think she'll relinquish the throne once he's married."

"But he's been gone for years and refused to take the throne in the past. *Why* is he going back now?"

Amira offers, "He told me he's done with Moon Crossing and its ways."

"*Pft,* he should have been done with that city long, long ago," Stryder huffs. "What else do you have to tell me? I can tell there's still something you want to say, Dom."

There's a moment of hesitation before Domenico complies. "What are your intentions with Locklyn, Stryder? I saw you two holding hands in the square so clearly, you don't seem to be just 'friends'."

I perk up at the mention of my name and keep still, my breath catching to hear what Stryder has to say—and why Domenico even cares.

"Locklyn is...well, the thing is—we're very close."

"Very close is too close." Amira says.

"Well, what am I supposed to do?"

"Tell us what your intentions are, Stryder," Domenico chides.

"I like her, okay? Is that so terrible?" Stryder retorts, the tension in his voice high-strung.

"Yes, it is because—has that window been open the whole time? *Blazes!*"

My heart pounds and I scramble away from the window as footsteps approach to close it. I slip around the corner of the building just in time and stand against it, my chest heaving with nerves. When I'm sure I'm not caught, I make my way back to Kaer and Clover's yurt and step back inside.

Vanne quirks an eyebrow at me. "You look like you've seen a ghost."

I run my fingers through my hair. "I feel like I almost became one."

Clover tips her head. "Were you eavesdropping on their conversation?"

"Maybe…"

"Locklyn!" Vanne protests.

"Don't you try to lecture me, Vanne, you're not my Protector anymore. And besides, why can't they talk about whatever they're talking about with the rest of us, huh?"

"Because people actually enjoy privacy," Kaer remarks, shooting me a quizzical look. "If I ever catch you eavesdropping on any of my meetings, know that I'll promptly kick you out of Wolves Creek."

"Mm, you really picked out a nice one, CC," I say and Kaer rolls his eyes. "Where are you from, Kaer?"

"The Pomanthean Empire," he tells me. "I'm from the Teals tribe, we lived outside of the provinces since we weren't welcome."

"Really? Why?"

Kaer shrugs. "The tribes in Pomanthea are nomadic and our beliefs differ from the masses. We're branded as heretics. I'm good friends with the Emperor's son, Prince Ezio. I should be since he's in love with my sister. But Ezio's a good man and when he becomes Emperor, I know he'll change things for the better in Pomanthea. People will have to accept 'heretics' if their Empress is going to be one someday."

"I'm glad to hear there's at least one noble leader in this world willing to make a change for the better."

"Only one?" He chuckles. "I've tried to change things for the better here in Wolves Creek."

"Of course. Two on the list."

"And hopefully more to come one day."

The yurt flaps open again and Stryder, Amira, and Domenico return. We all engage in lighthearted conversation for most of the morning, drinking tea and snacking on some rolls Clover made the other day. I smile and laugh along, but I wish I had heard what Domenico and Amira were telling Stryder about me. He seems fine as I glance at him and loops his arm around my waist, squeezing my hip.

I'll confront Stryder later but at least I know two secrets: that Councilor Cristol is a prince of Iluro, the city where Stryder hails from; and that his aunt, who I assume is Amira's mother, is sitting on the throne, which must make Amira a princess. Is Councilor Cristol her brother? Surely that would make sense. So Stryder must come from a noble family to have royal cousins. The web of his past keeps spinning itself and it intrigues me.

Amira is assigned to my yurt with Bibiana and I become incredibly suspicious of her as she sets up her bedroll on the left side of the yurt, away from me and next to Bibiana. I don't mind the space between us, but I'm still conflicted about what she was really doing in Moon Crossing and why she's dating Vanne. He's handsome, of course, but I'm sure that Amira could find someone who isn't a dorky redhead with the skills of an age-old 'perfect homemaker'. Vanne doesn't seem like a guy she would normally go for and that is *very* suspicious.

When Bibiana comes back and finds out that we have a new yurt mate, she insists we all stay up and hang out, have a little fun, and get to know each other. I'm about to object until I recall that some people spill critical information when they're sleepy and loopy. So I agree, hoping that Amira will be one of those people.

"What's your name again?" Amira asks Bibiana.

"Oh, I'm Bibiana Kendricks," she grins and shakes Amira's hand.

"Didn't you testify against Locklyn in the trial?"

Just like that, Bibiana's smile falls and she curls into herself, taking her quilt and wrapping it around her shoulders. "I wasn't testifying *against* her...I was relaying my side of the story to the Council."

"Ah." She produces a brand new bottle of Bliss from her bag with a mischievous smile. "Who's dying for some Bliss?"

"None for me," Bibiana states, pointing to her obvious baby bump.

"Locklyn? How about you?"

"I don't like to drink this late at night."

"More for me then."

We watch her pop the cap off the bottle of Bliss and take a swig. At this moment, she reminds me of myself back in college. I lean back on my pillows with my quilt tucked around me. If Amira gets herself buzzed enough tonight, I can try to get *something* out of her.

"You said you're from Spring Grove, right, Amira?" I ask after she's taken a few swigs.

Her hazelnut eyes narrow slightly and she quirks an eyebrow. "I never told you I was from Spring Grove, so who did?"

"Electra."

"Ah, I miss her. Working out at the gym together and having a girls' night out with Glory, too. Felt like college again."

My fingers curl into my quilt. "So you are from Spring Grove?"

"Originally, yes." Amira tips her head at me, her curls spilling over her shoulder. "Why are you asking?"

"I'm trying to piece something together in my head. Electra mentioned you had only been in Moon Crossing for a year and a half, is that correct?"

Her nose twitches as she glances at Bibiana. "Did she grill you like this when you first came?"

"Oh, uh, no, not really," Bibiana states, and gathers a pillow to her chest, glancing between us.

Amira sighs and holds her hands up. "You caught me. Yes, I've only been in Moon Crossing for a year and a half."

I nod. "So why lie to Commander Westing about being released from the Protectorship Program."

"That woman looked like she'd kill me if she knew I wasn't a citizen of Moon Crossing, so I made up a couple of names and *bam*, got her off my back. I didn't want her to have me deported."

"I guess that makes sense, Commander Westing would definitely deport you." I abruptly change the subject. "Can I ask why you're dating Vanne?"

Amira snorts softly. "Wouldn't you like to know."

"Who's Vanne?" Bibiana asks.

"He was my Protector in Moon Crossing," I inform her.

"Oh, okay. Continue."

With the Bliss still in hand, Amira stands to walk around the yurt. "I'm dating Vanne because he needs someone who will treat him *right*." She gives me a pointed look before going on. "He's charming, hilarious, sweet, and a superb cook. Handsome as ever and absolutely *incredible* under the—"

"*Blazing suns*," I cut her off, cringing, "we get it, Amira, no need to explain further."

She shrugs. "Eh, you asked. But why do you care?"

"I find it hard to believe that a woman like you would go for a man like him."

"You don't know me, Locklyn," she remarks with a suddenly somber expression, her hazelnut eyes becoming steel. "I've fallen for the wrong guys in the past, stupid, selfish, unkind guys. Vanne treats me like a person and respects me like one."

"Ooo, you've got yourself a keeper!" Bibiana grins.

Amira smirks and sits down again. "I like you, Bibiana. At least someone's enthusiastic about my relationship with Vanne."

Bibiana smiles and the light reaches her eyes. "You know, I never really had girlfriends to hang out with so it's nice that I have you two."

Amira looks touched and leans over, tossing her arm around Bibiana's shoulders as she hugs her. "Wayward souls have to stick together."

We all nod and I feel a sense of comfort. My suspicions of Amira are still there, however. She won't get off scot-free.

☽ ✧ ☾

It's strange to watch Vanne interact with the O'kshah of Wolves Creek. They've known him forever since his mom is from here. The bright copper hair is easy to find among the dark-haired crowd. He fits in with ease and even sits at Clover and Kaer's table in the mess hall, way up front, and set up on a long dais. I sit with Stryder, Amira, Bibiana, and Domenico near the back and sigh, swirling my spoon through my bowl of soup. I have yet to figure out a way to tell Electra the information I have, but my only idea is out of the question, and that's going back to Moon Crossing.

Next to me, Domenico asks Amira, "What is Vanne going to do once we all leave?"

"Well, he has to go back to Moon Crossing to get his affairs in order, and then he'll meet us in Spring Grove," she tells him.

I lean over. "When is Vanne going back?"

She glances at me. "He wants to go back next week so he'll have enough time to pack, move his things, and receive legal permission to leave Moon Crossing."

"So he's leaving for good? He's going to give up his citizenship?"

"That's what he told me."

I stand and make my way to the front of the mess hall, toward Kaer's table. Vanne notices me and gets up, stepping off the dais to meet me halfway. I take his arm and draw him outside of the mess hall, out of earshot of everyone else. We wait a moment for a few teenagers to make their way inside and I keep my voice low as I say, "I need a favor."

"Shoot."

"I need you to get a message to Electra. Do you think you can do that?"

"I suppose so. What's the message?"

As the mess hall fills with people, a line has formed outside, and I pull him around the back. Vanne leans on the wall, arms crossed. "Viktor Marsh poisoned Superior Cozeht and Superior Masoni."

Vanne's eyes widen and his jaw falls slack. Suddenly, he takes my hands. "Locklyn, this is good."

"Yes, I know, but I want Viktor to be arrested first. Oh, and tell Electra that he's guilty of kidnapping and attempted murder as well. Bibiana was his fiancée."

I don't want to give him too many details about Bibiana, because I'd rather not see her behind bars and have to deliver her child in a prison. I believe she was under Viktor's influence, blinded by love, one could say.

"Wait, Electra will want evidence. What evidence do you have?"

"Right, evidence." I worry my lip and draw my hands from his, pacing. "Bibiana knows everything, so I could have her record what she knows and send it with you. Electra might have to do some digging for the poison aspect *and* find the gun that Bibiana was shot with, too...she might have to hire a private investigator to help her."

"I'll help her. I'll be there for a few weeks, anyway."

I quirk an eyebrow at him. "You're not stealthy, Vanne."

"But I've been a member of the Deliverance since I was twelve, so I have *some* experience in espionage. Electra and I will come up with a plan and if we need someone stealthy, we'll ask Malini."

"I don't want you guys to get caught, especially if Viktor catches you. He'll kill you."

"We'll be fine. I'm going to guess he had accomplices, too, to help kill the other Superiors. We'll find them, Locklyn, I promise."

"Okay." I take a leveled breath and nod. "I'll ask what Bibiana knows about the plan and any evidence she may have."

Vanne removes a small recording device from his pocket. "Here, record it on this."

I take it and quirk an eyebrow. "Why do you casually have a recorder on hand?"

He shrugs. "Sometimes I like to record stuff. Just get everything Bibiana knows, okay?"

We head back into the mess hall and go our separate ways. I finish my soup with glee, knowing that with Vanne, Electra, and Malini on the case, they will find evidence to put Viktor away. I only hope that they'll be able to find his accomplices as well, but if they put away Viktor, both Bibiana and I will be glad of it.

A DROP OF TRUTH

THAT NIGHT, I sit down with Vanne's recorder and Bibiana in our yurt. My Mini is cozying up with Stryder so Moon Crossing's surveillance team can't tap in. Amira is out on a romantic rendezvous with Vanne, so we have plenty of time for Bibiana to tell me everything she knows. I plop down on my bedroll as she continues folding the clothes she washed today. When she notices me staring, she sits back and smiles.

"I've been talking with Rhyn about having a baby at this age since she was my age when she had Clover. Anyway, she said it was a challenge, but she made it through, even without a man at her side."

My brow lifts. "I thought her baby daddy helped her raise Clover?"

Bibiana shakes her head. "For a bit. She told me she decided she could raise Clover on her own when she was three or four and he left."

"Oh."

"Yeah," she cradles her belly in her hands, her smile strained now, "but if Rhyn could do it, I can do it, too. I don't need a man to help me. So I've been learning to do some typical household chores on my own."

"How are you going to afford the things you need for the baby and yourself?"

"I have savings from the restaurant...and Viktor always tipped me generously, so I have plenty to at least get started. When it runs out, I'll find a job."

I shift and click the recorder on. "Speaking of Viktor, can I ask you a few questions?"

Bibiana's face falls as she grows somber. "What questions?"

"I would like to know his plans for killing Superior Cozeht and Superior Masoni, how he obtained the poison, and who else he was working with."

"Oh." She begins to fold again as she inquires, "Are you gathering evidence so someone else can look into it?"

"Yes. Since Vanne is heading back to Moon Crossing next week, I thought he should take this crucial piece of evidence back with him. I'm sure that he and Electra, my lawyer cousin, as you know, can scrape together physical evidence against Viktor and put him away. I know Viktor hurt you, nearly killed you, for heaven's sake, so it would be very noble of you to testify against him. If I have your recorded testimony, you won't need to face him in court."

"So you want me to get revenge against Viktor."

"Yes, you could put it that way."

She falls quiet, focusing on the laundry, and I scoot over, placing my hand on her shoulder. Bibiana sighs. "What if he sends goons after me when he learns I'm alive? I can't risk putting my baby in danger."

"We'll protect you, Bibiana, and by the time he's convicted, you'll be with the Deliverance and they'll keep you safe. I promise."

"Okay." She glances at me, her hazel eyes filled with a strength I've never seen in her before. "I'll tell you everything."

"Great." I sit back. "Let's start with how he obtained the poison."

"He set up a meeting with a dealer a few weeks before the incident. By then, I had moved into his apartment so I noticed when he went out. Curious, I followed him to the Moonless Market but kept my distance so he wouldn't notice me. It was early in the morning and I couldn't quite see who he dealt with. All I saw was that they handed him a small case and exchanged some cash. I left before he headed back to his car and went back to bed, pretending I was asleep so he wouldn't be suspicious.

"When I was doing a little cleaning a week later, I found the case and opened it, thinking it was a ring box. But there were two vials of a clear liquid instead, not labeled, so I didn't know what it was. Viktor caught me snooping through his things and saw that I had seen the vials. He sat me down and explained that the vials contained a drug that enacted a coma-like effect. He told me that there were horrible people he needed to incapacitate. He said they had plans to enslave the people of Wolves Creek and brainwash them. So, I kept quiet about the vials and asked no more about it."

She takes in a breath before continuing. "I forgot about it for a bit and then Viktor showed up that night at the Cinnamon Lounge with the vials in his pocket. He pulled me aside and reminded me he was doing this for Wolves Creek, that the Superiors needed to pay. He asked for my help so I complied, hoping that I was doing the right thing and saving the people here from enslavement. I fetched two drinks, Viktor poured the liquid into each glass, and then when I was about to deliver them, he told me to come and get you, Locklyn.

"I did and you delivered them. Viktor took pictures as proof that you had delivered the drinks. I felt terrible when we went home, but he reassured me that what we did had been the right thing. The Superiors were terrible men and they needed to be taken down a notch. I didn't know the other Superiors were being targeted that night by his accomplices. Viktor didn't tell me. I found out it was arsenic poison later on."

I nod. "Did you ever meet his accomplices? Did you know any of them?"

Bibiana shakes her head. "Viktor had a private chat on his Mini, case sensitive, that kind of thing. I saw a few messages but thought little of them. I...I do know one thing...he was working with another member of the Elite Council and a police officer. The others were ordinary people."

"Do you remember any of the names you saw?"

"No, they had code names. Just...random animals. One was Hawk. Viktor was Scorpion."

A sense of disappointment overcomes me but I go on, "You have no idea who Viktor got the poison from, right?"

"No idea. Although, there was someone he mentioned who wasn't in the chat. Another code name, of course, but I always heard him talking about the Crow Overseer." Bibiana shivers. "I think he must have been in a secret order. I never knew of it, but I imagine that's what this was all about."

"How do you know he was working with a police officer and a Councilor?"

Bibiana gets back to folding. "I heard them on a conference call one night and they practically gave themselves away. They needed an inside person at the police station *and* two inside men with the Council, to get what they wanted."

"Hmm, yes indeed." I end the recording and set the recorder aside. "Thank you for doing this, Bibiana. It means a lot to me. I hope you can rest once Viktor, and anyone else he was working with, is behind bars."

"Of course." She smiles at me. "I hope it helps."

We hear footsteps approaching outside and the yurt flap opens a moment later. Stryder pokes his head inside and grins at me, then Bibiana.

"Good evening, ladies. Am I interrupting something?" he asks.

"No, we were just talking," I tell him.

"In that case, can I steal you away, Locklyn?"

"Sure."

I get up and walk over to the flap. Stryder steps back as I step out onto the tarp and tug on my boots. I wave goodbye to Bibiana and then take Stryder's hand as he leads me away from the yurt. There's a bonfire in the square, where a party has begun, and music flows from handmade drums and string instruments. I even see Amira and Vanne about to join in the festivities, their faces a little flushed. Stryder tugs on my hand when I angle toward the bonfire.

"Are we not going to the bonfire?" I ask, quirking an eyebrow at him.

"Nah, I was thinking we could spend some time alone tonight."

"We've seen little of each other these last few weeks."

He squeezes my hand. "I've been gone with the Blood Hunters a lot and you...what do you do with Clover again?"

"Um, I assist her with legal affairs and stuff...honestly, I zone out most of the time, anyway."

"Right, *and* you've been hanging out with Bibiana a lot. I'm glad you're getting along."

As we leave the residential part of the village behind, the moon seems to shine brighter on us and I soak in its rays. Moon Crossing was named so for a reason. The celestial mother always rested on the barrier after its descent through the sky, plump and bright. The first settlers of the land that would become my city believed the moon had healing rays, so they welcomed its crossing. Only when the first corrupt Circle of Superiors rose did the moon become bondage, like the people of the city it once protected. Now the symbol that is painted on everything that leaves or is claimed by Moon Crossing shows the true nature of the city. A full moon with a scythe caught around its belly, "guiding it".

He pushes aside branches as we wander through the thickening forest of trees still within the enclosed walls of Wolves Creek, and I can hear the small creek that passes through up ahead. Stryder helps me over a fallen tree trunk and we come to the creek banks.

"What were you and Bibiana talking about before I came?" he inquires as we sit on the grass and lie down.

"Oh, I forgot to tell you my plan. Since Vanne is heading back to Moon Crossing next week, I wanted to send him off with some information I learned from Bibiana to tell Electra. I was recording what Bibiana knew of the matter."

"What matter?"

"That if Electra and Vanne can gather enough information about Viktor Marsh's involvement in the deaths of Superior Masoni and Superior Cozeht, then he'll be locked up for a *long, long time*."

Stryder leans up on his elbow, eyebrows raised in surprise. "So Viktor Marsh is the Councilor who orchestrated all of this?"

"I don't know if he was the *main* villain, but he definitely had a part. And, as we know, he tried to kill Bibiana as well."

"What else did she tell you?" he asks, his almond eyes alight with interest.

I fold my hands on my stomach. "She told me he had accomplices. They had code names, though, and she didn't know who they were. There was also *another* Councilor *and* a police officer in on the entire ordeal. I'm not surprised there's corruption in the Council. The police, though, that was interesting."

"Yeah, it is," Stryder remarks softly. "I guess all I had to do was talk to Bibiana to crack the case." He chuckles. "I'm a terrible PI."

I shrug. "I doubt she would have told you anything when she was still loyal to Viktor. Now, his secrets are spilled."

"Mm, good riddance, too. I never liked him."

"Did you know Viktor personally?"

Stryder brushes a hand through his hair. "Not personally. He was, of course, good friends with Cristol in college so I always stirred up trouble with the two of them."

"Ah, Councilor Cristol," my gaze wanders away. "I feel like if Viktor was involved in this business, then he would be as well. He's incredibly intelligent and could certainly devise a plan like this. Maybe he's been working on it for years and needed the right opportunity to...to strike."

I sit up as revelation hits me and look at Stryder, my eyes wide. He remains quiet, his expression contemplative, and he lies down again, tucking his arm under his head.

"Could be."

"That's probably why he resigned." I breathe before I think and I gasp, clamping my hand over my mouth as I turn away.

Stryder sits up. "How did you know he resigned?"

"I—I saw it on The Moonlight Times website." I fib, trying to keep my voice from shaking.

His arm slips around my waist and he murmurs against my ear, "You eavesdropped, didn't you, *little fox*?"

My shoulders fall. "I know I shouldn't have."

"What else did you hear?"

I glance at him, timid now. "Is…is Amira a princess?"

"Not by blood, her mother was a trusted friend of the previous royal family."

"So Cristol isn't her brother?"

He shakes his head. "No, he isn't."

"Oh."

For a moment, Stryder reaches out and brushes his fingers through my hair and down to the nape of my neck. He brings my head forward and presses a kiss to my forehead. "It's nice to spend time with you," he whispers against my skin.

I smile and we lie down again to watch the stars twinkle in the ether.

☽ ✧ ☾

Though last night's atmosphere in the village was filled with jubilation, a cloud of gloom and doom descends on everyone this morning. Leaving the yurt with Amira and Bibiana, we come to find Kaer standing on a makeshift stage in the middle of the square. The O'kshah gather around him. Mothers hold their children tight while fathers and Blood Hunters alike are brandishing their spears and bows, calling on Kaer to fight. We find Vanne, Domenico, and Stryder quickly in the crowd and ask what's going on.

Domenico explains, his brow furrowed, "Scouts spotted Moon Crossing Recons and two commanders heading this way last night. They came back earlier this morning and now *Darga* Kaer has to decide what to do. He thinks they might be coming for the Recons still being held captive here, but the scouts said there were at least fifty of them with the commanders. No guns in Wolves Creek means the Recons could take all the Blood Hunters out quickly."

We turn to Kaer and my pulse spikes at the situation awaiting us. Kaer holds his hands up and barks at everyone to be quiet. With a little grumbling, everyone settles down and he glances out at his people, particularly focusing on Clover, who stands with Rhyn and Ezra, her blacksmith father, on the outskirts of the group. He draws in a breath and lets it go with a sigh. His expression turns solemn as he addresses us.

"All those that are able-bodied will be ready to fight at the gate *if* the need arises to attack. I will meet the commanders and Recons outside first with Mohe and Yansa. Attack *only* on my signal. I don't want a bloodbath today."

"What if they come on us guns blazing already?" someone asks.

"Then we fight. Clover will lead those who cannot fight through the back exit and to our safe camp. But I hope that this visitation is nothing short of business. Let's prepare for an emergency and keep our guard up, though." Kaer steps off the stage as the crowd disperses, flying into action to get things ready in case the Recons and commanders attack.

He strides toward us, to me, and his midnight eyes bore chasms. "I need you to accompany me to the Pit."

I learned a while back that the Recons, who had been caught over three months ago, were being held in a place called the Pit. It's an abandoned mineshaft embedded into the cliffs outside of Wolves Creek's back exit. Tunnels upon tunnels run through the mineshaft and one leads to an enormous pit, where prisoners are held until Kaer and Clover can give them a fair trial. I've been once and I don't like it at all.

"Why me?" I ask, shuffling back.

Kaer reaches out and takes my arm, turning me about. "I need you to talk with the Recons. They haven't spoken since we captured them and I want to know if they know anything about this battalion coming, whether they're coming for their comrades or if this is a planned attack."

I stumble after him as he drags me away. "Pft, how would I get them to talk? This makes little sense, Kaer."

On my other side, Stryder keeps pace with us. "I'm coming, too."

Kaer ignores him and tells me, "I need you to act like you're on their side. Certainly, they haven't heard about what happened in Moon Crossing with you, so they will see you as an ally. Act like you're here on their behalf and talk to them."

"Fine," I sigh and draw my arm out of Kaer's grip, "and I can walk by myself, thank you very much."

He says nothing and leads us past all the yurts, through the woods, and over a makeshift bridge crossing the creek. Not long after, we're met by the end of the protective wall around Wolves Creek and Stryder and Kaer pull open the gate leading out into the wilds. We all step out, close it, and head toward the cliffs where the Pit is located.

I keep an eye out for any Ar'iks that might be running rampant, and Stryder takes my hand, glancing around as well. Trees rustle nearby, but then a few deer pop out, blink at us, and continue to graze on nearby foliage. Kaer stalks ahead and we come to the mineshaft entrance, the wood rotted and the nails rusty. He takes a torch, lights it, and we descend into the mineshaft. It smells of dust, which makes me sneeze, and soon we'll be hit with the scent of unwashed bodies and waste. I despise the shadows that surround us and we stay close to Kaer, especially when we pass abandoned pits with no warning where they slope off from the forgotten coal cart tracks. Stryder switches sides with me, so I'm against the earthen wall as we scurry past.

It doesn't take long to reach the Pit and we're greeted by several volunteer O'kshah who rotate guarding the Pit. Torches are lit around the perimeter and carved-out earthen stairs lead down to where the Recons are being held. Each one has their own set of chains, fashioned by Ezra so I'm told. The Pit itself has an accompaniment of tunnels that branch off and lead to a makeshift mess hall of sorts and a natural spring that acts as a communal bathhouse. Currently, only the Recons are being held in the Pit, and other prisoners, if there are any, must be held in another part of the mine.

Kaer steps down into the Pit and glances around, his expression stony. "Who is your leader?"

None of the Recons answer him but one stands and I recognize him in an instant, an old friend from college. "Miss Harte?"

"Lieutenant Kulkari," I say with a gasp and ask on behalf of playing my part, "are you okay?"

"I would be better if we weren't stuck in this stuffy mineshaft."

"Of course." I step down next to Kaer and glance at him. "Could you give us a moment to talk?"

He grumbles, "Fine. I'm heading back to the village so Monroe can accompany you back."

"Thank you."

Once Kaer has ascended the stairs and disappeared from my sight, Stryder sits on the steps, nearly blending into the shadows. I walk over to Lieutenant Kulkari and we sit down. He looks suspicious of my presence here. His amber eyes narrow ever so slightly as he asks, "Why are you here, Locklyn? The Circle has never sent you out of Moon Crossing for business."

"I'm here with other Recons," I fib. "The Circle sent me to be the peacemaker since, well, we know how Commander Westing handles things."

Ravi chuckles. "Sure do." His gaze wanders past me to Stryder. "Who's the guy? Doesn't look like a Recon."

"My escort from Wolves Creek, but I trust him. We can talk freely. He won't say a thing."

He shifts and keeps his voice low. "You're here to free us then?"

"Yes, but other Recons are coming and I didn't call for backup. The Circle hasn't told me about their assimilation plans for Wolves Creek. Do you know why they're coming?"

Ravi works his jaw. "What month is it?"

"October."

"It can't be the march on Wolves Creek the District Patrol Division was planning then. That's supposed to be next month," he lifts his shoulders in a shrug and the chains around his wrists clink together, "so I don't know why they're coming."

I worry my lip. "The O'kshah are worried they're here to attack. I know that any talk of peace will be pushed aside."

Ravi nods. "If you let me get up there, I can meet them before they reach Wolves Creek and tell them to call off whatever they're doing. We need this village to be intact."

"I will talk to *Darga* Kaer when I return. Surely he'll cooperate."

I push myself up, ready to leave, when Ravi says, "Wait, Locklyn, I have a few questions for you."

I kneel at his feet and glance at him. His usually perfectly combed hair is in disarray and has grown to curl above his ears. Worry lines crease his brow and shadows of restlessness are nestled under his eyes. His uniform is dirty and unkempt but the insignia of the DPD is still clearly stitched on the breast pocket. Ravi's boots and cap lie nearby. He looks much older than he is.

"I still don't understand why the Circle sent you to be the peacemaker. You're their secretary and not a Recon by any means, no offense."

"None taken, and I know it seems strange. They should have sent Blake in my place to be a peacemaker, right? But the Councilors have been busy with other orders of business and I was free so they sent me. I have a few connections here."

His expression sours. "I saw Clover while we were being escorted here. Quite a surprise that was."

"Oh, it was for me, too."

"I don't know how *Darga* Kaer kidnapped her and bent her to his will, but if *you* could find that out, it would definitely give us a reason to remove him from his position."

I tip my head at him. "You think it's Stockholm Syndrome?"

"Likely. She seemed...happy, though."

I nod, watching Ravi's gaze wander away as he reminisces about something. There was a time in college where Ravi and Clover had mutual crushes on each other but were both afraid to admit it. So a couple of us arranged a "blind" date for them and...well, neither of them cared to reveal what had happened. They simply stopped talking to each other after their date.

"I will see what other information I can gather, Ravi." I reach out and set my hand on his shoulder as he glances at me again. "But don't worry, I'll get all of you out of here in no time."

"Thanks, Locklyn." He smiles and I stand again, turning away.

Stryder follows me up the stairs and past the guards. He walks on the dangerous side, his hand at the small of my back, and then we come to the entrance of the mineshaft. I sigh and sit down on a nearby rock, burying my face in my hands. He kneels in front of me, his hands on my knees.

"Hey, what's wrong, love?"

"I lied to him, Stryder. Ravi was one of my friends and I gave him hope." I lift my head as tears slip down my cheeks. "There's no way Kaer is going to let them go. Ravi knows Clover and he'll make up some case that Kaer kidnapped her. They'll be torn apart. Moon Crossing will claim Wolves Creek. Kaer will probably be imprisoned or executed..."

Stryder nods, solemn. "There are plenty of outcomes to this situation, but we need to keep our focus on the best outcome. Come on, let's tell Kaer what you learned."

He kisses me on the forehead and helps me up. We hurry back to the village and slip inside. It's a little hectic with emergency planning, but we soon find Kaer. He's sharing a private moment with Clover, so we hang back until he notices and waves us over.

"What did you learn, Locklyn?"

I relate what Ravi told me, and Clover looks away at the mention of our old friend. Then I ask, "Will you let Lieutenant Kulkari talk to the battalion coming?"

Kaer glances at Clover. "We'll need to discuss this further with the tribal council. I'll get back to you with a response as soon as I can."

With that, he takes Clover's hand and they head toward their yurt, calling on members of the tribal council as they pass. Ten people follow them into the yurt and the flap slaps shut. Instead of standing around doing nothing,

Stryder and I decide to help in the emergency effort until there's nothing left to do but wait.

☽ ✧ ☾

Kaer and Clover find me once they've finished their discussion with the tribal council and pull me aside from the rest of the crowd gathered in the square. Clover tells me, "We'll let you escort Ravi—Lieutenant Kulkari and *only* him—to meet up with the Recons coming. Kaer will come with, along with Mohe and Yansa as well."

"You want me to escort him?" I ask, my stomach turning at the thought.

She bobs her head. "You're the only person he trusts and he might find it strange if you didn't come along."

"If the commanders coming are Westing and Ore, they'll reveal that I'm no longer loyal to Moon Crossing and Ravi will know that I lied to him..."

Kaer sighs. "I'm sorry you can't keep up your moral character, Locklyn, but this isn't about you. It's about the safety of my people and they are my top priority."

"Yes, of course. I'll come. When are we heading out?"

"Right now."

I trail after Kaer to the stables and watch a few horses get saddled and led out into the square. I've never ridden a horse before, but luckily, Stryder volunteers to come along, and so I ride in the saddle behind him, holding on to his waist. We ride out of the gate and Kaer circles around to the Pit to retrieve Ravi. Stryder clicks his tongue and urges our horse forward in a slow trot. It doesn't take long for Kaer to join us once more with Ravi riding in his saddle and we head toward the well-worn road that leads to Moon Crossing at a thunderous gallop.

After a bit, I ask Stryder, "Why didn't we travel this road when we were coming to Wolves Creek?"

"On foot with just the two of us, there would've been a higher chance of being hijacked by highwaymen or the Ar'iks, so it was safer to travel along the river," he tells me and snaps the reins.

My gaze wanders to Ravi and he looks back at me. I feel queasy again and lean my head on Stryder's back, closing my eyes for the rest of the ride. I lift my head when we slow and eventually come to a stop. Leaning around Stryder, I see that we've found the Recons camp, and they have greeted us with guns. I duck back when Commander Westing and Commander Ore stroll over to our entourage and Kaer hops off his horse with Ravi. My fingers curl around Stryder's tunic as my pulse spikes.

"*Darga* Kaer Reeves," Commander Westing begins with a snarl, "and Lieutenant Kulkari..."

"Why are you coming to Wolves Creek, ma'am?" Ravi asks her.

"We were on our way to rescue your platoon, Lieutenant. It seems like you still need rescuing."

"If we give you your people, will you turn and go back to Moon Crossing?" Kaer asks.

Commander Westing doesn't answer and a moment later, a hand appears on my arm, jerking me away from the protection of Stryder's back. I look down at her and her nose crinkles. "Hello, little snipe. I can't say I'm surprised you're not rotting in Silverwater right now, but again, I haven't been monitoring your tracker. Why are you in Wolves Creek?" Her icy gaze wanders to Stryder. "And why hasn't your escort at least taken you to Arcane Cove?"

"It's monsoon season so Morlam Canyon is flooded," Stryder tells her, keeping his expression steady as he faces her down.

"Wait, Silverwater Penitentiary? Why does Miss Harte need to go there?"

Commander Westing flashes me a wicked smile as she walks back over to Ore and gives a signal for the Recons to tuck away their guns. She claps Ravi on the shoulder, pulling him away from Kaer. "I'll tell you all about Miss Harte's treason on our way back home. As for your proposition, *Darga*, I will take it. Give us our people and we'll leave your village alone."

Kaer extends his hand toward her and she takes it, her eyes never leaving his. "Do I have your word, Commander?"

"You have my word."

He turns to Ore. "And yours?"

"Yes." Ore shakes Kaer's hand as well.

"Good." Kaer swings back into his saddle. "And tell your Council to leave Wolves Creek alone. We want nothing to do with Moon Crossing."

Commander Westing's smile turns catlike, a hint of annoyance passing her expression. "I can't speak for the Council's future actions. Bring us Lieutenant Kulkari's platoon and we'll be on our way."

"Gladly."

At Kaer's signal, we turn and gallop back to Wolves Creek. I glance back before we're out of sight to see Ravi's puzzled expression as he watches us ride off. Commander Westing snatches his arm, turning him away to talk. I feel numb as we ride back into Wolves Creek and I'm dismissed for the day as Kaer gathers a group of Blood Hunters to bring the platoon to the other Recon camp. Bibiana and Amira drag me into the mess hall, where a meager meal has been prepared and we eat, even though I hardly have an appetite. Clover sits at the head table by herself, her shoulders hunched, expression grave.

I stand and walk to her table, sitting down next to her. She's hardly touched her food and blankly stares at the table. I nudge her. "Hey, are you going to be okay?"

Clover shakes her head. "Ravi's going to make up some story about how I came to be here, and then they'll be back to take me away. Kaer and I have no choice but to leave. Wolves Creek can't defend itself against an entire battalion of Recons so it'd be better if we don't remain here."

"Where will you go?"

"I don't know. If we go to Pomanthea, I know he'll continue to worry about our people here and whoever becomes the next *darga*. But at least we'd be out of the District, out of Mevania."

I reach across and take her hand. "Come with us to the Deliverance. They'll help, I'm sure."

She glances down at her belly, her eyes growing misty. "I left the Deliverance and pledged allegiance to Wolves Creek. I…I don't know if they'd help me. I practically ruined one of their missions in Moon Crossing. Kaer and I only want our child to be safe."

"Certainly they can forgive and forget. You made your own life outside of the Deliverance, they can't hold you guilty forever."

Her green eyes lift to mine. "Locklyn, you don't understand the Deliverance. Once you join, you stay for life. That's how it is. Spies are valuable assets and losing one creates a tremendous problem."

"Clover, come with us and see."

She works her jaw. "I'll talk with Kaer tonight."

As Ezra and Rhyn wander over to talk to Clover, I head back to my table and finish eating. The village is quiet as the afternoon sun blazes across the forest and people move about with solemn expressions, tired and aching from preparing for an emergency all morning. My yurt is warm, comfy for a mid-afternoon nap, and so I crash, falling asleep easily.

A STEP ON THE PATH

WITH THE ARRIVAL of the Recons and the departure of the captured ones, Kaer and Clover have decided to come with us to the Deliverance. But to ask for their help as soon as possible, Kaer wants to leave tomorrow, so I've packed my things and wandered to the garrison to see what Stryder thinks about the situation. As far as I know, the canyon is still being flooded by the constant rain storms moving through the area, but that's a two-day ride away and by the time the storm reaches us, it has lost all its heavy rainfall.

Walking through the garrison doors, I'm met with the potent scent of masculinity, and my nose crinkles. I pull my sleeve over my hand to cover my nose as I weave my way past all the cramped bunks and trunks at the foot of the beds. Stryder's bunk is near the back and he kneels in front of his trunk, packing the bag he was given in Moon Crossing. I hop on the bed and fall back on his pillow, looking up at the ceiling of logs above.

"Hey, love," he says as he stands and sits next to me.

I smile. "Hi."

"Looks like you have something on your mind."

"Always do." I sigh and glance at him, taking the hand settled next to me. "What do you think about heading to the Deliverance now with the canyon still flooding? It's so dangerous and yet...I don't know."

Stryder shrugs. "We can't go through the canyon, but we can at least make it to Arcane Cove and send scouts ahead. They have Hovercrafts there but flying is a whole different story in those storms."

"Yeah." I brush my fingers through my hair, letting out another sigh.

"Has your tracker been giving you problems?" he asks, tipping his head at me.

"No, has yours?"

"Kind of? The area gets warm sometimes and a numbing pain spreads to my shoulder and jaw."

I quickly sit up. "*What?* Stryder, that doesn't sound good. Let me see."

He turns his head, exposing his neck to me, and I reach up, tenderly touching the area where his tracker was injected. It is warm to the touch and looks a little puckered and veiny. My pulse quickens. I trail my fingers down to his shoulder, pressing softly as I ask, "Does this hurt? Can you feel anything?"

"A little."

"Did you talk to Rhyn about it?"

"Yeah..."

"And?" I prod, my eyes wide.

His almond eyes grow a little strained and he looks away. "She said the tracker injected in me may be a faulty one...meaning that it might release the poison regardless of being triggered or not."

My heart is in my throat and my vision blurs. "How long have you known this?"

"Only a few days."

"And you didn't tell me?"

"I didn't want you to worry."

I turn away, a sob escaping me as tears trail down my cheeks. He should have told me about this and we could have left sooner, gotten word to the Deliverance by now.

He places a hand on my shoulder. "Locklyn, I'm sorry—"

I squirm away and stand, facing him straight on, tears and all. "I love you, Stryder. More than I can even fathom and if you die—" I hiccup, cutting myself off.

Stryder moves over the bed and sweeps me into his arms in an instant, kissing my face and wiping away my tears. "I love you, too, Locklyn. I won't die, okay? I promise you that removing these trackers will be the first thing we do."

With my arms wrapped around his neck, I cry against his chest, soaking his shirt as he holds me tight. I can't believe I told him I love him when he, yet again, kept a secret. But right now, his life is in danger and we have to make it to the Deliverance no matter what.

☽ ✧ ☾

We leave at the crack of dawn with a caravan full of supplies, a few days' worth of food and water, and tired eyes. I walk with Stryder, my hands wrapped around his arm, as I lean my head on his shoulder. Clover and Bibiana are lucky to be pregnant because they don't have to walk and get to ride in the caravan. We could have taken another caravan but Kaer didn't want to in case those in Wolves Creek had to evacuate. So we're stuck walking, switching out with one another to ride in the caravan with Clover and Bibiana.

Amira had a tearful goodbye with Vanne and she walks ahead of us now, her head held high, curls spilling down her back. I hugged him and gave him the recording device. He'll keep me updated on whatever he and Electra find. Domenico walks with Kaer, chatting as if they're taking a stroll through the gardens, and they seem to get along pretty well. The day has dragged on, but at least we'll be stopping soon for the night.

"Stryder?"

"Hmm?"

"How do you know Domenico?" I ask, keeping my gaze on the strange man.

Stryder rolls his neck and shoulders back. "I told you, we had a few classes in college together."

"But how do you *really* know him?"

He hesitates, giving me a look. "Did you gather I know him better from eavesdropping?"

"Yes." I glance up at him. "So what's the truth?"

"We grew up together. His family worked near mine and we became friends. But we did actually go to college together, too."

"Why was he at the club that night? It seemed like you didn't expect him to be there."

"Because I didn't. Dom doesn't enjoy clubbing. I guess it was good for him to get out and experience life for once."

I look at Domenico again. "What does he do? Is he another PI?"

Stryder tosses his arm around my shoulders and pulls me into his side. "With all these questions about Dom, do I have to worry about you running off with him one day?"

I snort. "*Heavens*, no. I'm curious about him, especially since he spent his time at the club with one of my best friends."

"I'm sure they had a great time. Dom's not a creep. He's a gentleman."

"So what does he do?"

Stryder hesitates. "Dom...he's a soldier."

My gaze narrows ever so slightly. "Makes sense, he looks like one."

"Yeah."

"Is your family in the military as well?"

"My family's involvement is a little more complicated than Dom's family. But yes, we were."

Even though he doesn't elaborate on his family's involvement with the Mevanian military, I don't press further. I know Stryder doesn't like to dive into his past and when he's ready to, I'll gobble up all the information he shares. But for now, I don't want to make him uncomfortable. Personally, I know little about Mevania, except that it's a sovereign nation. We didn't learn about it in college, of course, because discovering that there's an entire world out there is something Moon Crossing didn't want us to know. So only those with government jobs are informed while the citizens are kept oblivious. I suppose now I know Amira belongs to a noble family. *What was her last name?* I turn to Stryder and ask.

"Solomon," he tells me, "why do you ask?"

"I realized I don't know who the sovereign family of Mevania is," I say, unscrewing the cap of my canteen and taking a swig. "I mean, I'm sure that the Circle knew. I only heard about a change in power that happened years ago."

Stryder drinks from his canteen too. "Maybe they thought it wasn't important for you to know."

"Probably, because they would have never sent me out of the District for business, so it was unnecessary information. Although, I've always been curious. I know Mevania is bigger than the District and its military must be impeccable compared to our Recons and police force, so why has Mevania never attacked the District?"

"Because Mevania wants to maintain the peace that we've had for years. The District proposed a peace treaty when the change of power occurred."

I stuff my canteen back in my pack and glance up at him. "Really? I never knew there was a peace treaty between Mevania and the District."

He nods, his expression grim. "The, uh, the previous Emperor and Empress were...killed by a District citizen so...Mevania was on the verge of war but the Empress Regent, Amira's mother, didn't want to be involved in a war so she signed the treaty and the citizen was...taken care of."

"What's her name?"

"Empress Regent Khione, married to Alastair Solomon."

"Khione," I repeat, "that's a beautiful name."

His brow creases. "What's that ahead?"

I follow his gaze to a group of at least a dozen dark silhouettes on the horizon and Kaer brings our caravan to a stop, easing the oxen as they snort and hoof the ground. The rest of us stop next to him and the silhouettes move, racing down the hill at us. A curse slips from Kaer's lips and he turns, rushing to the caravan. Domenico, Amira, and Stryder jump into action as well, but

I don't know what's going on. With my pulse spiking as the silhouettes near us, I run to the back of the caravan with everyone else.

"What's going on?" I ask as Kaer rummages through our supplies and starts producing many weapons; two swords, two crossbows, three knives, a bow, and a quiver of arrows.

Stryder pulls out a pistol from his pack and hands it to me with a handful of bullets. "Bandits."

I take the pistol and bullets, my hands shaking a little, but I hold it at my side and peek around the caravan. The bandits are nearly upon us. Kaer, Amira, Domenico, and Stryder pick up their weapons of choice and we move to the front of the caravan. Kaer has the bow, Amira has picked a crossbow, and Domenico and Stryder each have a sword and a knife. Which leaves Clover and Bibiana with a crossbow and a knife. My heart is racing in my chest, but I take in a deep breath and cock my pistol.

A shot rings out from the bandits and Kaer yells in some fashion, calling us to charge. I hold up my gun, aim, and fire at the bandit who is also holding a gun. He dodges my bullet, but it grazes his leg and his glare turns on me. The man dives behind a thick bush that leads into shrubs and trees nearby and I find my own bush to hide behind. I've never actually been up against anyone else in a gunfight and it's both exhilarating and absolutely terrifying. I have to make sure no one in my company gets shot by this bandit, which should be a simple task.

He leans out from behind his bush and fires a shot at me. I drop to the ground as it speeds over my head and my heart catches in my throat. I clench my jaw, adrenaline pumping through my veins, as I army crawl through the shrubs, keeping my eye on the gun-wielding bandit and his movements. He doesn't seem to know I've moved and I find an angle in the shrubbery that will give me a perfect shot without being seen.

I raise my pistol and aim, but as my finger curls toward the trigger, I stop. I still don't know the full details and circumstances revolving around why my father did what he did, but I can't help but wonder if this is how he felt.

Full of adrenaline and greed to be the one who makes it out alive. The bandit shifts in my sights, probably trying to find me, but he's hopeless because I have a perfect shot. My arms tremble, and I grip the pistol more firmly, trying to quell my anxious limbs. I'm not a murderer, that was my whole point in Moon Crossing, but out here, where there are no rules for life and death, am I willing to take that path?

The pendant around my neck feels heavy and I lower the pistol, glancing out at everyone else. Stryder and Domenico are holding their own pretty well. They don't seem to have any trouble injuring the bandits, cutting them down as they go. Kaer and Amira are defending the caravan, with Clover wielding the other crossbow. She loads bolts and shoots effortlessly, her expression controlled. I catch sight of Bibiana crouched by the caravan, her eyes wide and panicked as she tries to make herself as small as possible.

Movement out of the corner of my eye catches my attention and I glance to see that the bandit with the gun rolls out from behind the bush he was hiding behind. Amidst the battle, no one else is paying attention but me as he makes his way toward Bibiana. I hear her shriek as she sees him near and I don't think as I stand from the shrubbery, aim, and shoot him in the back before he can pull the trigger on Bibiana. The bandit falls, but he's not completely incapacitated.

His hand lifts with the gun again and I run out, shouting as I stand on his back, digging my heel into the wound. "Drop it!"

The bandit hisses and drops the gun, turning his head to glare at me. I train my pistol on him and look around. Most of the other bandits are occupied, but I see one tumble into the shrubs with a crossbow ready to fire. I press my foot into the bandit beneath me when he squirms and keep my gaze out for the crossbow. Bibiana has gone back in the caravan, finding it to be the easiest place to not get killed. With the distraction, the bandit beneath me sweeps my other leg and I trip, falling to the ground. My pistol falls out of my hand and I scramble for it, but he's quicker to reach for his, firing a shot before I can even register what's happened.

Searing pain and fire blaze through my leg as a bullet pierces my flesh and promptly exits into the ground beneath. I scream and nearly bite my tongue as I try to reign myself in, blinking away tears that come to my eyes and tentatively touching the wound. The bandit levels the barrel at my head. Before he can squeeze the trigger, a bolt pierces his neck and he squeals like swine to the slaughter. He collapses, his entire body twitching as blood spurts from the wound and fills his mouth, spilling onto his lips. I stare at the man, disconnecting from the battle around me and it falls completely silent. No one is screaming in pain anymore.

I feel numb, watching the blood drain as it seeps into the soil below. My leg still pulses with the gunshot, but I can't seem to focus. I didn't kill him. Whoever shot him with the crossbow did. My bloody fingers wrap around the pendant, and I don't care if I stain the stone. Nausea hits me when the pungent stench of blood does and I fall back, my eyes fluttering as the pain becomes unbearable.

☽ ✧ ☾

I wake on a firm bed under bright fluorescent lights and to the smell of antiseptic. I lift my heavy hand to shield my eyes against the lights and they dim immediately. A figure appears above, looking down at me with a medical mask over his mouth and red scrubs. Smile lines appear around his dark eyes and he sits beside me, so I have to turn my head toward him. My head feels fuzzy and I don't know where I am, who this man is, and what happened after I passed out.

"Glad to see you're awake, Miss Harte," the man says. "My name is Doctor Orlin Sosa."

My mouth opens to speak, but no words tumble out and I close my eyes, rubbing my forehead. Dr. Sosa tells me, "Don't worry, the anesthesia will wear off in a couple of hours and you won't feel so confused."

I hear a door open and shut and then someone takes my hand, warm and large compared to mine. My gaze travels to find Stryder there, leaning over me as he kisses my head. "*Blazing suns*, Locklyn, I'm so glad you're awake!"

Dr. Sosa snorts. "I don't know why you're surprised. I told you she was going to be fine."

Though Stryder lowers his voice, I can still hear him hiss, "Doing one surgery doesn't make you a physician, Orlin."

"At least I'm getting some experience."

What? He's not a physician?

I try to object, but Stryder smoothes my sweaty hair out of my face and explains to me, "We're in Arcane Cove, love. You passed out from shock after the battle with the bandits and we got here as quickly as we could. Everyone else is okay, with a few minor injuries, but nothing severe. A few scouts are heading out to the Deliverance, too, so everything's good, no need to worry. All you need to do is rest now."

I take a moment to process what he tells me and then I relax, bobbing my head. Stryder tucks a blanket around me and he and Orlin wander over to the door, where I can still hear them talk in soft voices.

"Despite your lack of a medical degree, I'm thankful you could set her femur, Orlin." Stryder grunts, his voice strained.

"Hey, stop boasting about my lack of a medical degree. I've been working in this clinic for years and studying since I was a *niño pequeño*," Orlin huffs, "but yeah, you're welcome. It's a good thing I got stuck here, too. I was going to head home to see how Padre is doing."

"Well, I'm glad you stayed. We were at the halfway point when we got attacked and rode through the night just to get here. But...we should let her rest. I think I'm going to stay for a bit."

"Don't get too crazy." Orlin clicks his tongue. "She's still healing."

"Get out, man."

The door opens, closes, and Stryder comes back. I gaze at him as he tentatively sits on the bed and rests his hand on mine.

"I'm sorry I didn't protect you," he whispers, "and tossing you right into battle was a terrible idea."

"It's...fine..." I whisper back, my voice raspy.

"I love you so much and when I saw you on the ground, I was—I was so worried I'd lost you." His voice breaks and a tear slips down his cheek, splashing on mine.

I reach up and rub away the tears with my thumb. I hope he doesn't beat himself up about it. It's not his fault I got hurt and at least I'm not dead. We have that to be grateful for. I may walk funny from now on, we could match, but it doesn't matter. I have my life and I have my sanity.

FOR GLORY AND GORE

O RB GOT OUT of bed, drew on his robe, and walked into the wash-room. Last night had been a busy one, beginning with his marriage to Glory and ending with his coronation as Emperor of Mevania. All under one sun revolution, he was a new man with a new life and he had plenty of changes to make around here. Orb showered, dressed, and approached the grand king bed once more. He drew apart the silk curtains surrounding it and leaned down towards Glory's face.

She was still asleep, her expression peaceful, and her hair mussed. He cupped her head, fingers slipping into her honey-blonde locks, and kissed her forehead. Glory Troisi was the love of his life. He knew so ever since he met her at the orphanage in Moon Crossing. The best news he had received a little over two weeks ago was that he and Glory were expecting a child—his heir to the throne once his brother was taken care of.

"I love you," he whispered against her skin and gazed at her a moment longer before stepping away.

The silk curtain fell back in place and Orb adjusted his royal robes, turning away as he exited their chambers. The corridors were familiar from ages ago when he was a mere child. Columned walls painted a soft cream with embedded gold leaf. The runner beneath his feet was of exquisite crimson and white thread, the design weaved into it simple with swirls and curves. Orb made his way to the war room, where he hoped to be spending plenty of time in the upcoming months. As he passed portraits of his family, he regarded his parents with a humble heart and his brother with a haughty glare. The fool, his cowardly act had gotten their parents killed and Orb would never forgive him.

Thankfully, the Iluro Senate was already waiting for him and they ceased chatting, standing as Orb entered. He took his seat at the head of the long oak table and nodded for the others to sit. His heart caught in his throat as he realized this would have been where his father sat. Orb gripped the arms of the chair, the animalistic carvings pressing into his skin, and glanced around at the best strategists in all of Iluro.

"Welcome back, Your Majesty," Arlo Amante dared to break the silence.

Orb's gaze glided to him. "Thank you, Amante."

Arlo had been his father's advisor and he thought it honorable to keep Amante on since he had been helping Khione as well. But the man had always creeped him out as a child, terribly skinny and tall with slicked back blonde hair, now graying, and sharp cheekbones that framed deep-set eyes. Orb remembered witnessing drama between Arlo and his parents. They kept it hush-hush in the palace. But he knew Arlo was in love with his mother, Aaralyn, and that his father, Keyon, did not like that one bit.

He turned away from Amante and announced, "I want to declare war on the District and destroy it for good."

The room was silent as they all stared at him and Orb waited, lifting an eyebrow. Admiral Luminosa Mezzanotte cleared her throat and spoke first, "Pardon my confusion, Your Majesty, but under Empress Khione we had a pact with the District and—"

He cut her off. "Khione is no longer in charge, Admiral. I would like to move forward with this plan and before we declare war, I would like to send for my allies still living in the District. I will write a list and we will get them out as soon as possible. Most will become part of the Senate as well. Do you understand me?"

"Of course, Your Majesty," the Iluro Senate replied in unison.

"Perfect. Now, let's discuss the state of Mevania since I've been gone for so long."

☽ ✧ ☾

After a long day of meetings, Orb wanted to take a hot bath and cuddle with Glory. But his aunt and uncle were going to make sure that didn't happen. Khione and her husband, Alastair, cornered Orb after his last meeting and insisted that he join them on the rooftop for a little chat—plus gelato. Orb sighed and followed them, a bit annoyed at their giddy and playful banter with one another. He was twelve when he left, but Khione and Alastair were always all over each other. He thought that getting married would have changed that but as he learned with Glory, Orb still lit up when she entered a room and she was all he could see.

"Oh, Al, you are too cute for your own good!" Khione giggled, eyes sparkling as she looked at her husband.

He had whispered something...or said something to her. Orb hadn't been paying attention. But as they passed by a few servants, Alastair asked for some gelato to be brought to the rooftop. They found their way outside and around the palace, where a metal ladder built by Alastair, back in the day, led to the roof. Orb climbed first, then Alastair and Khione, since she was wearing a gown. He grumbled as he sat down, feeling like a child again when Khione and Alastair would bring him, his brother, and their daughter up here on clear, starry nights to eat gelato, play games, and enjoy some time together. They were basically still teenagers at heart, but Orb wasn't a child anymore and his nose scrunched at the brightness of the moon.

"So, Orbbie Worrbie, tell me what you kids have been up to over in the District?" Khione started, smiling brightly. A dimple formed in her cheek.

She looked like his father when she smiled and he swallowed, glancing out among the treetops. "I attended Moon Crossing University and became a Councilor in the Elite Council."

"Really? I hadn't known that. Did you know that, Al?"

"I did not."

He shrugged. "I went by Orb Cristol instead of...well, you know."

Khione tipped her head at him. "I don't understand why you had to change your last name, darling."

Orb turned to her. "The Circle of Superiors would have known who I was if I used my birth name. I was undercover."

"Undercover? For nearly, oh how many years has it been? Fourteen years?" Alastair asked.

"Yes, it's been that long. I was infiltrating Moon Crossing, finding out who killed Makuahine and Babbo."

"And did you find out?" his aunt inquired, her voice suddenly cold and cautious.

"I did."

"Who?"

Orb clicked his tongue. "A man named Cicone Harte. The Circle executed him not long after."

He had, in fact, known for fourteen years who had killed his parents—Orb witnessed it himself. But he didn't want to divulge what justice he had wrought in Moon Crossing while he was there. Khione would be furious if she knew. Orb couldn't let it go. Cicone's posterity had to suffer for what he did to Orb's family, tore them apart forever, and made him watch it all unfold. With the knowledge of who killed his parents, they fell silent for a few minutes until a servant emerged with three bowls of gelato. Orb took one and set it in front of him, dipping his spoon into the gelato.

"Well, I'm glad he's gone," Alastair remarked softly. "At least we don't have to worry about a monster like that anymore."

"True. But I know why Makuahine and Babbo brought me to Moon Crossing. I'm not completely safe when the Eclipse Society is still hiding somewhere in Mevania. Neither is my child."

Khione nearly broke her neck as she whipped her head toward him, her golden-brown eyes wide and her jaw slack. "Your *child*, Orb? Did I hear that correctly?"

A sheepish smile came to his lips. "Yes, you did, Aunt Khione. Glory and I are expecting a baby."

"Didn't you marry only yesterday?" Alastair's brow crumbled in confusion.

Orb lifted an eyebrow. "Do I need to remind you that you got Aunt Khione pregnant before you married?"

He waved it off, but his voice held an edge to it. "She doesn't even know if I'm the father of Miri."

An awkward silence ensued and Orb smirked as he glanced between his uncle and aunt. When Khione was in her youth, she was being courted by Alastair. Then one summer, another young man, a former Recon, in fact, had vacationed in Iluro when the District and Mevania were on traveling terms. Orb was only a year old at the time, so he didn't remember what happened, but he heard about it later on. Khione embarked on a summer affair with both Alastair and the Recon and wound up pregnant not long after. Keyon was furious when he found out she was with child and gave Khione an ultimatum, to marry or be hidden away from the public eye to maintain the family's reputation.

She married Alastair and Amira was born, introduced to society as Alastair's daughter. Khione never had a paternity test done, but she always insisted that Alastair was Amira's father. Orb agreed they looked alike. Yet again, Amira also looked like the Recon Khione fooled around with. He only knew this because he had been acquainted with him in Moon Crossing. Cyrus Caine—now an impressionable detective.

"You are the father," Khione reassured her husband and shook her head. "But Orb, I'm so happy for you and I can't wait to see your baby toddling around these corridors soon. It's been a while since we've had children at the palace. Is Glory happy?"

"She wasn't necessarily happy at first, but she's content now," he stated, eating another spoonful of gelato.

"I should spend more time with her. She seems like a lovely girl. Where is she from again?"

"A little community outside Bountiful Hill called Doum."

Alastair asked, "And what of her parents? I don't think I saw them at the ceremony."

"They're dead. We met in the orphanage in Moon Crossing shortly after I...arrived there."

"Oh, poor thing," Khione sighed and threw her arms around Orb, squeezing him tight.

He tensed up until she released him and then he stood. "I should get back to Glory. It's been a long day."

"Of course." His aunt popped up and helped Alastair to his feet.

Again, she hugged him. His uncle patted him on the shoulder, and Orb shimmied down the ladder. They stayed on the rooftop, though, and he did not want to imagine why. With a rub of his tired eyes, he headed back into the palace and to his chambers. He hadn't seen Glory all day, which she probably didn't like, and he was sure she'd berate him about it when he stepped into the room. But that was perfectly fine. The only person he'd let berate him was Glory. She was his everything and his future. Back in Moon Crossing, waking up next to her on some mornings took his breath away. He had loved her from the moment he saw her and even more when she turned out to be the only person who understood him.

He cracked open the doors of his chambers and poked his head in. A slipper was promptly thrown at his head and he laughed, slipping inside. The doors closed with a click and he got a whiff of the candles burning, honey and lavender, and saw Glory standing in the middle of the expansive room, her hands on her hips.

"What happened yesterday, Orb?" she began, sauntering up to him.

His smile only broadened as she drew closer, eyes raking over her. "We were married, my love."

"If that's the case, then why haven't I seen you all day? Do we not have a honeymoon as emperor and empress of Mevania?"

"We do," he told her and took her hips, drawing her against him. "I needed to see the Senate today to get started on a few things. We can leave on a honeymoon by the end of the week, I promise."

Glory gazed at him. Her doe-like eyes were caught between a sea of freckles and perfectly arched eyebrows. She was impeccable, an incredible sight to behold, and he was terribly glad to have won her affection. Then her nose crinkled. "Why are you looking at me like that?"

"Because the sun began to shine when you were created," he murmured, leaning down to press a kiss to her lips.

She was stubborn for only a moment before she weaved her arms around his neck and kissed him back. Orb wanted a little more, but Glory pulled away. "But I'm being serious, Orb. Am I really not going to see you as often as I used to?"

"Being an emperor takes work, baby, it takes effort. I'll be in meetings a lot, but as empress, you also have the choice of sitting in on those meetings. We rule Mevania together. Our baby will keep you occupied as well."

"*Gah,* when I thought about being an empress, I imagined there would be extravagant balls, giant fluffy dresses, random luncheons in the gardens, and gossiping with other women of the court all day long."

"Do you wish it was like that?"

"No, I only have so much to gossip about." Her lips lifted in a smile and Orb stole another kiss before Glory eased him off. "Oh, stop, it's just me."

His fingers pressed into the small of her back and his gaze wandered as he bit his lip. "Exactly, and all I want right now is you."

"Is a bath included in that wanting as well? Because you smell like you've been running around the palace all day," she gibed.

"I have been. Join me?"

"Sure."

She took his hand and led him into the washroom. They talked softly as the tub filled with steaming water and Orb felt like a teenager again, giddy and hopelessly in love with Glory Troisi. She was the light in the darkness of his world and he would do anything to make sure she was safe from the Eclipse Society and Moon Crossing. If either came for her, they would have to go through Orb first.

☽ ✧ ☾

Stryder stood outside of Arcane Cove's clinic with his gaze turned toward the heavens. The rain clouds were heading toward Wolves Creek for the night, but the canyon was still flooding. Hopefully, the scouts would be safe in their endeavor to reach the Deliverance and bring word back. It irked him that he couldn't go, but with Locklyn's condition, he had to stay here, especially if Orlin did something wrong.

He snorted and shook his head, making his way to the large lodge he was sharing with everyone else in his company. Stryder had met Orlin when he first came to the Deliverance to see what they were all about and why they were asking for funding from Mevania and not Wolves Creek or Bountiful Hill. His aunt had sent him and he thought at first that it was a hopeless cause, but Orlin had convinced him otherwise, opening his eyes to the pain and torment Moon Crossing had caused in the other cities in the District, especially Spring Grove.

So he decided to help and became friends with Orlin, which also benefited him in becoming close to Orlin's father as well, Vicente Sosa, leader of the Deliverance. Stryder also, at one point, had a crush on Orlin's twin sister, Alita. She was kind, intelligent, and out of his league, just like Locklyn. The last he knew of Alita, though, was that she had been attending Bountiful Hill University to become a trauma therapist. An honorable profession that she definitely had the guts to take on. Stryder couldn't imagine listening to other people's problems all day long and not leave it at work. Alita could, though. She always listened to him when he had to vent.

Stryder climbed the stairs of the lodge and swung the door open. Orlin was kneeling in front of Bibiana and Clover as they sat on the couch, a stethoscope in hand as he listened to the babies inside them. Clover looked bored and annoyed, which must have meant that Orlin had forced them to let him practice being a doctor. But Bibiana couldn't seem to keep her eyes off of him and even genuinely laughed at his cheesy jokes.

After being with a guy like Viktor Marsh, Bibiana definitely deserved someone better, and well, if Orlin was her type, he saw no problem with it. The only thing might be the age gap. Nine years apart was too much for some people. Stryder moved into the kitchen but listened in on their conversation as he made himself a snack.

"So, Clover, I know you're Kaer's wife and were once in the Deliverance, but I don't think I ever saw you before," Orlin began, sitting back as he glanced up at the two women before him.

"I left before Spring Grove was destroyed. The Deliverance didn't even have its headquarters completely built back then."

"Ah, you're right."

Clover sighed. "Anyway, are you done with scoping out my baby? I'd like to spend some time with my husband now."

"Yeah, I'm done. Sounds like a healthy baby you have in there."

She rolled her eyes as she pushed herself up and then toddled up the stairs. Clover and Kaer seemed to spend an awful lot of time together, and Stryder wondered if that's what marriage was like. Your spouse was now your only and best friend in the entire world. He ducked into the refrigerator to grab the gallon of mixed berry juice and pulled a cup from the cupboard.

"She seems nice. What about you, Bibiana? What's your part in all of this?"

Stryder's shoulders tensed for a moment but then loosened as she said, "I'm trying to get to Bountiful Hill. Kaer was kind enough to let me tag along."

"Um, sorry if this seems too sensitive, but...what about the father? Is he still...a part of your life?"

"No," she answered briskly, "and he never will be again."

"Oh," Orlin cleared his throat, "if it isn't too forward then, I was wondering if maybe you'd like to grab lunch in town sometime?"

Stryder nearly burst out laughing, but he held it in, clamping a hand over his mouth. At least the kitchen was out of the way, so they couldn't see him with his shoulders shaking in laughter. *Oh, Orlin, always the fast mover.*

It sounded like Bibiana was smiling. "I would love to, Dr. Sosa, and then maybe you could tell me more about Arcane Cove?"

"I would be delighted to tell you about Arcane Cove and all we do here. And please, call me Orlin, I'm not actually a physician."

"You're not? Why did you tell us you were then?"

"Well, I was studying to be a physician, but these hands already know how to make miracles happen. Basically, I'm already the primary physician at the clinic here. I mean, it's just a piece of paper, right?"

Bibiana giggled. "I suppose so. But I would want a certified physician to deliver my baby."

"Understandable," he quipped.

It fell quiet for a moment and Stryder peeked out at them. They were gazing into each other's eyes and he shook his head. Orlin stood, helping Bibiana to her feet, and made his way to the door.

"I'll swing by tomorrow at noon if that works for you," he told her.

She shrugged. "I literally have nothing else to do so that works perfectly."

"Great."

Orlin gave her one last look and was out the door. Bibiana clasped her hands together, biting her lip as she tried to contain her smile from spreading wider. Stryder cleared his throat and she whipped toward him, eyes wide.

"Stryder!"

"Hi, Bibi," he waved and sat down at the table, finally able to enjoy his nighttime snack.

She wandered over, tucking her hands in the sleeves of her sweater, and tilted her head at him. "How long have you been there?"

"I walked in when Clover was still down here. I thought you had noticed."

Suddenly, worry furrowed her brow. "Do you think it's too soon to go on a date with Orlin? I mean, I only met him yesterday and sometimes I still think about Viktor, even though I *hate* it when he pops into my head. What do you think?"

"Why are you asking me about this?"

"Because you've been in relationships, asked people out."

"I thought I was in love with Inaya, who turned out to be a Worshiper. With Locklyn, we kissed on our first date/first time meeting each other. I don't know, should I tell you to kiss him?"

She gave him an annoyed look. "You're awful. I will not kiss him on the first date," a smirk lifted her lips, "not for thirty minutes."

"You'll be fine, Bibi, go on a date with him. I mean, you can't get pregnant again when you already are."

With a scoff, she reached over and smacked him across the back of the head as he chuckled. She glared daggers at him. "I don't know *why* my sister found you attractive."

"Inaya was quirky and thought I was too, just not *that* quirky."

"*Quirky* indeed."

Growing serious, Stryder asked, "Have you heard from her at all?"

Bibiana shook her head. "Not since she joined the Ethereal Might Convent in the Blooming Woods. She would scold me if she found out I was pregnant. I definitely don't miss her belittling me for not being 'righteous' and 'good' like her. Inaya was so different before she joined that cult."

He nodded. "Wild and independent, no one could talk down to her."

She inhaled and ran her fingers through her hair. "The past is the past. I probably won't ever see her again. So be it. I'm moving on from my life in Moon Crossing."

"Shouldn't we all."

Bibiana smiled. "Goodnight, Stryder."

"Goodnight."

She went upstairs and he was left alone, with his thoughts and with his snack, for the rest of the night.

PIECES OF THE PUZZLE

I GOT BORED in the clinic quickly, so I decided to write a letter to Vanne and Electra to see how things are going. Vanne should be back in Moon Crossing by now and hopefully, he has shared Bibiana's recording with Electra. His letter has just arrived and I turn over as I gently slip my fingernail beneath the flap and open it. Vanne's heavy-handed penmanship throws me off for a moment but I take a breath and clear my head. I squint as I read.

Locklyn,

I'm back in Moon Crossing and have touched base with Electra. We're going to try and do everything that we can to help you but...when I tried to play the recording, it didn't work. I had a trusted friend take a look at it and he said the device was waterlogged. For now, I'll leave it with him to see if he can fix it but there's a chance he won't. In that case, we need another recording. I sent you a new recorder in a separate package and this time, make sure it doesn't get damaged before you send it back.

Vanne

My blood runs cold and I clench the letter, glancing around the clinic. No one is paying any attention to me and I read it again, blinking in disbelief. I flip over on my back and try to think of what could have happened. After I recorded Bibiana, I left to hang out with Stryder. Surely, Bibiana wouldn't destroy the recording if she was willing to give it in the first place, right?

Maybe she freaked out and changed her mind. The only way I'll know is if I ask.

"Miss Harte, you have yet another letter," Orlin says and hands it to me. He leans on the wall by my bed, eyebrow raised. "I didn't think anyone sent snail mail anymore."

"Just trying to keep this information hush-hush," I tell him.

"Ooo, I'm intrigued."

I shake my head. "Including you."

Orlin chuckles and lifts his hands. "Alright, I get it."

He leaves and I open the letter. It's another one from Vanne but this time the message takes up the entire page. It's written in a rectangular form, lines crossing over others as it spirals into the center. My head already feels like it's going to burst just trying to decipher which sentences are first. There are even a couple of symbols scattered about and I can make out what looks to be a handgun and a purse.

I make myself comfortable and get to work. Slowly turning the page around as I read.

There's something I should tell you and this form was the only way I could think of. When A and I were on our first date, I noticed she had a gun in her waistband. I'm pretty sure it wasn't there at the beginning of the night when I picked her up. We were at our apartment, just hanging out, and A seemed totally normal. I didn't want to question her because it was the first date. I liked her, I didn't want to scare her away. But I asked anyway and she said it was for protection and slipped it into her purse. Another time, I joked about the gun but she didn't have it anymore because she trusted me. I believed her but it was still weird that she would bring a gun, of all things, on a first date. Not pepper spray or a taser. Every time we hung out, she insisted on coming over to the apartment afterward. I would talk to her but...you know, it's awkward. I thought I loved her but now I'm not so sure.

The letter ends and I drop it on my lap, pressing my palms against my eyes.

Amira Solomon, who in the blazes are you?

I know she's a noble. Her mother is Stryder's aunt and was ruling Mevania until Orb went back. I know she showed up in Moon Crossing a year and a half ago, but for what purpose? What is a noblewoman of Mevania doing in the District?

Amira and Vanne began dating about three or four months ago, a few weeks before my trial. She could have had access to anything in the apartment, including...including my gun. I swing my legs over the side of the bed and reach for the crutches I've been given. A nurse sees me trying to get up and rushes over.

"Miss Harte, what are you doing?" he asks, worry wrinkling his brow.

"I need to talk to Stryder. Do you know where he's staying?"

He ignores my request. "You shouldn't be getting up so briskly, you haven't walked without help since the surgery."

"Stryder Monroe, where is he?" I try again, shaking the nurse's hand off my arm.

"Please get back in bed, Miss Harte."

"*No!*" I protest and it draws the attention of the other patients, eager for some drama. Tears well in my eyes as pain shoots through my leg. "Just tell me where he is."

The nurse says nothing and instead sits me down and confiscates my crutches. I crawl under the sheets and pull them over my head, squeezing my eyes shut as the pain worsens. It spreads from my leg in both directions, numbing my foot with pain and causing my hip to feel on fire. It could be infected. I doubt Orlin really knew what he was doing. And yet, Stryder still let him operate on me.

Stryder.

He must know what Amira was doing in Moon Crossing—if she stole my gun and helped Viktor frame me. I don't know why; we don't have any bad blood between us. I don't even have bad blood with Viktor, so why am I the target? I suppose I was an easy scapegoat to blame since I worked with the Circle directly and knew all the awful things they planned to do. Maybe Stryder will clear up a few questions about Amira.

I whimper as the pain continues and someone pulls the sheet off my head, laying the back of their hand against my forehead. "She's burning up," a voice states, but it sounds so far away and I fade fast into a world of dark and numbing pain.

☽ ✧ ☾

I'm seven years old and I wait by the window for Papa to come home.

"Locklyn, honey, it's time for bed," Mama says.

I reluctantly pull away from the window and she gathers me close. I wrap my tiny arms around her neck as she picks me up and carries me to my bedroom.

"He promised he would tuck me in," I whisper in her hair. "I thought he was really going to tonight."

I hear the pain in Mama's voice as she says softly, "I'm sorry, honey. Maybe tomorrow he'll make it."

That's all she says, even when she lays me down and closes the door. An empty promise.

Much later that night, my father comes home and opens the door to my room. I lay motionless so he will think I'm asleep. The stench of something foul strikes my nose and I try not to let it crinkle in disdain. I hear him kneel by the edge of my bed and lean close to my ear.

"I've done something horrible, my sweet Locklyn. I'm so sorry. I pray you will forgive me someday for the wrong I've done. I love you. I love you with all my heart," he whispers, his voice breaking as he gently strokes my hair. "Remember the good times, not the bad." He pauses and I listen to him breathe for a heartbeat. "Remember me."

Then he places something on my nightstand and I hear it thud. He plants a kiss on my forehead and is gone.

In the morning, the police break our door down and I wake immediately, groggy. I slip out of my bed and cautiously walk down the hallway, but when I reach the end, I stop cold. The officers have my father pinned against the wall and they're handcuffing him. I'm anchored in place, unable to move. My mother cries near the kitchen, her sobs hitched.

"Papa?" I whisper and he looks at me for a moment, his gray eyes sorrowful, then back at the wall.

"No, no, no, no," Mama mumbles repeatedly.

They don't hesitate as they take my father away and leave me stunned and Mama crying. No explanation. Nothing.

That evening, a message comes over Mama's Mini. She sits at the kitchen table for a long time, reading the message again and again as tears silently slip down her cheeks. She won't let me read the message, though. But after she goes to sleep, I do.

Mrs. Maisie Harte, the Circle of Superiors has reason to believe that Cicone Harte is guilty of committing a major crime against the city of Moon Crossing. The Superiors will give Cicone a private trial beginning tomorrow, as this case is of the utmost priority, and you are welcome to attend. With someone as dangerous as Superior Harte has proved to be so far, we cannot promise the safety of the community and that is our foremost goal. If the Circle orders an execution, it will be a private affair that you have the choice to attend or not. The Circle of Superiors express their support for you and your children and our condolences if an execution order comes to pass.

I read the message over as Mama had, but only once. Then I go back to my room and pick up the object Papa left for me last night. It's a pendant necklace, the stone deep indigo with gold veins and held by a leather strap. I unclasp the necklace and put it on. Papa told me to remember him, so I will with his gift.

Every day, I'll wear my necklace in remembrance of Papa, but I'll hide it in my shirt so no one else will want to take it. I know I'm supposed to forget about him as everyone else will, but I won't. I will always *remember him.*

☽ ✧ ☾

I wake, feeling feverish and drift in and out of consciousness. Stryder stays by my side as Orlin and the other physicians try to decipher what's wrong. I can't remember what I needed to talk to Stryder about. My head is on fire and I don't even know what I ate last.

Stryder and Orlin have moved me to a private room. It's small, but it's much more accommodating and the other patients don't have to hear my moans of pain. They keep their voices low as I'm hunched under my blanket, eyes closed and numb for now, with the painkillers they've given me.

"We need Rhyn, Orlin, she'll know what to do," Stryder says, his voice strained with worry.

"I don't know if Locklyn can survive two more days of pain—"

"Send a Hover. If we send a Hover now, Rhyn could be here tonight."

Orlin sighs. "Stryder, I have no authority in Arcane Cove, especially over the Hovers. Talk to Sophronia Archer."

"Where is she then? Locklyn needs the best physician in the District because *you* screwed up," Stryder snaps.

"Hey, we don't know what's wrong with her and if it was because of my surgery."

"Which is why we need Rhyn and should have brought a certified physician out in the first place!"

"Stryder—"

"Tell me where Sophronia Archer is? That's an *order*."

Order?

Orlin is quiet for a moment before he relents, "717 Opal Way."

"Thanks," Stryder says, "I'll be back."

The door opens and closes; it falls quiet. I take the silence to sleep.

☽ ✧ ☾

Stryder donned a long coat lined with fur and set out to 717 Opal Way. The night was brisk as winter approached and he pulled his cap over his ears. He had a map of Arcane Cove on his Mini and walked through the paved streets. There were plenty of people out on the streets and music played in the square. Arcane Cove was a lively place, with circus tents, street magicians, and psychic services. It had an affinity for the supernatural and though Stryder would have liked to explore the town; he had other things to do.

It took him a half-hour to walk to Opal Way and he ascended the steps leading to the door with the golden number *717* nailed to it. He knocked and waited, glancing down the street to make sure no one was sneaking around to jump him. This part of Arcane Cove was dark and had a high level of criminal activity.

The door creaked open and a woman with teal hair and pale blue eyes appeared. Stryder asked, "Sophronia Archer?"

"That's me," she said, her accent hailing from the French nation, Amery, and gave him a once over. "What do you want?"

"I need access to a Hover. There's someone in Wolves Creek I need to pick up."

She didn't budge from the doorway. "Why?"

He clenched his fists, trying not to get upset. "My girlfriend had surgery earlier this week and now she's sick. Orlin told me to talk to you about getting a Hover and I need a certified physician to help her before it gets worse."

"Who are you again?"

"Stryder Monroe. I'm sure you've heard of me."

Sophronia worked her jaw. "I have. How much are you going to give me for my help?"

"We can discuss payment when we're on our way to Wolves Creek," he retorted.

"Fine." She grabbed her coat and they stepped down to the street.

Stryder followed in silence as Sophronia weaved them through the streets of Arcane Cove and to a large shed where a single Hover was housed. She pulled off the tarp, kicking up dust, and Stryder covered his mouth. The gleaming silver metal still looked relatively new, Stryder could see a hazy reflection of himself in it. Sophronia rounded the Hover, pressed a couple of buttons, and the hatch opened, thunking against the ground. They walked up the ramp and Sophronia took the pilot's seat, snapping on a cap and her seat belt. Stryder sat as co-pilot, the seat cushy, but hoped that he wouldn't have to help fly the Hover. He knew how to steer, but not that well, and couldn't even land.

"So what happened to your girlfriend?" Sophronia asked as she eased the Hover out of the shed, it crawled forward like a spider.

"We were attacked by bandits on our way here. They shot her in the leg and the bullet shattered her femur," he told her.

"*Oof*, sounds painful. Then Orlin operated on her and now she's sick?"

"Yes. It was stupid to let Orlin operate on her, but something needed to be done." He exhaled through his nose and pressed his fist against his chin. "You wanted to discuss payment?"

Sophronia pulled a lever and the Hover rose off the ground. "Sure, I'm thinking about 10,000 credits?"

"Pft, you wish. Give me a better number for only flying this Hover."

"Wow, you're kind."

"I'm stressed out, sorry, but really, I need a reasonable price."

"Fine, I'll take 5,000 credits."

"Deal." He withdrew his Mini, asked for her code, and friended her. When she accepted, he sent Sophronia the payment and her Mini pinged.

A smile came to her lips. "Thanks."

"Sure."

They left Arcane Cove behind and the Hover buzzed with life, the night vision windshield helping them see. It turned the outside world an eerie green and herds of spooked animals entertained them in the meadows below. The flight was smooth, as Stryder was lost in his head, sick with worry about Locklyn. Sophronia talked little and it only took them a half hour to reach Wolves Creek. Sophronia brought the Hover down outside the gate and Stryder departed once the hatch hit the ground.

Mohe and Yansa were half asleep in their tower as he approached, but he whistled and they woke, scrambling for their bows. Stryder held up his hands in surrender, keeping his distance as he announced himself, "It's me. Stryder."

The sentries blinked at him and then smiled, saying in unison, "Milk chocolate!"

Stryder rolled his eyes but stepped forward as they descended, dropping his hands. "I need to talk to Rhyn."

They nodded and opened the gate for him. Stryder strolled in and made his way to the blacksmith's shop. He didn't know whether Rhyn would still be at the clinic or at home. It was late, so he figured she'd be home. He walked up the two steps and knocked. It resonated through the wood door and he waited. It didn't take long for the door to open to a sleepy Ezra with a bedhead. He blinked a time or two and then rubbed a hand through his hair.

"Stryder? What are you doing here?"

"I need to talk to Rhyn," he said, wringing his hands together.

Ezra's eyes widened. "Is Clover okay?"

"Yes, she's fine. It's Locklyn."

The blacksmith stepped aside and waved Stryder in. "I'll get Rhyn."

Stryder nodded and waited in the shop part of the house. It still smelled like woodsmoke and soot, but otherwise, the blacksmith shop wasn't alive. A few weapons that Ezra was working on were laid out on the vast workbench in various stages of progress. The workbench was neat. Stryder suspected it was so because Rhyn had moved in with him. A light came on in the bedroom and then Rhyn emerged a moment later in her nightclothes, her hair also mussed with sleep.

"What's wrong, Stryder?" she asked, leaning her hand on the workbench as she rubbed the sleep from her eyes.

"We were attacked by bandits on our way to Arcane Cove and Locklyn was severely injured. A gunshot to the leg shattered her femur. Orlin Sosa performed emergency surgery. It's been over a week since and Locklyn suddenly got sick. I need your help, Rhyn, there's no certified physician there and no one knows what's wrong."

Rhyn's expression darkened and she turned away, heading back into their room. Ezra stood by the door, worry creasing his brow, and he asked, "Is everyone else okay?"

"Yes," Stryder reassured him. "It was just Locklyn who was injured."

Ezra bobbed his head and said nothing more. They stood in silence for a few minutes until Rhyn emerged with a suitcase, a medical bag, and a change of clothes. Stryder stepped out as she said her goodbyes to Ezra, telling him she might as well stay in Arcane Cove to deliver their grandchild and that she would let Ezra know so he could be there, too. Stryder and Rhyn made their way to the Hover and as they neared, Rhyn asked, "When Clover's ready to have her baby, can we have a Hover pick up Ezra as well?"

"Of course."

Inside, Sophronia stood from her seat and greeted Rhyn. "Hi, I'm Sophronia Archer, pilot of this Hover."

"Rhyn Parrish, it's nice to meet you."

"You as well."

"Let's get back to Arcane Cove," Stryder instructed and Sophronia slipped back into her seat, running through the takeoff diagnostics.

Stryder directed Rhyn to a private room and she said, "I'm sorry this happened to Locklyn and I hope I can help. Do you know if any x-rays were taken? I'd like to see what kind of femoral fracture I'll be dealing with."

"Yeah, I saved them on my Mini." He removed his Mini from his pocket and opened up the file of pictures he had on Locklyn's x-rays. "These are before the surgery and then after."

Rhyn took the Mini and slipped on glasses so she could see it clearer. She sat down on the bench lining the walls of the room and observed in silence. Stryder wandered over to the window and looked out as they lifted off. Wolves Creek's torches glimmered in the night and grew distant as they flew back to Arcane Cove. His shoulders were tight with worry and his foot tapped impatiently. He knew the flight wasn't long, but he was still worried about Locklyn and didn't know if her condition had worsened. Knowing she was in extreme pain hurt him the most. He was clueless about medical procedures, but Rhyn could certainly save her.

"So, she has a comminuted fracture, meaning that the bone broke into several pieces. You said Orlin Sosa performed the surgery?"

"Yes." Stryder turned on his heel toward her and cringed. "He's not certi-fied."

Rhyn gave him a motherly look of annoyance. "That was incredibly foolish of you to let him operate on her without being a certified physician."

"I know," he sighed, "but Orlin was the only one certified *enough* and she was losing a lot of blood. The bullet went straight through her leg. I didn't have any other choice."

"Stryder, you could have sent this Hover for me. I'm sure the clinic staff in Arcane Cove could have kept her alive long enough until I arrived."

"I wasn't thinking straight and Orlin offered so—"

"So don't decide that again," she interrupted and stood. "Regardless, he did a decent job of setting the bone. However, I figure that she's sick now because there's an infection. I'll have to go in, open the wound, see what kind of infection we're dealing with, and then treat it the best I can. How long has she been sick?"

"She only started showing symptoms two days ago."

"As long as it's not a septic infection, Locklyn should be okay."

"I hope so," he muttered, feeling a rush of emotions come to the surface as his eyes watered.

Rhyn reached out and squeezed his arm. "Stryder, she's going to be okay. You've got the best physician in the District now and she's strong, she can make it through anything."

Stryder glanced at her, wanting to believe every word she said. But it was difficult. He trusted Rhyn. He knew she was the best and that she would do everything within her power for her patients. But he was worried about losing Locklyn, the woman he truly loved and hoped for a future with someday. He had lost too many people he loved in his life already and he didn't want to lose another.

THE BONES OF LOVE

I'M ALIVE.

At least, that's what everyone is telling me. I don't quite feel like it since I've been bed-bound for the last week and a half. After Rhyn showed up and removed the infected tissue from my leg, I rested in the clinic for another day or two, then moved to the lodge where Stryder and everyone else are staying. It's a nice place and I have a room on the ground level. They made sturdier crutches for me, so at least I'm not completely immobile. I would like to be carted around in a wheelchair like a queen, but the lodge doesn't have wheelchair access and we won't be staying in Arcane Cove for much longer.

Since being in the lodge, I've been back in the loop on news. The Deliverance sent an entire force to Wolves Creek, a couple of days before Moon Crossing Recons marched on the village, as Ravi said. Wolves Creek is well fortified, but currently, there's a standoff. The Recons demand that they hand over Kaer and Clover, since the Elite Council ordered her back to Moon Crossing, but they don't know they're not there anymore. Right now, Clover's in the clinic with her mother and father, expecting to give birth soon.

The Deliverance has offered to send Hovers to pick us up in Arcane Cove, which will be an absolute relief. They'll be here to pick us up once the current storm passes and finally, we'll be able to get our trackers removed. I'll need two removals—my citizen tracker and my fugitive tracker. Stryder says his tracker hasn't been giving him trouble, but I often see him shake his hands out or rub his neck sometimes.

Being back in the loop makes me antsy again.

I sit in the living room on a window seat, the crutches lean on the wall next to me. I have a blanket tucked around my shoulders and a mug of spiced cider in my hands. Rain drizzles down the window and races down the streets. We never had this much rain in Moon Crossing, but whenever it did rain, it was my favorite.

"Hey, love," Stryder says as he approaches from across the room.

I glance at him and take a sip of my cider. He sits on the window seat with me, having me scoot over so he can fit, and then tucks an arm around my waist. I lean my head on his shoulder and rub the stone resting at the base of my throat. I've been conflicted about my father and his past for a while now, but I'll always remember the promise I made to him when I wore this necklace for the first time. I can't break that promise, even if it hurts to think about what he did.

Stryder leans his head on mine with a sigh. "What's going on in that head of yours?"

"A moral crisis of sorts," I admit softly, eyes glued outside again.

"I know what that's like. Care to talk about it?"

"I don't know what to think of my father anymore..." my eyes grow misty and I sniffle, my hands shaking as I bring my mug to my lips again.

Stryder sets his hands on mine, steadying them. I take in a breath and close my eyes. "I always admired him growing up and he trusted me with his secrets—apparently not all of them, though. I knew he engaged in illegal trading and I knew he planned on bringing two young boys into Moon Crossing. My father was so gentle and kind, but I knew he would do anything to protect his family. I don't know what happened that night. It doesn't seem right.

"I'll always love him, but maybe it's time to let him go. It's hard, though, harder than I thought and I feel like a child still clinging to the hope that he had a good heart. He was greedy and I didn't understand that when I was younger, but now I know it destroyed him. I wish I could get some answers but that's impossible so...I don't know, I'm babbling."

"No, it's okay. I can see why you're conflicted, it's a tricky situation when you don't know everything."

I nod. "I wish I could go back and convince him it was too risky to bring in the two boys. Maybe he would have listened to me or my mom, at least. I could have told her, but I didn't."

"Don't blame yourself for what happened, Locklyn, it's not your fault," Stryder says softly.

I lean into him, setting my mug aside on the window sill. "I know. Sometimes it feels like I could have done something. I thought I meant the world to my father and when he hurt me like that..." my voice breaks and tears stream down my cheeks.

Stryder pulls me into him and I wrap my arms around him, crying against his chest. I'm glad my emotional self doesn't scare him off and he's always willing to comfort me. I've been thrown for quite a trip ever since that night.

"If you keep blaming yourself for what happened, you're never going to get over it and it will destroy you. Believe me, I know what it's like," he whispers against my hair and his fingers curl around my blouse.

I hold on to him. "I love you."

"I love you, too."

I tip my head back, gazing into his almond eyes. Then, I draw his chin down and kiss him. He lays me back on the pillows of the window seat, mindful of my leg. My heart beats in my chest and I feel warm and fuzzy.

Stryder's hands glide down my sides and to my hips. His lips fall along my jaw and he says softly, "Will you come with me to Iluro once we get these trackers removed?"

I nearly melt in his arms. "Oh?"

"If you want to go, of course."

I draw back and smooth back his hair from his forehead. "Are there any more secrets you're keeping from me?"

Stryder takes in a breath, his fingers tapping against the pillow I'm lying against. "Well, there's something you don't know about me, Locklyn, something very important—"

"Are you two *finally* getting together?"

Startled, Stryder scrambles off me and I sit up the best I can, banging my elbow on the window sill. A curse slips from my lips and Stryder stands next to me, running his fingers through his hair. His face is red, mine feels like an inferno, and I shoot a glare at Amira, who smirks at us.

"Miri." Stryder clears his throat. "What do you want?"

"Oh, that's cute, trying to change the subject." She sits down on the couch and gestures for Stryder to sit, which he begrudgingly does. Amira's eyebrow lifts. "Did you forget other people are living here? I could hear you macking on each other from my room. So? What's happening?"

"*Nothing*," Stryder and I both quip and glance at each other.

Amira's not buying it, of course, but she shrugs. "Mhm, okay." She turns to Stryder. "Well, my mom called and she needs to talk to you."

He stands, alarm crossing his face. "Is everything okay?"

"She's fine, she needs to tell you something."

"Okay..." he doesn't move for a moment and then wanders over to me, leaning over to kiss my forehead. "We'll talk later, *little fox*."

"Okay," I mumble and watch him head up the stairs to his room.

My gaze travels back to Amira and I'm hit with the sudden feeling that I need to discuss something with her. I don't know what, I can't recall what I had stumbled upon before I fell sick, but I know it was something incredibly important.

Amira's nose crinkles as I continue to stare at her. "What's up with you?"

I tell her, "I have a feeling there's something strange about you and I can't remember what I must have figured out."

She shifts in her seat, uncomfortable, and crosses one leg over the other. "So you're back to suspecting me, huh?"

"I think so."

Amira leans on her elbow, a smile gracing her lips as she seems to relax. "You're one tough cookie to keep a secret from. You seem to know when someone is hiding something."

"Instinct. I know plenty of secrets I shouldn't." I pick up my mug again with my now lukewarm cider. *Besides Stryder's.*

"Care to share any?"

"No, I don't tattle."

"You must have been a dream student in school."

I glance away as Kaer walks through the front door, looking exhausted. I call out, "Everything okay, Kaer?"

He looks over at us and nods. "Yes. Rhyn sent me home to sleep. Clover's doing well, she'll probably give birth in a few hours."

"Did I ever tell you congrats on the kid?" Amira asks and he shakes his head. "Well, congratulations."

"Thank you." He shrugs off his coat and hangs it up. "I'm going up. Could one of you wake me whenever someone from the clinic stops by?"

"I will," Amira volunteers, "since we have Miss Crippled over here."

"Wow, you're so kind."

She stands, winking at me. "Trying my best to be. What do you want for dinner? I'm fixing to whip something up."

"Soup would be preferable, for me at least. I don't know about Bibiana, Stryder, or Domenico."

"They'll eat whatever I cook."

I lie back down as Amira gets to work in the kitchen, playing music from her Mini as she chops, fries, and stirs. The rain continues to come down as night falls and my eyes fall closed not long after. I drift off.

☽ ✧ ☾

Kaer and Clover have decided to stay in Arcane Cove with their baby boy, Calem, while the rest of us head to the Deliverance. Rhyn and Ezra will stay with them in the lodge. The storm let up after two days and we boarded the Hover sent. Orlin comes along with us since he's left Arcane Cove's clinic in expert hands with Rhyn, and he wants to show Bibiana around when we get to Spring Grove. The two of them have become quite close during our time in Arcane Cove and I even catch him slipping an arm around her when we hit rough air.

A strange pairing, but who am I to judge?

The flight to Spring Grove, specifically the Deliverance's underground facility, isn't long and we get there in record time. It makes me tear up a little seeing the destruction of Spring Grove, the ghost of a once-great city. My family traveled to Spring Grove a few times to go to the water park and now, seeing the empty ruins of it is chilling. The once towering slides toppled over and blasted to pieces. Moon Crossing did this and it's horrible. They must be stopped. If the Deliverance is large enough, powerful enough, then I'm sure we can bring the Elite Council to its knees. My only concern would be Blake's well-being but, since he's part of the Deliverance, I'm not worried. He'll be fine.

The Hover lofts down in an expansive meadow with daisies and a lush forest alike on the outskirts of Spring Grove. I stand at a window with my crutches and Stryder is next to me. He's been troubled for a few days now and I don't know why. But I imagine it's because of the tracker, which has been giving him more numbness and pain lately. Within our grasp is the solution, though, and I know I'm feeling much better about it. After this, we can talk and maybe make plans to go to Iluro. I hope by then, my name will be cleared with Moon Crossing.

The ground begins to rumble and Stryder slings his arm around my waist as the grass beneath the Hover shifts and lowers. My eyes widen as we appear in a gigantic Hover hangar and ours lifts off the patch of grass and to an open spot. There are at least hundreds of Hovers, of various shapes and sizes, parked in the hangar. All have the same symbols printed on the side: outlined hands, palm up, in a ring of blue fire. One hand holds the word 'justice', the other 'peace'. The symbol of the Deliverance.

Stryder squeezes my side and smiles as we make our way to the exit. "Welcome to the Aerie Compound, Locklyn."

I nod, still taking it all in and we descend to the floor below. The fluorescent lights are bright above and pilots, mechanics, and the like. They wander about, running diagnostics or sending out Hovers through the lighted tunnel on the far side of the hangar. An alarm sounds as one prepares to take off. I didn't know Spring Grove had so many Hovers. Of course, they were the technological genius of the District, but I thought Moon Crossing had taken all their Hovers and the tech for it. Aeronautical engineers must have escaped to the Aerie Compound before. I always thought everyone died and the Deliverance rose *after* the bombing.

An entourage approaches us as we walk toward the compound itself and Orlin leaps ahead to greet the man with a trimmed mustache and beard, silver hair, and sharp eyes. As we come closer, they embrace and begin speaking in Spanish. He ushers Bibiana forward, who converses with them as well, but the man greets her quickly before moving on to greet Stryder, Amira, and me. He drops into a bow before Stryder and Amira and I hear him say, "Your Highnesses."

My eyebrow lifts in confusion and Stryder stiffens next to me, placing a hand on the man's shoulder as he straightens. "It's great to see you again, Vicente. This is Locklyn Harte." He gestures to me.

Vicente glances me over and nods, looking unimpressed. "Pleased to meet you, Miss Harte." He turns his attention back to Stryder. "There is a skilled physician, who knows how to use an extraction gun, waiting for you in the infirmary, as you requested. However, when we attempted to test it, it wasn't working. The gun needs a chip of sorts to function properly."

Stryder frowns and we walk with the entourage into the compound. He grunts. "Where can we acquire this chip?"

"These guns have only recently been made outside of Moon Crossing. We stole a shipment just for this. But it would probably take another day or two to find where they manufacture chips and steal one."

As we pass through the iron doors and into the pristine halls of the Aerie Compound, something clicks in my head, and I gasp. "Wait, I think I might have one."

Everyone glances at me and I turn to a fellow carrying my bag. He brings it forward and I scramble through my things for the pouch where I keep my pendant and the chip that Blake gave me. I fish it out and hold it in my palm, leaning on one crutch as the other clatters to the ground. Stryder picks it up for me as Vicente examines the chip in my hand. His brow furrows, unbelieving, and he quirks a silver eyebrow at me.

"Where did you get this?"

"Blake Carmichael gave it to me before I left Moon Crossing."

Vicente nods. "Mr. Carmichael is one of our greatest assets in Moon Crossing."

I look at the chip. "He must have known we'd be injected with trackers and that we would need this chip to activate the extraction gun." My heart warms in my chest and I smile.

Stryder grunts again. "Well, what are we waiting for? Let's see if it works."

I snap out of my happy state of mind and he gives me my crutch, taking the chip. We make our way through the winding halls of the compound. It's clean and sterile, with swirled marble floors, light gray walls, and fluorescent lights. Those we pass are dressed in shirts or jackets bearing the symbol of the Deliverance. They look like soldiers, with stoic expressions and an agenda. A rebellion must always be serious, I suppose, especially with tensions rising around the District.

The infirmary doesn't look any different from the Arcane Cove one or any other infirmary I've been in. Stryder sits on one of the beds first and we all gather around as a physician inserts the chip into the gun. It beeps and the trigger glows a soft green, showing it's ready to go. He turns the dial to extraction and sets it against the place where Stryder's tracker was injected. It has become veiny and dark and he closes his eyes. The extraction is very simple and fast. A tiny pill-shaped tracker is pulled from his skin and clatters into a secure compartment on the gun. He is sent to another physician to make sure no poison was released and then I sit down. I tell the physician I have two trackers I'd like to get removed and he nods, extracting each. It feels uncomfortable, like a pin is being yanked out of my flesh, but I'm glad when each is gone and bandaids are placed on the small wounds.

Vicente's entourage has disappeared with Amira, Bibiana, and Domenico. Orlin and Vicente remain, along with a woman who keeps touching Stryder's shoulder as he's being checked and his head, neck, and shoulder scanned. I limp over on my crutches and she glances at me, cinnamon eyes a little cautious at my approach. I take her in as she takes me in, and I wonder how Stryder comes across all these beautiful women and still ended up with me.

"I'm Alita Sosa," the woman introduces herself. "Orlin's sister."

"I'm Locklyn," I say and glance at the physician. "Is everything okay?"

"Yes," she says and I feel a flood of relief. "My theory is that the tracker was on the verge of releasing its poison so it's a good thing we got it out now." The physician sops up the blood weeping from his wound, places some salve on it, then bandages it. "You might feel a little pain, but the salve will leech anything out of your skin that the tracker could have placed there. Come back later tonight and I'll change the bandage and check it, okay?"

Stryder nods and stands. "Thank you, Nela."

Alita walks next to us as we join up with Orlin and Vicente again. Vicente tells Stryder, "We need to have a conversation."

"Of course."

"Alita, can you show Miss Harte to her room?"

"No," Stryder sets a hand on my shoulder, gazing at me, "she can join us."

"But, Your Highness, it's classified information."

"I trust her."

I say nothing as I follow Vicente and Stryder to a luxurious suite and we sit down at the glass table in the dining area. I glance around, my jaw nearly dropping at the priceless art hanging on the walls and wonderfully crafted sculptures. These must have cost a fortune, which makes me wonder just who

Vicente is. He must have been one of the richlings in Spring Grove, but for what?

Stryder sighs and rubs his forehead as he leans his elbows on the table. "Before we talk, I need to clear the air with you, Locklyn."

I perk up and wait patiently, folding my hands in my lap. "About...what everyone's calling you?"

"Yes." He gazes at me once more, almond eyes as serious as the grave. "I'm a prince of Mevania. Orb—Orb is my brother. My parents were who your father killed."

Now, my jaw really drops and my eyes widen before the tears rush in. I quickly cover my face, my body trembling with my sobs. Stryder doesn't reach out to comfort me and he shouldn't. My father's mistake really is coming full circle.

He continues, "Orb and I were the boys he was supposed to bring in but I didn't go to the trade-off. There's an age-old cult in Mevania called the Eclipse Society and they have wanted to see the monarchy fall for years now, claiming the Monroe family are not the rightful heirs to the throne. They're led by someone called the Diviner, whose identity is still unknown. My parents decided it was best to hide us in the District, specifically Moon Crossing, where we would be the safest. But I was convinced the District was a horrible place and I didn't want to leave Iluro. Unfortunately, my absence ultimately killed my parents and it was devastating. Orb remained in Moon Crossing, as you know, but changed his last name and hid his accent.

"I stayed in Iluro for a few years after, and then came to the District. I learned of the Deliverance and began funding it, so we could take Moon Crossing down. I also tried to convince Orb to come home, since he's the first-born and rightful heir to the throne of Mevania, but he refused. So I stayed here for a bit, learning about the District, making connections, and helping in the best way I could."

I look up at Stryder, blinking as the tears streak my cheeks. "I—I don't know what—why?"

"I know it's a lot but you need to know."

"If you knew all this, why didn't you tell me in the beginning?" I ask, my voice breaking.

His expression shadows over and he spreads his hands flat on the table. "I didn't know if I could trust you with my true identity yet. I needed to get you out of Moon Crossing and here. The Deliverance can't have any contact with Blake in case the Council finds out, so we need your knowledge. He's not necessarily willing to give up Council information either so he doesn't commit treason, but he was all for getting you out of Moon Crossing and helped convince the Council to send you to Silverwater."

My heart is shattering in my chest as I look at him, cold and unfeeling. How could he betray me like this? I thought love and trust went hand-in-hand and my stomach twists as panic flares in my chest. What if he doesn't even love me?

Quietly, I croak out, "I feel like I don't even know you anymore, Stryder."

Stryder's jaw clenches and he looks away, silent.

Vicente clears his throat. "Shall we discuss our next topic, then?"

"Yes," Stryder murmurs and straightens, focusing his gaze on Vicente. "I've heard that my brother has stopped sending funds to the Deliverance and that he plans on declaring war with the District."

Both mine and Vicente's eyebrows rise in surprise and he asks, "War? For what purpose?"

"Orb wants to get rid of the District and the people here. I know Mevania has been at peace with the District since my aunt reigned and this isn't much land to take over. It'd be silly to declare war on such a small portion of the country."

"And yet he does. No matter what, there's no way that the District can withstand the forces of Mevania. We would all be obliterated."

Chills race down my spine at Vicente's tone and I ask, a little warily, "What about you, Stryder? Won't he care that you're here? Or Amira? Or anyone else he cares for?"

Stryder shakes his head. "Orb doesn't care about me. He despises me. As for Amira and others, I imagine he has a plan to get them out of the District before he attacks."

"So what are we going to do?"

He glances at each of us. "We'll fight back, of course, join forces with the other cities and make sure the District remains standing."

Vicente grunts. "Moon Crossing would never team up with the likes of the other cities and *especially* not the Deliverance. But they have the best military force and we would need them."

"Oh, they'll join once I explain their impending doom. I still have black-mail on each of the Councilors and if they don't want that information to get out, they ought to have their military pick up arms and fight."

I tuck my hands in my lap and zone out as Stryder and Vicente talk a bit more. I'm still in shock from what Stryder revealed to me and I can't be completely sure that I trust him. Like Amira, he's become suspicious and how do I know, or any of us know, that he isn't in cahoots with his brother? Why does the District even matter to him if he can rule the entire country? What do we mean to him? I take him in, knowing he's hidden a lot from me, and I can't be sure he's the fun-loving, goofy guy I fell in love with.

Maybe it was an act after all.

A SOUL SPLINTERED

AFTER STRYDER GETS his second check-up of the day and we've fed ourselves, we're shown to our rooms. They are conveniently next to each other and I expect him to say goodnight fairly quickly, but he helps me into my room and closes the door behind him. I sit on the little chaise by the window, aching for a bath. He leans on the door, arms crossed, mind elsewhere. I wait patiently.

Finally, he states in his soft timbre. "I should have told you sooner. About everything."

"So why didn't you?"

"I thought you would see me differently. I know my life isn't normal, that I'm a prince, but I wanted *someone* to love me for me."

I blink slowly and fold my hands in my lap. "You said you love me and you don't even tell me who you are. How am I supposed to believe that now?"

"Locklyn—"

"I'm serious, Stryder. Being a prince and the fact that my father—" my hands tremble and tears well in my eyes, "that he took away your parents' lives has to have shaped the man you've become. Not knowing that—I don't know what to think."

He doesn't budge from the door, even as the tears spill and I cover my mouth, trying not to let the sobs escape. I squeeze my eyes shut and turn away from him, curling up on the chaise the best I can.

I babble, "I'm sorry, Stryder—I'm so, *so* sorry for what he did. I could have stopped it—" I hiccup and the tears keep flowing.

"You couldn't have, Locklyn," he tells me, his voice solemn. "I don't know what horrible trick was being played, but I learned my lesson to cherish everything and everyone in life because you don't know when they'll be gone. It could happen in an instant..."

For a long while, we sit there in silence, unable to face or comfort each other. I feel like he should have hated me from the beginning when he first found out my name, but as far as I know, he doesn't. How will this change our relationship, though? Will we go our separate ways and never see each other again? It would break my heart into a million shards, but it would be for the best.

I'm startled when Stryder sits down behind me on the chaise and I curl even more away from him now. He sighs as he recalls, "I remember when my parents sat Orb and me down in our room and told us their plan. It was a few days before we were supposed to leave and I was so upset, I ran away from the palace and into the forest. There's a cottage that's been in my family for ages and it's been uninhabited for a while, but that's where I liked to go to be alone. So I sat there, among the dusty portraits and the gaudy pillows and tapestries, crying. I didn't want to leave Iluro and I hardly knew anything about the District, only that it was far away and much different from my home.

"My parents found me and dragged a reluctant Orb along to comfort me. My dad started a fire in the hearth and my mom fanned out some blankets and wrapped us all in them. I remember leaning my head on her shoulder and she would stroke my hair, singing a song from her homeland that always calmed me down. We didn't talk about the plan anymore or the fact that the Eclipse Society wanted us dead. We recounted memories we had made and it was one of the best nights of my life, sitting in that cottage with my family, warm fire at our feet, and some hard candies Orb had found," he chuckles before continuing.

"The next few days, I asked around the palace about the District and I received mixed responses. What frightened me the most was what my father's advisor told me. He said they would brand me as a servant and toss me into some rich household to work until my hands cracked and bled and I was fatigued. He said that the other children would look down on me because I didn't speak the language well. I was going to be an outcast, bullied, never accepted, and worst of all, they could still hand me over to the Diviner anyway, regardless of my parents' wishes. Amante made it sound like hell and I believed him. So I stayed behind. I locked myself in my closet and refused to go. Reluctantly, my parents left me in Iluro and took Orb...you know how that went."

"Why don't you hate me?" I whisper, lifting my head from my arms and propping my chin up.

"I wanted to, believe me, but when I met you, I couldn't. You're not a terrible person, Locklyn. You don't have an ounce of evil in you and I've known that from the beginning."

I sit up and turn to him, unable to meet his gaze, however, and I wipe away my stray tears. "I don't understand how you could even let yourself associate with me. I despised the Superiors for taking my father away with no explanation. Yet, I still worked for them but...deep down, I hoped they would fall one day."

"We all have feelings, Locklyn, and some people feel differently than others. I wasn't raised to hate those that hurt me—my mother made sure of that—she was always gentle and kind, stern when she needed to be. My father kept his contempt on the down low and I know he wasn't a perfect man either. He did what he had to do for our empire and his family. I don't blame you for anything that happened. I blame myself and whatever evil forces did the damage."

"I'm sorry—"

He tilts my face up to his. "Stop saying you're sorry. It won't fix anything. It doesn't change my feelings for you, Locklyn. *You. Are. Not. To. Blame.*"

A beat passes before Stryder leans away and stands, turning his back to me as his shoulders tremble. I reach for his coat and tug, urging him to sit down again. He does, burying his face in his hands, and I run my fingers along his back, pressing gently. My brow knits as I close my eyes. His soul has splintered.

☽ ✧ ☾

I wake to find that Stryder is gone and he tucked a blanket around me. I feel a little cold and detached from reality as I lie there and stare across the room. Can I live with the knowledge of my father's crimes and still face Stryder daily? Still kiss him, touch him, hug him, laugh, and enjoy life with him? His parents died at my father's hand and it seems cruel that it has brought us together. We are products of tragedy. Spinning two tales, interwoven by fate. He even kept a calm demeanor when I was sad and babbling about my love for my father. How could I rub my admiration in his face?

Numbly, I stand with the help of my crutches and make my way into the bathroom. I flick on the tub's spout and adjust the temperature as warm water fills the porcelain base. I lean on the wall alongside my crutches as I strip out of my clothes and hop to the tub before easing myself in. It's painful, as I have to use my still healing leg. But with a sense of relief, I sink into the water, shut off the spout, and relax. A bar of soap wrapped in plastic packaging awaits me, but I wait a few minutes before scrubbing myself clean.

In my head, I map out my next steps. I'm free of both of my trackers and I assume they've been activated and destroyed themselves so the Council will think Stryder and I are dead. I have a clean slate before me and I can be whoever I want. I don't know if I'll stay in the District for long, but I have to visit Jesse, Mom, Oisin, and Nadia in Bountiful Hill before I leave. Then I'll make a new life for myself and leave this one behind. Leave Stryder, too. I can't bear to be a reminder of his pain and suffering for so many years. I'll live a quiet life, maybe find someone to marry, and have nothing to do with conspiracies or rebellions or murder ever again.

TO LIVE OR TO DIE

ELECTRA, MALINI, AND Vanne had been hot on Viktor Marsh's trail when he completely disappeared one day. Electra tried to ask around the Council, but they said that he had resigned from the Elite Council. Even Blake Carmichael wasn't much help.

A few days later, with no luck in discovering Viktor's whereabouts, Electra received a letter in the mail. The envelope was of shiny, fancy material and the seal on the back was that of the Mevanian Empire. Electra knew little about Mevania, but she had taken a few cases from immigrants trying to gain citizenship in the District. Her boyfriend, Drew, was sitting next to her as Electra cracked the seal and slipped the letter out. She recognized the delicate handwriting of Glory and read quickly. Everyone in Moon Crossing now knew that Orb Cristol was actually Orb Monroe—heir to the throne of Mevania—and that Glory was now his wife. Electra was sad to have missed the wedding, but it had already happened by the time she found out about it.

Electra's eyebrow lifted as she read. Glory was asking her to come and visit Iluro, the capital of Mevania, and where the palace was located. She wrote that Electra could bring one guest along and that Glory really wanted to see her again. Electra knew this was Glory's handwriting, but it seemed strange. She was an empress now. Why did she want to invite her old friend to the palace? Glory finished the letter by saying that she had a few things to tell Electra and she could only tell in person. Strange. Glory used to tell her everything.

"What's that?" Drew asked.

Electra handed it to him. "From Glory."

He read the letter and tipped his head in curiosity. "What do you think she has to tell you?"

"I don't know, but I hope it's not something insane. We still have Locklyn's case and that's my top priority right now."

"Well, she didn't say how long we have to stay, so let's go, clear your head a little. Maybe Vanne and Malini will have better luck while we're gone."

She didn't like to pause in the middle of a case, but this one was a headache. No one wanted to talk because no one wanted to incur the wrath of Viktor and whoever else he conspired with. She wasn't getting anywhere and a break seemed well-deserved. She had never been outside the District before and had been told Mevania was beautiful and lush with life.

"Okay, we'll go, but not for long," she told him and stood, folding the letter back up and setting it on the coffee table.

Drew pushed to his feet as well and caught Electra's hand before she headed to her room. She looked at him, his hazel eyes concerned. "Are you going to relax or will you continue to obsess over this case?"

She drew her hand away. "I'll relax, I promise."

He wouldn't let her go that easily though and trailed after her to the bedroom. "My sunflower, light of my heart, you have hardly relaxed a day in your life."

Electra dragged a suitcase out from under her bed, popped it open, and started tossing clothes in. "Drew, you've known me professionally for three years. Personally for one. You know I love shopping and going to the salon and sweating in a sauna. I am perfectly capable of relaxing."

"But you were working on cases that weren't as big as this one or as personal." He leaned on the door frame with his arms crossed. "Just a couple of days, that's it, no legal stuff."

She let out a sigh and glanced at him. "Fine, now help me pack."

☽ ✧ ☾

Since Glory didn't give them a day to come, they left the next morning in Drew's truck with an all-day road trip ahead of them. They were permitted to leave the barrier of Moon Crossing when the watch guards realized the invitation was from Mevania. They drove through the Blooming Woods, eerie with its constant mist and skeletal state. The trees could have woken like monsters in the night and pierced the cab of the truck. Drew drove over the speed limit until they reached Bountiful Hill. The road to Mevania wound around the city, but Electra saw they were setting up for a festival. Banners flapped in the autumn breeze from businesses and workers flooded the streets with barrels and carts heavy with the harvest.

Electra settled her hand on his leg and leaned her head on his shoulder as they left the District behind. It was pretty desolate. Besides the occasional villages and aspiring cities they passed, tucked behind soaring hills of swaying grass. There was forest everywhere, the massive trunks the size of two or three lanes, and colorful leaves bursting from the branches. There were plenty of lakes and ponds with glistening clear water and canals snaked in and around the villages. Olive tree groves could be spotted miles from the road, the plants neatly lined and full, almost ready to harvest. It was certainly different from city life, but Electra found comfort in the Mevania's serenity.

"Are we staying in the palace?" Drew asked, wrapping his free arm around her shoulders.

"I imagine so. I'm sure there are plenty of spare rooms in the palace."

"Do you want to stay in a room with me?"

A smile crept onto her lips and she glanced up at him. "Of course."

He gave her a look and a smile that warmed her belly with butterflies.

Sometimes, it still felt unreal that she was dating Drew Holloway. He was a hot-shot lawyer in Moon Crossing who she had always kept her eye on. He wasn't bad to look at, with burgundy waves and freckles, but he had also been her biggest competition. One night, they met properly at Arrow's Bar and Grill downtown. Electra drank, he drank, and they wanted to take each other home but both passed out before the debate could be won. When Electra saw him hanging around her apartment complex the next day, she didn't know what to think. But Drew asked her out properly and their love began from there.

Their chemistry was electric, more electric than she'd ever felt with anyone else. Drew was a sweet guy and he would do anything for her. Electra felt secure with him and he admired her intellect first, before her beauty, which she had craved for so long. For someone to see beyond the pretty face.

"I love you," she whispered as she kissed his cheek.

"I love you with everything that I am," he declared softly and leaned his head on hers. "Electra, I know it's cliche, but you've made me the happiest man alive. I never thought I could be with someone like you. You're wonderful."

Electra ran her hand along the nape of his neck, giddy with love for him. Drew hadn't been a fan of the fame that came with his career and though they were both successful lawyers now, Electra helped quell his anxieties. He wanted to live a quiet life, away from the city, and spend time with the family he hoped to create one day. Electra wanted that, too, and she wouldn't mind giving up her career to work on a farm with him. Drew was her everything and she wanted nothing more than to be with him.

☽ ✧ ☾

Iluro was beautiful. The palace sat on a hill surrounded by a grove of trees. It was breathtaking. They entered the eastern gate with the letter Glory had sent and drove down into the valley where Iluro's residents lived. As they passed, Electra was glad to see children running around, smiles lighting their faces and eyes, and content adults chatting with one another. There didn't seem to be any unrest or prejudice here. Mevanians were happy and at peace. Nothing like the District, especially Moon Crossing. There was always something to worry about.

The palace glittered in the waning light. The golden roof was slanted, the panels perfectly cut into thin pieces and placed. Terraces of gardens accented the palace's columns of swirling marble. The gardens were beautiful, well-kept, and sported many species of flowers and plants. A small, marbled obelisk stood in the middle of one and Electra wondered what was etched on the front. As they drove up to the palace and passed the watchtowers, her gaze shifted elsewhere. The palace itself was open to the air and the colonnade wrapped all the way around. A canal wound around three sides of the palace, leaving the front open, and they rolled into the courtyard. A gardener glanced up and smiled, warm and welcoming. Electra felt content.

A man with graying blonde hair and sharp cheekbones wandered down the palace steps a minute later as they departed from the truck. He wore a white tunic and brown trousers. A sleeveless cloak clung to his slight shoulders and nearly touched the ground. Sandals were strapped to his feet, and he was holding a Mini in one hand.

He lifted the Mini and tapped away, glancing at them. "Are you Miss Electra Harte?"

"Yes, and Glory said I could bring a guest, too," Electra said as Drew slipped his fingers through hers.

"Your name, sir?"

"Drew Holloway."

The man tapped away and then tucked his Mini against his side again. "My name is Arlo Amante, royal advisor to Emperor Orb."

"It's lovely to meet you."

He nodded and turned on his heel. "Follow me."

"What about our bags?" Drew asked as Electra tugged him along.

The man responded by whistling at three lingering servants and he spoke to them in Italian. The boys trailed down to the truck and opened it, taking their bags out. Drew didn't like people getting in his truck, so when they were done, he locked it. Electra rolled her eyes as he pat his keys in his pocket and smiled at her. She loved teasing him that his truck was his other girlfriend. He agreed wholeheartedly.

"How is Glory?" Electra asked, just to fill the silence and the awkward slap of their shoes on the marble as they walked down the lavish corridors of the palace.

There were tapestries hung on the walls and sunbursts etched in gold into the marble floor. The ceilings soared and vaulted like a cathedral, mural and all. It was beautiful and pristine, and she was kind of jealous that Glory lived here. A light breeze even passed through the corridor and ruffled her hair on her shoulders.

"Her Majesty is doing well," Arlo stated simply.

"Good."

They turned down another corridor and came to a solar, where Glory sat on a chaise. Music trilled from her Mini and she was eating tiny cakes with a glass of lemonade. Orb was working at a desk, his brow lined as he thought. Electra felt a little defensive seeing the former Councilor cozy in his palace, far out of Moon Crossing's jurisdiction. She was sure he had something to do with framing Locklyn since Viktor was involved, but she had yet to find any evidence connecting him to such a crime.

Glory's doe-like eyes widened when she saw them and she stood, beaming from head to toe. Electra ignored Orb and grinned, hugging Glory.

"I'm so glad to see you."

"I'm so glad to see you, too!" Glory was bubblier than usual and Electra had to give her a once-over.

"So what did you want to tell me?"

"First, introduce me to you know who." Glory's gaze strayed to Drew.

Electra turned to him and took his arm. "As you know, this is Drew Holloway, my boyfriend."

"I'm glad to meet you in person, Drew." She reached out and shook his hand. "I always heard about you through Electra's complaints."

Drew chuckled. "Is that so?"

"I complained *a lot.*"

Glory directed them over to the chaise, but Drew went over to Orb's desk and they chatted. Electra took Glory's smooth hands in hers and lifted an eyebrow at her best friend. "So?"

Glory giggled, a strange sound from her, and told her, "I'm pregnant, Electra."

No wonder she was glowing.

Electra hugged her again. "Congratulations! That's so exciting!"

"Thanks, I feel so airy, you know? This baby has made me happy." Glory leaned back and tucked her legs beneath her.

Electra kept her voice low as she asked, "Has Orb been making you happy?"

"Of course. He makes me very happy and I'm glad to be here. You would never think that two orphans could make it this far."

"Well, he was born into it so it is believable."

Glory sighed. "Me then. I made it this far."

She shrugged. "You fell in love with the right man."

Her friend's expression grew solemn and she glanced at her husband before scooting a little closer to Electra. "There's something else I need to tell you later. Without the boys around."

This made her stomach turn and she nodded. "For now, tell me what you've been up to as the Empress of Mevania?"

Glory dove into everything that had happened and Electra listened intently. At the back of her mind, though, she still wondered about Orb.

☽ ✧ ☾

That evening, Drew and Electra were shown to a dressing room. They had been invited to dine with Orb and Glory, but they needed proper clothes. A couple of servants shuffled in with neatly folded outfits in their arms and stripped them down. Electra blushed as she and Drew shared a glance. The servants didn't seem to care about modesty, but she did.

They dressed Electra in a satin pastel gown with a tight bodice and off-the-shoulder sleeves. Pink wasn't her favorite color, but she didn't want to complain. Glory and Orb were showing their hospitality so she had to take it in stride. Drew wore a finely tailored suit, dark gray with a matching pastel pink bow tie and shoes that could shine for days. He looked sharp. His hair was combed and gelled. Electra enjoyed seeing Drew dressed up, even though he always dressed up for work. Even so, he knew how to work a suit.

When they were deemed presentable enough, Electra took Drew's outstretched arm. They made their way down the corridors and to the dining hall. They strolled into the empty room and were seated. The lavish table was bare, but Electra admired the craftsmanship that had been put into its construction. There were floral details engraved along the edges, with the matching chairs, and the feet of the table looked like lion paws. Drew sat across from her and they shared a glance, trying not to laugh at the delicate nature of the dining hall. It was elaborately decorated and furnished.

All the air left Electra's lungs when the next guest entered. He slinked in like a snake, jet-black hair slicked back into a knot at the base of his neck. He was dressed in a suit as well, which wasn't unusual, but Electra didn't like to see him here all the same. Even Drew was on edge as Viktor Marsh took a seat next to him and she stared at him, her blood boiling. Electra was about to open her mouth and say something before Glory and Orb breezed in, well-dressed and happy as they took their seats. Glory sat on Orb's left, while Viktor was on his right. Electra didn't like that placement.

Viktor cleared his throat as they were served the first course and he had a snake-like smile on his face. "I'm glad I don't have to dine with just you two now."

Orb snorted, but Glory retorted, "Believe me, we're glad, too."

Viktor's gaze traveled to Electra, though, and lingered on the neckline of her dress. "I'm not surprised to see you here, Electra, but I am glad you came."

"I only came for Glory." She stated and reached out for her friend's hand, squeezing it gently.

"Speaking of which, we will definitely need to schedule some time away from all these men."

"Do you hate me that much, Your Majesty?" Viktor asked, batting his eyes at her.

She only pursed her lips. "Hate is a strong word. I don't hate anyone."

He turned to Drew and held his hand out. "Mr. Drew Holloway. Now, I'm surprised to see you here. What brings you to Iluro?"

"I'm Electra's guest," he said as he reached out and begrudgingly shook Viktor's hand.

"Really? Well, that's interesting. Two hot-shot lawyers on a trip outside of the District? Must be something more no one's telling me."

"They're dating." Orb rolled his eyes, apparently tired of Viktor's games already. "I'd much prefer to talk about the reason I've brought you here and what you will do for me."

Electra shifted in her seat, uncomfortable by the way Orb's tone sounded too serious and a hint deadly. He looked at each of them with those pretty blue eyes and continued. "I need allies. Powerful allies from the District, specifically. Electra, I've known you as long as I've known Glory and though you are cousins with that wench Locklyn, I'm willing to overlook that."

She had a troublesome time keeping her cool and asked through her teeth, "What do you need allies for?"

"A war."

"A—a war?" Drew sputtered, fear shining in his expression.

Orb nodded. "Yes, I plan to wage war against the District."

"Why?"

"I'm tired of the District. Now that I rule Mevania, I don't want to keep allowing them to think they're free from my judgment. This land belongs to my family, the District was created out of dissension years and years ago, and I want unity again."

Electra spoke up, "If you wage war on the District, won't people die?"

"That's what happens in war, Electra," he flatlined, an annoying curl to his lip. "But there's another thing I discovered. The District has been in cahoots with the Eclipse Society. They have been operating out of an underground black market in Moon Crossing."

"What's that? The Eclipse Society?" Viktor asked.

"The original enemies of Mevania and, specifically, the crown. The Eclipse Society is a cult that broke from Mevanian allegiance generations ago and has been a growing weed since. Our army has yet to find its central headquarters. They must have been moving around the country for years."

"What were you doing in a black market?" Glory asked, her eyebrow quirked.

Orb's expression softened when he looked at his wife. "My brother was undercover as a private investigator and he stumbled upon the Moonless Market. I did some investigating myself and found out the market owner was involved with the Society."

"You could have taken the Moonless Market out as a Councilor," Electra said, still puzzled at where this was all going.

"Yes, but the District wouldn't have the might to fight against retaliation from the Society. Besides, the silly resistance in Spring Grove, the Deliverance, probably would have joined forces with the Diviner. I have much more power here and I can wipe out all resistance that faces me in this land."

Viktor's laugh started low at first and then turned into an outrageous howl. Everyone stared at him and Orb's hand gripped his spoon like it was a dagger, ready to slash Viktor's vocal cords. But when he calmed, he simply said, "You're a genius, Orb."

The Emperor's grip eased and an autocratic smirk curled his lips. "Of course I am."

Glory set her hand on Orb's arm. "Why are you telling Electra and Drew? What can they do?"

Orb nodded. "You two are lawyers. As an Emperor, I am within my jurisdiction and therefore, the District cannot touch me. But I have allies and they will need your help."

Electra swallowed. She didn't like where this was going. "Who?"

"You'll find out. I plan to declare war once I and my army are prepared."

"What do we get out of this?" Drew inquired. He looked like he might be sick.

Orb's gaze was dark and his prideful demeanor washed away as he told them, "You get to live."

☽ ✧ ☾

Electra and Drew felt like they were trapped when they convened in their room after dinner. They sat on the bed, swathed in silken nightclothes, and kept their voices low as they discussed what they'd stumbled upon. Orb was going to declare war, the District would be destroyed, and no one would see it coming.

"We can't join him, he's mad!" Electra whispered harshly, eyes wide with fright.

"I know, I know. But what will he do to us if we don't join him, Electra? I want to live and I especially want *you* to live," Drew replied softly and he reached for her hand, caressing her palm.

Electra wanted to say Orb was bluffing, but when he told them his plans, she knew he was telling nothing but the truth. She sighed. "I want us to live and I want the District to live on as well. Orb will destroy everything, he doesn't care. So, I think we should get out of here as soon as possible."

"I agree. What are we going to do when we return to Moon Crossing?"

"Tell the Elite Council what he's planning. He wasn't dumb enough to give us a list of his associates, but maybe I can scourge that up from Glory. *Blazes,* Glory! I can't believe she married this man *and* she's having his child!"

"It didn't seem like she knew this before and Orb would do nothing to her."

Electra nodded. "Maybe so. He won't hesitate to hurt everyone else, though. We *need* to tell the Council regardless, Drew, so the District can at least prepare for some level of attack."

"Orb would kill us if he found out and would probably attack sooner," he lamented, shadows of doubt crossing his expression. "I don't know that we can save everyone *and* save ourselves at the same time."

She straightened and with no tremor to her voice, told him, "Then we sacrifice ourselves for millions of others. We're only two people, Drew, and I'm willing—"

"*No*," he cut her off and shook his head, "*no*, Electra, I'm not willing to—"

"But we have no choice!"

Drew leaned closer so their faces were inches apart. She had never seen such a storm rage in his hazel eyes. "If we tell the Council, Orb will know. He'll have us hunted until we're found and killed. I always wanted something more than being a lawyer in a big city." His voice broke and the hair rose on her arms. "I want a life with you, Electra Harte. I want *everything* with you and if we can't even have that then—no, we will. We're getting out of here, out of Mevania, for good. We may have to change our names or dye our hair but we are *not* getting involved in this war."

She remained silent, feeling chastised and conflicted. Drew sat back and turned away, running his fingers through his hair. Electra reached for his shoulder and then stopped, dropping her hand to the bed. She wanted a life with him, too, but it still felt wrong to not warn Moon Crossing. Then an idea came to her and she wrapped herself around his back, pressing a kiss to his cheek.

"I have an idea, love, that doesn't involve us going back to Moon Crossing."

Drew didn't look at her, but he perked up a little. "I'm listening."

"We can send an encrypted message to Vanne and Malini. They can inform the Council, both about the war and about Marsh hiding away here. The Council can order him back to the city and Orb wouldn't be able to do anything about it. Marsh is still a citizen of Moon Crossing. We've gathered enough evidence against him to bring him to trial and I'm sure we can get *someone* to crack. But we won't have to go back."

"Electra, if Orb finds out it was Vanne and Malini who tattled, then he'll kill them. You're putting their lives at risk."

"Vanne already plans to disappear from Moon Crossing soon and Malini will certainly do the same. The Deliverance will protect them and I'm sure they won't miss life in Moon Crossing."

"What if they're still caught?"

Electra let out a frustrated sigh and moved back, laying her head against his back. "I don't know, Drew. It was just an idea. Vanne and Malini will have to be smart about it. I'll detail how important it is that they get out before havoc is raised."

He said nothing for a long moment. She trailed her fingers down his spine and around his waist. Drew took in a sharp breath and turned in her arms. Electra gazed at him and he brushed her hair behind her ears. "So what do we do?"

"I think we should play along, for now, snoop around the palace for any plans or evidence, and then leave Iluro. I'm sure we could stow away on a ship at Hollow Key Harbor."

"My sunflower, Hollow Key Harbor is the District's largest port. They will search those ships first."

"Then we should learn what other harbors there are in Mevania. But, that's the plan I've got so far."

"We'll work on it," he promised and kissed her forehead.

Electra closed her eyes, feeling anxious about the situation. If it worked, they would leave everything and everyone they'd ever known behind. It twisted her heart to think about it. If Electra and Drew wanted to live—together and unharmed—they would live.

Viktor didn't like what he was hearing from the listening device he had placed in Electra's room before they had arrived in Iluro. He didn't know she was still irked about her cousin and he especially didn't like that they were on to him. If they got a message back to Vanne or Malini, he and Orb would be done for. Orb's jurisdiction and role as emperor couldn't protect him from committing treason in a city when he was a citizen. And without

Orb's protection, they would execute Viktor as well. So he found Orb alone in his study and relayed to him what he had heard.

"So?" Viktor asked once he finished.

Orb was pacing by the window. His expression was thoughtful, but his soul was vacant—as usual. He always had an eerie silence about him that used to freak Viktor out, but it was useful when they were committing murder and treason. Orb was stealthy, intelligent, and wicked. Losing his parents had surfaced something sinister lurking deep inside him. Orb didn't care what he did. It was all in the name of vengeance, for the sake of his parents and their untimely murder. Viktor admired Orb's thirst for blood and his lack of remorse. He had always felt the same, but he enjoyed causing trouble for fun. It energized him, fed him, and even murder was thrilling. Though Viktor preferred a hands-off murder. Bloodstains in his clothes were the *worst* to clean out.

"For now, we'll do nothing."

Viktor blinked. "What?"

Orb turned to him, blue eyes calculating. "Let them send a message to the Elite Council."

"Doesn't that defeat the purpose of everything? Like swooping in when they least expect it?"

"Yes, but I knew they would take it back to the Council."

His fists clenched. "Orb, they plan to tell the Council what we *did*. You can't protect yourself when you committed a crime as a citizen."

"I never said that the Council would *receive* the message, Viktor. You should listen. We still have allies in Moon Crossing who will do anything for a hefty reward of credits. I want you to contact Caine and the others and make sure they track the movements of Malini Russo and Vanne Heppin. They may receive the message but our allies will make sure they never deliver it."

Viktor grinned. This is what he admired about Orb, and he shivered just thinking about the blood that would be spilled. "What about Electra and Drew? What are we going to do with them?"

"Let them snoop around if they want, but I'm charging you with monitoring them. When they run, don't let them leave Iluro. I'll send word to the sentries in the watchtowers to make sure they're not let out. Capture them, bring them back here, and I will deal with them myself."

"Won't Glory be mad if you kill her friend?"

"Glory won't know anything. When she finds out Electra and Drew are dead, I'll play it off as an accident."

Orb turned back to the window and dismissed Viktor. They were terrible men; they knew. But with Orb in charge, they could get away with anything.

VEILED AFFECTION

I GET TO know the Deliverance's facility pretty well within a few days and I find little nooks and crannies I can hide in. Right now, I fit snugly in a small nook near the ceiling of the mess hall. It's been my favorite place to be alone with my thoughts and eat without everybody staring at me as I limp around on crutches. Stryder has been busy, but he still takes time to see me in the evenings, or at least make sure I'm still alive during the day. I've yet to tell him I can't be with him anymore. I don't have the heart for it yet.

I've decided not to leave the safety of the Deliverance until I'm healed, and Electra and Vanne have been able to work on my case in Moon Crossing. Bibiana's recording was able to be saved, thankfully. Since then, I've heard little but I assume they're working hour by hour. I'm not worried about it. They'll do everything they can to clear me and bring the actual murderers of the Circle to trial. I don't think a sentence to Silverwater Penitentiary will be in the plans either.

Down below, it grows loud as people fill the mess hall for dinner and gather at tables with their friends. I haven't acquainted myself with anyone else, really, since I've been here. I've spoken to Orlin, his sister, Alita, and then the band I came with, minus Amira. I catch them all down below, besides Amira, sitting together like they're in college, already laughing at whatever Orlin says. Bibiana leans on his arm, glowing with a smile. Stryder sits by Domenico, the other side of him empty where I should be. I don't really feel bad about it. He knows I need my time and my space.

Not far into the meal, my gaze catches on a girl with teal hair wandering around the mess hall, her eyes scraping over everyone. When she finds who she's looking for, she perks up and hurries over. I bristle as she sets her tray next to Stryder's and plops herself right next to him. *Too close for my comfort.* I sit up in my nook and peer down, eyes narrowed. Of course, I can't hear their conversation, but at first, Stryder looks surprised to see her. They fall into their own conversation. She doesn't touch him or fawn over him, but the fact she gets to smile and not have a care in the world when she's talking to him makes me jealous. I wish things were normal, that Stryder and I could have fun and tease each other, but we can't.

We never can again.

At the end of dinner, I kick my tray aside and stand, leaning heavily on my crutches as I do. Stryder and the teal-haired girl are still talking while almost everyone else has cleared out. I stagger down to the mess hall and try to be graceful as I make my way to the table. But Stryder notices my approach and stands to help. The girl turns to me and I get a sense of disgust as pity fills her eyes.

Ugh, I must look like a fallen bird—broken, battered, and in need of help to even live. Pathetic.

"Where have you been?" Stryder asks as he helps me sit and takes a seat next to me, completely forgetting about the teal-haired girl.

"I was elsewhere," I say softly and rub my hand along my leg.

"Did you eat already?"

"Yes."

"Oh," his expression grows distraught as if he really wanted me to eat with him.

I'm about to reach up and pat his shoulder when the teal-haired girl stands abruptly, her hand already in my face as she introduces herself. Her accent is foreign to me. "Sophronia Archer. Hover pilot from Arcane Cove."

I reluctantly shake her hand. "Locklyn Harte."

She rocks on her heels, her head tipping toward Stryder as she tucks her hands in the pockets of her joggers. "He told me about you. I brought over the physician from Wolves Creek. How's your leg?"

"Fine."

Sophronia nods and after an awkward moment of silence, Stryder fills it. "Anyway, Locklyn, what are you doing tonight?"

"Nothing, why?"

"Sophronia was telling me that there's a meteor shower tonight. Several of us are heading to the surface to see it."

I think of my leg for a moment but then I recall the look of pity in Sophronia's eyes and I lift my chin. "Sure, I'll come."

Stryder grins. "Great."

Sophronia shuffles aside, as quiet as a mouse, and someone calls Stryder away to talk to him for a moment. Sophronia glances me over, says nothing, and walks away.

A minute later, Stryder comes back and helps me to my feet. I walk with him as we make our way over to a group in the corridor that will head up to see the celestial show. Of course, Orlin and Bibiana are tucked together by the wall, his fingers grazing her belly as they whisper to each other. I'm surprised Amira's not here and I look around again. She doesn't show. We stuff into several elevators in groups and ride up to the surface.

"Where's Amira?" I ask Stryder quietly, since I'm basically pressed up to him in the elevator's corner.

He tilts his face down to mine and I can see the flecks of gold in his almond eyes. "I don't know, I haven't really seen her all day."

"That's strange."

"Maybe she's been chatting with Vanne all day. Or her mom. Aunt Khione can talk."

I shrug. "Well, it's too bad she's missing out."

"Yeah." His expression softens and he reaches a hand up to touch my hair before dropping it. "I'm glad you're with me, though. I feel like we spend little time together anymore."

The elevator dings and people shuffle out into a weapons warehouse. Stryder and I follow as I say, "We should talk soon."

"Is everything okay?"

"No," I admit.

Stryder stops and turns me toward him, grabbing my shoulders. "Locklyn, talk to me."

I open my mouth to spill everything, but I look at him, so concerned about what's bothering me, and I can't. I shut my mouth and try again, a wobbly smile on my lips. "It's nothing to bother you with right now. Just keep me warm as we watch. That's all I need."

He observes me for a moment longer and sighs before he drops his hands. "All right, but we will talk later, I promise."

I nod and we move outside of the warehouse. My jaw falls slack as I look up at the sky. It's beautiful. Hot, white meteors blaze across the sky like falling stars...or an imminent alien invasion. Stars sprinkled against the canvas of the ether gleam. I've never had the chance to witness a meteor shower before because of the light pollution in Moon Crossing, but I always heard that it was an otherworldly experience. And it is.

We find a patch of grass away from everyone else and Stryder sits first before pulling me down on his lap. I lean back into his chest and he wraps his coat across me before securing me with his arms. I feel like a child watching in awe and I know my brother would have liked to see this. Jesse was always fascinated with space, the above and beyond. He even started a degree in astronomy once he was in college but without enough kids interested in the program, they shut it down. So he turned to marketing, a grounded career choice.

Stryder leans his head on mine and presses light kisses against my hair. He's being a bit more affectionate than usual. Does he suspect what I need to tell him? I have done nothing special for him and occasionally, I've been avoiding him. I don't mean to make it tense and awkward, but I suppose that's how I feel now. I feel none of those impressions from him.

For now, though, I'll take this time with him and get lost in the celestial show above.

☽ ✧ ☾

Though there are clocks and calendars available to stare at, I still lose track of time while we're in the Aerie Compound. Every once in a while, Stryder and I go to the surface for some fresh air. I also began physical therapy with the therapist in the infirmary and trauma therapy with Alita, which both have been going well. I'm reluctant to tell Alita what's been bothering me the most, though. She says when I'm ready to talk about it, she'll be there to listen and help me along. It's nice to have her support and guidance.

The only thing I've heard from Vanne is that Electra and Drew have been in Iluro for the last two weeks, invited by Glory and Orb. He doesn't know when they'll be back. He and Malini stumbled upon some things, though, but wouldn't tell me what they discovered. I don't mind, as long as I'm exonerated soon so the burden can be lifted off my shoulders. I haven't seen Amira and Stryder tells me she's gone back to Iluro, even though she was supposed to meet Vanne at the Aerie Compound. I find it strange but she must long for home.

I sit in the lounge with a book on my lap, wrapped in a cozy, warm blanket. We've had our first snowfall and I've heard winter can be unkind, even when you are underground. It never really snowed in Moon Crossing.

Out of nowhere, Sophronia shows up and sits in the armchair across from me. She has her Mini out and hums as she taps away. I set my book on a side table and wrap my fingers around the mug of steaming wild berry cider I acquired earlier. I lift it to my lips, take a sip, and let the warm liquid roll down my throat and warm my belly. With a soft sigh, I snuggle into my blanket and lean my head on the plush chair, staring at Sophronia.

It takes her a moment to tense and glance up. Then, her lip curls as she asks, "What are you staring at?"

"What are you doing here?"

"Relaxing. Is that a problem?"

"Maybe." I wiggle my socked toes beneath the blanket as the warmth hits them. "So, where are you from?"

"The Amery Nation."

I haven't seen many maps that contain other nations besides Mevania but I nod anyway. "How did you get to Mevania?"

She cuts her eyes at me. "I came as a bondservant. To pay for my voyage, housing, food, and medical care, I worked in Arcane Cove as a performer. But that's never where my true passion lied and I hated it. I much prefer to work with machinery and manipulate it into something better. And thanks to the generosity of Stryder, I paid off my bond and came here."

"What generosity?"

"He paid to pick up the physician from Wolves Creek."

"Oh. Why would you come to Mevania?"

Sophronia shifts, gaze narrowing as her nose twitches. "I was forced to leave my country—banished, if you will."

"What did you do?" I probe further.

"You want to know everything, don't you?"

I shrug. "I mean, you don't have to answer me, of course."

She stares at me a moment and then shakes her head. "I made a mistake and now I can never return to my country."

I remain quiet, intrigued by what she could have done. Sophronia squirms as my gaze bores into her. "I had an affair with the chancellor of Amery. When his wife found out, she was pissed and ordered my banishment. So I was and Mevania was the closest country to sail to."

"Well, I'm not for cheating but banishment seems like a hefty punishment."

"Oh, I was branded as well." She lifts her sleeve and shows a brand of the letter 'A' on her forearm. "But, to tell you the truth, his wife should be branded as well. She's been sleeping with the Tsar of Saunia for who knows how long."

I nod, having no clue who any of these people are, and I say, "Sounds scandalous."

"Very much so." Sophronia rolls her eyes. "Heloise got what she wanted, though, and I guess I got something better. I loved Bastian, but I love mechanics more so she did me a favor."

"And you can always find someone who's not married or already taken," I point out, quirking an eyebrow.

She laughs. "I suppose so. I've always been the woman on the side. I think I'm cursed."

Now a frown creases my mouth. "That seems awful."

Sophronia drops her gaze, rubbing her hands together. "It is sometimes, especially when I'm found out. I had to make a living somehow, though."

I catch what she means and my eyes widen. Here in the District, and as far as I know in Mevania, her previous line of business is strictly forbidden. Even women or men who didn't have jobs didn't have to resort to that profession. There was always someone willing to hire them and welfare programs to help.

"How did you get into mechanics?" I ask, hoping to lighten the mood.

It works and Sophronia's face brightens, diving into her story about her lifelong love of mechanical things, especially Hovers.

THE HUNT

ELECTRA AND DREW had been on the run for the past week and it was *exhausting*. There had been a listening device in her room, which Electra felt stupid for not thinking to check for after Viktor showed his face. She and Drew had been moving back and forth between the villages in Iluro since they were not allowed past the gates by Emperor Orb's order. Viktor was hunting them down, desperate to bring them back to the palace. They had laid low with the addition of ditching their regular clothes and taking up the everyday garb of Iluro's working class. Electra had a modest head wrap to tuck her strawberry blonde hair into and Drew had cut his curls, grown out some stubble. They were currently being hidden by a kind farmer and his wife—the de Palma's—and to stay hidden, they worked on the farm.

Neither Electra nor Drew had ever had to get their hands dirty before so it took some effort to wake up at the crack of dawn and file out of the farmhouse with the other farmhands the de Palma's employed. Electra learned that their younger son, Domenico, was a dear friend of the prince and had become a soldier in the *Speranza Cremisi*, or the Crimson Hope, Mevania's elite military force. Their eldest son, Donte, was to inherit the farm and continue their service to the crown. But thankfully, the de Palma's weren't too keen on Orb's rule. Electra was shocked to find out that Stryder Monroe, the man Locklyn had been seeing, was the prince they were loyal to.

Though they were safe with the de Palma's, Viktor's search grew more desperate and warriors of the *Speranza Cremisi* were sent to lock down each village, force everyone out of their homes, and find Electra and Drew. The de Palma's weren't protected then and when Electra and Drew were forced out onto the farm with the other farmhands, Viktor was there pacing with rage boiling in his veins. He barked orders at the warriors like he was their commander and they listened, not fearing him, but the wrath of their Emperor if they didn't obey.

They brought each farmhand to their knees and Viktor approached with a lantern to see their faces against the moonless night. Electra's heart pounded as Drew, a few people away, was brought to his knees and ripped his cap off. He blinked against the lantern light and scowled. Viktor grinned. "Found you, Holloway."

He whistled at two warriors and they dragged Drew out of the lineup, holding fast to him as they locked shackles around his wrists and ankles. With Viktor's overbearing confidence, he continued his search until he came to Electra. She clout him across the jaw before he could order her arrest and scrambled back up on the porch, reaching for a handgun that sat on the swing. She swung around and pointed it right at Viktor's chest as he pounced up the stairs toward her.

"You b—" he started but Electra pulled the trigger without a second thought.

He dove, but it tore through his shoulder—spewing blood and fleshy bits—and he let out a howl of expletives. Electra cocked the gun, but Viktor was faster, somehow, and snatched it away from her, tossing it off the porch. She pressed back against the house and Viktor's hand clamped around her throat, his thumb digging into her flesh. Electra clawed at his hand, gasping for air. His dark eyes were wide and manic, fighting through the pain of his wound. Drew shouted and thrashed against the warriors holding him.

A woman dressed in a crisp crimson uniform pulled Viktor off, her brow lined. "Emperor Orb wants the fugitives alive!"

Viktor glared at Electra and a low growl emitted from his throat. He stood and clutched his shoulder, blood spilling through his fingers. "Fine, but I want to kill her myself."

The woman didn't acknowledge his lust for blood and instead helped Electra to her feet, eyes disconsolate as she shackled her wrists and ankles. Viktor turned and marched down the steps of the farmhouse. The de Palma's were standing to the side, holding each other as they stared at what had just occurred on their lovely little farm. Electra had a feeling that Viktor wouldn't let them go unpunished, but he breezed past them and picked up the lantern. He strode out to the fields and the warriors followed, with Drew and Electra in tow. There was a Hover parked in the meadow, ready to bring them back to the palace.

About halfway through the fields, Viktor tossed the lantern to the ground and it shattered. The fire immediately caught on the crops nearby. Electra could hear the de Palma's shriek as the flames quickly raged over their crops. Mr. de Palma shouted at his farmhands and the warriors quietly walked by. Her stomach roiled with spite as she watched Viktor merrily walk away from the fire and once they were at the Hover, he had a smile on his face as he ushered them up the ramp.

"You'll pay for this soon, Electra darling," he quipped, gesturing to his shoulder.

She shrugged.

Viktor growled again and the woman hurried her up the ramp. Electra cast Drew a look as they were brought to a white-walled room and surrounded by warriors. They sat on a cushioned bench next to each other and he took her hand, their shackles clinked together. The woman who had rescued her shut the door and the Hover buzzed as it came to life. She pulled up a chair in front of Drew and Electra and sat, keeping her voice low.

"I'm Admiral Luminosa Mezzanotte, leader of Mevania's Navy and member of the Iluro Senate. Emperor Orb didn't debrief us on why he wanted you captured, but I can't imagine that it's because he wants to make amends." She removed her cap and shook out her honey-brown hair, which was cut a little past her ears. "I don't like the direction Mevania has been heading in, so I must know why Emperor Orb didn't want you to leave Iluro."

Electra and Drew shared a glance. Neither of them knew whether they could trust her, but she seemed to be just and civil, rather than barbaric and whiny like Viktor. So Electra told her, "We found ledgers of Emperor Orb's expenses made in the District when he lived there. Some of those transactions were marked in code, but upon deciphering them, we found they were illegal and made by both the emperor and his right hand, Viktor Marsh. Drew and I are lawyers back home and they framed my cousin for the murder of our leaders. We've been working since, with a confession leading to Viktor being heavily involved, to prove that he and Emperor Orb were behind it and we finally got our evidence. We sent a message to our associates and planned to flee from Mevania. Emperor Orb doesn't want us alive to bring his truth to light."

Admiral Mezzanotte nodded slowly. "I see. What is your cousin's name?"

"Locklyn Harte..."

Her eyes narrowed. "Daughter of the man who killed Emperor Keyon and Empress Aaralyn fourteen years ago, correct?"

Electra's eyebrows rose. That didn't sound right. All she remembered was that he was executed for illegal trading outside the barrier, treasonous in Moon Crossing. Drew spoke up. "What are you talking about?"

The admiral stood. "I don't know what's been happening in the District, but Emperor Orb has brought that infection to Mevania and I won't see this dear country fall into the likes of the District's twisted ways. I hope you two have some entity to pray to, Emperor Orb will not be kind."

She swept her cloak as she turned away and left. Electra and Drew blinked. The Hover lifted off and lofted down again when they arrived at the palace. They were escorted back inside and to one of Orb's studies, where Electra had snooped and found the ledgers. Orb was seated at his desk now and he steepled his fingers as they entered. Viktor pranced over to his side and Orb's gaze strayed to the bullet wound in his shoulder.

"Who shot you?" he asked, voice unnervingly calm.

"Electra," Viktor sneered and flipped her off.

She rolled her eyes and that seemed to annoy him even more. Orb stood and moved out from behind the desk, one hand suspiciously tucked behind his back. Drew pulled on his restraints as Orb tipped Electra's chin up with one slender finger.

"I knew I couldn't trust you, Electra, but Glory wanted to bring you here, anyway. A weakness, I'd say. She has to let go of the District and everyone in it." He dropped his finger and gripped her jaw, tilting her head to the side. "Who tried to choke you?"

"I did after she shot me," Viktor confessed.

Orb glared at him. "You idiot." He moved over to Drew and Electra saw what was in his hand, a dagger that gleamed in the light of the lanterns, the edge sharp and the handle encrusted in gold and crimson whorls. Her pulse quickened as he shifted the dagger, holding it so that if he slashed at Drew's neck, it would make a perfect cut, deep enough to kill him in an instant.

Electra screamed, "GLORY! GLORY, HELP US!"

A soldier clamped a hand over her mouth and they waited. A few moments later, Orb shuddered and the dagger disappeared in his cloak. Electra tried to crane her head, but Glory strode past them and shoved her husband back. He stumbled, catching hold of the desk and he curled his fingers around the edge until his knuckles were white. Glory turned to them, her tawny eyes alight with anger, and she ordered, "Let them go."

"Glory—" Orb started.

She held a hand up to silence him. "I don't know what's going on, Orb, but this is not the way I'll have my guests treated! So let them go."

"I can't."

Glory glanced at him, her voice near dangerous. "What do you mean you can't, Orb Monroe?"

He cringed at the use of his family name. "Electra and Drew have stumbled upon...delicate information that simply can't reach Moon Crossing, my darling. If the Elite Council knew what they knew, then they would order me back. My power and position wouldn't protect me. It wouldn't protect *you*."

"What do they know?"

"Darling—"

"*What do they know?*" Glory had turned on him, her hands on her hips as she gazed up at him.

Orb swallowed and Electra saw the conflict in his mind play across his expression. He didn't want to lose Glory, but he didn't want to be exposed either. Electra never thought she'd see such fear on his face. Orb never showed fear. Finally, he crumbled Glory up in his arms and whispered in her ear. She held still, listening intently, and then drew back. Her expression was stricken with confusion and grief as she said, "At least imprison them then."

Electra's eyes fell closed and Orb gave the order. They were taken away, guided to the prison vault of the palace, two towers at its back, and locked in separate cells right next to each other. The cell was small, poorly lit, and the stone was cold beneath her. Drew sat on the side of the bars he shared with Electra and leaned his head back, sighing. She joined him, their backs almost touching if it weren't for the bars, and she pulled her knees to her chest.

"At least we're not dead," she said solemnly.

"Yeah," Drew replied. "But Electra, we won't stay here forever. When Glory's not around, Orb will have no problem executing us."

"Then we should make sure she stays around."

They fell silent then, contemplating what would happen if Glory left for a day, maybe to go shopping in one of the villages. Or when Glory would have her baby and be recovering. Orb had the power and will to do anything he wanted, but as long as his wife was around, they were safe. Electra didn't feel safe, though, and she wished they had made it out of Iluro much sooner. If they hadn't snooped or Viktor hadn't heard what they were plotting—she had found the device the morning after—then they would be in Moon Crossing. Safe behind the barrier and untouchable.

Yet, they were here, in mossy-smelling cells, cold and damp. Guards brought food, blankets, and pillows for the cot fastened into the wall. They told them that the far section of their cells contained a place to take care of their human necessities. They could shower and use real bathrooms if they were on their best behavior. If they fell ill, then a physician would be available. The service was exemplary, which surprised Electra, but she had seen the hospitality of the Mevanian folk in her time here. Of course they would treat their prisoners well, too.

As Electra stood to crawl into her cot for the night, Drew reached through the bars and took her hand. She turned to him as he rose and cupped her cheek, his features tired and loving at the same time. He cleared his throat and told her, "Electra, I'm sorry I couldn't protect you. You're the woman I am deeply in love with and I should have *tried*...but I didn't and I will regret that for the rest of my life. For now, I hope you can forgive me because I want to promise you I will protect you, I will make sure we don't get tangled up in a mess like this, and I want to give you the life you deserve, the love that you deserve. I'm unworthy of you and the fire in your heart for justice. I'm terrified but with you by my side, I can make it through any day."

"Drew..." she trailed off, tears glinting in her eyes as he fished through his coat pocket and knelt on the ground of his cell, still holding her hand in his.

"I'll love you to the day I die and I hope that day is nowhere near. Electra, if we make it out of here alive and well, will you do me the honor of becoming my wife?"

Her heart fluttered in her chest and she nodded. "Yes, Drew. Most definitely yes."

He opened the box and she held her hand out as he slipped the ring on, a beautiful round cut diamond set into a twisting silver band. It wasn't the ideal place she thought she'd get engaged, but it was perfect. Electra reached through the bars and hugged him the best she could when he stood again. She wanted to kiss him, wrap her arms around him without the bars in the way and reassure him he was worthy. That he was good to her. And promise her heart and everything to him. But she couldn't, so she told him through the bars instead.

Drew grinned and he kissed her fingers, pressing them to his lips. "I love you to bits, Holloway."

"I love you, too, Harte."

Electra smiled. "We *will* make it out of here alive, I promise. We will fight if we have to but we won't go down without one."

TRUE COLORS

V ANNE ARRIVED AT the Aerie Compound a few weeks ago—Malini in tow—but he's been distraught about Amira's absence. I don't know why she left before he came, but they've been in contact since. Vanne is still annoyed and complains about his woes to me. Bibiana is due to deliver her baby in a day or two, so Sophronia, Malini, and I have been accompanying her to the bathhouse to relieve her stress about birthing a baby into this world. My leg has healed completely, and physical therapy has helped me splendidly, but I walk with a slight limp now. Just like Stryder.

Today, we're lounging in a private pool, clad in swimsuits as the steam fills the air. Bibiana runs her fingers over her belly, breathing in and out slowly. Sophronia and Malini are talking about her gang days and I sink into the water, leaning my head back on the stone of the pool.

After a couple of minutes of bliss, Bibiana whispers, "I'm scared."

My eyes flutter open and I turn my head toward her. "Scared about the baby coming?"

Bibiana bobs her head. "But I'm also scared that Viktor will find out I'm alive and come for us. He knows I'd be terrified to testify against him in court, but if he found out..."

I reach out and take her hand, squeezing her fingers. "Viktor won't ever find out, Bibiana. I know his secret. Electra, Vanne, and Malini know his secret. He can't hide forever."

"Have they collected the evidence they need?"

"Yes, but Viktor sent some goons to take out Vanne and Malini and…" I trail off. "I don't know where Electra is."

I haven't heard from my cousin in a couple of weeks and usually, I wouldn't worry because Electra gets busy. I'm hiding away in a rebellion compound and so our communications are limited. But not even Vanne and Malini know where she is. They know she left town with Drew Holloway, who I learned was a rival lawyer of hers turned lover. So they must be somewhere safe, feeding information to the Elite Council because recently, they've called for Viktor's arrest and I couldn't be happier.

Justice is so close and yet, so far.

Bibiana worries her lip. "I don't want to remain in hiding forever. Orlin and I want to leave Spring Grove."

My eyebrow quirks in surprise. "Oh? You and Orlin?"

A blush colors her cheeks despite the steam. "Yeah, if you haven't noticed, we've grown quite close. He treats me so well and doesn't even care that I'm carrying the child of another man. I know it's only been a few months, but he takes care of me, he loves my baby as much as he loves me."

"I'm happy for you, Bibiana," I say with a smile. "Besides the fact he's a rotten physician, he's a kind person and much better than Viktor Marsh could ever *hope* to be."

"I want a life with Orlin. I hope Viktor doesn't swoop in and screw that up."

"Lie low until he's charged and they find his associates, okay? Everything will be fine."

She looks at me. "You have such great faith in your friends, Locklyn, and it sounds like things will work out for you."

"They better," I tell her with a light laugh that feels more sobering than amusing, "because beyond this, I have nothing else."

We lapse into silence once more and soon Sophronia and Malini fall quiet as well.

I'm on my way back to my room after the dip in the bathhouse pools when Vanne appears out of nowhere and latches to my side. I startle and lay a hand on my chest, giving him a sharp look.

"You scared me, *heavens*."

Vanne is unfazed. "Do you remember when I told you about Amira bringing a gun on our date? I've been mulling over what I could've done wrong for her to leave before I even got here and I was reminiscing on that. I hate to say this, but what if Amira had a part in framing you?"

My memory is jogged and I gasp, thinking of how Amira showed up out of nowhere. She must have targeted Vanne specifically to get into our apartment. Taken the gun and replaced it after the murder of Superior Dunn. I eagerly turn to Vanne. "I bet you she did. Why else would she show up and insist on going over to the apartment? And the silencer, I never purchased one."

We come to my room and step inside, settling down on the small couch.

"Right." Vanne's expression crumbles and his shoulders hunch. "If Amira was working for Viktor, she could have snuck the gun from your room, kill Superior Dun, and then snuck it back into the apartment at a later date, leaving the silencer as further evidence it was used to kill him."

"I hardly ever checked my gun so it worked. Why would she work with Viktor though?"

"That's what stumps me. She made no indication of knowing him when we were at the courthouse."

We sit there, gears grinding in our heads as we try to think, and I say, "She could have been doing it for one of their other associates, whose identities we still don't know."

Vanne leans back on the couch and sighs. "Yes, that is a likely possibility. She went home to Iluro and I know she's a princess, but not in line to inherit the crown. Cristol is the Emperor now and I don't quite know the connection between them."

"He resigned right after I left, which is strange, don't you think? A win like that would have boosted his chances of re-election and yet, he left."

"Do you think he was in on it, too?" He asks.

"I've had no reason to believe otherwise." I fold my arms and tilt my head at him. "Still, I don't understand why. I've done nothing to Orb or Amira or Viktor in my lifetime."

He nods and wonders. "If you did nothing, then who did? What are we missing here?"

I still for a moment as a piece of the puzzle clicks into place. "Wait, wait, wait, Orb is Stryder's brother. They're the heirs of Mevania and…and my father killed their parents…"

Vanne's head snaps to me and his eyes widen. "Revenge!"

My pulse quickens beneath my skin as another thought generates. "Orb and Stryder are brothers; Amira is their cousin. Viktor has always been Orb's goon and Bibiana was caught in the crossfire. But…if Orb sought revenge for his parents' death then wouldn't—"

"Stryder seek revenge as well?" Vanne finishes, his tone sober.

The room tilts suddenly and I curl against the couch, my skin chilling to my core. *No, he wouldn't do that to me, would he? He loves me…but this all happened before he knew me. It started with my father and is supposed to end with me.* My breathing quickens as thick tears roll down my cheeks. I love him and he very well could have betrayed me before that fact was a reality. *No, it can't be.*

"Locklyn, calm down. Take a deep breath," Vanne soothes, making me look him in the eye. "We don't know anything for sure, okay?"

I bob my head, but it doesn't help and I continue to cry. Vanne holds me, letting me sob against his shoulder. He's quiet, not denying that Stryder could have been involved. He shouldn't deny it anyway because it's probably true and even though my heart twists thinking about it, I have to confront him. I need to know whether all of this was a ruse; his feelings, the kisses and sweet moments, the tears and tender stories. Has he been pulling one over me this whole time?

Have I been made a fool?

I hear the door creak open and Vanne turns to whoever stands there. Vanne jumps up as I slowly push to my feet. I blink through the tears and look up into Stryder's blurry face. In a flash, I see twisting horns grow out of his head. His frown turns into a smile with razor-sharp teeth and his tongue flicks out, forked.

A monster.

I gasp and scramble away, falling to the floor as my whole body shakes with sobs, and an ache shoots through my leg. Vanne stands in a halo of light, watching, and Stryder kneels, reaching for me.

I claw at him, rasping, "Leave me alone! Don't touch me!"

He stops and his hands fall on his knees, brow furrowed in confusion. "Locklyn? Talk to me, love."

"Don't call me that," I hiss and hiccup with another sob. "You don't love me, you only wanted to use me!"

Surprise appears in his almond eyes and yet, he remains calm. "What do you mean?"

"Vanne and I made the connection, Stryder. You were part of the scheme, you helped frame me."

I rub away the tears with the sleeve of my sweater so I can see his face. He gulps and sits on the floor, his shoulders slumped forward now. Vanne doesn't move and I'm glad he's there, in case Stryder finishes the job.

"Tell me the truth, Stryder Monroe."

In a quiet voice, he confesses, "I was part of the scheme—in the beginning. The three men who kidnapped Adume comprised of me, Orb, and Domenico. After we released Adume, I wanted out. Orb called me weak, childish, and dishonorable. Your father had killed our parents in cold blood and even though he paid with his life, that wasn't enough for us. We needed *everyone* your father had loved to suffer as we did.

"I went along with it because I thought I had to make up for being a coward in Orb's eyes. It was my fault they died because I didn't go. Orb had fueled me with that rage for years and I was desperate to release it. But in my heart, I knew it wasn't what my parents wanted, so I tried in vain to opt out. When I wanted you to come to Bountiful Hill with me, I was trying to give you a reasonable alibi so you wouldn't be in Moon Crossing when the murders occurred. But you wouldn't go," his voice trembles.

"Orb wanted to kill you but I suggested Silverwater and then lied that I would make sure you didn't get there. He gauged my true feelings for you and had the trackers inserted. I've been trying to make things right, Locklyn, but I've been confused, manipulated, and used by people I trusted with my life, with everything. They all betrayed me and now...I've betrayed you."

"Who else did you work with?" Vanne asks, sounding almost too afraid to learn the truth.

Stryder's eyes fall closed. "Amira, Detective Cyrus Caine, Domenico, Orb, Viktor, and Bibiana. I didn't kill anyone, I couldn't, but I helped scheme the framing and I'm sorry. I tried to stop the killings, but Orb knocked me out and tied me up after I saw you. I'm worthless now as I was when I let my parents die and I can never redeem myself from that."

"Why did the others do it?" Vanne steps back into the room and we all know the unspoken question on his mind, *Why did Amira?*

"Orb and I are obvious. Losing our parents broke us and neither of us will ever be the same. Domenico and his family have always been loyal to the Monroes and he's my dearest friend, he was very close to my parents. Amira is their niece. Detective Caine may be her biological father, but no one knows for sure, and she was hurt by their loss as well. Caine wanted to help because if he did, he hoped Amira wouldn't be caught. Viktor is Orb's right-hand man and Bibiana was helping because she thought he loved her."

Something clicks in Vanne's hand and I glance at him as he holds up another hand-held recording device. "I need to get this information to Blake so Locklyn can be free. Surely you understand that, Stryder."

I can't look at him but he stands, defeated. "Yes, and we will all pay for what we've done. I'm willing to accept that."

"Does Vicente know what you've done?"

"No, and it's not something I'd like to discuss with him if the Deliverance and Mevania are to continue an alliance."

A mirthless laugh escapes me and I push myself to my feet again, leaning on the bedpost for support. "There won't be an alliance if Orb destroys the District, Stryder."

"I know," his cheeks color in embarrassment, "but whoever takes up the helm once Orb and I are gone will probably want to ally with the Deliverance. There's no bad blood between us. What we did in Moon Crossing has nothing to do with the Deliverance."

"Gone?" I glance at him.

His almond eyes are devoid of the light that once shone in them, now replaced with darkness and despair. "They will execute us, no doubt."

My heart leaps into my throat and I shake my head. "You didn't kill anyone though—"

"I'm a foreigner," he interrupts. "I schemed. I kidnapped Adume. I even bought some supplies that were used in the murders. Moon Crossing will see nothing but trouble. The Council won't give me a second chance, Locklyn, no one will."

"What about Blake? Surely he knows you help fund the Deliverance—"

"He doesn't know because he hasn't been here since I began funding the Deliverance. He's one Councilor out of ten. I'll take my punishment in stride, I deserve as much."

"No—"

"Locklyn," Vanne says sharply, "why are you still trying to protect him?"

The tears spill again. "I—I don't know…"

He gestures for me to come over and I limp to him, unable to meet Stryder's eye again as I pass. When I'm by Vanne's side, he abruptly whips out a sleek pistol and aims it at Stryder. I gasp, grabbing his arm, but Vanne holds firm, his finger hovering above the trigger. Stryder turns to see and he raises his hands in defeat.

"Go ahead, shoot me."

"No!"

Vanne sneers. "I would like nothing more, believe me. For the way you've hurt Locklyn and for how Amira hurt me...you both manipulated us. Your brother sent goons after Malini and me when we were still in Moon Crossing. They nearly killed us. But we passed Electra and Drew's message to Blake. I'll pass on your confession to him and you will all go down for what you did."

"You're a spy for the Deliverance," Stryder says, his voice dismal, "you should despise Moon Crossing, despise the Circle of Superiors and the Elite Council. Everyone else here is glad the Circle is dead."

"I don't care about the Circle, I care about what you did to Locklyn. What you did to Adume and what your brother has probably done to Electra and Drew. These people are my friends and seeing what they've been put through is unacceptable." He drops the pistol, slipping it into his waistband once more. "But a fair warning, Stryder, if you don't leave Locklyn alone, I'll kill you before the Council even hears of your involvement in this scheme. Do you understand me?"

Stryder only stares for a moment and then moves past us, out of the room. I try to take in deep breaths, but the gulps turn into sobs and I step away from Vanne, leaning against the wall. He wraps his arms around me. I shove him off. I don't want his comfort or anyone's. My world is crashing down around me and I need space. I need answers, but that requires talking to Stryder and I can't watch Vanne kill him for it.

"Leave me be," I grumble, and after a moment, Vanne does, closing the door behind him.

I slide the lock in place and trudge over to my bed, crawling atop the blankets. My view through the window that reflects outside shines brightly with stars. I feel sick after Stryder's confession and annoyed at my need to still protect him. My love for him is a conflicted flame in my heart that I know I should snuff out, but I'm still hesitant. Always hesitant. Just like my love for my father. What he did caused this to happen. All this pain and suffering that so many of us have endured. Stryder, Orb, Amira, Jesse, Mom, me.

A never-ending hurricane of misery.

Eventually, I sleep, but my dreams are full of Stryder's face and the demon in him. I wake up screaming and whimpering and am doused in sweat. Afterward, I'm unable to close my eyes.

HEREAFTER

I T DIDN'T SURPRISE Orb when the truth had wiggled out of its hole and he learned that Moon Crossing had set a bounty on his head. Viktor had gone back, like a fool, and been caught. So had Cyrus Caine and Orb wondered why he ever associated with imbeciles who couldn't evade the law. So he had taken Glory and fled to the royal safe house, Goldridge Estate, which lay on the western coast of Mevania. It was tucked into a canopy of trees with its own private beach. It couldn't be seen from the skies and was protected by a fortified wall, occupied with the best *Speranza Cremisi* warriors.

He was taking a stroll along the beach, bundled in a long coat, when Captain Matteo Crews of Orb's Invictus Guard approached and dipped his head in a bow. "Her Majesty has requested your presence in the royal chambers, Your Majesty."

Orb swept past him and back into the manor, depositing his coat in the hands of a waiting servant. It was decorated for happier travels with a teal and white theme, sculptures of sea creatures, and black and white designs on the tiles both beneath his feet and above on the vaulted ceilings. The Monroes had come to Goldridge for vacation during the summer and Orb ignored a couple of portraits of his family as he passed. It was still too painful to look at his parents caught in the canvas, smiling and breathing. All he saw now were flashbacks of that night. He repeatedly heard the gunshots and saw the bullets tear through his father's chest and lodge deep in his mother's stomach. He saw the blood spurt out, their bodies fall, and Cicone Harte's terrified face as he realized what had happened. Orb's hate had been born in a split second and it would never be quelled.

Their chamber doors were open and he strode with caution, peeking inside. Glory was clutching her back as she paced across the room, breathing in and out as her physician told her to. Orb quickly walked in and asked, "Is everything okay?"

"Yes," Dr. Vilaro said. "Just some swelling. Nothing to be worried about, though."

Orb came to Glory's side and she stopped, resting a hand on her round belly. "Don't look at me like I'm a wounded animal. I'm fine."

He grunted and Dr. Vilaro slid out of the room like a snake, closing the doors behind her. Orb helped Glory to the bed and she climbed on, sitting cross-legged as she leaned back against the multitude of pillows they had. She was only wearing her undergarments, and a fan wafted in the cool air. He shivered. It was the dead of winter outside and though it wasn't as cold as it was inland; he preferred the heat of summer.

"I don't like it when you talk to me like that when others are around, darling," he said as he pressed his fist into the bed.

"You know I've been having wild mood swings and right now, I'm annoyed."

"At me?"

"You, the baby, everything. I miss Iluro."

He removed his boots and sat on the edge. "We can't go back to Iluro."

Glory's nose twitched. "Thanks to you."

It felt like an ice pick was slowly chipping away at his cruel, frozen heart whenever Glory didn't give him the time of day. She had been angry about imprisoning Electra and Drew, angry when she learned Moon Crossing had placed a bounty on his head, and angry that they had to come here with minimal staff and a not-so-skilled cook. But he couldn't be caught, not yet. He wanted to spend more time with Glory and needed to perfect his plan of attack. His mind had been scattered, though, with rage at one of his associates for confessing everything. He didn't know who had done it but he had a pretty good idea. Stryder was weak, he knew, and being around Locklyn had given him some sort of hero's complex. It was foolish, like everything Stryder did.

"I'm sorry, my love." He leaned down to press a kiss against her knee, but she wasn't having it.

Her doe-like eyes narrowed on him. "I've been watching the news, and I've heard rumors about you. People say that you're wanted for purchasing anonymously from the Moonless Market, is that true?"

"Glory—"

"Tell me the truth. You trust me, don't you?"

"Of course I trust you." His brow furrowed and he began to feel himself sweat. "But I don't want you to think differently of me."

"I listened to you pour your tiny heart out as a child, seeking revenge, and I'm married to you today. Do you think I'd suddenly hate you?"

"Yes," he breathed and his shoulders hunched forward. "You would hate me and leave me, I'm sure of it."

Glory shifted, looking uncomfortable. "What did you do? Does it have to do with Electra and Drew? You told me they knew something that would take you away from me and our baby..."

Orb gazed at her. He had loved her since he was twelve. His chest tightened. He was heartless to an extent, but with Glory Troisi, he would gladly fall at her feet. He couldn't bear to see her hate him, so he settled for confessing the least of his crimes.

"I have made purchases from the Moonless Market."

"What did you buy?"

"Does it matter anymore?"

She pressed her lips together. "I suppose not. But why?"

He cringed. "I just did, Glory. Electra and Drew found the ledgers. They were going to expose me. Unfortunately, the message got back to their associates in Moon Crossing and was taken to the Elite Council. So now I'm wanted."

"Surely the sentence for that wouldn't be long. Maybe a couple of years?"

Blazes, if she only knew all that he had done.

"Probably, but I don't want to leave you," Orb reached out and settled his hand on her belly, "and I won't miss the birth of our child."

"You better not," she sighed, "but we can't continue to hide here, Orb. You have a country to rule. Can't you be pardoned as the emperor of Mevania?"

"I committed crimes there when I was a citizen, not as the emperor of Mevania; therefore, by law, I have to be held accountable no matter what. I hoped my power here would defy that, but it doesn't, not for certain crimes."

"So you'll be taken away despite your birthright."

"That's what it's chalking up to be."

"Who will rule in your place? Your brother?"

Orb snorted. "Definitely not. I'll appoint Khione again. I trust her to take care of the empire. And then, when our baby is born, he'll take my place."

"He?" Glory shook her head. "That's something I wanted to tell you, darling, we're having a baby girl."

Orb froze and dread filled him. He took a step back and whirled away, running his fingers through his hair, not caring that it was now unkempt. In Mevania, the eldest boy would be the heir to the throne. It was the way it had been done for centuries. Of course, he could enact that his daughter would inherit the throne. Orb needed to have a son to keep his legacy on the throne and family name. He knew they would execute him when he was finally caught and wouldn't have time to produce another heir with Glory. As long as Stryder died right beside him, the next heir to the Mevanian throne would be his cousin, Amadeo, Amira's brother. But he wasn't fit to rule.

The Mevanian Empire was doomed.

"That's not the reaction I expected," she said.

Orb inhaled deeply and faced her again. "Only a son of mine can inherit the throne."

Glory snorted now. "How dumb. Why can't your daughter inherit? She'll be *just* as capable as any son of ours."

It hurt to hear Glory talk about future children when this little one was likely to be their only. But he didn't let it show. "It's tradition, the way the Monroe family has done things for years and to keep our name."

"Don't worry about it, then. Maybe we'll have a little boy next time. We have plenty of years ahead of us."

He shuffled closer and leaned forward to kiss her forehead. "Of course, my love."

"You should bathe. I need peace to think of names for our precious little girl."

Orb obeyed, dreading the future of Mevania.

☽ ✧ ☾

Amira's nose crinkled as a chilly wind whipped at her face, spraying seawater. She never had the taste for traveling by sea like her little brother, Amadeo, did. He was a sailor and captain of the *Fairlight*—his ship commissioned by the throne to travel to other nations and trade. Even though Amadeo was only three years younger than her, he had been sailing the Glass Sea for nearly five years now. Whenever he came into port was the only time she ever saw him these days.

She leaned back against the ship's thick railing and glanced around. Amadeo was greeting his crew for the morning and confirming they were on course for their next stop in the Reyes Kingdom. Amira had been lucky that Amadeo was in port when the news broke in Moon Crossing and she'd learned a bounty was placed on her head. She didn't tell her brother about it, only told him she wanted to spend some time with him out on the open sea. See what being a sailor was all about. They would be gone for a few months, so she said her goodbyes to her parents, to Orb, and left.

Since Amadeo didn't want her sleeping below deck with his crew, who consisted mostly of men, they shared the captain's quarters and it was strange because they never had to share a room in their lives. The palace was far too large for that and Amira knew she would miss the luxuries of being royal, but she would have to suffer now. When everything seemed on track, Amadeo walked toward her and leaned against the railing as well.

He had a sunny countenance, like usual, and his curly hair was sticking out from beneath his cap. "It looks like it's going to be a beautiful day. Everything is in order and we're on our way to Reyes."

"Glad to hear it," she murmured.

Amadeo tipped his head at her, his honey-colored eyes a tad concerned. "I know you're not very fond of sailing, but there seems to be more to the problem. Why did you suddenly want to leave Mevania, Miri?"

She tensed and cast her gaze across the deck. "It's nothing, Ama. I told you I wanted to spend time with you."

"I've been out on the seas for five years and *now* is the time you want to see me?" He shook his head. "What's going on back home? I know Orb was crowned emperor, I was at his coronation, and that he married a woman from the District. I'm not up to date on everything, though."

"They're having a baby."

"Oh? Congrats to them, then. I'm glad Ma's the younger sibling so I wouldn't have to be Emperor. Orb and Stryder are certainly fit to rule. It's not the life for me."

"Me neither," Amira admitted.

Amadeo nudged her. "You're still troubled about something and I'm going to be the annoying little brother until you tell me."

She huffed and looked at him again. "I'm in trouble back home with the District. But it's not just me; Orb and Stryder are, too."

"What kind of trouble?"

"The worst kind. But I was never a citizen so they really can't hold me accountable. Stryder and Orb had citizenship, the dummies, those two have always been trying to one-up each other."

"It's more like Orb has been trying to one-up Stryder all his life," he said and shook his head. "I don't know why Orb hates him so much. Poor Stryder has done nothing to him. They both lost their parents and I thought that would bring them closer."

"You know how Orb is, he's always dancing on the very edge and he wants to prove how intelligent he is." She rolled her eyes. "We all know he's smart, always has been, but this time, we went too far."

Amadeo lifted an eyebrow at her. "What exactly did you guys do?"

Amira felt a little sick to her stomach thinking about it but waved him to the captain's quarters. "Better I tell you in private."

Her brother followed her back to the quarters they now shared and they sat on the bed. Amira knotted her fingers together and pulled them apart, nervous about what Amadeo would do once she told him. He could very well turn the ship around and drop her off in Mevania again, refusing to let her run away from her problems.

"You know Uncle Keyon and Aunt Aaralyn were murdered in Moon Crossing, and Orb witnessed it all. The man who killed them was Cicone Harte, but he was executed years ago. He has a daughter in Moon Crossing who worked for the Circle of Superiors and Orb, Stryder, and I all wanted to exact our revenge for taking away Uncle Keyon and Aunt Aaralyn. So we framed his daughter for...for the murder of the Circle of Superiors."

He was quiet for a moment and she glanced at him. His honey eyes were shadowed over, mouth pulled into a frown. "The three of you killed the Circle then?"

"It wasn't just the three of us. Domenico wanted to help and...Cyrus Caine, as well. Orb had an associate in Moon Crossing who is as mad as him, a fellow Councilor, and then a naive server."

Amadeo's eyes widened. "Cyrus Caine? You *worked* with that man?"

"Yes." She still felt ashamed about it, especially after she learned what he had done to her mother.

"So you're wanted for murder and you worked with the man who *drugged* and *defiled* Ma, *who might be your father.*"

"I know it's bad, Ama, and that's why I needed to leave. There's a price on my head. Moon Crossing has already caught two of us, and I'm sure Stryder and Domenico will turn themselves in."

He stood and paced the width of the cabin, ripping his cap off and crumbling it in his hands. "Let me guess, Orb was the mastermind behind all this."

"Of course. Stryder even tried to opt out and I should have, too, but...I was afraid of what Orb might do to me."

"What still irks me is that you worked alongside Cyrus Caine, *gah*." He whirled on her. "Do Ma and Pa know about this?"

"No. I'm sure they'll learn soon enough. Orb probably already fled as well."

"Do you really think Uncle Keyon and Aunt Aaralyn would have wanted this? The death of what, five people, in their names?"

Amira curled into herself. "No, they were better people than that. It hurts, though, and Orb and Stryder have it worse. Aunt Aaralyn was always so kind and loving. Uncle Keyon was funny and wise. They taught us so much and loved us as much as Ma and Pa do, but they were taken too early and in such a cruel manner. I thought I was doing the right thing when I joined Orb, but I wasn't. He wanted bloodshed, he wants war even now. He's lost it."

"And now he's in charge of Mevania." Amadeo sighed, rubbing his eyes. "This is why I would never want to rule, that amount of power is too tempting to abuse. What exactly did you do, Miri?"

"I began dating Locklyn Harte's Protector, Vanne, to gain access to her apartment. I needed her gun, so I stole it. Cyrus shot one of the Superiors and I returned the gun so that when the police found it, they would link it to Locklyn."

"You dated someone to help commit a murder?"

"Yeah, but he's a member of the Deliverance, a rebel resistance in what used to be Spring Grove."

"So you didn't actually *kill* anyone?"

"I didn't. Cyrus was the one who pulled the trigger."

"*Ugh*, I hate hearing his name. Where is he now?"

"In prison in Moon Crossing. The likeliest sentence we'd all receive is execution."

"So…if you, Orb, and Stryder were all to be executed, that would leave me as heir to the throne unless Orb has a son."

"Pretty much."

Amadeo groaned and plopped down next to her. "I leave and the three of you get yourselves in this mess."

"Orb was going to do something anyway," she said with a shrug, "but we didn't get away with it as he planned. Someone slipped. I know the server did for Orb's friend in the Elite Council and he's in prison now as well. But for the rest of us, I'm not sure. I'm betting on Stryder, though."

"Stryder has always had a good heart, he'd face what wrong he did and take the punishment."

"He also fell in love with the girl we framed so that probably broke him. Knowingly hurting someone you love is tough to deal with…" she trailed off, thinking of Vanne's bright smile and his soft hazel eyes.

"It sounds like you fell in love with someone, too. The Protector?"

Amira's cheeks flushed in embarrassment. "Vanne was *everything* I could have hoped for and more, but I built our relationship on a lie. I fell in love with him, but I knew I had to leave before I got caught. Breaking up with him was horrible. I betrayed his trust, and I'm sure he hates my guts."

"Probably," Amadeo said bluntly.

"So, what are you going to do with me?"

"I know it might be stupid to harbor a fugitive, but you're my sister and we have to look out for each other. I love Stryder and Orb, but I can't help them. Domenico, too. You might never return to Mevania, though, Miri. If the problem arises about a proper heir…then I'll go back, get married, and have a kid."

"Ama, you'd be giving up your life on the seas, your crew, the *Fairlight*."

"I know, but my first duty is to my family and Mevania. Without a proper heir, the Eclipse Society will swoop in and destroy Mevania as we know it.

Our people would be miserable. A civil war might rage." Amadeo straightened his coat. "I must do what I have to if it comes to that." He smiled at her. "Do you think Admiral Mezzanotte would want to be my empress? I feel like she's always flirting with me when we have our trade meetings."

Amira snorted. Amadeo has had a crush on Admiral Mezzanotte since he decided to sail the Glass Sea. It surprised her he still fawned over her as he'd risen in the ranks and obtained his own ship. The admiral was six years older but not married yet, claiming that the sea was her partner and the Mevanian Navy her children. Amira didn't understand her and Amadeo's love for the sea, but at least they shared that.

"Maybe, Ama, if you receive permission from the sea to bind her inland."

"Hey, it would bind me inland, too, so we'd be miserable together."

As he headed for the door, she said softly, "Thanks for letting me stay."

Amadeo's sunny expression was back in place. "That's what siblings are for."

☽ ✧ ☾

Viktor flexed his fingers and took another spoonful of the slop they had given him for dinner. He didn't know how long he had been in the holding cell at the police station downtown, but it felt like a while now. Orb had said it would be foolish to come back and he had been right. Viktor was looking to get in with mercenaries from the Moonless Market and instead had been caught and arrested. The baker who reported him must have been overjoyed to receive twenty thousand credits. Whoever found Orb or Stryder would certainly receive more.

He wasn't much of a strategist like Orb, but he would not go down quietly or smoothly. There would be a fight. He needed help from the Moonless Market and now that he had been arrested, that option was slim. No one in the Market wanted to get involved with someone who was foolish enough to get caught. At least he wasn't alone and his gaze traveled to Cyrus Caine in the holding cell next door. He had been surprised when Orb brought the former Recon on, but Viktor never learned why Cyrus even wanted to help kill the Circle of Superiors. He'd kept close to Orb's cousin, Amira Solomon, so maybe she was the reason.

On the wall across from his cell were several TVs lined up in a row, displaying the bounties that had been set. Viktor scowled as Bibiana's face appeared on the screen, her large eyes innocent and her smile adorable. He grunted when he saw they had set the bounty higher. The longer the rest were missing, the higher the reward became. But Viktor knew no one would ever find Bibi. He and Orb had made sure of that. He pushed his bowl back onto the tray by the little dispenser door and walked over to his bedroll, lying down. Some nights, he could still hear her scream as she fell into the raging river below and though it should have given him joy, it had all been for nothing. Someone talked and he would still wind up dead.

Bibi hadn't been cut out for the job; she was too naive and supposedly in love with him. He hadn't even known about Orb's plans when he met Bibi at the Cinnamon Lounge and was only looking for a good time. But she had proved to be a little different from some of the other girls he spent nights with, and he knew he definitely shouldn't have gotten attached. Bibi was a leech and he had to admit, he enjoyed her company and even made the absurd choice to propose to her. He hoped it would keep her quiet, but alas, Bibi was a terrible liar.

After they'd shot her and thrown her into the river, Viktor felt conflicted. He had not only killed Bibi but also the budding life inside her, his very own child. It haunted him for weeks and still did. But he was loyal to Orb, not some girl he'd gotten himself tangled up with. Now, it only angered him when he saw her face plastered on the screens, and heard her name from the murmurings of the other prisoners. He thought by now, the child would have been born and he was glad to not have such a responsibility. Viktor had never wanted children. They were messy, loud, and bothersome, and you had to watch and feed them for ten years. It was far too expensive for his liking. Yet, when he thought of Bibiana and their baby, something inside him...melted.

Viktor shook his head. *No, she was dead; the baby was dead, and soon, he would be, too, if he didn't get out of here.* So that's all Viktor thought about, a way to escape to the Moonless Market.

☽ ✧ ☾

They had arrested Cyrus while he was working on a case, which had been embarrassing. Commander Keeva and Commander Ore had come for him themselves since the case of the Superiors' deaths fell into their hands. She had been overly excited, which he always found strange, and wondered if she was just as mad as the kids he'd plotted these murders with. In all honesty, he only joined when he learned Amira had gotten herself tangled up in this mess. He still had lingering feelings for her mother, Khione, princess of Mevania, and though he knew she despised him, Amira still had the possibility of being his child. So he wanted to protect her.

Now, he had no clue where she had gone, nor where Orb, Stryder, or Domenico were. He had only been acquainted with Khione on his summer vacation in Mevania the year Amira was conceived and then briefly acquainted by Alastair's fists. Keyon and Aaralyn Monroe meant little to him, but Khione was more. Orb even lied and said that Khione wanted him to do this, to protect Amira and avenge her brother and sister-in-law. So Cyrus had complied—like an idiot. Now his reputation was ruined and they would execute him.

Shooting Superior Dunn hadn't affected him, only because he'd been a Recon before being demoted to a detective and had to kill people before. He didn't agree with the Circle oft times, but this was the city he loved, and now he had betrayed it. Cyrus knew he shouldn't have joined forces with the young Councilor and thrown his life away like this. He thought of Locklyn Harte sometimes and then of her father, Cicone, who he had grown up around but was never really acquainted with.

Cyrus had been a minor detective on the case at the time and followed his superiors to the Harte's house to arrest Cicone. They had the testimony of a little boy, who Cyrus now knew had been Orb Cristol, and when the ballistics came back from the lab, Cicone Harte was guilty. He had done it. Not only murder but he also had a lengthy history of illegal trading and his greed had boomeranged. Cyrus had attended the execution with his fellow detectives on the case, along with the Superiors and Councilors, and cringed when the bullet tore through Cicone's chest and pinged off the bulletproof glass behind him.

Cicone had fallen to a knee, his hands shackled so he couldn't staunch the bleeding. He had tilted his face heavenward, murmuring something as tears streaked his cheeks. The last prayer of a dying man who had gone too far. He died quickly and his body was unshackled and removed. The executioner, who wore a black mask and cloak, had simply holstered the gun and climbed off the stage, disappearing into the crowd. Cyrus still remembered Cicone's ashen face as they checked to make sure he was truly dead and tossed a sheet over his features, wheeling him off to be cremated.

Cyrus had the boring task of going through Cicone's clothes and found a picture of the Harte family. Beautiful Maisie held a little Locklyn in her arms while their son Jesse stood with a brilliant smile as Cicone rested his hands on his son's shoulders. The picture had been taken at a beach called Sapphire Point, and they looked content. He had pocketed the picture with the intent to return it to Maisie Harte. She cried when he did.

That had been the only act of kindness he'd given the Harte family because then Locklyn started getting into trouble. Her father's death tormented her, and Cyrus had a job to do. He would give anything to go back if he could. Refuse to be part of Orb's scheme and reveal him to the commanders. But now, he was stuck with this fate and Cyrus hid his face in his hands, knowing he would never see Khione or Amira again.

A FORMATION OF SNOWDRIFTS

S TRYDER HAS SUCCESSFULLY avoided me for the past few weeks, but I'm still desperate to know if his feelings for me were a ruse, to get me to trust him. Vicente wanted information on the Circle's previous plans and I obliged, for the sake of knocking Moon Crossing to its knees. But I want to know how Stryder feels. He doesn't carry himself as confidently as he used to, especially now that Moon Crossing has a price on his head. Bounty hunters have been dispatched from the city and even Orb and Glory have disappeared for the time being. Viktor was caught and is in prison now, awaiting trial until they can find the others.

Vanne has been following me around to make sure Stryder inflicts no more pain, but he has become an annoyance. I'm surprised he doesn't seem as hurt by Amira's betrayal as I thought he would be. Maybe he's just hiding it. He finally leaves me alone when Kaer and Clover come to visit and Vanne gushes all over their baby boy, Calem. After an hour of playing with their adorable baby and visiting with them, I escape with the claim that I'm heading to bed. Instead, I send a message to Stryder and tell him to meet me on the surface in fifteen minutes.

Vanne will kill me, he replies.

I'll make sure he won't. I need answers, Stryder.

With a reluctant pause, he messages, *Fine.*

I change out of the clothes I've been wearing all day—which have a little slobber from resting Calem on my shoulder—and pull on a heavy sweater and trousers with boots. Winter is upon us now and the ground above is covered in snow. There's a small shack that used to be a hunting hut and with a small fire blazing in the hearth, we should be able to keep warm. I shrug a winter coat, tuck my Mini in the pocket, and pull a wool hat over my head. I look both ways before I slip out into the hallway and make my way to the elevators. The hallways are all but deserted, because of a strategy meeting Vicente is holding in the main cavern. The Deliverance hopes to launch an attack on Moon Crossing soon. Everyone knows about the bounty on Stryder's head and I'm surprised people aren't scrambling over each other to shove him in a Hover and take him back to the city. Loyalty runs deep in the Deliverance and since he funded them for so long, they wouldn't betray one of their own. Besides, being caught could mean execution for them as well.

The elevator pings as the doors slide open and I step inside. It rises slowly as I lean back on the wall, my arms crossed. I feel a little anxious about being alone with Stryder, but somewhere deep down, I know he won't hurt me. At least, physically. Emotionally is a whole different story and I've come to terms with what he did to me. I should feel used since I was so vulnerable and blinded to see what he might have been doing, but...I don't. Maybe my love for him is still making my head fuzzy and logic has clearly never been in play with Stryder Monroe.

I'm deposited into the warehouse above and I wait in the shadows, listening to the wind whistle through the derelict wooden slabs all around me. After a few minutes, another elevator opens and Stryder steps out. It closes with a soft clang and I wave him after me. We leave the warehouse behind and brave the frosty wind. Snow falls around us like gentle rain and it's not as bright as I thought it would be since the clouds are so low. There are few lights on the surface, anyway. The door to the hunting hut is unlocked and we slip inside. I drop the plank in place so it doesn't spring open if the wind catches it and Stryder sits on the bare ground, leaning against the wall.

I kneel to start a fire in the hearth and he watches me, which makes my skin crawl, as he asks, "Why are you starting a fire?"

"Because I don't know how long we have but I want all of my answers tonight."

Once the spark catches on the kindling and I set a few pieces of dry wood atop, I brush my hands off on my pants and seat myself opposite of him. The orange glow of the fire casts light on only half of his face, leaving the other side in shadow. I burrow into my coat and slip my hands into my sleeves as I draw my knees to my chest.

"Do you love me?" I ask quietly.

"Locklyn, I already told you that my feelings for you are genuine. I wouldn't tell you I loved you if I didn't mean it. Playing with your heart was never my intention," he tells me, smooth and calm.

"I don't understand it, though. You knew what was happening—what would happen to me—so why would you pursue a relationship?"

His brow knits and he tips his head back against the wall. "Because I'm stupid. At first, I was being kind and I wanted to help you escape my brother's wrath. The Deliverance needed to know what you knew. Then I developed feelings for you and it felt like something more. I needed to protect you and though I couldn't stop what happened, I still needed to get you out of Moon Crossing. I wasn't doing it for the Deliverance then. I did it for myself because I'm selfish. I didn't mean to fall in love; it just…happened. You've become incredibly special to me and it pained me every day knowing what I did and how it ruined your life. So I'll pay for it. I'll take a thousand bullets for you, Locklyn."

Stryder pauses, looking at me again, his almond eyes haunting. "I'm not afraid to die. Until I do, I'll regret what I put you through. I knew I would break my heart and yours when the truth finally came out, but I couldn't stop myself. You became my world."

I swallow. "So it wasn't a ruse to bring me to the Deliverance."

"No. Honestly, after I fell in love with you, I only wanted to come here to get the trackers removed. Then I planned to whisk you away to Mevania so we could have a life together. But, of course, that was never a realistic option. I still have to face what I've done and when you found out, I knew you would never want to be with me again. I'm surprised you even asked to talk."

With a bob of my head, I gnaw on my lip. *What am I doing here? Why did I ask him to talk? For answers, of course, but it feels like something more, too.* The wind picks up outside and the fire crackles. Woodsmoke drifts through the chimney above.

"I've been thinking all month and now, I know where we stand."

"Are you going to leave?"

I nod. "Soon."

"If I were you, I would have left a month ago."

"Yes, that seemed like the reasonable thing to do but—" I take in a shaky breath and gulp, "somehow, I'm still in love with you after everything. My heart is broken, but I hope you can redeem yourself in my eyes. Would you ever turn yourself in?"

His voice is soft and reflective. "I would have weeks ago. But I felt there were unspoken words between us and we both needed closure. I suppose we have that now."

"Wait," I breathe, "if you turn yourself in, you'll never have a chance to tell Orb how you really feel. I think you need closure from him as well."

Stryder looks a little baffled. "Orb doesn't care."

"He will if the Deliverance teams up with Moon Crossing to face him. Orb is wanted just as much as you are, but if you help them bring him to justice as well...maybe the Council will be lenient with you."

"You want me to live?"

"Yes," a blush colors my cheeks, "call me selfish and delusional, but I feel like it's my turn to save you, Stryder."

"Why?" he asks, his interest piqued.

"You were hurt as a child, manipulated and used. I still wonder how my father could lose control like that, too. He was greedy, but I never thought he would pull the trigger on anyone."

"The only person still alive who witnessed it was Orb."

Stryder and I stare at each other. "So we should figure out what Orb saw that night. What he might not be saying."

"If the Deliverance teams up with Moon Crossing and I'm at the head of it all, that will definitely draw Orb out. He can't resist a chance to kill me."

"Vicente still trusts you, then?"

He shrugs. "If I explain, I'm sure he'll help."

"I hope he does, we can't do this without the Deliverance at our backs," I tell him. "Vicente's holding a meeting in the main cavern right now, maybe we should go pose our idea."

We stand and I'm about to snuff out the fire when I hear the door slam open. I glance back and Stryder stands there, holding the plank in his hands as a storm rages outside. It blows snow in, the world completely white, and he pushes the door closed, dropping the plank in place again. The wind rattles the hut and for a moment; I fear it might collapse on us. But the structure holds, despite the severity of the snowstorm outside. We haven't even been here long, maybe a half-hour.

"Looks like we might be stuck here for a bit. The storms around here are too blinding and cold to go out in, even if we are just a short distance away from the warehouse."

I glance around the small structure as it shudders. "Will we be okay in here?"

"If it's been able to withstand these winters before then I'm pretty sure we'll be okay, Locklyn."

He sits next to me in front of the fire and unzips his coat. I tap my fingers against my legs, glancing at him. "So...now what?"

Stryder's gaze glides to me. "Well, as for us...I don't want to cross any boundaries you're uncomfortable with."

"I'll need time and...and distance."

He nods. "Of course."

And then we sit there, across the hut from one another but feeling like we're a world apart. I lean my head back on the wood and close my eyes. This is for the best. I need that space to heal. I've been too naive with him, believing he couldn't possibly cause me any harm. Our romance was a dream and I was silly and sick in love with him. That won't happen again. I won't lose myself like that.

Neither of us say a word for a long time and when the storm lets up, we go our separate ways.

EYE FOR AN EYE

VICENTE WASN'T TOO thrilled about the idea Stryder and I conjured up in the snowstorm. But he has agreed to help us. We are on our way to Moon Crossing for negotiations with the Elite Council and we're hoping they won't have us killed on sight. So Stryder and I wear cloaks and Vicente has brought his best fighters, who carry guns strapped to their backs as well. Vanne got a message to Blake to have the Council meet us and now he's hovering around me again. Thankfully, he never learned of my little rendezvous with Stryder in the hunting hut and neither of us plan on telling him about it. We keep our distance from each other but share concerned glances as we near Moon Crossing.

The Hover has to land outside of the barrier, there's a light dusting of snow on the ground. The Council is already waiting, their bodyguards armed and the commanders with them as well. My stomach rolls at the sight of Commander Westing. I wonder if she still thinks I'm responsible for the deaths of the Superiors, even with Stryder and Bibiana's confessions. She's hardly a forgiving woman and looks a little too comfortable with the guns at her hips, her gloved fingers resting on them. Commander Ore looks sharp, accessing us as we approach, and he shuffles closer to his wife. I know they'd die for each other. Their close partnership has always made that obvious, and in some twisted way, it's adorable.

We come to a stop at a suitable distance from the Council and Blake is the first to step forward and greet Vicente. "Welcome, I understand you come with a proposition?"

"Yes, my associates would like to explain," Vicente says and waves us forward from his group of fighters.

I follow Stryder as we come to where Vicente is, my heart beating erratically in my chest for fear that they won't listen and kill Stryder on sight. He seems to be fearless, though, because he removes his hood, and the Council gasps. Commander Westing's jaw clenches and she unholsters her guns, preparing for an attack. Stryder holds his hands up in defense and then glances at me. I remove my hood as well and Blake's eyes flash with surprise. He must have not expected me to come along.

"So you're both still alive," Councilor Graves sneers.

"Yes," Stryder drops to a knee and I do the same, "and we mean no harm. I know I am wanted after my confession, but I also know you've only caught two of my associates. I want to help."

Councilor Ridge looks skeptical and crosses his arms. "How can you help? You schemed to kill our Superiors."

"As you know, Orb is my brother. Our parents were Emperor Keyon and Empress Aaralyn of Mevania. He blames me for their deaths and so if Moon Crossing will work with me, we can draw him out of wherever he's hiding. I will turn myself in. Domenico de Palma will, too."

"What of Bibiana Kendricks?" Councilor Zimmer asks. "We heard her confession, too."

Stryder's jaw clenches slightly. I know he was hoping they would keep Bibiana out of this, but she also agreed to turn herself in. Only a month after the birth of her baby girl and now...well, who knows what the Council will decide.

"She will as well."

Commander Westing strides forward and Commander Ore sticks to her side like a leech. She glances at the Deliverance fighters. "Are Mr. de Palma and Miss Kendricks hiding underneath hoods as well?"

"No."

"Then how do we know they'll turn themselves in?"

Stryder levels a look at her, almond eyes speaking the truth. "They will, you have my word."

"What of Amira Solomon?" Blake inquires.

"I don't know where she is. She might have fled Mevania."

"Coward," Commander Westing spits and holsters her guns again.

Councilor Fraze ambles forward, looking down on Stryder. "How can we trust you?"

"I came here, didn't I? And I confessed. I'm here to right a wrong and will take whatever sentence my sins have granted me."

"How do you intend to draw Orb out? How do you know he'll even come for you?" Commander Ore's eyebrow quirks, doubtful.

A sneer twists Stryder's mouth. "He hates me more than anyone in the entire world. If I find out where he's hiding, I'll send a message that I'm here and I'll reveal his location if he doesn't come and face what we did. He'll come if only to try and kill me, and he won't want to put his wife and child in danger, that's for sure."

I glance at him in surprise. I didn't know Glory was pregnant. Orb is solidifying his bloodline on the throne with an heir. Smart move.

"He married Glory Troisi, correct?" Blake asks, and Stryder nods. "Does she have any idea what happened?"

Stryder shakes his head. "Orb would never put her in that kind of danger. He'll come to be rid of me once and for all. Glory will be none the wiser, I'm sure of it."

"Will he also release Electra Harte and Drew Holloway?"

My head snaps toward Blake. "*What?*"

"They traveled to Iluro a few months ago and have yet to return. We think they are being held captive upon discovering evidence against Orb."

"Or they could be dead," Commander Westing flatlines with a shrug.

I bite back a snarl and Stryder takes up the reins again. "I wasn't aware of their disappearance. Once Orb is captured, either Glory or our aunt will take the throne until a proper heir ascends. They'll release them."

The Council convenes out of earshot to discuss the alliance and I look to Stryder, tears pooling in my eyes. "What if he killed them?"

His almond eyes glide to me as we stand. "I don't know the circumstances, but if Glory's there, she wouldn't let him kill Electra, right?"

"Of course not. I don't know their dynamic, though, he's an Emperor, royal by blood. Nobody tells him what to do."

"He'd obey Glory and only her. He worships her, always has."

I gnaw on my lip, still uncomfortable that Electra could be rotting in a cell somewhere, or worse, already dead and her body decayed. I should have kept tabs on her, she's the only one who went missing, and I've been so self-absorbed that I never even bothered to send her a message. *Blazes, she could very well be dead.* I can't live with that, knowing I was so careless about her safety. *Electra, where are you?*

The commanders approach us and I stay close to Stryder's side, though Commander Westing isn't sneering at me this time. Her piercing emerald eyes are trained on Stryder. "You're a disgrace to the entire human existence. You, Orb, and everyone else. I always knew he and Viktor were trouble but I trusted your cause."

"Orb and I both justified that it was for our parents. They were taken from us too soon and in such a horrible way," he laments.

A flicker of pain crosses her face and she actually reaches out, settling a hand on his shoulder. "My father and little sister were murdered, too. I understand your pain."

"I'm sorry you had to endure such tragedy as well."

She drops her hand; her gaze cutting away. "It was years ago."

Commander Ore's brow furrows in concern for his wife and he says to Stryder, "I hope you are right about your brother."

Then he guides her away, his hand at the small of her back. As they leave, I see the rounded shape of her stomach beneath her coat, just barely noticeable to anyone paying attention. No wonder she actually seemed quite affectionate and Ore's being so protective of her, they're expecting a child. I look to Stryder, but he's lost in his thoughts and eventually, the Council joins us again.

Blake is the one to shake hands with Stryder now. "We agree to the terms. You find Orb and bring him here. Along with Mr. de Palma and Miss Kendricks."

"I will."

He looks at me. "Locklyn, you are no longer exiled and are free to take up your old apartment again."

I stiffen. "I don't want to stay in Moon Crossing."

"Where else are you going to stay? We will hold Stryder at the police station with Viktor and Caine."

"I mean, I don't want to be alone."

"Stay with me then. Harper could use some company since I've been working so much."

"Who's Harper?" Stryder asks, shuffling closer to me.

Blake holds his hands up. "Harper's my dog and I promise, there will be no funny business."

"Better not be," he warns, his voice a little too deadly.

I sigh. "Thanks, Blake."

He fishes through his pocket and extracts a key card, handing it to me. "I'm sure you remember the number. Westing and Ore are heading near my complex after this and I'll probably be back later."

I take the key card, ignoring Stryder's heated glare, and slip it into my coat pocket. "You have food, right?"

"Always. Please feed Harper, she's probably starving."

"I will."

Blake wanders away to talk to the commanders and several armed officers approach to take Stryder into custody. The Council welcomes Vicente and his men to camp outside of the barrier and he sends a salute to Stryder, wandering away. I turn to Stryder, tuck my arms around myself, and he tilts my chin up.

"If Blake even *touches* you—"

"He won't, Stryder. He is decent and respects me. You have nothing to worry about. I'll only be there until the trial and then...I guess I'll go to Bountiful Hill."

Neither of us wants to acknowledge that his execution is imminent and if I don't think about it, the less real it will seem.

He draws my face closer. "We probably won't ever be alone again, but I want you to remember how much I love you and always will. You're every-thing to me, Locklyn, and I'm sorry for all I've done that hurt you. You deserve better, you always have, and I hope you find it."

I step forward and hug him, leaning my head on his shoulder. Stryder holds me for a moment, his face buried in my hair.

"Goodbye, Locklyn," he whispers.

An officer clears his throat and we part. I sniffle as they handcuff him and walk him into the city. The Council has already departed and the comman-ders are waiting by the gate for me. I trudge forward and once we're all inside; they close the gate. Their patrol car is the only one left and I climb in the backseat, feeling like a kid on the way home from the police station, about to be scolded by my mom. None of us talk on the way to Blake's apartment. I grumble my thanks and get out when we arrive.

I have the pack I brought when I was first exiled, but I'll be glad for a fresh pair of clothes. I can't think about shopping, though, especially when it makes me think of Electra. She loves shopping and now I have no clue where she is or even if she's still breathing. I feel horrible for involving her, but she wanted to see justice served, the real culprits taken to court. Unfortunately, she's not here now, and...one of the culprits is the man I'm in love with. I'll have to ask Blake what the Council will decide. Many of the Councilors are old enough to have been trained by the Superiors and to have been their friends. To them, it wouldn't matter that the Empress and Emperor of Mevania were murdered just outside Moon Crossing's barrier. Their mentors had died because of it.

When I open the door to Blake's apartment, I hear a low growl from Harper before I flick the lights on and she recognizes me. She attacks me with a wagging tail and props herself up so she can try to lick at my face. I laugh and ease her down to the floor. She promptly flips on her back, her tongue hanging out of her smiling mouth, and I scrub my hands along her furry belly. When she's satisfied, I stand and close the door. Harper trails after me and I prepare her some food and fill up her water bowl as well.

As she laps away, I snoop through the refrigerator and find that Blake has an extra carton of leftovers from one of our favorite restaurants, Dragon Delights. I dump the orange chicken, fried rice, and spring rolls onto a plate and warm it up in the microwave. He would always take an extra carton home because it's his favorite. Hopefully, he won't mind me eating his leftovers. I flip on the TV to drown out my thoughts and plop down on the couch with my heated food. Harper lies at my feet and snoozes.

After eating, I make my way to the guest bedroom and am glad Blake still keeps it so tidy. I shower as my laundry is going and steal an old t-shirt of Blake's to wear until my clothes are done. I lie on the bed and scroll through pictures on my Mini of Stryder and me. Sometimes, I liked to catch him off-guard and snap a pic. I laugh at the goofy expressions he always struck. The tears come again as a wave of melancholy crashes into me. I already miss him. We used to be together constantly, and now I feel the void of his absence. Maybe Blake will work some magic and keep him from the execution stage. Then Stryder will just serve time.

Once my clothes are done, I change into regular nightclothes and crawl into bed. Harper ambles into my room, sleepy, and curls up at my feet. It takes a while in the deafening silence to fall asleep, but I do, a picture of Stryder still pulled up on my Mini.

WISH ON THE SUN

I T'S STRANGE TO wake up in Blake's apartment, but it's not an un-familiar feeling. I roll out of bed, muss my hair, and wander out into the kitchen. Blake is awake, despite his late night, and dancing around the kitchen as he cooks. I take a seat at the bar and Harper licks my ankle in greeting. Blake startles when he turns around and sees me sitting there with a smile. A blush colors his cheeks and he clears his throat, pushing his glasses up.

"Good morning, Locklyn."

"Good morning, Blake. You're in a good mood."

He shrugs, turning back to the stovetop and flipping over his famous buttery pancakes. "I'm all right. Glad you're okay."

"Well, I'm surprised I even slept last night," I sigh and prop my arms on the bar, "because I already miss him."

"I can tell."

"Blake...do you think he'll be executed?"

He plates a couple of pancakes, smears on cinnamon whipped cream, and tops it with strawberries before handing the plate to me. I grab his hand before he can pull back and he looks at me, midnight-blue eyes a little sad.

Blake gulps. "Murder usually leads to execution, Locklyn."

"But he didn't kill anyone," I mutter, releasing his hand. "He shouldn't have to die."

"Stryder is in a sticky situation. They killed the *Superiors*. It's kind of difficult to get someone to walk when our leaders were the targets, you were the only exception. Now the Council has a confession. I don't know what I can do."

"I love him, Blake." I bury my face against my hands, embarrassed that I still feel that way after everything.

"I know," he says softly, "and I want to help, but…I don't know if I can this time."

I push off the stool and move toward the guest room, tears brimming in my eyes, but Blake stops me, his finger curled around my arm. "Wait, Locklyn, talk to me. Don't run away."

With my vision blurring, Blake sits me on the couch and I hiccup, attempting to calm down. He rubs my back and I take a deep breath. I don't know how I'll survive however long the trial process will take. My mind will replay all my memories with Stryder and my heart, every feeling.

"Are you ready to talk?"

"Yes." I curl my fingers against my knees. "I don't understand why you were so willing to help me, and yet, you don't even want to try for Stryder."

Blake's hand falls from my back. "The Council wasn't convinced you worked alone and that's how we were able to sentence you to Silverwater, but now there is a team that confessed to carrying out the murders. Silverwater won't be enough."

"You still didn't answer me, Blake."

He sighs. "I know you, Locklyn. I love you. I didn't want to see you dead and I knew you were innocent. Stryder…Stryder isn't innocent and I can't keep trying to save criminals."

"Did you know he had been funding the Deliverance until Orb became emperor?"

Blake stills. "No, I didn't know that."

"He would help free the District. He would take care of this country better than Orb."

"How do you know that for sure?"

I huff. "Stryder wants nothing more than to do what's right. He's nothing like Orb and if they are both dead, there is no heir to the throne. There might be a war. The Eclipse Society has people in the Moonless Market; who knows who else is corrupt? The District could be brought into the war and destroyed. So many people would die, Blake."

"If Stryder walks, we could prevent a civil war?"

"I don't know if it would be prevented or if such a thing would even happen, but I'd rather have Stryder in charge than Orb or the Diviner."

He drags his fingers through his hair, tousling it. "Is there no other worthy heir in Mevania?"

I shrug. "There may be, but I'm unsure. Orb is expecting a child and Stryder has no children. The only other heir I know of would be their cousin Amira, who has gone AWOL."

"It would be years before Orb's child could inherit the throne."

"Exactly, so a war could break out until then. If the Council goes forward with the Circle's plans to control the entire District, then the Deliverance will attack. Whose side are you going to be on when that happens, Blake?"

"I'll stand with the Deliverance, of course." He rubs Harper's ears and her tail wags, happy as can be.

"Why don't you stand with the Deliverance now? What more can you gain from being in the Council?"

His shoulders hunch. "I've been undercover so long that it'll be strange to leave…Moon Crossing is the only home I've ever known."

"It was to me, too, but this city isn't getting any better and I doubt it ever will. Things need to change and you can help." I rub Harper's other ear. "You helped with the trackers. You saved both of us, and I'll always be grateful for that. So help me save Stryder. He can save the District and Mevania."

"I'm terrified of what would happen to us, Locklyn, if anyone found out and I—"

I take his chin and tilt his head toward me. His midnight eyes flash with fear and I cup his cheek. "I know you're terrified and I am, too, but I would feel worse if I sat back and did nothing to save him, to save our very country. I would do the same for you, Blake Carmichael, so please, do the same for me."

He closes his eyes briefly and nods. "Okay, I'll help."

I drop my hand and kiss his cheek. "You're a good man, Blake, and I know you have the heart to do what's right. That's one quality I loved about you."

"*Loved*," he grumbles, fingers flexing on his thigh.

I roll my eyes. "Fine, I still love it and you, but in a way of deep appreciation and trust."

"I know, I feel the same."

"So let's make a plan."

A Return to Light

THE HOLDING CELL that Stryder was in was nicer than any Silverwater cell he could have imagined. Unfortunately, his neighbors weren't the best—Cyrus Caine and Viktor Marsh. Viktor had snarled expletives at him. Cyrus had only curled up in his corner with a troubled expression on his face, paying no heed to the world around him. Stryder noticed the officers treated Cyrus with far more cruelty than him or Viktor. They had been his friends and he betrayed them—their pain ran deep.

They had authorized Stryder to use his Mini to locate Orb, but he guessed where he would have gone, anyway. Goldridge Estate. It was their family's safe house, completely secure and only the most loyal to the crown knew about it. When the Emperor was out of the palace, the advisor took up the helm, and as far as Stryder knew, Arlo Amante wasn't aware of the safe house's location. Maybe his father had a reason for such secrecy.

He couldn't give away the location of Goldridge so he spent a few days pretending like he was really doing PI work. In reality, he was communicating with Locklyn and making sure Blake was keeping his hands off of her. Jealousy had never really been a problem for Stryder because the only other girl he would have been jealous over was Inaya. She had been a free spirit, a little weird, wild—a mix of everything. When she got angry, which was rare, she would speak rapid Spanish that felt like bullets of which he couldn't understand. When she was calm, she would dance and tease him with kisses, barefoot, and as happy as could be. Everyone in Wolves Creek thought she was mad, but Stryder was blinded until the truth was revealed.

Now Locklyn was sensible, but she had exes who fawned all over her. She was *very* lovable. So what worried Stryder the most was her staying with Blake—her *ex-fiancé*—and the fact that their break-up had been because of Vanne, not either of them.

But according to her reports, she and Blake were stirring up a plan to make sure he at least stayed far away from the execution stage in Prime Tower's pavilion. At least Locklyn was still thinking of him. He knew her love ran as deep as his, but her hope that he would live through the ordeal was unbearable to witness. Locklyn saw the broken part of him—the frightened little boy who, at the moment he learned of his parents' deaths, had a chasm of despair break open in him. She was taking pity on him and usually, he wouldn't have wanted that, but he loved how kind-hearted Locklyn was. Orb was a fool for choosing someone like her to frame for murder. Her character simply couldn't allow such a thing.

Stryder heard the clomp of boots outside his cell and he glanced up from his place on the bedroll, knowing they were expecting a report on his progress. Commander Ore himself had come this time—his partner nowhere in sight—and Stryder stood as he addressed him. "Mr. Monroe, I hope you have an answer for where your brother is."

"I do." He tapped his Mini against his palm. "Would you like to watch me send the message?"

"Yes, the Council has asked me to."

Commander Ore swept his clearance and tapped in a code for the cell before the glass door breezed open. He strode inside and Stryder assessed him. They were about the same height, but Ore was slim and limber, while Stryder was broad and clunky. The Commander had pushed his sunglasses on his head. His whitish-blonde hair was neatly parted and combed. A single lock fell out of formation. He always seemed to wear a mostly stoic expression. A small crease between his brows showed only a little indication of what could have been on his mind. Stryder had heard Keeva Westing was the fiery one, but once upon a time, he heard that Anton Ore was fiery, too. He must have had to tame himself to deal with Westing.

Stryder pulled up his messages and typed in Orb's Mini code. He had erased all the old messages with his brother out of spite, trying to forget what they had done. Ore stood at his shoulder and watched closely as Stryder typed:

As you know, I've made my confession and it's time for you to come forward as well, Orb. I'm in Moon Crossing and the Elite Council has entrusted me with finding you. I know exactly where you are and if you don't come and make things right once and for all, I'll reveal your location. Makuahine and Babbo wouldn't want blood on their fine black and white tiled floors, would they? Glory would be safe, your child would, and you could even have the chance to bleed me dry. Come, Falco Sol, Makuahine and Babbo will not rest in peace until you finish what you began. I'll be waiting.

Ore whistled low. "Sounds like quite the threat. Are you sure that's enough for him to show up?"

"If I promise the shedding of my blood at his hands, he'll be here. Orb can't resist a fight with me."

"You two have a very strained relationship."

Stryder shrugged, but a frown tugged at his mouth. "We're brothers, but we've been through a lot. Orb is vengeful and I enjoy baiting him sometimes, maybe a little too much."

He clicked send and Ore stepped aside but didn't leave the cell yet. "I know the Superiors were...our leaders, but what you and your brother went through was horrific. As Keeva—Commander Westing said, she understands your pain and I understand a bit as well. But, laws and morality govern our world, so I wish you the best of luck, Mr. Monroe."

He was surprised, just like when Commander Westing actually appeared to be human, and he nodded to Ore. "Thank you."

The Commander slipped out and the door closed with a soft thunk. Stryder sat down on his bedroll and waited for Orb's reply.

☽ ✧ ☾

Orb was absolutely *furious.*

So much so that he picked up a beautifully crafted vase and hurled it across their chambers, startling Glory from her sleep as it shattered against the wall. His pulse had spiked, sweat beaded on his brow, and he shook with anger. His little brother had the *audacity* to send such a scathing message, mocking him *and* threatening him. It was an obvious trap but—*ugh*, Stryder was one pest he couldn't get rid of.

Maybe once, Orb had loved his brother, but those days were gone and would never return. At every turn, Stryder screwed everything up and he'd done it again with his confession. Orb had expected it, that's why he fathered a child to maintain his bloodline on the throne. There wasn't enough time now to produce a proper heir and Stryder was rubbing the fact in his face. It drove him mad. *Stryder* drove him mad. Calling him *Falco Sol* was a punch to the gut as well. The childhood nickname his parents had lovingly given him hadn't been spoken in years. Orb hated it. Hated how Stryder acted as if he cared about Makuahine and Babbo when he couldn't care enough to go to the trade-off.

Orb knew Stryder had been lied to and tormented about what the District would do, but his brother should have been brave. He should have been smarter to see what kind of danger they had been in. Spies from the Eclipse Society had even taken Stryder *hostage* when he was a toddler. It was brief. The ransom was paid, but sometimes Orb wished they would have killed him then. It would have caused him less of a headache now that he still had to deal with the twerp. Alas, he didn't know if he could bring himself to kill Stryder. His eyes reminded him of Babbo. His easygoing manner was like Makuahine's. His silly belief in doing what was right had fueled Mevania for years. Orb couldn't deny that.

"What are you doing?" Glory asked as she stumbled out of bed, her hair a mess, her silk shirt hiked up over her protruding belly.

Orb turned away. He couldn't deal with her wrath right now, and she found the Mini on the desk. She picked it up and read as he still boiled over with anger. He didn't want to leave her. Their baby was due in a couple of weeks. Despite having a girl, Orb had fallen in love with the first kick, the sound of her heart beating. He wanted to hold his daughter in his arms. He wanted to kiss her little nose and play with her toes, see her open her eyes for the first time, and attempt a smile.

Would she smile at a monster like him?

"Orb...what is this? What is Stryder talking about?"

A wave of spite and grief washed over him and he felt like he was drowning. His words caught in his throat, choking him, and Orb rushed for the door. He couldn't possibly tell her how much of a monster he was. He had never intended for her to find out. Glory called his name as he raced down the corridor, his bare feet slapping against the marbled tile—black and white and black and white. The portraits he passed haunted him and he grit his teeth as unexpected tears filled his eyes. He hadn't cried in a long time—he had always been too wrapped up in anger to do so. If he had been given the chance to grieve properly for his parents, would he still be afraid to express emotion?

The guards near the garden doors wore wide eyes and troubled expressions as he shoved past them and out into the gardens. They were beautiful, a near replica of the ones back at the palace. The ones Makuahine had designed not long after she married Babbo. He tore through them, his robe flapping in the sea breeze and the cold seeped through his nightclothes. Snow scattered the path, but Orb didn't care. He made it to the small greenhouse, wrenched the door open, and hunched against the wall. His hands were shaking as he ran them through his hair and he cursed because the tears wouldn't stop. Emotions were never a thing he could control and he hated it. He had spent years repressing them around everyone else except Glory.

Orb tucked his head between his knees and tried to take in measured breaths. No one swung open the greenhouse door to look for him and his nose was filled with the scent of roses and azaleas, lavender and orchids, and all the other flowers his mother had loved. Her favorite was the pikake, native to her homeland, and she often wore one in her hair. His father would pick them and give them to her. A secret smile shared between them that spoke of their love for one another. Orb had admired his parents, loved them with every part of his soul, and he thought he had honored them correctly in exacting revenge, but...he had only made a mess. They would be ashamed of him. They would not rest in peace. He couldn't change what he had done.

Moonlight broke through the skylights above and he shed his robe and shirt, gazing at the hawk tattoo that swirled around his right bicep. The words in Italian felt foreign to him and he knew he had not upheld the promise he had made to his Ancestors, his parents, and his country. He had gotten into his head, ignored his feelings, and now he would pay for it. It would leave Glory a widow, his daughter fatherless, and the very air from his lungs would be expelled. Orb bowed his head, his shoulders hunched, and he clutched a stray pikake flower that had drifted to the ground. He rolled the stem along his palm and let out a sigh. His tears fell like raindrops on the petals.

Quietly in Italian, he spoke to the silence, "I—I'm sorry, Makuahine and Babbo. I'm so sorry..."

No one answered, but a warmth spread through his chest and the hawk tattoo seemed to glimmer in the moonlight. He sobbed as arms of light enveloped him, and he heard his mother's voice in his ear saying, *"We forgive you, our little Falco Sol, and forgive Tigris Sol. It wasn't his fault. Now go, make things right, and return to your true self."*

☽ ✧ ☾

Bibiana trailed her fingers over Isidora's head and leaned down to kiss her tiny nose. She was seated in a rocking chair that was given to her by another mother in the Deliverance and Orlin had got a crib for Isi. Bibiana smiled as

Isidora sighed softly and curled against her. She was finally asleep and after a moment, Bibiana rose and gently set her down in the crib. Orlin slipped through the door and she held a finger to her mouth, telling him to be quiet. He joined her, slipping an arm around her waist.

They looked down on Isi as she slept and Bibiana was in love. She was a beautiful child, with round cheeks and dark hair sprouting on her head already. Her eyes were wide and lovely—tilted just a hint—but she resembled her mother more than her never-to-be-mentioned father and Bibiana was glad for it. Isidora had been a tempered baby so far, and it pained Bibiana to think about leaving her soon. She covered her mouth and turned away, trying not to wake Isidora with her sob and Orlin rubbed her back.

"It will be alright," he told her, knowing exactly what she was thinking about. "Before you know it, she'll be back in your arms."

Bibiana nodded, but she wasn't sure it would be all right. As an accomplice to two Superior murders, she could be taken away from Isidora permanently and she couldn't bear that thought. So she turned to Orlin and looked up into his lovely eyes. "I'm going to bathe. If she wakes, rock her a bit. Maybe sing a song."

Orlin smiled. "You know I'm wretched at singing."

She leaned into him, kissing his chin. "I'm sure Isidora's not much of a singing critic."

Before she could pull away, he tilted his face down to hers and gave her a proper kiss, murmuring, "I love you, Bibi, and I'll stand by your side. We can make it through this together."

Her heart somersaulted in her chest, and her fingers reached out, curling around the hem of his shirt. "I love you, too, Orlin," she breathed, relieved to say the words she had been thinking about for so long.

He kissed her again, and then she headed into the bathroom to shower. When she emerged, her hair wrapped up in a smaller towel, Orlin was still standing by the crib, gazing lovingly at Isidora as he gently stroked her cheek. Bibiana couldn't have been more in love with him then, the perfect father to a child that wasn't even his. She took his hand and he kissed Isidora's head before following Bibiana over to the bed. She dried her hair the best she could and then turned off the lamp. Orlin had insisted on staying overnight in her room after the birth to help her with Isidora. When she was too fatigued, he would get up and take care of her. Sometimes, he took her for a walk down the hallway until she calmed.

Bibiana couldn't have asked for a better man than Orlin Sosa to step in and rescue her.

His arms reached out for her in the dark and she moved toward him, accepting his embrace. She tucked her head against his chest and closed her eyes. Warm and safe. Orlin's fingers glided through her hair as he pressed his lips to her forehead, humming a song that always seemed to make her drift off into sweet oblivion. Bibiana moved closer and he cradled her head.

Here in his arms, she didn't worry about what lay ahead, didn't think about it. Her mistakes dissipated, and all that mattered was little Isidora and Orlin—her family. Bibiana hadn't felt true love in her life, but she had it here in this room. Her home was with them. She finally belonged.

☽ ✧ ☾

Domenico flipped over on his back, letting out an annoyed sigh. He couldn't sleep. Worry wrinkled his brow, and it was far too hot in his room. He tore off his sheets and sat on the edge, running his hands over his buzzed hair. Once Orb showed up in Moon Crossing, he and Bibiana would travel there and turn themselves in. It was nerve-racking, but he was a soldier. He would serve the crown he promised to until the end, even if it meant his own life was taken. Dom would have at least liked to see his family and the farm again, but he had photos on his Mini. That would have to be enough.

He got up, dressed in a tank top and shorts, and left his room behind. The Aerie Compound was made of concrete and unadorned, but that didn't bother him. He was used to living in drab compounds, anyway. Although here, there were no posters of Mevanian pride and no flag flapping in the wind above the compound. He missed Iluro, missed running drills, and ordering his comrades. He was Lieutenant de Palma and rising in the ranks. Now, he was nothing but Dom, a farm boy following two princes.

The day he met Stryder had changed his life forever and Dom reflected on such with a smile. They had been eight years old and the Monroes were visiting his family's farm. Dom had been a rambunctious child with a gap-toothed grin and a mop of dark hair. Stryder and Orb had been groomed, of course, dressed in white tunics, black leather coats lined with fur, crimson trousers, and snow boots. Stryder had a crimson cap with a golden sunburst and though he walked around with a bored expression, he lit up when he caught Dom releasing the chickens to wreak havoc. Stryder had gladly joined.

The chickens were squawking and flapping about, but rushed into the back meadow as Dom and Stryder let them out. They giggled and hid behind the coop to watch his older brother, Donte, squeal and try in vain to gather the chickens. Their parents were in the house enjoying cider, fresh soup from the recent harvest, and visiting with all the farmhands. Orb was standing on the porch, his arms crossed and eyebrow quirked as he watched Donte flutter about. Dom and Stryder couldn't keep quiet, and he waved him to the little playhouse he and his father had built.

Inside, Dom wrapped a blanket around himself and they hid out in the insulated playhouse. "I'm Domenico," he said with a smile.

"Stryder," his newfound friend said. His smile fell a little lopsided, crooked. "Do you think your brother can gather all the chickens?"

"Nah, there's too many." Dom shuffled over to the window and peered out. A few farmhands had discovered the chickens' escape and were helping Donte now. "Bummer, that fun didn't last long."

Stryder joined him at the window. "What about the goats? Horses? Sheep?"

Dom's cheeks flushed and he shook his head. "I tried to release the horses once but they nearly stomped all over me."

"Oh."

They settled back and Dom climbed a rope ladder to the small second floor of the playhouse. He cracked open the chest of wrapped sweets he always kept stocked. He tossed down a few chewy candies, fresh sweet rolls from that morning, and two ice-cold bottles of juice.

Stryder was chewing on a candy, his almond eyes almost thoughtful, when Dom joined him. "I wish I lived on a farm sometimes."

"Why?" Dom asked as he pulled apart a sweet roll and the buttery scent nearly made him gobble it all in one bite.

"The palace is big and lonely." his new friend cast his gaze aside. "I don't have anyone to play with but my brother and my cousins."

Dom shrugged, savoring a large bite of his sweet roll, and he flapped his arms at his sides. "I only have my brother to play with but he says he's too old to play baby games anymore."

"Don't you go to school?"

"Nah, Mama teaches us at home and when I'm old enough, I'll go out with Papa and Donte to work on the farm."

Stryder picked up his sweet roll and delicately peeled away the wrap. He didn't even have dirt under his fingernails, and Dom cast a self-conscious glance at his own. He didn't know what it was like to be a prince, but he supposed it wasn't hard.

"Do you want to be my friend?" Stryder suddenly asked, his eyes wide and then a blush crept along his cheeks in embarrassment. "I mean, you don't have to—"

"Sure," Dom told him enthusiastically. "I want to have so many friends that Papa and I will need to build a new playhouse!"

The young prince looked relieved. "Me too." Then he winced and Dom cocked his head at him, "But...I don't know when we can play."

"I'll come to the palace," he said. "Mama said I can start making deliveries so I'll bring food to the palace kitchens."

"Won't she want you home after though?"

Dom stuffed the rest of his sweet roll in his mouth and spoke around it, "Mama won't mind, she likes me out of the house sometimes and if I'm doing deliveries, she can't complain."

"That would be fun," Stryder lit up again, "and you could meet my cousins! Amira and Amadeo want a new friend, too."

"We're going to be best friends, Stryder."

The young prince seemed to be over the sun, and they gobbled and talked until it was time for him to go. Dom was sad to see his new friend depart, but it lifted his spirits when his parents agreed to let him deliver to the palace.

"You can start in two weeks," his mother said as she pulled him onto her lap, "that's when the *Gala di Capodanno* begins and the palace will need *plenty* of food."

"Why aren't we ever invited to that?" Donte asked, pouting as he plucked a feather from his coat.

"Because we're common folk, son, and this year is special. The young Prince Stryder is to be marked by the Ancestors."

"What does that mean?" Dom's seafoam eyes were wide and wondering.

His mother nuzzled his head. "It means his Ancestors will descend and bestow a blessing upon him—he will receive his Spirit Guide for life."

Dom remembered hearing about the age-old traditions the royal family had upheld, but he always wanted a Spirit Guide himself. Maybe when he went to the palace, he could sneak in and see the Ancestors blessing Stryder. Donte would be *so* jealous. But for now, he was glad to have made a new friend today.

He was shaken from his memories when he caught sight of Malini Russo lounging in one of the many libraries. This particular one was dedicated to military warfare, and he gulped, hesitating at the door. He knew she despised him, she had shown as much in her scathing glares every time they passed each other in the compound. She loathed him for framing Locklyn, one of her best friends, and he often cringed thinking about it. Dom and Malini had...somewhat of an inkling of romance between them. He had only gone to the club that night to tail Stryder—see what he was up to because Orb had asked him to—and then Malini approached him.

Dom had felt like lightning had struck him. She was beautiful, with her chocolate-colored hair and light eyes, freckles spanning her nose and cheeks. He thought they'd flirt, have a couple of drinks, dance, and then she'd leave, but Malini had insisted they go to dinner. Dom didn't want to leave Stryder alone with Locklyn, but Malini had been quite convincing, and he knew Stryder could handle himself.

So they left and enjoyed the rest of the evening together. Orb had punished him for leaving his post, so Dom didn't call Malini back. He distanced himself. She probably hated him for that, too.

He rolled his shoulders back and strode into the library. Malini was sitting on a cushioned chair, a bottle of Bliss in hand, and a book propped open on her lap. She was humming softly; her socked feet kicking, and the moonlight filtered through the skylights above.

As he neared her, she seemed to sense his presence and glanced up. He paused as she glared and made to chuck the book at him. "Get out of here, you scumbag."

He held his hands up. "I mean no harm."

Malini snorted. "As if. What do you want?"

"Nothing...I couldn't sleep so I thought I'd walk around and then...ended up here."

"Well, don't let me keep you from your late-night adventures." She dismissed him with a wave of her hand but kept a wary eye on him as he rounded her chair and sat across from her.

He picked up an extra book on the table and didn't even bother to read the cover. With the book open on his lap, he lounged back and stole small glimpses at her. She had delved back into her book, but the easygoing, comfortable pose of her body was gone. Malini was on the defensive now, and though he didn't know if she could ever forgive him, he hoped to make amends.

"What do you keep looking at?" she sighed and snapped the book closed, setting it on the table between them.

"I'm sorry," he said softly, looking away from her spiteful eyes. "I'm not that kind of person—"

"What kind of person?" she interrupted, "A murderer? A scumbag? *What?*"

Dom cringed. "I've done things I regret, yes, and I've hurt many in the process. In the end, though, I'm a simple farm boy, and second, I'm a soldier to the Mevanian crown."

He had learned that Malini's mother was from Iluro and that she was a servant in the palace. She took a trip to Bountiful Hill with a couple of other servants on holiday and met Malini's father. She didn't know what trouble she was getting herself into. He had been a gang leader, looking to take territory in Moon Crossing, and she followed willingly, bearing him a daughter who eventually took up his ways. Malini ran with the Russo gang as a child until they were caught on a heist and thrown in prison. Malini and the other children went into the Protectorship Program after a lengthy stay at a correctional facility. Her mother had returned to Iluro and her father was in Silverwater, unable to escape. So Malini had known all about Mevania, more than plenty of other citizens of Moon Crossing, and that was something they connected on. Their mothers were even from the same small village.

"Do you expect my forgiveness? For any of it?"

"No, I only wanted to express how sorry I am. I'll live with this guilt for the rest of my life—however long or short that may be."

Malini was quiet for a moment and then sneered. "Why are you cowering here in Aerie? Why didn't you turn yourself in with Stryder?"

Dom sat up and smoothed his hand over the surface of the book. "We're trying to draw Orb out and Stryder insisted that Bibiana and I wait until Orb comes. He wanted to give us a little more freedom before we get locked up and probably executed. Bibiana gets to spend more time with her daughter and I...get more time to reflect on my life. I wanted to go, but he ordered that I stay."

"And you follow orders like a dog."

"Like a soldier." His brow furrowed as he glanced up at her. "I've vowed to stand by his side, by Mevania, in everything. It's my home and he is my prince."

Malini rolled her eyes. "Warriors' pride and patriotism, I don't get it."

"Didn't you feel that way when you ran with your father's gang?" he bit out.

She stiffened, casting another glare his way. "That's different. We were a family."

"You don't think Mevania is as well? The warriors and our sovereigns? I think of Stryder as a brother. His parents were kind to my family and they helped us when there was a famine. They kept us alive." Dom paused and took in a measured breath. He was getting emotional. "I respected Emperor Keyon and Empress Aaralyn. They were good people and they didn't deserve to die."

"If only we could all believe that, but alas, things happen in this world. It's unfair, it's cruel, and you all shouldn't have moped about it."

Dom blinked at her and stood. "This is pointless."

Malini watched him, her eyebrow quirked. "What? I can't forgive you for what you did to Locklyn. So don't come looking for it again."

THE BLOOD OF THE FALLEN

BEFORE BLAKE AND I can come up with even half a plan to free Stryder, Moon Crossing is tossed into a battle with Mevania. I hear sirens wail early in the morning and stumble out into the hallway. I bump into a groggy Blake as we scramble for the living room to turn on the TV. A newscaster pops on over an early daytime show, showing a live feed of all four gates of Moon Crossing where Mevanian warriors are using battering rams to take them down. Others scale the barrier, climbing over and deftly avoiding the shots being fired at them. There are thousands of warriors surrounding Moon Crossing, dressed in the crimson and gold uniforms of the Mevanian military.

"We are under attack," Blake points out, rubbing his eyes to wake up from his sleepy stupor.

"This is bad," I say, my hands trembling as I rub them along my arms. "Orb wars with us instead of handing himself over."

"I mean, did we really expect him to give up that easily?"

A frown creases my mouth. "No. He wants to stay alive to rule and destroy the District and Stryder. He won't go down without a fight."

"Neither will we." He turns and heads back into his room.

I follow and am shocked to see Blake produce a rifle and several handguns from his closet, along with plenty of ammo and bulletproof vests laid out on his bed. Blake never seemed like the guy who would be ready for an apocalypse and yet, here he is, ready and armed.

"Rifle or handgun?" he asks, glancing over at me.

"I'm better with a handgun. The rifle has too much kick."

"Come pick what you'd like then."

"I haven't even showered this morning and now we're going out guns blazing." I shake my head as I walk over to him and survey the handguns he has.

I pick up two semi-automatic handguns, grab a double holster belt, a bulletproof vest, and hopefully enough ammo. Then I head back to the guest room to get dressed. I know we won't be the only ones fighting out there. The police and Recons should be defending the barrier right now. I wonder if I'll see Commander Westing and Commander Ore, especially since I learned she's carrying their child. She wouldn't risk it to save this city, would she? No, she'd have to be insane to do something like that. But without one of them or both, there go two of the best sharpshooters in Moon Crossing.

Once I'm dressed and Blake's ready, we head out into the city. His apartment sits smack dab in the middle, so it should be safe from the invasion. The city is deathly quiet as people hunker down and take shelter, hoping that no Mevanian warriors break down their doors and kill them. We drive on the empty, frosty streets and park a couple of blocks from the southern wall, which has yet to be breached. There's a police station nearby and the barrier is swarmed with Recons and police officers alike. They stand in lines, guns at the ready, as the gate continues to be battered. Recons are gliding along the top of the barrier, from watchtower to watchtower, shooting down any warriors that fire back at them.

Stryder is being held in the police station on the west side of the city and I wonder why we didn't go there first. We could easily break him out, but as I turn toward the west, an explosion rattles the ground beneath us, and the buildings around shudder at the impact of the shock wave. It throws us all off our feet and ringing fills my ears. A large plume of black smoke rises near the west gate and I push myself up, holding a hand to my bleeding ear. Blake is up, too, and we look back on the southern gate. The blast has blown the Recons from their posts, either outside or back into the city, and some remain still. A fall like that is fatal.

Another explosion rocks the city from the north and then the east. Blake and I dive to the ground behind a concrete structure just in time as one takes out the southern gate. I feel dizzy as I sit up again and cough into the crook of my arm. Through the dust and smoke, Mevanian warriors march in, their heads covered in protective helmets, visors clear and swords drawn. The disoriented officers and Recons try to jump to attention, but the Mevanians are quicker and cut down anyone who stands in their path. They can even deflect bullets off their swords and we duck as some ricochet, striking those who pulled the trigger.

"We need to get Stryder!" I yell fiercely to Blake.

His breathing has become erratic, and he removes his glasses, pinching the bridge of his nose as he tries to calm down. Once he nods, I take his hand and we bolt for the city streets, running back to the car. A dull pain shoots through my once incapacitated leg and I grit my teeth, carrying on. The screams and shouts of the fallen behind us twists my heart but we can't help them. Our bullets are basically useless if the Mevanians are skilled and quick enough to deflect them. Who knew that swords would win in a gunfight.

As we're running, a barrage of arrows flies toward us and we slip around a corner just in time. We stop, and Blake whips his rifle off his back and stands against the building, peeking around the corner to see who is shooting at us. I crouch down and look, too. Two Mevanians have noticed our departure and one has a bow with three arrows nocked to it. I've never seen a bow like it before, beautifully crafted and alabaster, the arrows as dark as death itself. The other Mevanian has twin swords drawn, already dripping in blood.

"Have you ever killed anyone?" Blake asks me as he cocks the rifle.

"No, and I never intend to. We should only hurt them enough so they can't follow us."

"Then I think your bullets will do less damage."

He stands down and gives me the corner. I take a deep breath and then turn at the corner, firing at their abdomens with both of my guns in hand. The Mevanian with the swords deflect my bullets and they shatter the windows of the building. One bullet tears the leg of my cargo pants and I hiss as it grazes my skin. But I continue firing and three arrows sail toward me. I retreat behind the corner and they breeze past. Blake hands me two full magazines and I release the empty ones, reloading. I can hear the clap of their boots as they run for us and I step out again, firing multiple rounds at them. The swordsman isn't fast enough to deflect all my bullets and one catches him in the side. He grunts but doesn't fall. The archer is less protected and two bullets plunge into her abdomen. She stumbles and falls to a knee, nocking three more arrows in one swift movement.

The swordsman roars something in Italian and marches on. Blake and I wheel back as he slides around the corner and nearly slices both of our heads off. We duck and roll, guns at the ready, when I face him again. The rifle goes off and the swordsman pauses, his body shuddering as blood blooms in the middle of his tunic. He swings his swords once more with less force now and cuts my cheek, too close to my eye, while he snags Blake's arm. We scramble back and the swordsman slumps to the ground, muttering something under his breath.

A small ball appears in his hand and it clicks. Blake and I surge to our feet and run as the grenade detonates. It hurls us to the ground, and I protect my head from hitting the pavement. I groan and can barely hear Blake now as he asks if I'm okay, and we stand once more. How many bombs are we going to run from today? But there's no time to dread the possibility of more and we make it to the car. Blake can't drive with the deep gash in his arm, so I take up the wheel as he tends to his wound. We head for the western gate and I hope Stryder isn't already dead.

☽ ✧ ☾

The explosion of the western gate had the police station shuddering like a child in the dead of winter, and Stryder was glad the structure didn't collapse on their heads. He had been sleeping and startled awake, as were the others. He stood on the bench by the small window, looking out of the cell, and couldn't believe what he saw. From the black smoke emerged a man riding on a black stallion, while *Speranza Cremisi* warriors flooded in behind him. He had his own swords drawn and his stallion stomped on anyone in his way. Though Stryder was too far to make out his face, he knew it was Orb. The armor his brother wore had belonged to their father—crimson and gold—and was made from the finest and strongest metal of Mevania's quarries. Bullets simply pinged off the armor. His ebony cape fluttered in the breeze and his swords shone in the morning light, bloody.

Stryder cursed and hopped down to the floor. He hurried to the cell's door and tried to kick it out but it didn't budge. In the cells next door, Viktor seemed unbothered while Cyrus was practically chewing his fingernails off. The station was relatively quiet, but the few young officers left behind to watch the prisoners were shaking in their boots, sweating at the imminent invasion. Stryder knew Orb would come here and kill him—which is why he didn't want to be defenseless against his brother.

"Orb is going to *kill* you when he gets here," Viktor snickered, casting a devious glance at Stryder.

He ignored him and Cyrus spoke up, "Orb might not just kill Stryder, you know, he could kill us, too."

Viktor snorted. "Maybe you but not me; Orb and I have a bond like brothers."

Now Stryder turned to him. "*I'm* his actual brother and he hates my guts! You may be friends, but you let Bibiana slip away and let her confession get back to the police. You let him down. Orb will only see you as weak."

The former Councilor gnawed on his lip, looking a bit more worried now. Stryder wiggled his fingers through the bars, trying to reach the access pad to type in the code he'd seen Commander Ore type. He could get up to his wrist out but then his arm got stuck. He bent his wrist and punched in the first number. Viktor was at the door of his cell as well, trying to reach through the bars.

"What's the code?" Viktor asked.

"04965," Stryder told him.

"That won't work," Cyrus said from his cell with a shake of his head. "They change the codes out every day and generate different ones for each cell. Even then, you'll still need card clearance before."

They drew their hands back, expressions grim, as Viktor snapped, "Why didn't you tell us this before we looked like idiots?"

Cyrus shrugged. "Didn't cross my mind until now."

"Sure it didn't."

Stryder dropped to the ground and ran his fingers through his hair. "Well, this is the end for me."

No one said a word. They waited. Three more explosions rattled the city, and Stryder stood to check how the fight was faring. More police officers and Recons than Mevanians were littered across the ground, their bodies still and bleeding. He couldn't find Orb among them, which was sort of a relief, but then the door to the station banged open and he could hear people approaching. If it was the police coming to free them, they would run. Orb wouldn't run. He would let Stryder breathe for another minute or two before he either stabbed him, beheaded him, or both.

He turned toward the cell's door as Orb came into view, flanked by several masked *Speranza Cremisi* warriors. Apparently, their uniforms had been upgraded to provide more protection. Orb removed his helmet and tucked it beneath his arm, no smirk on his face, as Stryder expected. He didn't move from his spot in the cell and Orb didn't move to open it up. His brother had yet to draw his sword as well, but Stryder knew it would only be a matter of time.

"I see you're laying siege to Moon Crossing."

"I thought I would make my presence known."

Stryder took in a deep breath, his fingers flexing at his sides. "You've come here to kill me, right? I know you're not one for small talk so let's just get this over with."

Orb's mouth twitched and he swiped a clearance card, typed in the code, and the door slid open. He was the only one to enter the cell and Stryder's pulse quickened, his blood rushed, and he thought of Locklyn as he brought his fists up, ready to at least give himself a fighting chance. Orb neared closer and Stryder felt uneasy at the expression on his brother's face. There was no homicidal rage, no malice. Orb's expression held no emotion and Stryder stiffened as his brother, awkwardly, pulled him into an embrace.

It had been a very long time since Orb had hugged him. Stryder blinked, his confusion nearly unbearable. But Orb simply drew back and held Stryder by the shoulders, looking him right in the eyes. In Italian, he told him, "I'm sorry for treating you the way I did for so long and for blaming you for that night. There's something you need to know that I never told anyone, but I need to get you out of here first."

As Orb stepped back, Stryder couldn't believe what he just heard. He remained still, wondering if he was dreaming. "What? You're not going to kill me?"

"No," his brother kept his voice low, "I...believe that Makuahine and Babbo visited me from the world of spirits. It has made me reflect on what I've done. You were scared. I was too, but I thought you were weak when really, you weren't."

"I...I don't know what to say."

Orb rolled his shoulders back. "We can discuss it when we're safe. Let's go."

☽ ✧ ☾

When Blake and I arrive at the police station Stryder is being held in, we're shocked to find that the door has been blown to bits. I get out of the car and run for the entrance, hopping over the debris that has fallen. The rest of the station is untouched, but my blood runs hot as I make my way to the cells.

I don't want to find him dead. If only Orb and Stryder could make up and be brothers, not enemies. They both lost their parents. It isn't fair that Orb thinks he's the only one who cares.

I walk down the corridor of the cells, knowing exactly which one Stryder is being held in, and I pause briefly to compose myself. Then I continue. Only one prisoner remains and it's not Stryder. Cyrus Caine sits in his cell, back against the wall, eyes vacant. Viktor's cell is empty and so is Stryder's but there's not a drop of blood anywhere and no stench of death. Blake joins me as I stare into Stryder's cell. He looks as confused as I am. I tear away and march over to Caine.

"Where is Stryder?" I ask, my voice a little squeaky with nerves as I turn my uninjured ear to him.

"He let them out," Caine replies with a raspy voice.

"Orb? He didn't kill him?"

"No." His brow knits. "In fact, he hugged him."

I blink. *What is going on?*

Blake speaks up. "Where did they go?"

"Who knows? Orb and his warriors came in. He spoke with Stryder, and then let him and Viktor out. He left me here to die."

"But you were his accomplice. What does Orb have against you?"

Caine's shoulders crumble forward and he sighs. "I'd rather not get into the details but I have the possibility of being their cousin's father."

"Amira?" I ask.

He glances up at me. "I didn't think you knew her, but yes, she might be my daughter. But the circumstances of it weren't...ideal and so Orb and Stryder don't like me."

"Why work with them if they don't like you?"

"I wanted to protect Amira, or, at least, I thought I was. She's gone AWOL now and I'm here, awaiting my trial and execution so...I suppose she's protected but not safe yet."

I pace in front of the cell. "Do you know which direction they went?"

"Orb came in through the western gate so I imagine that's where he'd leave through, too," Cyrus tells us.

"Let's go then," Blake says.

I move past the cell, casting a glance at Cyrus. "Thanks for your help."

"You have nothing to thank me for," he broods and turns away, hunched over.

Blake pats my shoulder and we leave Cyrus behind. He dug his grave when he agreed to work with Orb. I hope that the same fate doesn't come to Stryder. But as we near the western gate, all is quiet. The Mevanian warriors have already moved through here, leaving bodies of Recons or officers behind. Some warriors have fallen as well, but I'm sickened by how many bodies there are in general. If Stryder was in charge, this slaughter never would have happened.

We keep quiet and alert as we weave past all the fallen and I keep my eyes up, knowing my stomach wouldn't be able to handle seeing the dead up close. Blake does the same, but he looks a little green in the face anyway. They blew the western gate to bits, like the other three, and we approach with extreme caution. Being on the western side of Moon Crossing, we're met with the beginnings of the Blooming Woods. I shudder at the morning mist still obscuring the ground. The Blooming Woods is the place where nightmares live, where Worshipers dance and supposedly summon the dead. As kids, Mom always told Jesse and me that if we misbehaved, an ill-willed spirit would emerge from the Blooming Woods and snatch us up in the middle of the night.

We pause outside the destroyed gate and I glance at Blake. "Do you think they escaped into the Woods?"

"Probably." He shifts on his feet and adjusts his grip on the rifle. "I would imagine that they came in Hovers so if they're not parked outside the barrier then they must be hiding in the Woods."

"Good point."

Neither of us moves and we both let out nervous chuckles as Blake says, "Are you thinking about nightmarish spirits emerging and stealing our souls, or is that just me?"

"Our souls? My mom told us they would just snatch us up."

"Then your mom spared you the true horror of the Blooming Woods." He holds his hand out to me. "Together?"

I take his hand. "Together."

We face the mist-filled woods and step into its confines.

STRANGE HAPPENINGS

STRYDER KEPT LOOKING at his older brother as if he were seeing a ghost. The Orb he was witnessing now differed greatly from the Orb he had known for the past fourteen years. Before their parents died, Orb had been a regular big brother who thought his little brother was annoying. Although he acted dignified and like an emperor already, Stryder knew the real Orb had a fondness for books, swimming in the lake, and even scaling trees with him. Stryder was more of the risk-taker, while Orb calculated the logical choice. For the past fourteen years, his brother had become a phantom, only addressing Stryder out of spite.

Now he actually stood next to him. He did not walk ahead with his head held high, as always. They were traversing through the Blooming Woods, side by side, as warriors trailed after them, a respectable distance away. They had arrived in Hovers, and Orb's stallion was being led by a lanky stable hand. Stryder stepped over unruly roots and clutched the coat he'd been given. It was chilly in the Blooming Woods, hoar frost glistened on the bare branches and he could see his breath. It was very quiet, too, an empty silence in the Woods. Stryder shivered, he wanted to get on a Hover as soon as possible. Even the crunch of fallen leaves beneath his boots was eerie. They hadn't been followed out of Moon Crossing, since there was no one left alive at the gate to follow them, but Stryder still thought about Locklyn. He didn't want to leave her behind. But she belonged to this world—the District—and he belonged to Mevania.

He was glad Viktor had stayed and suspected he would run off to the Moonless Market. His friendship with Orb was on the rocks, and Viktor didn't want to face Orb's wrath if he screwed up again.

"What did you want to tell me?" Stryder finally asked.

Orb inhaled deeply and glanced at him with their mother's eyes. "I saw something that night that I've never told anyone. Not even the detectives when I gave my witness."

"What did you see?"

His brother's brow creased and his voice dropped low. "It wasn't Cicone Harte who pulled the trigger. I mean, he did, but he didn't mean to shoot at Makuahine and Babbo. There were three people in masks that had appeared out of nowhere and they forced Cicone's hand. One of them used Makuahine as a shield, then another killed Babbo himself." Orb's voice grew raspy, still pained with the memory, and he continued, "I saw a symbol on one of their cloaks, Stryder. It was a sun in eclipse with twin shooting stars."

Stryder stumbled over a root and caught himself on his brother's shoulder. He looked at Orb, almond eyes narrowed to slits. "The Eclipse Society."

"Yes. During my time as a Councilor, I discovered that not only is the owner of the Moonless Market in cahoots with the Eclipse Society, but the entire Circle of Superiors was as well."

His jaw dropped. "*What?*"

Orb bobbed his head. "Masoni, Wells, and Dunn had been with the Society for at least sixteen years. They were pro-anarchy and hoped that if the throne was overthrown, the District could expand into Mevania and they would work side-by-side with the Diviner. Cicone had refused to join in the past and threatened to reveal them from time to time. So the Diviner thought to take out two birds with one stone and they set up Makuahine, Babbo, and Cicone. The Circle knew about his trading—that's how the Diviner found out—and set up the meeting. I'm convinced that there were spies in the palace and in Moon Crossing to make sure Babbo and Cicone agreed."

It was an overload of information and Stryder blinked, trying to wrap his head around it. "So…Cicone was framed for their murder and executed. Two birds with one stone…"

"Yes. What I'm confused about is why the Society's spies didn't kill us. They didn't even attempt to take my life that night and no one ever came for you either, correct?"

"No. That *is* strange."

Orb shrugged. "I suppose our own hubris and grief was to be our downfall."

Stryder ran his fingers along his arm, thinking of the tiger tattoo on his back. "You knew all this before we framed Locklyn, didn't you."

"I did. I was still confused and figured that Cicone had something to do with it after all. I even wondered if Locklyn was in alliance with the Society. She was the perfect target, though, even if she is or isn't."

"She isn't."

"How would you know that?"

Stryder tucked his hands in his pockets and lifted his chin. "She's not that kind of person. She would never side with an organization that kills to get its way."

"And yet, she was the Circle's secretary," Orb retorted.

He bristled. "Locklyn would never be a spy for the Diviner."

His brother sighed. "Maybe, but how can you trust anyone these days when life is about deceit, greed, and lust? I think it best if we leave all this behind."

"How can we do that with bounties on our heads?"

"I'll take care of it. I have a plan."

Stryder snorted. "Will your plan work this time?"

Orb shot him a glare. "I'm sure. The District will most likely wage war on us, along with the Diviner. The Mevanian military has much more fire and manpower than either will ever have. I've been working with Admiral Mezzanotte and Captain Lain to prepare for an attack, both on the seas and land. Mevania has the most land and the most harbors, so we will win this war."

"There's that hubris again."

"This isn't hubris, this is a fact. I *know* we will win."

"Prove it—"

"Pardon me, Your Majesty, but we must hurry to the Hovers," Captain Montgomery Lain suddenly said behind them and the brothers jumped.

Orb recovered quickly and turned to the captain. "I didn't think we were walking that slow."

"We're being followed by two civilians."

"Why haven't they been taken care of?"

Captain Lain glanced back at the other warriors standing there, awaiting orders. Stryder looked past him to where the two civilians were, crushed between the overly large and muscular Mevanian warriors, and his heart stuttered as he recognized both. Locklyn and Blake, both bloody and covered in soot. He breezed past Orb and Captain Lain, his eyes only for Locklyn, and her gaze met his. She had a small cut on her cheek and dried blood crusted her ear. She broke free from the warriors and stepped into his open arms, albeit a bit stiffly as she was limping. Stryder enveloped her, his hands trembling in sheer joy—and panic. *Why did she follow them?*

"Locklyn," he whispered and drew back a breath, keeping his voice low so only she could hear. "What happened? What are you doing here?"

"I came to find you," she whispered back and glanced over his shoulder, eyes narrowing on Orb. "Why are you with him?"

"Don't worry, I'm in no harm. Orb and I are fine."

She looked unconvinced and lifted a dark eyebrow. "You two aren't going to kill each other?"

"No."

"So...what now?"

"We must be on our way," Orb said, and Stryder held Locklyn a little closer, ignoring his brother.

"I need to go home." He cupped her cheek, her blood staining his fingers. She was the best thing that had ever happened to him and she deserved to know about her father. Stryder turned to his brother. "Tell her what you just told me."

Orb hesitated a moment and sighed. "Fine."

He gave his spiel and Stryder watched as tears filled Locklyn's eyes. "My father was framed?"

"He was. The Diviner was behind all this. I targeted the Circle because of their affiliation. When your father was taken out of the picture, the Diviner recruited Roman and Cozeht to their 'cause'. I believe the Diviner also had blackmail on the Superiors so it gave them another reason to join."

She sniffled. "Who is the Diviner?"

Orb tsked. "I have yet to discover that, but I believe it's someone in the palace. When I go home, I intend to weed out all the traitors and execute them for treason and conspiring against the crown." He took Stryder's arm, "So now, we must go."

Stryder resisted, like a child not wanting to go yet. Desperately, he gave it one last shot. "Locklyn, come with me. We can have a normal life together in Iluro."

She gazed at him, eyes watery, before shaking her head. "I can't."

Locklyn took a step back and though his heart ached, he knew she still needed her time and space. Distance. Their relationship was over. He flinched before he let himself be drawn away from Locklyn.

They walked to the wide-open meadow surrounded by a wreath of trees. The Hovers were cloaked in an invisibility shield, and Captain Lain gave a signal to the pilots to reveal them. The Hovers materialized out of thin air and it was a comfort to see the Mevanian sunburst and laurel crown painted on each Hover. He hadn't been to Iluro in a while and he ached to walk the corridors of the palace again, run his fingers along the tapestries and study the portraits of his Ancestors as he had as a child.

There were at least a dozen Hovers in the meadow, but he knew that there would be more outside the other destroyed gates of Moon Crossing. A couple of warriors walked around the royal Hover to make sure it was still secure and then they were ready to board. A wave of relief overcame him as they made their way to the Hover.

Blake and Locklyn had been ushered along and Captain Lain asked, "What am I to do with these civilians, Your Majesty?"

Orb waved an indifferent hand. "Let them go."

Stryder glanced back at Locklyn, wondering if he should hug her goodbye. She accepted his embrace before but didn't return the gesture. Now she stood shoulder-to-shoulder with Blake, the both of them looking like deer in headlights.

He hoped that someday, when she had healed, she would come back to him. But that hope was minuscule, as it should be after all he'd done.

Stryder lifted a hand and gave the both of them a wave, his gaze trained on Locklyn. The corner of her mouth lifted, drawing his attention there, and she waved back. Blake simply nodded. With his jaw clenched, Stryder followed his brother.

Orb was striding ahead, a few warriors flanking him, and they began their ascent up the ramp. Something caught Stryder's eye as he neared. A tiny spark zipped beneath the ramp. His eyes widened as he realized what was about to happen and he shouted at his brother, "Orb! A bomb!"

Orb turned and lifted a brow—always the skeptic—as the royal Hover exploded.

☽ ✧ ☾

Every part of his body was fire or ice.

Stryder blinked, willing himself to wake up. He couldn't move. He was in so much *pain.* Above him, a geometric mobile turned slowly and a fan whirred somewhere near his head. It was quiet but for the fan and he was unsure where he was. He heard no other breathing and determined that he was alone. But where was Locklyn? Where was Orb? They had been too close to the bomb, especially Orb, and his throat constricted with anxiety.

No, Orb couldn't be dead. He had only begun to redeem himself—in a way.

Stryder wasn't ready to lose his brother after they'd finally made up. He needed to get up and make sure Orb was okay, that he was still breathing. They would not leave the Monroe line with only Stryder at the helm. He couldn't bear to lose another member of his family—not after his parents. Tears welled in his eyes. He knew he was helpless. The two people he loved and appreciated the most *had* to be alive.

THE DAWN OF DISCORDANCE

MY HEAD LOLLS to the side and a slamming door startles me awake. The morphine dripping into my veins is strong as I feel no pain. I crack my eyes to see who has barged into my hospital room. Mom and Jesse rush to my bedside. A red-haired man and his daughter stand apart, glancing at us with worry creasing their brows. I've only met Mom's new husband once and my gaze trails to the girl, who bears the same smoky eyes as our mother and she stares right at me. Nadia.

"Oh, sweetheart, are you all right?" Mom asks, taking my hand in hers and brushing my stringy, sweaty hair away from my forehead.

I nod and croak, "I think I'm fine. Where am I?"

"Bountiful Hill," Jesse says, sitting on my other side. "They found you and Blake in the Blooming Woods next to a smoking Hover."

I struggle to sit up and Mom helps me, setting another pillow behind my back. I wince as the medical gown pulls taut against the burns along my torso, but that pain doesn't compare to my confusion. "Just me and Blake? Where's Stryder? The Mevanian warriors?"

Jesse and Mom share a look and he asks, "What are you talking about?"

I blink. *Was it a dream? No, it couldn't have been a dream. I'm in a proper hospital with real burns and bruises, my arm in a sling. The disaster in Moon Crossing still happened, right? I watched Stryder wave goodbye...I instinctively ran toward him when he shouted about the bomb.*

"Haven't you heard about what happened in Moon Crossing?"

"The full details haven't been broadcast yet, but we know the city was attacked," Jesse says.

"Mevania attacked, er, Emperor Orb did, I guess."

"Emperor Orb as in Councilor Cristol?"

"Yes, but he's not Orb Cristol, he's Orb Monroe. Heir to the Mevanian throne."

Mom tips her head at me. "Why would he attack Moon Crossing?"

I take one weak hand and run it through my dirty hair. "I don't know, to wage war on the District? But I need to figure out where Stryder is. Where's Blake?"

"The room next door. He didn't sustain burns like you but was knocked off his feet from the blast. What were you two doing out in the Blooming Woods anyway with a Hover?"

"Trying to run away together?" Jesse suggests.

I roll my eyes at him. "No. But, I need to know where Stryder is and if he's okay. Please, take me to Blake."

She tsks. "We'll bring him to you since he's much more mobile. Hold on."

As she stands and leaves, a nurse wanders in and sees that I'm awake again. "Ah, Miss Harte! I'm glad to see you're awake. How are you feeling?"

"Numb."

"At least the morphine is working. You've been near quite a few explosions, as your friend informed us. I'm surprised neither of you sustained too much hearing loss or shrapnel damage."

"But we sustained some?" I ask.

"Yes."

Mom returns with Blake and the nurse departs. Blake also has his arm in a sling. His hair is a mess. He has soot smudges on his face, but he looks okay. Blake sits on the edge of my bed and I shoo everyone else out so we can talk in private. My business with Stryder is a tricky one and I'd rather not have Mom snoop and find out the true story of how things went down. Although, one day I will tell her that my father was framed by his own coworkers and friends. And the Diviner. For now, I have to know if Blake knows anything I don't.

"Hey, Locks, you good?" he asks, genuine concern in his eyes.

"Well, I'm still alive. Do you know what happened? My brother said it was just us and the blown-up Hover that was found in the meadow."

"That's what I was told as well. The last thing I remember is hearing Stryder shout about a bomb and then diving to the ground for cover. I woke up here, same as you."

I scratch an itch on my slung-up arm. "Maybe someone isn't telling us the whole truth. No one else seems to be startled about what happened in Moon Crossing."

"The Council censored what happened. I was watching the newsreel earlier and they're playing it off like it wasn't a big deal. Which is odd. If you look toward Moon Crossing, you can clearly see the black smoke rising into the sky." Blake rubs his whiskerless chin. "I imagine they'll try to blame the bombing of the barrier on the Deliverance."

"Why wouldn't they say it was Mevania that attacked the city? The rest of the District should know what happened."

"I'd say it's a political move. If everyone else learned that Mevania attacked instead of the Deliverance, Moon Crossing would be seen as too weak to keep its barrier properly fortified and immune to being bombed. They took each gate out in a matter of minutes. They mowed officers and Recons down with *swords* while they wielded guns. The Council must be scrambling to cover it up. They can't be seen as weak."

"Do they know you're here?"

"Yes, and they've dispatched a Hover and a slew of bodyguards to retrieve me once I'm discharged." Blake looks down as he rubs his hands together. "I think I'll resign and go to the Deliverance. I have no clue if Orb is still alive. If he is, I know that he's not finished with the District."

"I wouldn't want to be here if he is alive and returns to finish what he started. If he could wreak that much havoc on Moon Crossing then imagine what he could do to the entire District."

"You're right, I'd hate to be here. The Deliverance has been in Mevania's good graces for the past several years so I hope we can ally with whoever sits on the throne." Blake pokes my hand. "What are you going to do when you get out of here?"

I think for a moment, gently leaning back on the pillows stacked behind me. "I think I'll stay here. Crash at my mom's house for a bit until I can get back on my feet again."

"You don't want to come to the Deliverance?"

I glance at him, those midnight blue eyes a gentle reminder of better times. "I want to live a normal life, Blake. I don't want to be involved in conspiracy and anarchy and revolution. I'm tired of fighting—and I'm too old to be tossed around and beaten up."

He laughs. "You're only twenty-one, Locks, *hardly* in your elderly years."

A smile lifts my lips. "*But* I'll be twenty-two soon." My smile turns somber as Blake stands to go. I tell him, "Thanks for trying to help me, Blake, and for being my friend."

"I'll always be there for you, I promise. I'll try to dig up what happened with Stryder, too."

"Thank you. Truly."

Blake hugs me and wanders over to the door. Before he steps out, he glances back and gives me a little wave. "See you around, Locks."

With Blake gone and my room empty and quiet, I let the silent tears break free.

☽ ✧ ☾

"Your Majesty? How are you feeling?"

Orb's eyes slowly fluttered open and it was as if his body past his waist was numb. It took a moment for his gaze to focus and above him were Dr. Agosti and Glory. Neither had a pleasant expression on their faces and he closed his eyes again, not wanting to hear the bad news. His hearing was different, as he had already noticed, and with nearly his whole body numb, he was probably just a torso and head now. No one would accept such an emperor. But that wouldn't be the only reason Mevania wouldn't accept him anymore. He had most likely begun a war and hundreds of the *Speranza Cremisi* were dead, loved ones lost to a silly cause while Orb remained alive.

He had not wanted to leave Glory. To leave their child behind and his Empire—his people.

"Orb," Glory said, her voice was trembling and he felt her cool hand on his arm. "Open your eyes, my love."

His brow lined and he opened his mouth to speak, but no words tumbled out. Orb gazed up at her. The halo of light framing her head made her look like an angel. If the afterlife included angels like Glory, then he would have gladly gone if he wasn't done with this world yet. She had tears in her doe-like eyes and leaned down to kiss his forehead.

"I'm so happy you're alive but...Dr. Agosti has something to tell you."

When she leaned away, he looked to Dr. Agosti, who was worrying more lines into his face, and Orb recognized he wasn't worried, but fearful. The physician feared Orb would retaliate against the news he had to share. That he would be sent to his death, or worse—his family would. All in the name of not being able to help Orb, but...he didn't want to be that kind of Emperor, one who ruled by the fear of his people, and so he tried to look as kind as he could.

Dr. Agosti took in a quick breath before he began. "Your Majesty, as you might have noticed, you've suffered some hearing loss. Being so close to the blast, I'm surprised you survived. When you were brought in, we had to perform emergency surgery for your lumbar spine. Currently, everything below your waist has been unresponsive, but this doesn't mean that the paralysis is permanent. We've done all we can for now and will have to monitor you and see what happens."

Orb blinked. *Paralysis.*

That was one thing he thought he would never be told in his life, and his chest felt heavy with grief. Though Dr. Agosti tried to reassure him it might not be permanent, Orb knew paralysis was serious. Even if it wasn't permanent, the process to gain his legs back would take a long time. He wanted to run to the greenhouse again and hide like a little child, afraid and unsure. At times like these, he needed Makuahine and Babbo the most. Makuahine to comfort him and show him the motherly love he missed. Babbo to tell him to be brave and be strong. That he would make it through the terrible and the sweet if he trusted in his own ability.

"I think we need to be alone for now," Glory gently told Dr. Agosti.

The physician nodded and left; the door closing softly behind him. Strange tears welled in Orb's eyes and he reached up to brush them away, not wanting Glory to see. But she was sitting next to him and held his hand. Most of his body was bandaged from the burns he had sustained, and Orb felt so weak. *He hated it.*

After a bout of silence, Glory spoke again, "I'm so sorry, Orb—"

He shook his head. *It wasn't your fault;* he wished he could say. *I was selfish. I wanted to be done, but I made things worse.*

Glory picked up a small notebook and pen from the side table and handed them to him. "Write, darling."

Orb took the notebook and pen but his grip was weak so Glory helped guide his hand. It was pathetic that he had been rendered so useless that he couldn't even speak or get up from the bed or write without help. Glory stayed a little longer and she told him she was due in two weeks. Orb hoped he would be well enough to be there for the birth. He was eager to hold his daughter. Then, after a while, Glory left to let him rest.

But Orb couldn't.

As he thought more about the Hover incident, a thought came to him. It *had* to be sabotage, and Orb knew the number one enemy to Mevania was still alive. The Diviner: the mysterious cult leader of the Eclipse Society. Even if he was permanently paralyzed, he would not rest until he found out who the Diviner was and killed the weasel himself.

EPILOGUE
Two Weeks Later

S INCE MY INJURIES weren't too severe, I was released from the hospital earlier than I thought. My arm is still in a sling, sprained from falling on my shoulder during the blast, but my burns have almost healed completely. I have scars, but that doesn't bother me as much as Blake's silence. He only sent me two messages, one to tell me he made it to the Deliverance and the other to tell me he couldn't find anything on Stryder's whereabouts. I cried for hours after the last message, my heart aching from not knowing where he could be or if he's dead. I've had nightmares since—seeing his cold and ashen face lying next to me, no sign of life in him. I can only hope that he somehow survived. *If I did, then he had to, right?*

Bibiana and Domenico turned themselves in—regardless of Stryder and Orb's absence. They were sentenced to Silverwater. Detective Caine is sentenced to be executed. I hope Bibiana survives to see her child once more.

My heart swelled with joy when I learned that Electra and Drew had been released and returned to Moon Crossing. I won't be able to see them until they come to Bountiful Hill and I get antsy every day my cousin remains in that wretched city.

Mom and her husband, Oisin, have let me stay with them until I can get back on my feet again. I have my own room and have been ordered to rest from the ordeal I've been through, but I feel like I can't rest with my mind racing. There are so many things that went into play with my father, the Circle, everything. The situation is much more complicated now and though Moon Crossing hasn't declared war on Mevania, there are rumors they'll order a draft from the District. And if people don't comply, they'll be imprisoned.

The Elite Council, or what's left of them, is in charge of Moon Crossing now. They will hold an election in a couple of weeks since they've decided that no Circle of Superiors will ever be needed again. It's a risky move, taking on all of Moon Crossing as the Elite Council, but with more sensible people in charge, maybe the city will fare better.

I try to spend time with Mom, Oisin, and Nadia, but I am often in my room still, either crying or in a daze. I want to tell Mom what happened to Dad, but I'm not sure I've fully processed everything yet. It doesn't surprise me that the Circle was involved with the Diviner, but it surprises me they betrayed my father like that. I never would have thought the Circle would have been involved, and yet, they were more involved than I could ever imagine.

I see now that everyone's true colors come to light in the end.

THE END

THE DUSK OF GREED
FOURTEEN YEARS PRIOR

*C*ICONE HARTE.

Father. Husband. Superior.

He had all that he needed, all that he wanted, and yet, greed ate at him. Gambling in underground clubs was his retreat during lunch breaks and trading outside the barrier—his vice on weekends. The night he lost control was one gamble that he shouldn't have made.

Cicone left work well into the night and started for home. He took the main road to ease suspicion and then turned right into an alleyway that led to his meeting spot at the barrier, the wall of defense that surrounded Moon Crossing. Once Cicone got the boys and the payment, he would take the boys home and set them up in his office. Then he would tiptoe into Locklyn's room, kiss her goodnight, and crawl into bed with Maisie. He would slip in as easily as night had slipped in while he was in the Circle's conference room.

He made it to the barrier just as the watchtower shut off its searchlight and the guard descended from his post. It was common knowledge among his trading buddies at the barrier that the night watch guard always cut their shift short of one in the morning, so Cicone waited in the shadows, the SUV off and deathly silent. He never reported this to the Circle of Superiors, of course.

From his seat in the SUV, he could make out a few figures emerging from behind the foliage once the guard was gone, but he remained in his car. The barrier was twenty-eight feet tall, a feat to climb without gear.

He then leaned across the console and popped open the glove compartment. Inside were the registration papers and manual for the car, but underneath that, Cicone always kept a revolver, just in case. He shuffled through the papers and his fingers slid over the grip. He pulled it out and the revolver's satin finish glinted in the moonlight. He pocketed six bullets, in case he needed to fire off a warning.

Cicone pulled himself out of the car and tucked the gun into his waistband. He came to the southern gate and punched in a code only the guards knew. It cost him some money to even get such information so he patiently waited until it opened. He approached the figures waiting on the other side. Once he got close enough, he recognized the man, who had now brought his wife and clinging to her was a boy. Cicone suddenly felt disconcerted at this change. Where was the second son? Didn't the man discuss two boys to smuggle in?

The man, Keyon, Cicone remembered, stepped forward. He had broad shoulders and tan skin paired with caring almond-colored eyes. He looked different from the last time Cicone saw him, no longer concerned and open about his sons but stern and cautious. Sweat glistened on his brow and dark circles nestled beneath his eyes. He looked like he hadn't slept since their first meeting two weeks ago when Keyon told him there was a threat to his sons, some cult or something that was after them. Cicone glanced again at his wife, a beautiful woman with dirty blonde hair and baby blue eyes, which her son had inherited.

"Cicone, this is my wife, Aaralyn, and our eldest son, Orb." Keyon said, gesturing to his family. His accent was heavier with lack of sleep.

He nodded in greeting and then lifted an eyebrow. "What about your youngest?"

"My youngest refused to come. I did my best to convince him it was for his good, but he wouldn't listen. He was…terrified to come to a new place," Keyon informed him.

Cicone shook his head. "You promised two boys and double the original sum. I won't take only one in. This wasn't the deal."

"Yes, but my son—"

Cicone grabbed Keyon by the front of his crimson tunic, nearly lifted him off his feet, and growled, "I don't want to hear excuses about your other son. I was supposed to bring in two boys and receive my payment. What do I get now?"

"I'll give you only half. That's all I brought," the man said through clenched teeth.

Rage welled in him, ignited by greed, and it consumed him, wrapping its scalding tendrils around his heart and squeezing tight. He shoved Keyon to the ground and impulsively drew the revolver, feeling a little lightheaded as red flashed before his eyes. "Give me what I asked for and I won't hurt you."

It was unfair to only receive half when he was promised every credit, and he intended to keep that trade true.

Keyon stood and held his hands up. "We don't want any harm. Just take Orb into the city and we'll bring our other son tomorrow night."

Cicone lowered his hand. "Do you promise then?"

"*Yes.* He's just afraid but we'll bring him."

"And then you'll pay in full?"

Both Keyon and Aaralyn nodded vigorously.

Cicone sighed, "I need to pay for my debts. But I can wait another day," he held his hand out to Orb, "come on, son."

Orb cowered away from him, his gaze still on the gun, and then he closed his eyes. Aaralyn moved to stand behind her husband. Cicone was about to tuck the gun away when he heard heavy footsteps approach from behind. He whirled and lifted the revolver, his nose twitching as he blinked. Had Keyon set this up as an ambush? Was there a guard around who saw them? Cicone waited. The gate creaked as it was pushed open a bit more.

From the dark appeared three masked people, no weapons in hand, eyes sharp and cold behind their silver masks. They weren't guards. Cicone's brow knit and his shoulders tensed up. He cast a glance at Keyon, who was staring at the strangers blankly. Cicone couldn't tell if he knew them or not.

Clearing his throat, he shouted, "What business do you have here? I am Superior Cicone Harte and the barrier is off-limits to civilians."

The masks said nothing and Cicone turned so he didn't have his back to Keyon anymore. He glanced at the man and asked, "Do you know them?"

A single shake of Keyon's head made Cicone's stomach drop.

He swung the revolver and pulled the trigger as one of the strangers rushed him...only to remember that he hadn't loaded it. Ducking beneath the man's arm, he jabbed his elbow into his side and groped for the bullets in his pocket. Out of the corner of his eye, he saw Keyon and his family run to the foliage. The other assailants followed and Cicone opened the action, loading the bullets. An elbow jammed into his spine and he gasped, falling to a knee as pain burst through him.

With the revolver loaded and his hands shaking, he lifted it but black fabric enclosed his head and cinched tight against his throat. His chest heaved and he clawed at the fabric, desperately trying to tear it away. It only tightened until he was left gasping for air and the revolver fell from his hand.

Tears leaked from his eyes and he could feel the assailant ease him to the ground. The man leaned his mouth against Cicone's ear, his breath radiating warmth through the fabric as he spoke in a low, gravelly voice. One that Cicone swore sounded a hint familiar.

"You're going to pick up your revolver again and follow my lead."

"Or...what?" he wheezed, teeth grinding as his head began to feel light.

The assailant's knee dug into his back. "Or my associates and I will go to your house, find your wife and that little brat of yours and gut them where they stand. Little Locklyn's screams will be sweet to my ears."

Cicone bucked and grabbed the assailant by the shoulders, hauling him over him. The man landed with a thud and a groan in front of him and the cloak fell away. He scrambled for the revolver but a boot slammed down on his wrist and held him in place. Cicone looked up. Keyon and Aaralyn were being held at gunpoint, their son still hiding in the foliage and staring with wide eyes.

"Don't fight," the assailant hissed. "It's them or Locklyn and Maisie."

Nostrils flaring as his heart skipped in his chest, Cicone closed his eyes. He knew what that meant.

Slowly, he nodded.

The assailant swept the revolver from the ground and stepped back. Cicone pushed to his feet and walked to where Keyon and Aaralyn stood. Her eyes shone with tears and she trembled, sniffling as he came closer. Keyon stared at him, not pleading for his life to be spared or that of his wife's. The masked man handed Cicone the revolver and he felt another gun barrel digging into the back of his head.

Lifting the revolver, he aimed for Keyon's chest first. If Cicone were in his shoes, he would rather die first than watch Maisie be shot. Cicone's finger curled toward the trigger as Keyon lifted his chin, unafraid as he kept eye contact with the man about to kill him. A breath or two passed and Cicone exhaled slowly, letting his chest deflate before he shifted and aimed for the assailant behind them. The man had impeccable reaction time as he grabbed Aaralyn and pulled her in front of him like a shield. Cicone flinched as the bullet tore through her chest and her mouth fell open, bright blue eyes wide. The assailant swore as the bullet passed through her and struck him in the chest. He dropped her to the ground.

Keyon made his move and knocked the revolver from Cicone's hand. He stumbled back, staring at Aaralyn lying on the ground, a hand to her chest as blood spilled through her fingers. She was looking at her husband and in the foliage, their son was screaming. The boy rushed forward as Keyon shouted something in a language Cicone didn't know. Orb stopped but he was trembling terribly and Cicone took another step back. The assailants didn't bother to have Cicone fire off another shot, they decided to kill Keyon themselves. One grabbed Keyon by the nape of his neck and kicked the back of his knee so he knelt. And then they shot him.

Keyon slumped forward, blood blooming on his tunic. His eyes glazed over and he tilted his head toward his wife, his brow knitting as she reached a hand toward him. The boy was screaming again. The assailants vanished without another word. Cicone felt immobile as his head spun with what just happened and his legs grew weak, taking him to his knees. Orb rushed to his father's side and helped him lie down, putting pressure on the wound. He glanced frantically at his mother and went to do the same, tears streaking his cheeks. Cicone blinked and snapped back to himself. He had to get them to the hospital, even though doing so would likely cost him his freedom.

Cicone gripped Keyon beneath the armpits and dragged him to the SUV, setting him against the car window. Keyon coughed and blood dribbled down his lips. He was looking paler by the second. But Cicone ran back over to Aaralyn and was about to sweep her up when the boy lashed out at him.

"You shot her!" he accused, his eyes angry with tears.

"*Shh,*" Cicone countered, "I'm going to take them to the hospital."

"No!" Orb cried.

"*They will die if I don't,*" he hissed and grabbed Aaralyn, running her over to the SUV.

Orb followed, hitting him and demanding that he let his mother go, but once she was in the car, he lifted Orb and tossed him into the passenger seat. Before the boy could scramble out or protest more, Cicone sped away from the barrier. He raced down the streets of Moon Crossing and screeched to a halt right in front of the hospital's ER entrance. He ran inside and quickly explained that two people had been shot and they needed medical attention immediately.

They brought two gurneys out, but when the physicians saw the clothes that Keyon and Aaralyn were wearing—the clothes worn by the Mevanians on the other side of the barrier—they paused. A nurse asked, "Who are they?"

"I don't know." Cicone claimed. "I heard gunshots and found them like this."

Orb glared at him from the passenger seat, but Cicone ignored the boy. When they still hesitated, Cicone boomed, "*THEY ARE DYING*! It's your job to save people!"

After that, the physicians and nurses moved quickly, bringing Keyon and Aaralyn into the ER. He paced and ran his fingers through his hair in the waiting room. Orb was curled up in the corner, still crying but silently now, and he glared at Cicone, fury burning in his eyes.

Cicone felt like he was out of his mind.

It was an accident. He didn't mean to shoot Aaralyn. Now he would go to prison until his co-workers held a trial. This night was a mess and he knew he was in big trouble. *Oh, blazing stars. Locklyn, he had failed her.*

He felt like he had no heart anymore.

After a few hours of waiting, a physician finally emerged, her expression crestfallen. Cicone stood to hear the news and hoped the boy was out of earshot as the physician said, "I'm sorry, but we weren't able to save either of them. Their bleeding was too excessive. Do you know who they are, sir?"

Cicone had to sit down for a minute and he buried his head in his hands, tears stinging his eyes. Regret and panic flooded him. *What had he done?* That little boy was truly an orphan now, along with his brother. It had been so *selfish* to take this trade, so selfish to gamble when he had his whole life ahead of him. So selfish to only think of himself, really, only to get what *he* wanted. Maisie never asked for his gambling debt. Neither did Locklyn or Jesse.

"Sir?" the physician asked again, setting her hand on his shoulder.

He flinched and stood again, wiping at his tears. "They have no ID but the boy," he gestured to Orb in the corner, who was staring at them, "he said they were his parents."

The physician wandered over and knelt in front of Orb, gently explaining that his parents couldn't be saved and were gone. He broke out of his ball of fear and wailed, getting up and trying to run back to see them. Cicone caught him and pulled the boy close. Orb kicked and thrashed, screaming for his parents.

"I'm so sorry," Cicone murmured to him. "I'm so sorry..."

When Orb relented and let Cicone carry him, he promised the physician he would bring Orb to the orphanage. They trusted him. As a Superior of Moon Crossing, a righteous leader in their eyes, trust was all they had. In the car, after a long silence, Cicone asked, "Why didn't your brother come?"

Orb's hands fisted in his lap and he stared out the window. "My brother is a coward."

In those five words, Cicone could tell that the boy held resentment toward his brother. The tension in the air only confirmed it and it made him sick with grief. He couldn't take the boy to the orphanage just yet. He would need a promise of silence on his part. They came to Cicone's cozy home and he parked the old SUV in the driveway. All the lights were off in the neighborhood and all was quiet. Cicone and Orb quietly snuck into the house and to his office, where Cicone set up a bedroll for Orb. The boy flopped on it and curled into himself, his shoulders trembling as he cried again.

"Stay here until I come and get you in the morning, okay?"

When Orb said nothing, Cicone sighed and stood, draping a blanket over him. Quietly, Orb hissed, *"You're a monster."*

Cicone paused for a moment, a frown creasing his mouth, "I am, aren't I."

As he was about to leave, something caught his eye by the door. Cicone bent over and picked up the stone that the boy must have dropped. It was a *lapis lazuli*, beautiful and rare. Without a second thought, he pocketed the stone, knowing that his precious Locklyn would love it.

PRONUNCIATION GUIDE

Aaralyn — air-uh-lynn

Adume — aah-doom

Alivi — uh-live-ee

Amadeo — ah-ma-day-oh

Amery — am-err-ee

Ar'ik — our-eek

Babbo — bah-bo

Calem — kay-lum

Cicone — sih-cone

Domenico — dom-eh-knee-co

Iluro — ih-lure-oh

Inaya — in-eye-ya

Kaer — kay-er

Keyon — key-on

Khione — key-oh-nee

Luminosa — lou-mi-no-sa

Makuahine — mako-ah-he-nay

Malini — muh-lee-nee

Mevania — meh-va-nee-ya

Morlam Canyon - more-lamb

Oisin — o-sheen

O'kshah — oak-sha

Parrish — pair-ish

Ravi — rah-vee

Reyes — rays

Rhyn — rin

Saunia — saw-nee-ya

Shikoba — shh-ih-co-bah

Speranza Cremisi — spur-anza crem-ee-zee

Tiran — tear-ran

Troisi — troy-ee-zee

Vanne — van

THE SEQUEL...

Book 2 in the True Colors trilogy is...

DARK GAMES

ACKNOWLEDGMENTS

*T*rue Colors has come a long way since the idea first sparked in my mind ten years ago, but it wouldn't be what it is today without help from others. I'd like to thank my family and friends for cheering me on and for reading early drafts of *True Colors.* I'm grateful for my husband, who has supported me throughout this publishing journey and gets to listen to me jabber on about my books. I'd like to thank my alpha and beta readers for providing excellent feedback that really helped me see this story in a new light and helped make it the book I wanted it to be. I'd like to thank the writing community as well for spreading the word about my book since marketing is not my forte.

About the Author

L oren S. Olsen has been writing intriguing young adult and new adult fiction since she was twelve years old. She enjoys writing dystopias, space operas, and fantasy novels with lovable characters. Loren graduated with a degree in English, and an emphasis in Creative Writing, from BYU-Idaho in 2023 and is excited to continue exploring her passion. She is an avid reader and spends her time "studying" other YA and NA books, scribbling a couple of lines in her current works, and drawing fan art of her own original characters. *True Colors* is her debut New Adult novel.

Instagram: lsolsen.author